To Sarah:
Thank you for
putting my book
on your she
xoxo
Stacy

THE HAUNTING OF BARRINGTON COUNTY

A BARRINGTON COUNTY NOVEL

Stacy Charasidis

BY STACY CHARASIDIS

First Edition – April 2012

ISBN
978-1-77097-360-2 (Hardcover)
978-1-77097-361-9 (Paperback)
978-1-77097-362-6 (eBook)

Cover and Map Design: Samuel Lampron

Published by:

FriesenPress
Suite 300 – 852 Fort Street
Victoria, BC, Canada V8W 1H8

www.friesenpress.com

Distributed to the trade by The Ingram Book Company

table of Contents

Dedication v
Barrington County Town Map vi
Family Lines vii
Past ix
  Prologue xi
Present 1
  June 2
  July 5
    Nathalie & Dean 6
    Sadie & Luke 33
  August 74
  September 207
  October 297
Future 367
  Epilogue 373
Acknowledgements 377

Dedication

This book is dedicated to my parents,
Ellis and Mary Anna Charasidis.

To my father because he understood the value of education after only finishing Grade 8, and insisted I go to university to ensure I could do anything I wanted... and to my mother who set a great example by finishing university at night with three small kids. My guiding lights...

Love you, miss you.

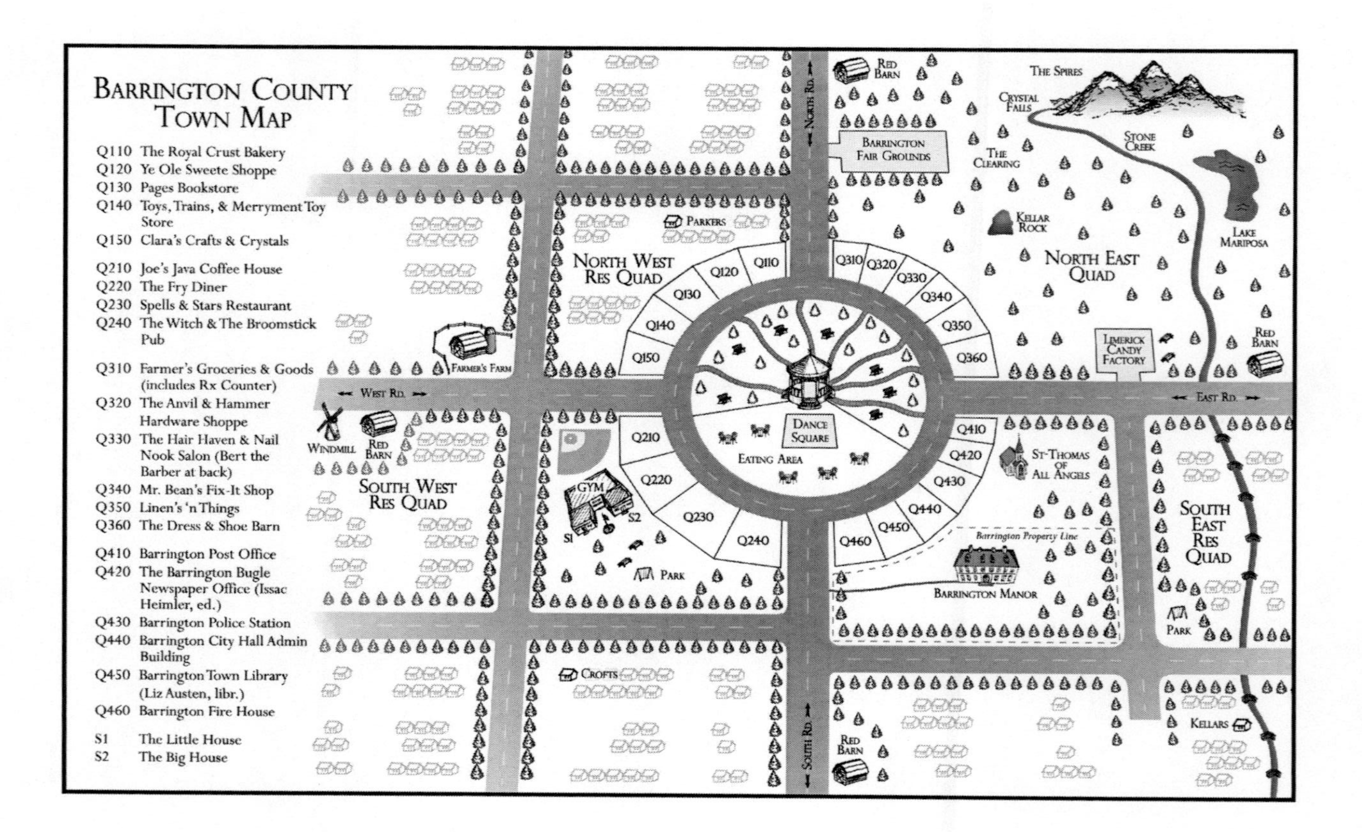
BARRINGTON COUNTY
TOWN MAP
Q110 The Royal Crust Bakery
Q120 Ye Ole Sweete Shoppe
Q130 Pages Bookstore
Q140 Toys, Trains, & Merryment Toy Store
Q150 Clara's Crafts & Crystals
Q210 Joe's Java Coffee House
Q220 The Fry Diner
Q230 Spells & Stars Restaurant
Q240 The Witch & The Broomstick Pub
Q310 Farmer's Groceries & Goods (includes Rx Counter)
Q320 The Anvil & Hammer Hardware Shoppe
Q330 The Hair Haven & Nail Nook Salon (Bert the Barber at back)
Q340 Mr. Bean's Fix-It Shop
Q350 Linen's 'n Things
Q360 The Dress & Shoe Barn
Q410 Barrington Post Office
Q420 The Barrington Bugle Newspaper Office (Issac Heimler, ed.)
Q430 Barrington Police Station
Q440 Barrington City Hall Admin Building
Q450 Barrington Town Library (Liz Austen, libr.)
Q460 Barrington Fire House
S1 The Little House
S2 The Big House
RED BARN
NORTH RD.
BARRINGTON FAIR GROUNDS
THE SPIRES
CRYSTAL FALLS
STONE CREEK
THE CLEARING
KELLAR ROCK
LAKE MARIPOSA
NORTH EAST QUAD
PARKERS
NORTH WEST RES QUAD
Q110
Q120
Q130
Q140
Q150
Q310
Q320
Q330
Q340
Q350
Q360
LIMERICK CANDY FACTORY
RED BARN
FARMER'S FARM
WEST RD.
EAST RD.
WINDMILL
RED BARN
DANCE SQUARE
EATING AREA
Q210
Q220
Q230
Q240
Q410
Q420
Q430
Q440
Q450
Q460
ST-THOMAS OF ALL ANGELS
SOUTH WEST RES QUAD
GYM
S1
S2
PARK
Barrington Property Line
BARRINGTON MANOR
SOUTH EAST RES QUAD
PARK
CROFTS
SOUTH RD.
RED BARN
KELLARS

Family Lines

Bakers: Cindy & Noah (parents), Reginald (17), Austin (15)

Barringtons: John & Claire (parents), Raphael (27), Gabriel (24), Michael (22), Tristan & Jack (20), Luke (17), Max (15)

Browns (extinct): Jedidiah (17) d. 1860

Crofts: Josephine & David (parents), Dean (17), Ella (15), Bessie & Fanny (7), Eddie & Zach (5)

Farmers: Barbara & Bill (parents), Hannah (17), Savannah (15)

Kellars: Liora & Boris (aunt & uncle), Sadie (17)

Parkers: Mary & Steve (parents), Rain (20), Nathalie (17), Nick (6)

Smiths: Sarah & Daniel (parents), Tess (17), Harry (15)

Sweets: Anna & Eric (parents), James (17), Bella (15)

Past

"Our name will be forgotten in time,
and no one will remember our works;
our life will pass away like the traces of a cloud,
and be scattered like mist
that is chased by the rays of the sun
and overcome by its heat.
For our allotted time is the passing of a shadow,
and there is no return from our death,
because it is sealed up and no one turns back."
Wisdom of Solomon 2:4-5

"Well, that's what we expect to happen, anyway."
-Ella Croft

Prologue

June 21, 1595 – Day of the Summer Solstice

The six stood in the clearing in a semi-circle in front of the gallows, their blazing torches smoking in the early evening light. The sun had not fully set and a storm was brewing. The wind was rising, trying its best to blow the hats off the heads of the men gathered there. One woman stood in the shadows under the trees. She was there to observe and remember.

On the gallows was an incredibly beautiful woman. Her long black hair and dress whipped around wildly in the wind. Her violet eyes blazed in a pixie face as she stared with hatred and loathing at the townspeople below her, while her slender, willowy body twisted and writhed in an attempt to free herself from her bindings. It was a futile effort, for the woman who would record these terrible events was also the woman who had carefully studied the lore required to bind a demon's mistress.

While innocent women around the counties were being falsely accused, charged, and executed for witchcraft, somehow Dame Willow Kellar had slipped the noose until now. How could such a vicious and obviously powerful witch escape death for so long? Dame Parquhar smiled grimly at the answer as she watched the gathered men. She knew many men could not bring themselves to put such an inhumanly beautiful woman to death, especially one of whom they had carnal knowledge. Barrington men were no different.

That Willow had seduced many powerful men was well known but not spoken of. Early every day Dame Parquhar passed the Kellar cottage on her way to the bakery where she worked. As chief bread maker, her strong, thick arms made short work of the daily baking. The walls of the Kellar cottage were thin, and there were many mornings where she heard the creaking of bedsprings along with the grunting and moaning of fornication. Just as often she overheard the pleading tones of a desperate lover newly scorned, begging Willow to change her mind. But once Willow had what she wanted, or once she grew bored, the unfortunate male was discarded. Many marriages in Barrington were strained, and the unfaithful hung their heads in shame as they went about their business. A couple of men had killed themselves — one of them leaving his widow with young babes. It was such a pity.

Willow often looked at Dame Parquhar speculatively, probably wondering how much she knew. She always looked back at Willow with a vapid wide-eyed stare. It just didn't do to have Willow Kellar think you knew her business. She was just glad her own Henry had gone before that witch had graced Barrington. All she could do was mind her own business and pray to the good Lord that the next time Willow Kellar batted her eyelashes to bewitch a male, the man would have the good sense to avoid the snare. So far, she was still praying.

The mayor had never done anything about the shameless and sinful behaviour exhibited by some of his townsmen. However, when the sixth child of Jenna and Saul Croft went missing, Dame Parquhar snapped.

"Poor little tyke," the young female assistants sympathized as they knead dough. "She just disappeared."

Dame Parquhar listened as the girls whispered, and she burned with righteous anger and fear. She knew Willow Kellar was responsible. This was the third child missing in the two years since Willow had arrived in Barrington. Each one had gone missing just before the summer solstice, which was tonight. She'd seen this pattern before, and despite her fear, she would act!

After the day's first loaves were put in the huge bread oven she left the bakery, and in a panic, humbly presented herself to the Mayor at his home and spoke out.

"This is a very serious accusation, Dame Parquhar," Jacob Barrington said with shock. They were sitting in the visitor's salon of Barrington Manor. It was a gorgeous room, full of red velvet and crystal.

"The punishment for these crimes is death. The woman will be tried as a witch, hung and burned at the stake. If you are wrong, Dame Kellar can have you put in the stockade for false accusations, or worse, have you tried as a witch yourself," he said quietly, his face creased with consternation. He looked uneasy.

Dame Parquhar shook her head. "I will take that chance, your honor," she said with determination. "A dangerous witch roams our town and now a child's life is at stake," she said urgently. "We *must* act now, before the summer solstice comes to a close."

During their conversation, Jacob's wife had been busily preparing tea. "What say you of all this, Jane?" he asked. His wife had an uncanny sense of intuition that baffled and amazed him in its accuracy.

Jane poured tea and looked thoughtfully at her husband. "I've known Dame Parquhar all my life. She has never uttered a falsehood. She has been an exemplary member of this town." She stopped speaking as she handed out cups, but then continued. "But mainly, she has no reason to lie. Willow has not done her a wrong, and so has no other conceivable reason to say these things except for revealing the truth and exposing evil."

Jacob was pacing, and Jane put her hand on his arm to stop him. She looked into his face. "Surely you see the truth, husband?"

He nodded, and that was that. Jacob sent messengers to gather the influential men of the town and they planned her capture for that very night.

"We can't delay," Dame Parquhar said anxiously, wringing her hands. "Today is a powerful day for witches. The child will lose her life when dark falls."

At dusk the mob headed to Willow's house, torches burning. A group of townsmen waited at the side of the Kellar cottage, ready to apprehend her if she tried to flee. The plan was to have Jenna and Saul Croft distract Willow at the front door by confronting her and making a scene by demanding Willow return their child. At the back, Jacob Barrington and Dame Parquhar would sneak in and search the house.

They found little Livey Croft barely alive, bound and gagged in the root cellar. She had blood markings on her face, wrists, and feet. They also found the remains of at least one other child. It was a horrific sight.

Jacob cried the order and the men rushed to the front and grabbed her. Willow just laughed. "No human prison can hold me, you fools," she had hissed. Her violet eyes had turned white.

The men were terrified. "Demon," they whispered as they backed away and crossed themselves superstitiously.

"Bind her," Jacob barked when he arrived. He could see the evil flickering inside Willow and eating away at her immortal soul. They had captured more than just a witch.

"We should burn her house too, Jacob. It is a place of evil," one of the men could be heard saying as they bound Willow's wrists and legs with carefully prepared rope.

"We will come back when the wind dies down and cleanse this place," Jacob said, looking back at the house.

The mob dragged her off.

The Crofts were sobbing and hugging their child. Dame Parquhar put her arms around them. "Take your child home," she said softly. "There is only violence left here this night."

At the county law office the room was in an uproar—packed with people shouting. The trial itself was merely a formality considering the grisly evidence found at Willow's home. She was condemned to die, and sentenced to hang and burn as a witch immediately. No banns would be posted and no crier sent to relay the news. The townsfolk cried their approval as the decree was recorded in the ledger...and they found themselves here.

Dame Parquhar's drifting thoughts were brought back to the darkened clearing, which was being torn apart by the wind. She looked around at the gathered men. Only a select few had come. Jacob had forbidden the townsfolk to follow due to the dangerous nature of the witch. No judge and no doctor were present either because they were, unfortunately, former lovers of hers...tsk...but Tobias Baker and Alaric Sweet were there. Tobias looked longingly at Willow, like an alcoholic looks at a bottle of spirits, even though he knows the vice will kill him.

Dame Parquhar had known of his indiscretions with Willow. Unfortunately, so did his wife. *Well, at least he's here. He made the right decision by supporting the verdict, and is acting like a responsible,*

God-fearing man, she thought with grudging respect. *Alaric on the other hand...* she shuddered.

Jacob Barrington, owner and mayor of Barrington County, stood in the middle of the men. The torchlight cast a harsh glow so that his gaunt face looked almost skeletal. He raised the scroll of arrest and execution and unrolled it. He raised his voice to be heard over the wind.

"Today we execute the witch, Willow Kellar. Her crimes include consorting with the devil, the murder of two children, Peter Knotts (still missing) and Jenny Stone, whose remains we found at her residence, and the attempted murder of Livey Croft, aged two years. We, as a community, have observed that by her actions she has forfeited her soul, and by the law granted unto me by the Lord, has now forfeited her life. She will be hung and burned, and her remains will be buried in unconsecrated ground for all eternity."

The wind was howling now and it was fully dark. The moon was just beginning to rise, but did not cast much light. Through the torchlight the trees could be seen bending with the force of the wind. The men muttered and one of them spit on Willow.

Willow stopped her struggling. She looked at the gob of spit on her skirt and stared directly at the man who had insulted her. "Ezekiel Smith," she said. She turned her gaze to each man in turn, "Alaric Sweet (who sobbed), Michael Farmer, Joshua Brown, Tobias Baker, Jacob Barrington..."

She smiled. Her white eyes glinted.

"Hex," she hissed at them while they stood there, staring at her as if enchanted. "I hex you," she mouthed in the wild wind, yet everyone in the clearing could hear her voice clearly in their heads. "There will come a time when you will all gather again, and I will return. When I do, I will destroy your families and erase your family lines. I will bathe in their innocent blood, and I will show no mercy."

Dame Parquhar was stunned. Willow was cursing the idiots and they were just standing there, listening! "Kill her!!!" Dame Parquhar screamed, breaking from the trees and running towards the men to be heard over the wind. "Release the gallows," she screamed frantically, breaking the semicircle and grabbing Jacob Barrington's arm.

As if coming out of a trance, Jacob nodded and touched the bramble underneath Willow with his torch while the executioner released the lever.

In the second it took for Willow Kellar to fall, and her neck to snap, she looked directly at Dame Parquhar. "You'll watch," she whispered.

She was burned where she hung. The flames from the witch's pyre could be seen from town. Eerily, her body turned to ash and scattered with the wind. There was nothing left to bury.

From that time on, no living thing ever grew in that clearing again. Jacob Barrington had a tall rock placed on the dead earth, with a warning on it, chiseled in Latin: "Be warned. All he who consort with the Devil shall perish utterly."

Haunting

After the Kellar burning, the men responsible for the judgment and execution of Willow Kellar began to be haunted by their dead.

Jacob Barrington was pacing in Father Joshua Brown's living quarters at St. Thomas of All Angels, the town's small church. "What the hell is going on here, Joshua?" he asked in an aggrieved voice. The tension in the small, dark paneled room was palpable.

"Watch the *'h'* word Jacob. This *is* a house of God," Father Brown said wearily from behind his desk.

"The good people of this town—our friends—*your parishioners*—have become crazed with fear." Jacob ran his hands through his hair and rubbed his eyes. "They think the town has been touched by the devil. This is completely unbearable," he said desperately. Ghosts haunted his footsteps during the day and Willow's white eyes plagued his nightmares at night. Jacob looked haggard. Building a life in the middle of the wilderness had been a struggle for all the families. Every one of them had lost a member somewhere along the way. Seeing them reappear was deeply unnerving.

Father Brown looked at the visitor in his office. So far the apparitions had only appeared in the graveyard or around town, but none in the church itself. He had called in a specialist. Another priest was present in the room, dressed in black garb and priest's collar. He wore his black hat squarely on his bald head. Besides being a priest, Herman Mitchkovik was a specialist in the occult.

At this point Herman cleared his throat and shook his head at Joshua's desperate look. "You have been hexed," he said in his heavy German accent, "and not just you. Every member of your family vill be stained vith this curse until it comes to fruition. There is no escaping it or removing it." He shrugged.

Jacob stared at Herman. "That's helpful..." he trailed off weakly and turned to look at his friend. "That leaves you the lucky one Josh, with no descendants forthcoming," he said, his voice strained.

Father Brown took a deep breath and sighed. "Not true, Jacob. I wasn't always a priest. I became one after my wife died in childbirth. The child survived."

Herman nodded.

"Oh." Jacob Barrington was stunned. "Damn it, man, this is *awkward*. Why didn't you tell me this?"

Father Brown laughed. "What difference does it make now? I took Holy Orders and I'm a priest. I can't go back. My son has no idea that I'm his father. He thinks I'm his uncle."

Herman cleared his throat to speak again. "Ya. Vith Villow Kellar's hex marking your bloodlines, anyone involved vill draw death. Think of her curse as a vedge in a door that no longer closes fully. It is like that," he said simply.

Jacob looked confused. "What door? What's a veg?"

Father Brown sighed again. "That's 'wedge,' not 'veg' Jacob." He stared at Herman. "So vhat do ve...er...what do we do now?"

Herman was thinking out loud. "Of course, proximity is an important factor."

Even Father Brown looked mystified now. "Of course, so..."

"So, move your graveyard," Herman said, as if this was the most obvious thing in the world.

In the end Jacob Barrington and the Mayor of Limerick, The Honourable Sean Kirkman, came to an agreement and Barrington's small graveyard was painstakingly moved by carriage to a plot of land in the tiny settlement of Limerick. Father Brown worked tirelessly consecrating the ground for the new graveyard and then blessing each grave as it was moved. It took six months to complete. In Barrington, a new, larger church was built on top of the old site, and Father Brown once again blessed the ground that had been torn asunder.

The haunting stopped and peace returned to Barrington, but not to the six men. They convened and formed a secret group called The Circle. The Circle was responsible for protecting their descendants from Willow in the future. They strategically redesigned the layout of the town and put in a special warning system to alert future circle members to the presence of evil. Dame Parquhar recorded it all, as did Jacob Barrington.

Unfortunately, like all things journeying through the passage of time, the gravity of the hex faded and became a myth—a traditional "town" story told by the campfire. The fear faded. The lore passed on to the six's children became family ghost stories, losing its purpose as a means to transmit important knowledge. Like the Salem witch trials, the Kellar burning became a famous historical event for Barrington. Instead of fearing the hex, the town capitalized on its chilling potential, and Kellar Rock became a famous site to visit. Dame Parquhar's "Book of Record" was boxed for storage and lost for a time. Although Barrington boys were always given Jacob's diary to read every generation, and it was cared for as a precious heirloom, the contents were no longer taken seriously...

Until now.

Present

"Every town is famous for something.
For some it's hot springs, for others it's ruins... but not us. Nope.
Barrington, well, we burned a witch who hexed
our asses until the end of time.
It's a creepy story that draws a lot of morbid visitors to The Rock every year.
Crazy right?
Is it?
No, I don't think it is.
See, I've been watching what's been happening in our town.
You know what I think? I think that crazy witch wasn't kidding."
-Excerpt from Ella Croft's Diary

June

"Seasons come and seasons go in an endless cycle,
circling ceaselessly with time,
never changing,
always following the same earthly dance.
However...
Every so often cracks appear in the endless cycle that present opportunity.
Cracks with edges that open and multiply power.
The opportunity is not for good or for evil,
for that is defined by the caller.
It is just opportunity,
if you can find the crack."

Friday, June 21—Day of the Summer Solstice

The windmill stands at the town's western boundary, situated on West Road leading out of Barrington County. No one knows how long it has been there or when it was built, only that it hasn't worked in over four hundred years. One of the town's precepts is that it is never to be torn down, and so it remains.

The base is shaped like a lighthouse—fifty feet of grey, weather beaten wood supporting huge metal blades rusted in place. It sits alone at the edge of a rolling meadow and casts an ominous shadow in the path of the setting sun.

On June 21, during a wild storm, an incredible metal scream unfurled into the night as the windmill's blades began to turn for the first time in centuries. The groan of unoiled steel went unheard, drowned out by the crash of thunder.

To their credit, the townspeople did notice the next day that the windmill was spinning, but were not fazed by the phenomenon. What they found spooky was the fact that the windmill didn't make any noise, and it spun without any wind.

Nathalie's Journal – Entry for Friday, June 21

Today Dean and I spent the evening making our way through town, window shopping, buying candy and fudge, and eating our favorite greasy food at The Fry Diner. It was a wild night. It had been windy all day, and I don't mean a gust here and there, but gale-force as evidenced by my severely tangled hair. It tapered off a bit in the evening but then around midnight started up again. We raced home because the sky was black and seething with streaks of what appeared to be blue lightening flashing across the sky. It looked as if the sky was trying to crack itself open. At one point Dean and I were so startled at a flash of lightening and a crack of thunder, we just bolted for my front steps. By the time we got there (Dean before me), we were laughing, especially since I started making chicken noises and calling him yellow. He hates lightening, my good-natured teddy bear. Like usual he just laughed and hugged me, and we stood there for a while, just like that, and watched the sky bust open. That moment was the best part of my day.

July

Nathalie & Dean

Whether you become friends,
Or you become lovers,
In some way,
You are falling in love.

Nathalie's Journal - Entry for Tuesday, July 2

Today a new temp started at our office working in the mailroom and doing part time reception. Her name is Bethiah Lacey or "Beth" as she likes to be called. She must be at least nineteen, so a bit older than me. I've never met anyone like her before. When Shaemus introduced her around the office, Dean and I were getting coffee in the kitchen. She seemed so nice at first, and I could tell that Dean was impressed when he slopped coffee on himself. (Mind you, he does do that all the time.) However, being the authority on Dean on account of the fact that we've been best friends since we were five... the guy was impressed, not clumsy. And so was she. She giggled and breathed all over him. She touched, no *fondled,* his arm. He looked a little dazed, but he denies it.

Okay, there's no doubt that Dean is a cutie. Tall, broad shoulders, dark brown hair cut short to hide the "girly" curls, soft chocolate brown eyes, long black lashes, white pale skin like the popular vampires these days...yes, yes. Tra la la... I tried not to raise my eyebrows (but I did) and looked right at her. But here's the interesting part. Beth gave me the most unfriendly smile after Dean put his arm around me and introduced me as his pal, Nat. She turned her big blue eyes on me and asked me if I were named after some kind of BUG! I said, "nooo, my full name is Nathalie," and all the while I was thinking, *did she just say that to me?*

Shaemus and Dean just laughed. Men! Idiots! Anyway, *I* was shocked. She just met me! I was waiting for her to say she was kidding or *something,* but she never did! She sorta *humphed* and then grimaced when she offered me her cold white fingers and shook my hand. I swear I heard her say "squishy" under her breath! Dean says I'm imagining things, but I'm not.

Later on Beth left a phone message on my desk and spelled my name GNAT. Unbelievable. What NERVE. I told Dean to address me by my full name from now on, but he just laughed.

Seriously, what a witch!!

Nathalie's Journal – Entry for Wednesday, July 3

The company I work for during the summer is really great. They make candy, all types, but mainly chocolate. As I am in charge of designing candy boxes and wrappings, I get to come up with slogans and colour patterns. The owner, Shaemus O'Malley, employs students because he figures we know what's "in" for kids these days. Dad says it's because we're cheap labour, but whatever. I got Dean a job in sales and he does very well. I remember Shaemus being a little skeptical at first because he's a teen, but Dean has really proven himself. He's in charge of candy store sales in Barrington and Limerick, and he knows what kids like and want to buy. (He's the eldest of six.) The factory's candy is delicious, and with Dean's no-nonsense sales approach, it has been a winning combination. His clients just love that adorable face of his and his earnest disposition. I always tease him about it.

In our office, the first Wednesday of every month is batch-testing day. Shaemus puts out samples from the factory and we spend the day trying the different candies. It's my favorite day because Dean and I spend the day arguing the different merits of the candy (colour, texture, taste, blah blah) and then have a picnic lunch together outside. We're lucky because the factory is close to Barrington but still completely surrounded by woods. The picnic tables at the back are in a clearing with a few huge maple trees for shade just before the dense wood starts. Shaemus even had paths cleared so his employees could take walks in the woods during breaks. It's very pretty.

Anyway, this new girl Beth tagged along with us while we were doing our candy rounds. Dean always reserves that time for *me* and makes sure he's not out on a call so we can sample together. Beth asked if she could join us and my first instinct was to say no. She did not come across as very nice yesterday, but when I reread my journal this morning (for some perspective), it did appear that *perhaps* I had overreacted. No one could be THAT rude, could they? She was probably just trying to be funny, right? Maybe her sense of humour is just way off. Dean hesitated too, but when I agreed, you know, with a "the more the merrier" attitude, along with (I have to admit) a fake smile, he smiled and agreed too.

Boy, WAS THAT A MISTAKE. OMG!!!

We went around the tables trying different chocolates and then stopped to have our regular debate over the merits of caramel vs. fudge filling (I prefer caramel, he prefers fudge). Beth was licking her fingers when she interrupted us. She put her hand on Dean's arm and tells us how she's so full and how she's impressed, "I can eat so much."

That's what she said. I looked at her, certain I had misheard her, but I hadn't, TRUST ME. I said, "Sorry, what?"

And with the most innocent expression on her face, Beth told me she noticed that I eat a lot and that it *explains my size*. All the while she has this sympathetic look on her face while she's staring at me.

I looked at Dean and I could tell that he was shocked and uncomfortable. My face felt like it was on FREAKIN' FIRE. I must have been so red I was almost purple. (Unfortunately, there's no doubt that's true since my face does go extreme colours.) Then... she smirked at me. No wait, not a smirk, but a small malicious smile. Well, I'd never seen anything like that before. She narrowed her baby blue eyes and I knew right away that for whatever reason, this girl did not like me at all. I don't know why but I instinctively backed away from her a couple of steps.

Dean hadn't caught that fleeting look. His eyes were on me and his face was flushed with concern and anger. He defended me! He took my hand and stood beside me, forcing Beth to remove her hand from his arm, and asked her what her problem was. He told her she was being rude and that her comment was completely inappropriate.

"I am *so sorry*," she said to us with a light laugh and a shake of her head, tossing her long blond locks behind her shoulders. "I did not mean to offend."

(Oh, did I mention she has incredibly thick and long wavy blond hair? She looks like a mermaid from the back!) She turns to me and tells me that I'm beautiful just the way I am and laughs again, but her eyes are as cold as ice as they look at me.

Dean muttered, "you're damn right. Nathalie, let's go have lunch." Beth just raised her eyebrow at me. (And no, she does not have a unibrow. I only wish she did.)

In the end I didn't eat lunch. I went back to my desk to, well, hide and sulk. I was more upset than I let on. She had embarrassed me in front of Dean. It didn't help that now Dean was mad at me too. He wanted to have lunch and go for a walk, and when I wouldn't, he just stomped back to his desk with our lunch bag. Or so I thought. My desk is near a back window and as I was staring out, brooding, I could see Dean and Beth head to the forest. She had obviously smoothed things over with him. I watched her take his arm and I burned with anger at her meanness!

After work Dean waited for me and we biked home together in silence. We sat on my porch for a while and discussed what had happened today. I asked him why he walked with her at lunch.

He just shrugged. "Did it bother you?" he asked me.

Yes! I yelled in my head but to him I said, "a bit. You're *my* friend," I emphasized the "my."

"You ditched," he said and he shrugged again, not looking at me.

So I asked him if he thought I was fat and he said "nope." I asked him if he would tell me if I was fat and he said "nope." Exasperated, I asked him if he was lying and he said "no," but he finally looked at me and smiled. I could tell he had forgiven me for dumping him at lunch to pout. I asked him if he thought Beth was pretty. At that he took my hands and said, "yes, Beth is very pretty," but then he told me that I was the most beautiful girl he'd ever met since kindergarten. Before that the only gal in his life was his mom.

Okay, he was staring at me with his gorgeous, long lashed chocolate brown eyes. I thought he was teasing, but when I looked into his face, he was serious. Then he smiled and my eyes went to his mouth. His teeth seemed whiter and his lips redder against the five o'clock shadow of his beard. For a split second I actually thought Dean was going to kiss me, and I could not breathe. But then he put his forehead against mine instead and sighed. It was a real let down. I realized right there that I think my best friend is really hot, and I wanted him to kiss me. I mean, I always *knew* he was attractive, but I never, well, *experienced* it before.

We sat there for a couple of minutes, mainly because my heart was still hammering, and then mom showed up. *Greeeeaat timing.* We pulled apart and it was annoying because we looked so *guilty*—for *nothing*! I could tell she saw us head to head because she had this really big, stupid grin on her face when she walked up the steps and invited Dean for supper. He couldn't stay, of course, because he plays basketball at the high school on Wednesdays with his buddy, Luke Barrington. I was kind of glad. My face was red/purple again for the second time today. I felt awkward and my hands were sweaty and I needed to think about what had just happened. I think Dean could tell I was flustered. He kissed the top of my head and *sauntered* to his bike. To me, he seemed very pleased with himself.

After Dean left I helped mom with dinner and then went upstairs to relax, but I was too restless. I debated going to watch Dean play basketball, like I'd done *a million times* before, but now I felt shy. I tried to reach Tess—I really needed to talk to one of my girlfriends, but she was working.

I thought about what happened today and looked at myself very carefully in the mirror. Long shiny brown hair, thin face, green eyes, white teeth with a slightly crooked right canine, a few freckles... not ugly, I decided, and certainly slim enough. I snorted when I remembered Beth's comment, and an image of her with her long blond hair and extreme slenderness formed in my brain.

Do I have a rival?

Nathalie's Journal – Entry for Thursday, July 4

Dean was not in the office today. He was in Limerick (a town about twenty kilometers from Barrington) doing a tour of the candy stores with another sales guy. I was relieved in one way since I needed some space. I wasn't sure what my face would show and Dean was an excellent "Nathalie reader." At the same time the office was pretty dull without him.

In the morning I had a strange encounter with one of the girls in my office, Emma. I don't normally chat with her much, just the typical social conversation, like, "how are you?" and that type of thing. I was getting a coffee when she sidled up to me. She looked around to make sure we were alone and casually asked me what I thought of Beth. I was a bit startled; after all, Beth had only been with us for a few days. Apparently, yesterday Beth had made a comment about Emma's "healthy" body weight.

"You mean to tell me she subtly implied you were fat?" I asked her.

"Yeah, I think so." Emma confided. Now, Emma isn't fat, she's like me, normal! "There's something else," Emma added. She lowered her voice and looked at me with round eyes. "She made a comment about you too. A mean one. Beth said she wonders how Dean can stand to be around you considering your, er, fleshy shape."

"She—my what?" I whispered, horrified. I was shocked. I mean, what is that girl's problem? What a witch! I'm pretty sure my face got really red—again.

"I don't like her," Emma said decidedly. "She's mean."

My day didn't get much better after that and continued to follow the same theme. At lunch I had an appointment to see Dr. Peabody for my annual checkup.

"You're a perfectly healthy girl, my dear," he said to me, pleased, as he scribbled in my chart. "Don't gain any weight though," he added, "nobody will marry you." He chuckled at his own joke.

Oooh, I thought to myself, angrily. My face was definitely fire engine red.

The doc didn't notice.

"I'm only seventeen and a half. I'm not getting married," I muttered under my breath.

He didn't hear. "And make sure you exercise. Students who work at candy factories get fat." He hollered for his wife. Mrs. Peabody is the town nurse and dietician. (Apparently they were both married when they met and then ran off to Barrington to be together and escape social censure. But I digress.)

She arrived with the healthy eating guidelines and a recommended exercise plan. "Try and avoid sweets," she told me with a warm smile.

"Again, I work at a candy factory," I informed them.

"Yes dear. Remember, a moment on your lips, forever on your hips," she said lightly, patting my arm as she handed me the papers. "Don't overindulge."

"Don't eat that crap at all," was the doc's advice. He closed my file and sent me on my way.

When I got back to the office, the first person I saw was Beth. She was wearing a form fitting black dress with low-heeled black pumps. Nothing extravagant, but her slenderness and pale colouring made her appear willowy and ethereal. I studied her. She was thin, but almost unnaturally so, like she had been starving or was malnourished. It didn't take away from her beauty, but if you looked closely, it struck me as an odd thing this day and age. She must have felt me staring because she turned and smiled at me. Not a nice smile, a sly one, and then she sort of bared her teeth. I hid the papers from Mrs. Peabody behind my back and decided that now was not the time to confront her about her mean comments. I gave her an insincere smile instead.

Dean was waiting for me on my front steps when I got home, leaning back on his elbows. His tie was loose and the top two buttons of his shirt were open. He looked relaxed and his face broke into a smile when he saw me. My heart started to race and I could feel my face flush.

"Your father asked me if I've moved onto these steps permanently," he said with a laugh. I saw the bag beside him and smiled myself. We don't have a Chinese food restaurant in Barrington, so Dean always picks it up when he's meeting clients in one of the outside towns. Thursdays my parents eat at Joe's and then go dancing in the church hall, so we had the house to ourselves. I parked my bike and we went in. I broke open some cans of soda and we ate, Dean telling me all about his day (which was very successful). "You're quiet today," he said, looking at me with his beautiful, lashy, chocolate eyes.

"Same old," I told him. I wanted to tell him about my visit to the doctor, but I decided not to. I did tell him what Beth had said about me.

Dean just laughed. "Ignore her, Nat. She's a temp. She'll be gone in no time."

If only that were true. I have a feeling that a lot is going to happen before she leaves. That girl's going to be trouble.

Nathalie's Journal – Entry for Friday, July 5

Thank God it's the weekend. At lunch Dean and I went for a walk to the lake and back and I went in the bathroom to freshen up afterwards. I keep a hairbrush, toothbrush and toothpaste at the office in case I need them. I was brushing my hair when Beth walked in. When I cleaned the hair out of my brush and threw it out, Beth was looking at me aghast.

"You just leave your hair in the public waste bin?" she asked me. She seemed horrified.

I looked at her. "Why on earth not, Beth?" I asked her, curiously. "What do you do with your, er, hair?" God knows she had enough of it.

She seemed to recover slightly, as if realizing her behaviour was odd. "Oh, just some silly superstition from when I was growing up. I had a grandmother who followed the old ways, you know."

I didn't, but she continued.

"According to the lore, your hair and nail clippings can be used against you, to hurt you, should someone know the right spells, so you don't leave them lying around," Beth said.

I really didn't know what to say to that. *What a screwball. Used against you? Lore? Spells? What is this loony toon talking about?* "Er, well, I haven't had any negative experiences yet," I told her in my most positive tone.

She considered me for a minute with narrowed eyes. "I see," she said before she turned and left the washroom, her curls bouncing behind her.

She is definitely a strange one.

Later I went to see Dean at his desk to show him my newest designs for the Halloween packaging and saw Beth sitting at his cube, swinging her legs and laughing at what he was saying. Dean was flushed and looked completely enthralled with her. What a gorgeous couple they would make. Both tall, she was slender and light and he was broad and dark. I felt something dark roll inside me and I could feel my eyes narrow. I knew the feeling was jealousy. We were only best friends, but I'd been feeling more possessive over him in the last year, and the feeling was magnified a hundred fold at the moment. I was about to back away and hide when Dean saw me. His face lit up and he called me over. Beth was looking at me with dislike, and she didn't smile.

"Hello bug," she said to me.

Dean laughed a little awkwardly. "Is that a nickname?"

Beth and I stared at each other. Not a nickname, a perception. To her I was annoying, a pest. Something to get rid of. She had just drawn the line with me on one side and her on the other. We were not going to be friends. We were enemies. This girl barely knew me and yet, without a single doubt, hated my guts.

Dean pulled me down onto his lap and was completely oblivious to the hostile female undertone going on around him. The goof was talking to me in his evil, dastardly villain voice, "I see you have brought me some new wares to consider, minion, but theeese weeel not be good enough…"

I squirmed to get off his lap.

Beth looked down at us with disgust and left.

I *almost* got free but Dean pulled me back and wrapped his arms around me. I sometimes forget how big he is. At six feet two inches, he's not a small guy, and it's hard to escape his large hands. I stopped struggling and hissed at him.

"We're in the office, Dean! *What are you doing?*" I said with a wild look around. I started smacking his hands. He let me go, and when I turned to look at him, he was grinning.

"Don't worry about these dorks."

"Hey!" someone yelled.

"They know how much I love you," he said casually. He looked down at the marketing proofs I had brought. "These are awesome, Nathalie," he said sincerely, flipping through them. "You truly have a gift for concept and colour."

Someone started making kissy noises behind us.

I tried to appear nonchalant and hide my extreme pleasure at his comments, but it was hard. I watched him concentrate on my work, giving it its due, and I realized that I was completely head over heels in love with my best friend.

"Gotta go," I said, and fled.

Nathalie's Journal – Entry for Saturday & Sunday, July 6-7

What a great weekend! I spent Saturday morning shopping around Town Circle with my mom. We got groceries and we stopped in Ye Ole Sweete Shoppe, where we got ice cream cones. At Clara's Crafts & Crystals I picked up some new tarot cards while my mom got a new latch-hook kit. I needed to see what my fortune was telling me.

"Don't let Father MacGunne see you with those cards," my mom said, looking around the store furtively. "You know what could happen."

I do. Father MacGunne and Clara Innes have argued loudly for years over some of the contents of her shop. To our town priest, tarot cards and other such paraphernalia are the Devil's tools, and to parishioners caught with such paraphernalia, a strong suggestion to attend mass and confession usually follows. To Clara, they're just for fun. It must be the Irish in them because even though they argue loudly, and frequently, they always seem to be thoroughly enjoying themselves.

We stopped in Pages Bookstore to say hello to my manager dad and to browse for some new books. I found an interesting history book on our district, covering the three counties of Barrington, Limerick, and Superstition. I probably could have taken it out of the library, but it looked so interesting that I bought it. I noticed that the book covered the Kellar witch burning of 1595 and I wanted to read up on it a bit more, especially since the Kellars are members of our community (even though they claim they aren't directly related to Willow Kellar herself). After that, maybe I'll send it to Rain.

Dean came over for supper and then we played cards on the porch. He kept winning so I made him play fifty-two pick up before I stalked off. We debated walking to town to listen to the band that plays every Saturday from July to August (before the festival starts), but we were too lazy. Instead, we sat on the front porch swing with the lights out, looking at the stars and trying to catch the lightning bugs flying around us.

Dean took my hand and we curled our fingers together. Dean and I have been doing this since that fateful summer day in the park, all those years ago, when our friendship was formed.

Hiding under the slide, we held hands, which symbolized our joined forces against Reginald Baker, who was throwing sand at us and getting it in our eyes.

Our plan was simple. "Just drag him behind the slide so his mom can't see (not that she was paying attention to the little brat anyway), I'll sit on him and you rub his face in the sand. Then we'll spit on him so the sand sticks. No, wait, spit on him first."

"Okay," Dean whispered and nodded.

"Betcha he'll cry like a little baby," I told Dean confidently.

He nodded and scrunched up his face determinedly and we executed "Plan Sand Job." It worked like a charm, but contrary to my prediction, Reg didn't cry. Nor did he go whining to his mom. He took his licks then left the park. He never bothered us again. Instead, a few days later, he asked if he could play with us.

"Should we let him join?" I asked Dean. My fierce expression keeping Reg at a distance as he waited for our verdict.

"He ain't so bad," Dean said, scuffing his toe in the sand.

I nodded and beckoned for Reg to approach. Dean knew what he was talking about. I had utter faith in him.

We laughed as we remembered that day.

"It's interesting, isn't it?" said Dean. "Things have pretty much gone our way since," he mused, looking up at the stars.

It's true, I thought as we rocked quietly in the darkness. Since I met Dean I've never been alone or lacked anything. I hadn't failed at anything either. I looked at the sky feeling really, really lucky.

Sunday morning we walked to The Spires, our local mountain range, and hiked up Crystal Spire, which is the most western mountain. In the afternoon we swam at Crystal Falls, the waterfall at the base of the mountain. The weather was great, hot and sunny, but the water was ice cold. I jumped in but was out in seconds. Dean likes the cold so he stayed in longer, splashing around like a big kid in the bath. It was always a bit of a shock to see Dean without his shirt. His skin's so white it glows, which is why the contrast with his dark hair can often be startling, as I observed while he splashed around. I tried not to stare at him, even though I wanted to. My newfound realization that I was in love with him was making my eyes roam all over his body behind my sunglasses. I had to control them. I also felt self conscious in my bathing suit. After all, bikinis are only outdoor underwear.

The falls were absolutely gorgeous. Completely surrounded by trees, with bushes and wildflowers growing in wild profusion in between, the pool at the base of the falls was completely private. Ringed by tumbled rocks, the water cascades down from a spout in the mountain about a hundred feet up. They call it Crystal Falls, not only because the water is so clear you can see the bottom of the pool, but because the cascading water sends out droplets of mist that look just like crystals in the sun.

The sun, shining through the trees, created patches of light all around the falls and surrounding forest. It was so beautiful and peaceful—except for the crazy boy splashing around like an idiot, of course.

"Could you make a little more noise?" I asked Dean teasingly as I lay down on one of the wide, flat rocks. It was warm from the sun and felt great on my back. I was tired from the hike and my feet were hot and throbbing from my hiking boots, so I endured the cold and left them dangling in the water.

Dean swam over. "Poor Nathalie," he said, smiling. He lifted one of my feet out of the water and rubbed it. I think I moaned as his hands worked out the soreness. When he was done he kissed the bottom of my foot and held it to his mouth, which was very warm.

I went still and excitement fluttered in my belly. I wasn't sure what to do, exactly. I raised myself on my elbows and looked at him. His beautiful eyes were watching me, one eyebrow slightly arched, as if to say, "yeah, I kissed you. What are you going to do about it?" I stared at him for a long moment.

"Don't forget my other foot," I said as I hauled it out of the water, wiggling my toes as I lay back down. He laughed quietly as he rubbed.

I'm not sure what we would have said or what would have happened if we hadn't been interrupted right then by a family of swimmers with a picnic basket. Regardless, the spell was broken. Dean dove into the water and swam a few very rigorous laps before laying his towel beside me in the sun. We didn't speak. We just curled our hands together and snoozed.

Dean had his usual Sunday family dinner to attend so we parted after he walked me home. As the eldest of six kids, Dean was usually pretty busy helping out. He lingered as he gave me a kiss goodbye on my forehead, his hands on my shoulders and mine on his waist.

When I went in my dad was barbequing, wearing an apron that said "IF IT'S DEAD, I'LL COOK IT" in big letters. Mom stood by with the fire extinguisher. She calls it our Sunday burn-B-Q when daddy's cooking. Mom always makes a pasta dish in case the meat isn't edible.

My little brother was in the backyard battling his imaginary foes, vanquishing them, and as always, declaring himself the victor. He had his superman cape around his neck and was attempting to fly across the yard.

Nick is six. There are eleven years between us. He was mommy and daddy's surprise gift when she was forty. Now I understand what that means, but back then I thought it kinda sucked as far as gifts went. Rain didn't mind, but she knew everything being my big sister and three whole years older. Now twenty and an aspiring writer, she saved all year so she could spend the summer in Superstition County, writing a paper on the history of that community.

"Don't you think Superstition is a wild name for a county, Nathalie? Not one history book provides the name's origin. It's so odd. There must be a reason why it's called that, and I'm going to find out." That's exactly what she said and that's where she is right now, and I miss her. She rented an old barn in Superstition and is spending the summer there doing research. I heard that one of Luke Barrington's older brothers was there as well, but I had no idea which one, or why. I made a mental note to ask Luke the next time I saw him.

When Nick saw me, he stopped flying around the yard and ran up to me with some interesting news.

"Natlee, me 'n mommy saw a girl named Beth in town today," Nick said. He took my hand with his pudgy one. "She was in the candy store and mom said 'hi' because she saw Beth's pass for the candy factory. She thought maybe you and Beth were friends." Nick looked at me very earnestly. "She doesn't look right," he whispered to me. "There's something black inside her. I couldn't stop staring at her." He fidgeted with his cape as if to give himself courage and started again. "While mom was talking to Bella and buying our candy, Beth was looking at me as if she was mad. Her eyebrows were in a V like this," he whispered, scrunching up his face to show me.

The wind blowing through the yard sent chills down my back despite the day's warmth. Intimidating a six-year old! Unbelievable!

"She was mean to me, Natlee, when mom wasn't looking," he told me in a trembling voice. He obviously had not said anything to mom. "She told me that kids like me get hurt if they tell stories to adults. You're not an adult yet, are you?" Nick's eyes held fear, and knowledge.

"Only in a few months," I said reassuringly. "You can tell me anything."

All of a sudden his expression was not that of a six-year old, but something way older. "You stay away from her, Natlee," Nick said with a frown of his own. "She's a bad kid inside." Then he was off running and mom was yelling for us to come to dinner.

So now I have a few questions. What is Beth's problem? What did Nick think he saw? And more importantly, what's up with Dean?

Superstition County
July 4

Dear Nathalie,

Hey little sister! How are you? I'm doing great. I'm hoping this letter actually gets to you since it'll leave the post office via horse and not by mail truck! I miss you so much (who would have thought, you pest) and have so much to tell you.

Did you know that you can't drive a car in Superstition? This town is nuts. I had to exchange my car for a HORSE at the town gates because the roads are for horses and carts only. I actually had to ride the animal to the "farmhouse" I'm staying at. (It's actually a converted barn.) I bounced on that bastard until I thought my ass was going to break! Thank God the people in this town are so nice. They may have snickered at my equestrian skills, but they got a cart and unloaded my car for me and helped me get settled. Not only that, they made me so many welcome meals that I'm still eating them! One thing they have allowed me is a fridge and stove that run on gas. I think they think I'm going to starve otherwise (and I absolutely would), or burn down their barn if I tried to use the fireplace. They use huge blocks of ice to keep things cold. It's a wild and different life here. I miss my hot shower!

There is a Barrington boy staying next door to me. He's really interested in my research. It's one of the middle ones, Gabriel. I think he's more interested in my fridge and stove, though. It's like he's moved in. He tells the townspeople that he cooks on his hearth. Right... (this would be sarcasm). If opening a can of beans and eating raw hotdogs is cooking on the hearth, then he gets a gold star! Actually, we've struck a deal. He helps me out with some of the stuff around here, like caring for Popper (my horse) and fixing things falling off the barn, and I cook for the both of us when I'm home. When I suggested he spring for the groceries since he's rich, he agreed in a very desperate manner! It could have been my incredible sexy charm, but I suspect it was the banana bread I'd just baked helping him with his decision. I'm such a stinker!! But don't feel too bad for him. He ate almost the whole thing by himself. He was moaning! I think he's missing his momma. Anyway, so far our arrangement has worked well (and no, I don't make him buy everything). The barn I'm in has not fallen down around my head and he doesn't look like he's starving or dying of scurvy anymore. The townspeople are none the wiser, so mission accomplished.

I spend most of my days at the town's archives, or in the library doing research. Nothing is on computers, of course, so I have to read through piles of paper with archaic writing. It's pretty neat, even if I have to handwrite everything. Really though, people in the past couldn't spell for shit.

Oh, and I got a dog. I rescued her from the town brats. I just love her! Her name is Abbey and she's really fat for a stray. Surprisingly, I love Popper too even though cleaning up his giant poops makes me gag!! Hey, I'm changing and growing here. Soon I'll be a country girl!

Otherwise, not much exciting happens. There was a bit of a kerfuffle when I first arrived. A young teenage girl, Tilly Black, went missing from the town. She's your age. Apparently she's not quite "normal" in the head, if you know what I mean. They are still sending search parties in the woods to see if they can find her. It's so sad. Her parents are beside themselves.

Please write and tell me your news. How's Dean? You know the guy is absolutely crazy about you, right? Objectively, I can say he's hot, but let me clarify that with an "ew" since he's, like, my little brother. But he is HOT. So... anything interesting happening? Anything at all?? Write me!

Love you,

Rain xoxoxo

PS: Say hi to Nick and the "rental" units, and give him a big kiss for me!

Barrington County
July 10

Dear Rain,

Hello beloved sister! I got your letter yesterday. It arrived safe and sound! I was so excited to hear from you! All is well here in Barrington County. Your family sorely misses you, but we certainly enjoyed your news. It made us laugh so much! Mom showed the letter to Claire Barrington (who photocopied it after mom blotted out all the swear words). Apparently Gabriel calls occasionally but doesn't write, so she has no idea what's happening with her son, and you know how Mrs. B is about her boys. She was obviously desperate for information and reread your letter a few times. Mom said some of his brothers snickered at the starving part. If you have any influence over him, get him to write his mother for God's sake!

Not much happening here except for a new girl in town, named Beth, causing me grief. She has been nothing but mean and hostile towards me. She's just a temp at our company but she's already caused so much trouble there. She's hitting on Dean big time. At first I thought I wouldn't mind if Dean had a girlfriend. We've always just had each other but now that we're seventeen, it's inevitable that we, you know, branch out. But when I saw her flirting with him, and them laughing together, something inside me snapped. I realized that I'm completely in love with my BEST FRIEND! I don't know what to do! I feel so shy and obvious. I wish you were here. I really need someone to talk too! He's also been doing some romantic things. He kissed my feet at the falls, he holds me longer, and we stare at each other.

Of course, enter Beth, the tall, pale, slender witch (excuse my language), who is going around telling people they're fat or ugly, and in the office! It's not a high school! The power of suggestion is incredible. People are very unhappy, including me. So I ask you, why would sweet, beautiful Dean, want to date me?

Anyway, I'll sort it out. I was happy to hear about your new pets. Check and see if Abbey is pregnant. Strays are usually thin from starvation. Either that or someone was feeding her. As for Popper's poop, well, it's rich with nutrients so... use it in your garden. You have a garden, right? Don't people pay lots of money for manure? Better yet, sell it!! Ha ha, no, I agree, that was not funny.

Oh, one last thing about the witch... she picked on our little brother. Apparently she threatened him. He said she's evil. You know Nick, for a six-year old he's pretty damn intuitive, and we've had some very interesting experiences with him in the past exposing liars. Don't worry; I'll keep a close eye on him.

That's my news for now. Back to work tomorrow (yay—not). I found an interesting book at the bookstore. I'll send it to you when I'm done reading it. It's research on the three counties of Barrington, Limerick, and Superstition, sort of along the lines of what you're doing.

Let's hope this letter gets to you! Onward, horsie!

Love you,

Nathalie

Superstition County
July 15

Dear Nathalie,

Quick but important note, babe.

You are awesome. Don't let anyone tell you otherwise.

AND

Nobody, but NOBODY messes with a Parker. You tell that bitch that Rain Parker will make a special trip home to kick her skinny white ass if she so much as looks at Nicky again.

You tell her!

Rain

Nathalie's Journal – Entry for Thursday, July 11

Thank God tomorrow is my last day of work before my vacation. Beth is completely out of control. I've worked at this candy company for two years part-time and as a full-time summer student. The environment has always been friendly and fun. Shaemus O'Malley (the owner) has always been the most jovial and generous man I know, and not only that, always encouraged his people to do the same. Hell, I've been here full-time since mid-June and I can tell something has seriously changed. First of all, Beth has accumulated a gang of *minions* and they're going around the office picking on people. Someone wrote "FATTIE!" on my lunch bag in permanent marker. When Dean saw that he got so mad he wanted to kill someone.

I wasn't the only victim.

Another girl, Nadia (who admittedly has a larger than normal nose) had a giant nose and the words "SNOT BAG" written on *her* lunch bag. Again, in permanent marker! That's just not cool, and that's only a couple of examples. Beth and her pretty girl tag-alongs are whispering and snickering at others as well.

I went to hide in Dean's cube and told him about the razing and the insult gang. "Who cares about what they think, Nat? Ignore them."

"Nathalie," I corrected automatically, looking over his cube wall for the roving bitches.

"Nathalie," he smiled. "Hey, look at me," he said, shaking my arm.

I did. What a dreamboat.

"Maybe she comes from a place where they were really mean and competitive. Anyway, if she chose all the pretty girls to be in her 'gang,' then why didn't she choose you?"

Dean's innocence of the female gender was astounding, and I had to smile at him. When he smiled back, I couldn't help but stare at his beautiful mouth, and the warm expression on his face. It was one of those moments again where we sort of looked at each other for a time. Of course Beth chose that *exact* moment to interrupt. The witch.

"I wish I had time to chat," she said, and laughed, but I could hear the spite. I looked at her with dislike, hoping to get rid of her. She didn't leave, so I decided to be intrusive myself.

"Actually, we were talking about you," I informed her, turning around. "We were wondering where you came from and how you ended up *here*." *Lucky us.*

Beth looked at me suspiciously. Why, I have no clue. None of her responses make any sense to me. "I come from Superstition," she informed me rather warily.

"Superstition, eh? Where are you staying in Barrington? There aren't any boarding houses or hotels here," I quizzed. I put my hands on my hips for emphasis.

There was no inn in Barrington County and no graveyard either. The joke is "no strangers and no ghosts." I think a few residents tried to propose both at one point, but the town council turned them down flat. It's not even a proposal you can make anymore. Well, it's John Barrington's town and he can do what he wants with it. The lack of an inn makes it hard for people who want to spend a few days visiting our Harvest Festival. The fairgrounds are huge, with lots of things to buy, eat, see, and do. People come from all over to set up shop and hawk their wares. Thousands of visitors flock to the fair but they have to stay in the surrounding towns. Superstition has some quaint lodging for those who like to get away from modern conveniences, but it's really far north. It's Limerick that booms when the fair opens in August. The good thing is that Barrington compensates with shuttle buses from different points in Limerick and Superstition that leave every half hour, but our visitors get annoyed anyway. Barrington is small but picturesque, and people want to stay in town. The Harvest Festival makes August through October the most exciting three months of the year in these parts. The festival opens August first and closes on Halloween.

Dean interrupted, "Nat…thalie, isn't your sister…" he started when I stepped back onto his foot. "Ow ow ow ow ow ow ow ow," Dean said, pushing me off him, comment forgotten.

For some reason, I didn't want Beth to know that my sister was in Superstition. I looked curiously at Beth and waited for her to answer my question.

"I'm currently boarding in the room above Clara Innes's shop for the summer."

"Really? Interesting. Why come to Barrington?" I asked. The folks in Superstition didn't often encourage their young people to leave and work in modern society. In fact, it was deeply frowned upon.

Beth was starting to look irritated. "I wanted to work at the candy factory and have some different experiences," she said, rather defensively. "Mr. O'Malley was kind enough to offer me work." She smiled at me insincerely. "Not that it's any of *your* business, Miss Nosey Pants."

I was looking at her intently while she spoke and noticed that she looked healthier since she started at the factory. Her face was not so gaunt and starved looking. She really was pretty. Too bad she was such a bitch.

"Well, that was very lucky," I told her. "Knock on wood," I said, knocking my fist on Dean's forehead.

Then Beth did the strangest thing. "You invoke the wood?" she asked in a panic, looking around for wood, and knocked her fist on Dean's desk.

Dean and I stared at her, a bit surprised. "You okay, Beth?" he asked her curiously.

"I'm fine, just fine," she said, clearly annoyed with herself.

"You superstitious, like your town?" I couldn't help it. I smirked at her.

She frowned at me. "You really shouldn't mess with things you don't understand," she said ominously and turned to leave, but then stopped and turned towards us again. The floozy *smiled* and leaned towards Dean, smoothing her dress down and making her bust pop out!

"Looks as if you're going to need a friend while GNAT is gone for the next two weeks, *honey*," she breathed at him. "But don't you worry," she said, patting his knee, "I'll take *very good* care of you while she's gone," she purred.

Dean blushed. BLUSHED! She was looking at him as if she had stripped off all his clothes and all there was left was a handsome lollipop ready for licking. I shook the image out of my head, and pursed my lips. I tried really hard *not* to have a reaction, but I couldn't help it.

I looked at him with disgust and he shrugged. "What?" he muttered.

All of a sudden I was overwhelmed. I didn't want to go on vacation anymore. My parents take us to the beach every year, but now I had a very bad feeling.

Beth was looking smug and was smiling at me in that sly way of hers. "See you later," she said and walked away, swinging her backside suggestively.

I looked sharply at Dean and he looked at me, guiltily. "What??" he muttered again in an aggrieved voice.

"Well, *really*," I said frostily and stomped back to my desk. When I got there I opened the cupboard in my cube to get my coffee cup, and I swear, huge black spiders came tumbling out in a rush. I screeched and jumped back, and everyone around me came running.

"Spiders!" I yelled, and everyone recoiled, checking the floor around their feet, but then they drifted closer when *not one spider* could be seen. They had completely disappeared. I looked around frantically, but there was nothing! NOTHING!

"Sorry, everyone," I said, a bit sheepishly. I was starting to feel really silly. Hallucinations now? I did need a vacation.

Emma was there. She looked around and then sidled up to me at my desk. "I don't like slugs," she told me, looking around with huge eyes. She lowered her voice conspiratorially. "They're moist," she shuddered. "They give me the creeps. Anyways," she paused and looked around again, "had a whole bunch at my desk earlier today after a run in with You Know Who, and then they were gone." She looked at me straight in the eyes. "Something weird is going on here Nat. It's that girl. Watch your back." She drifted away just as Dean appeared, panting, with his fly swatter.

"What on earth are you going to do with THAT?" I asked with a laugh. It was shaped like a shoe and said "SMASH!" whenever it was used. Unfortunately, it seemed to be broken since it kept saying "SMASH!" over and over again, without one bug being swatted.

"I heard there were spiders...but you obviously don't need my help," he said, looking around curiously, kicking aside the shoes under my desk and checking under papers. He looked at me and said loudly, "brave old Peterson called me."

Peterson, who sat beside me, scowled and gave him the finger.

I played along. "I thought I heard a high-pitched shriek," I said, looking at Peterson and laughing. He laughed at that because it was true. He had a paralyzing fear of spiders.

"Hey, if you can't help, get help," he said smugly.

"False alarm," I told Dean, still slightly miffed with him, but at the same time, pleased that he had come to my rescue. It was very warm in the office. His hair was damp at his temples and his tie slightly askew from running.

"You dropped this," Dean said in a strangled voice, after I straightened his tie and ran my fingers through his damp hair. He was a bit flushed as I smiled up at him and took the item from his hand. It was a sachet, bound with ribbon, and it *stank* like something had died in it.

"That's not mine," I said quietly, picking it out of his hand. A chill ran over me and I felt afraid. It looked and smelled...evil. "Ew," I said and tossed it in the garbage.

Dean picked it up, looked at it curiously and then pulled it apart. Inside were dried plants and herbs along with a large dead spider and someone's...

"Hair," I said, looking at the mass of brown strings.

"Okay, that's gross," he said, tossing it back into the garbage.

A second later I yelped as my garbage went up in flames.

"Better to burn that," Peterson said quietly, standing there with some matches.

We stared at him as if he was crazy, but deep down I agreed.

"Maybe it'll start the sprinkler system," he said, looking up at the ceiling hopefully. "It's damn hot in here."

But within seconds the fire was out and there was nothing left but ashes.

"Fire is the great cleanser," he said, going back to his desk.

He's weird, but then Dean put his arm around my shoulders and kissed the top of my head and I didn't care about Peterson anymore. Beth passed by, a venomous look on her face, but she didn't stop. Somehow, I knew all of this was connected to her in some way.

When I got home mom and dad were arguing over vacation supplies. Nick was packing his cape, his sand toys, and his stuffed animals in his Sponge Bob backpack. We're leaving tomorrow night, right after I finish work. The plan is to arrive Saturday morning, eat a hearty breakfast, and sleep on the beach before taking possession of our beach house in the afternoon. Normally, I am so excited, but the thought of leaving Dean was really upsetting me.

I was still standing at the front door, assessing the level of chaos when it swung open and smacked me in the arm. I looked behind me and there was Dean, already changed out of his suit into tan shorts and a white tee with black lettering that said, "Bros before hoes" (with a garden implement pictured).

"Are you kidding me?" I said when I saw it. I had to laugh.

"Sorry, Nat," he apologized—rubbing my lower back where he assumed the door hit me.

"Er, um, actually, that would be my arm," I pointed out dryly. He just grinned and smacked me on the bottom.

"What are you doing here?" I asked him, smacking his hand away.

"Your parents invited me for dinner," he said, and then mom called us.

"Come and eat, you three." She looked at Nick, who had just declared he was packed. "Your clothes and everything?" she asked curiously.

"Clothes?" he said blankly. Mom sighed.

"Let's eat and sort out the travel plans, and the packing," she said and headed for the kitchen.

Dean and I followed. My dad had been barbequing, but this time the meat actually looked edible. He had purchased a new, top of the line, Grill Master 4000 barbeque. My mom has told him repeatedly not to blame his tools, but he does anyway, hence the new equipment. He took off his apron, which said "MEAT FEAR ME" and sat down, rubbing his hands together.

"Wash up," my mom told him.

"Real men don't wash," he replied in a loud voice, looking at his meaty successes.

"WASH UP!" my mom yelled at the top of her voice. We all bolted for the bathroom, laughing. My father beat us all there. Once we were all seated again, and the food had been served, my father started talking.

"Nathalie, we have a surprise for you," he said primly. I looked up from my plate where I had been stuffing my face with meat, which was surprisingly good. My cheeks were puffed out like a blowfish full of water. Dean laughed, trying to poke me with his fork.

"We've invited Dean to come on vacation with us, and his parents have graciously given their permission," my mom said. At this point I was frantically trying to swallow my food, but was choking a little. Nick started slapping me on the back.

"Mmm fne," I mumbled, waving his little arm away. I got my food down and I JUST BEAMED WITH HAPPINESS. "ARE YOU SERIOUS!?" I yelled, looking at Dean.

He was laughing. "My bag's in the car!!"

"That's SO AWESOME!" I yelled. We jumped up and down with glee. Wow!

My dad "harrumphed" a little. "Okay, okay, settle down kids... there are RULES," he told us sharply, his eyes slit and shifting between us. "This is a vacation and not pandemonium. It will not be all fun and games." My mother was rolling her eyes. My dad stopped when he realized what he'd just said, but then he went on. "Rules will be presented to you both tomorrow in the car, once I write them. You will study said rules. You will *obey*." My father was rubbing his hands together again.

Rules, smules! My father was all talk. Dean was coming with me! HA, sucks to be Beth! I can't wait to *inform* her tomorrow.

Nathalie's Journal – Entry for Friday, July 12

We're off! It's late now. We've been on the road for a few hours and we left later than we thought. We sang some songs, ate some junk food, but now Nick and Dean are dead to the world. In the front, dad is driving and humming to himself. Mom is asleep. In the back, Dean is drooling on the window on the driver's side, I'm snuggled against him, writing in my journal, and little Nick is curled up against me, clutching his orange dino. I'm so happy right now. Everyone I love is with me (except for Rain, but four out of five isn't bad). Dean is so cuddly, like a giant teddy bear. His hand is warm on my leg and my stomach feels all fluttery. I have this incredible urge to kiss his adorable face.

Of course, dad's trip rules are nonexistent, as I expected. "I'll make 'em up on the way," he said. He's the worst troublemaker out of all of us. It's too much of a task to catalogue all your sins to make sure no one else commits them!

To note—Beth was hopping mad when I casually informed her that Dean had been invited on vacation with us. I must have looked so smug and self-satisfied! She didn't even respond when we bounced out the door, shouting our goodbyes. Boo hoo! God, she's such a witch, but one I won't be seeing for two whole weeks! Yahoo!

Nathalie's Journal – Entry for Sunday, July 28

We're back from the beach. Wow, what a vacation. I'm going to try and record how wonderful it all was.

When we got there Saturday morning (two weeks ago already!) we were all lying on the beach by eleven in the morning. Our beach house was only available in the afternoon, so we were killing time. Of course my dad wouldn't let any of us get anything out of our bags to change.

"Are you crazy?" he asked us with wild eyes, pointing at the precariously packed car. "I move one thing and it's over! We'll be hauling everything ourselves."

So, we found ourselves sitting in the sand in our clothes. A group of girls had settled beside us with their towels and bikinis. I felt so self-conscious in my rolled up joggers and tee-shirt. They were giggling and one of them was gorgeous. So gorgeous that even I could appreciate what a perfect figure she had. Unfortunately, she took one look at Dean and you could tell right away that she had found herself a prospective summer fling. She started chatting with us and pumping Dean for information about himself.

Dean's my best friend and I wanted him to have a great time, so I tried to be nice, but I just ended up being quiet. I felt sick and heartbroken the whole time. Dean was *mine* and I didn't want to share him. I just got him out of Beth's clutches! I hated that he laughed at her stupid comments. I struggled to hide it. My dad finally whistled for us to hit the road, and even though Dean had his arm around me and was trying to cajole me into a better mood, I was despondent.

Carrie (her name), the airhead, asked us to meet her at the pier that night around seven, and she would take us to a beach party.

"You can meet the gang," she said smiling and putting her hand lightly, but possessively, on Dean's arm. She *liked* him. The worst? I could tell she knew *exactly* how I felt about him, and she didn't care. "Maybe we'll find a nice guy for you."

Now Dean wasn't smiling.

"Perhaps," I had replied in rather unfriendly tones. Maybe it was the lack of sleep that made me chilly with our new friends, but after we unpacked and went to the pizza parlor on the main strip, I cheered up. No point in being a party pooper. No one ever wants to hang around those people.

Afterwards, Dean took my hand and suggested a walk on the beach. Some people were still sunbathing, but most looked as if they were settling down for romantic picnic dinners. Dean curled his fingers with mine and we headed down the beach, looking for stones and shells, not really talking about anything but just enjoying each other's company. I was very conscious of the time, having made up my mind about things, and as his best friend, decided that his fun was more important. We were pretty far from the pier when I suggested we turn around.

"Why?" Dean asked me. He had planted himself in the ocean with the waves lapping around his ankles, burying his feet deeper and deeper in the sand.

"I thought you wanted to meet Carrie," I said, looking at him. He wasn't smiling at me. He looked, well, exasperated.

"What??" I asked, putting my hands on my hips.

"Where did you get that idea? I never said that," he replied, annoyed.

I hesitated. "I don't know, you seemed to like her..."

He huffed loudly. "Well, I do NOT want to meet Carrie. Nor do I want to go to a stupid beach party," he added through clenched teeth. He looked at me. "Come here for a second," he said and reached out his hands.

I looked down and his feet were pretty stuck. I stepped forward. I could feel him staring at me, but all of a sudden I was feeling shy. I just took his hands but he bumped our hands underneath my chin, forcing my face up and rested his forehead against mine.

He sighed. "Nathalie, do you have any idea why I wanted to come on vacation with you and your family? Do you know why I was so happy?" I looked at him. His eyes were so warm, his smile made his mouth so... inviting.

"Why don't you enlighten me," I said softly. I knew something big was coming. (Okay, I hoped something big was coming.)

"I came so that I could spend every waking minute with you. No going home and wondering what you're doing or if you're going to call. No basketball where I constantly eye the door to see if you're going to come and watch me this week. No more daydreaming about beautiful Nathalie because Nathalie will be with me all the time, to swim, build sandcastles, hold hands and walk on the beach. When I sleep will be the only time we're apart, and even then you'll be in my dreams. That's why I came here. Not to meet other girls or hang out with other people. Just you, you and your family."

Then Dean pulled me close and he kissed me. His mouth was warm and salty and I was kissing him back. I slipped my arms around his neck. I wanted to inhale him. When he slipped his tongue into my mouth I literally melted against him. What a sensation. Of course we realized that we were making a spectacle of ourselves.

"When it's dark," he promised, hugging me really tight.

"Yes," I whispered. The ocean was running over our feet. Both of us were stuck in the sand together.

So, vacation ended up being sunny days languishing on the beach, our hands entwined just waiting for night to fall. The evenings were long, warm, starlit summer nights making out on a blanket in secluded dunes covered by the thick black of night without streetlights. He was so hot, his lips, his mouth, his tongue. He ran his beautiful large hands all over my body, his feverish skin pressed against mine, his mouth kissing my neck, my mouth, my eyes, and holding me so tight. The sensations running through my body were unbelievable. I couldn't get enough, and the hours of the day waiting to be held and loved by Dean began to be torture. At one point I thought that the pleasure of our secret sessions would break me apart and I would splinter into a million pieces.

One evening it rained and I knew that my private time with Dean was not going to happen. I was not happy. I kept trying to sit on Dean's lap to snuggle but he kept pushing me off and looking at my father with wild eyes. Thank God my father is easily bored, and so is Nick. He announced that he was leaving for the pier to become king of the arcade for a few hours. Nick squealed with excitement. I desperately prayed my mother would go along. She looked up from her book and *volunteered* to go along to make sure daddy didn't spend all our trip money. Dad looked at us and enquired whether we wanted to attend.

"Not me," I told my dad. "Bo-ring. I'm just going to stay here and read."

"No thanks, Mr. Parker," Dean said with a smile. "I'll keep Nathalie company," he said, looking at me. Dean's smile had turned wolfish, and I wondered if I were wearing a lamb suit.

"Duds," my dad said, turning away.

Dean looked at me. His eyes were burning. I was breathless and my stomach was fluttering with excitement.

There was confusion while they got organized to leave. *Go, go, go,* I thought desperately, getting my brother into his rain jacket...and then the door slammed shut and we were alone. Within seconds I was in his arms and he was crushing me against him. His kisses were hot and wet. His large, warm hands were running up my back, under my shirt, up to my neck, holding my head tightly so he could attack my mouth with his tongue. We ended up in his room for two blissful hours, making out, touching and pressing against each other in his soft bed. It was heaven.

What an incredible time. My vacation was a haze of beach and Dean. We've decided to keep our change in relationship a secret for now. Less prying eyes, or should I say, suspicious eyes, if we want to be alone together. Right now our parents think nothing of us lying on my bed together with the door closed (because we'd been doing it since we were kids), and we want to keep it that way.

When we got home Dean was desperately smooching me up on my porch before heading home. I was laughing and he just kept saying how beautiful I was.

I can't wait to see him tomorrow. It'll be in the office, but there are plenty of private rooms...I wonder what happened with Beth while I was gone? I can't wait to tell her that Dean's *taken*.

Sadie & Luke

*"**Nurse**: His name is Romeo, and a Montague;*
The only son of your great enemy.
***Juliet**: My only love sprung from my only hate!*
Too early seen unknown, and known too late!
Prodigious birth of love it is to me,
That I must love a loathed enemy."
-Shakespeare's Romeo & Juliet, Act 1, Scene V

Sadie & Luke

Sadie closed the door to the farmhouse quietly and locked the door. She stood there for a moment, her slim shoulders sagging slightly in relief, before straightening her spine and turning sharply on her heel, calmly walking down the front steps. Not one emotion showed on her pale face. Her long black hair, cut Cleopatra style, fell to her waist, perfectly brushed and perfectly straight. Her skin was white like alabaster, and unlike many of the seventeen year olds in town, without blemish. Her eyes were a dark violet surrounded by long soft black lashes in a long angular face with a wide mouth and red lips. Sadie was as pretty as a heroine out of a fairy tale, but without the smiling and the "singing to birds" part. Sadie never smiled. Her white summer dress clung to her slender form and buttoned all the way up to her neck. Sadie had no friends and was never teased or bothered. The other kids called her "The Ice Witch" because of her heritage and frosty manner, and people joked that she was like air conditioning. You were always cold around her.

Sadie did not care what anyone thought about her. She was not allowed to have friends, so she didn't bother. Right now she had a problem and she was headed to the library to see what information she could find to solve it.

Sadie was a Kellar, and while her family claimed that they were not descendants of *the* Willow Kellar, the notorious witch the town burned over four hundred years ago, that was only partially true. Only Sadie was from Willow's direct line, but they kept that a deep secret. Who knew what would happen if the town found out? She certainly wouldn't lose any friends since she didn't have any, but it was the hex that kept the Kellars quiet. The Kellars have been protecting Willow's direct descendants for over four hundred years in the hopes that the hex would be activated. The famous hex—the last words Willow Kellar had uttered before she died.

On top of her own problems, in the last few weeks, Sadie had noticed a change in her Aunt Liora and her Uncle Boris. While there was never much love between them, they always took good care of her and followed the social norms required to keep prying eyes away from their home. Now, however, things seemed to be changing. Her aunt was acting strange. Sadie could hear her chanting and meditating, lighting candles and drawing diagrams on all the floors around the house. She was treating Sadie like a possession and not a person, constantly asking her where she was going and who she was spending time with.

"I don't have any friends, aunt," she would reply mildly. Liora would look at her with narrowed eyes.

"What about boys then, girlie? You're a mighty fine looking lass, like your ancestor Willow, who could turn a few heads. You've the look of her, from what I understand." Liora would laugh, baring her long yellow teeth. Liora did not inherit the legendary beauty of Willow Kellar. "Crone" was a better description of her.

Sadie frowned, her expression tight. "*Boys* do not interest me," she would say coldly, looking straight at her aunt. "I have no use for them."

"That's probably best," her aunt would reply without a smile.

Her uncle was more withdrawn than usual. But as strange as her aunt and uncle were, Sadie could live with that. What she couldn't live with was her new problem. In the last week Sadie had started missing time. Almost two hours she could not account for. She had no idea what she did or how she had arrived at her destination (The Rotunda in Town Circle). Sadie was meticulous with her person, her time, and her things.

Sadie had also been feeling strange. Someone was whispering to her at night, just before she fell asleep and then again, just before she woke up, in those in-between times of almost consciousness. She was frustrated because she couldn't remember what the voice was saying. She was frightened because the voice was insidious, persuasive and beautiful. Yet behind the words were such determination, anger, and power. It wanted something from her. Sadie felt her person was under attack, and she needed help fighting it.

Sadie headed towards the main strip of town. She walked because she hated bikes, the main means of transportation in town. She felt they were for tomboys and hooligans. Sadie lived in the south east corner of Barrington. The center of town was not far, but it was a good fifteen-minute walk. She could have shaved off a few minutes by cutting through Barrington land, but she didn't. The Barringtons and the Kellars had an age-old animosity, which had begun with the murder of Willow Kellar.

Sadie arrived at the library and walked up the thirteen steep steps to the old door and pulled it open. The wonderful smell of books and old building hit her and she was instantly comforted. Barrington's town center wasn't large. Many of the buildings were hundreds of years old and appeared to be squeezed together, which was part of its incredible charm. Like most of the business buildings on Barrington's Main Circle Road, Barrington Library was no exception and looked like a tall and narrow English townhouse. The outside was decorated with dark wood paneling and brass trim with a sign perpendicular to the building. Inside it had four narrow floors completely crammed with books. The only concession to modernity was the huge librarian's desk and two computers found on the main floor near the front door. This is where you could search for a book or an article, but mostly the librarian did it for you. The library was never that busy. The two top floors had reference books, articles, and both fiction and non-fiction works. The main floor held magazines, children's books, and more reference materials. The bottom floor held the archives. Seating was available on every floor, and there were quiet nooks among the stacks.

It took a few seconds for Sadie's eyes to adjust. When she did, her heart dropped, although not one emotion showed on her face. Luke Barrington was the librarian today. *Luke,* she thought wistfully, but then she felt anger stir inside her and again had that odd sensation that she was experiencing someone else's emotions. Out of all the boys in town, Sadie had always liked Luke despite his heritage. As a gawky bookworm, he was often picked on when he was younger. When they were five Sadie remembered defending Luke against one of the bigger playground thugs. She threatened to curse him with a giant painful boil if he ever laid his hands on Luke again (he was so small then). Even then the children were scared of Sadie. The boy had backed away from her muttering, "ah, he's not worth it."

Luke had simply thanked her, looked at her in his owlish way, pushed his glasses up, given her a small bow, and left with whatever dignity his five-year old body could muster. To this day, Luke still inclined his head with respect whenever he saw her in the halls at school. He was tall now, much taller than her, and Sadie had to tilt her head up to look at him; but, he was still a bit owlish and gawky with his big eyes and glasses.

What made Luke special was his nature. He was very kind and he always had a nice word or a warm smile for everyone. He was also the smartest boy in their school. This made him popular with the idiots on the football team because he tutored almost all of them, and she suspected he had written more than a few of their papers. She knew that some of the girls in her class sighed over him. His eyes were an intense blue under a mop of blond hair. He had an angular face and a wide smile—a smile so endearing it prompted you to smile back. But it wasn't Luke's looks. He had a gentle way about him, and he always told the truth, even if it got him beaten up, usually by his older brothers.

Sadie steeled herself and walked over. There was no time for self-consciousness. She couldn't do this herself. While she'd been hoping Miss Liz, the town librarian, would be here to talk to, she wasn't. Luke it was.

Luke looked up and was startled to see Sadie Kellar standing across from him. The girl of his dreams, the enchanting black-haired beauty he secretly mooned over. He took a moment to compose himself, just allowing himself to stare *briefly* at her hauntingly beautiful face, before he smiled and spoke. "Hey Sadie. Can I help you?" In a heartbeat he would have missed it, but he didn't. He never missed anything when it came to Sadie Kellar. She had fidgeted and he knew right away she was not at ease. Sadie did not fidget or twitch.

"Hello Luke," she said formally. She noticed he was staring at her. "Perhaps you can assist me? I'm working on a project and I need some rather... unusual material."

"Sure, I can help you with that," he said. Luke had read practically everything in this library. Being a genius level IQ, and a bookworm, he read voraciously.

"Great," she said softly. She hesitated before pulling a list of topics from a small pocket near the waist of her dress, hesitated again, and then handed it to him.

Yep, she's uncomfortable. Luke took the list from her white, slender fingers. He noted they were ice cold. He unfolded the paper and had a look. His face never changed expression as he read the list written in her neat handwriting: *Astral projection, witchcraft and incantations, possession, mental illnesses.*

Sadie was tense. She had locked her fingers together, and if it were possible, they were getting whiter by the minute due to a lack of blood. Luke looked up at Sadie and said very professionally, "follow me. Why don't we start in Psychiatry?"

They spent the morning looking for the books she was interested in. There were tons on mental illnesses. He tried to probe a little. "You're going to have to go through them to find what you're looking for. Is it anything in particular? I can try and index..."

"No, that's okay. I'll use the indexes in the books," Sadie replied evasively. Even she didn't know what she was looking for.

Luke shrugged. "Well, when you figure out which disease you're looking for, I can get you more specific books to read on the subject rather than these broad topic ones."

There were a lot of books on witchcraft and incantations in the library. "This section is well stocked. This was a very popular subject hundreds of years ago. We have fairly recent reprints of some pretty old books on witchcraft and spells. After all," Luke joked, "one of the most famous witches did live here."

Sadie raised her eyebrows. "And died here."

"Er, yeah, well, I know, we killed her. Uh... I'd better go help those kids," Luke said in a rush and disappeared.

She shook her head and allowed herself a small smile. Luke still tripped over himself. Sadie looked through the volumes but saw right away that most of them were shams. She needed a family's spell book. *Ahhh, here we go,* she thought to herself. *"Spells & Hexes – The Von Vixen Family Book of Magic"* by Elanah Von Vixen. Sadie knew of her. *A book by an actual witch... in the library. Priceless,* she thought, skimming through the pages. It was an original. Not many family spell books had escaped burning by the witch hunters back then. Elanah had escaped the noose. *She was very lucky,* Sadie thought. The Kellars had their family spell book and Willow's grimoire. They had always been available for reading in the house. Sadie had been encouraged to study them, but she had resisted. It was bad enough that she was already an outcast because of her last name and family affiliations, which of course, no one could confirm.

Clutching Elanah's book, and a few psychiatry compendiums, she walked to the librarian's desk where Luke was checking out books and rating them at the same time. The kids waited in line nervously.

"Good, good, boring, good, not bad, too old for you," he said, taking a racy romance novel out of the girl's stack.

"Hey!" she said, frowning in outrage. "I'm old enough!"

Luke frowned back. "You are not. Plenty of time for that kind of action, WHEN YOU'RE OLDER," he said sternly.

"What! That's not fair! You can't stop me Luke Barrington," she said, reaching for the book, but Luke was faster.

"Oh yeah? How old are you? Fifteen this past June? So *old*. Get your mom in here and have her read page 113 for a start, and if SHE thinks it's okay, then I'll be happy to check it out for you," Luke said disapprovingly.

"Really!" the girl huffed in disgust. "Forget it. Keep the book," she said, taking her bag and books and stalking out.

Sadie was trying not to smile. "Er... wasn't that..."

"My best friend Dean's younger sister, Ella. She's a brat. Has middle child syndrome, like me." He laughed and added, "but I'm not a brat." When he was done checking out books, they started computer searches for the topics they couldn't find. Books on astral projection and possession were non-existent in Barrington's library. Luke and Sadie searched the online catalogues to see if any of Barrington's sister libraries had some.

"Limerick's library has some good books on astral projection and incantations," Luke told Sadie. He was paging through book lists on the computer. Sadie stood there quietly, watching behind him.

"I'm requesting the Barrington Library borrow them. They'll send them to us as an interlibrary loan," Luke said, filling out the request form on the computer.

"Don't bother with the books on incantations. I've got a good book here," she said, showing him Elanah's book.

Luke took it from her and looked at it. "You got this off the shelves? This should have been locked in the room with the rare book collection."

"Obviously someone was looking at it. Maybe it was mistakenly put back into general population?"

"Certainly wouldn't have been me or Liz." Luke shrugged. "Well, finders keepers. I'll let you borrow it. I know you'll take good care of it."

"I will," she said, secretly pleased at his instant trust.

"Superstition has a very large religion section with many books on possession." Luke looked through the list and selected a few. "I've read some of the writing...these two are probably your best bet to get started. Samuel de Rochefort was a practicing exorcist, and his book *'Possession'* describes his experiences in detail. He also includes some theory."

Wonderful, Sadie thought with a mental sigh. "So, you read romance novels and books on possession in your spare time?"

Luke blushed, but quipped back. "Isn't being in love like being possessed? I was doing research for when I got older."

"Right," Sadie said dryly.

Luke laughed. "I'll also bring in a book of witch rituals. Can't hurt," he said cheerfully.

"I thought that Superstition didn't have computers," Sadie said.

"They don't. The librarian at Superstition sends the Limerick Library a list of new or removed books for electronic recordkeeping once a month. Limerick keeps Superstition's library listing separate." Luke was typing at breakneck speed.

"Why would they do that?" Sadie asked curiously.

"Because Superstition has quite a few rare and out-of-print books that need keeping track of. They allow the Limerick Library to lend them out. Gives them some prestige, I guess."

"Thank you Luke," Sadie said quietly. She gathered up her books, which Luke had checked out for her. "I appreciate the help." Sadie hesitated and put her hand on Luke's arm. "Also, if we could keep this to ourselves, I'd appreciate that as well."

Oh my God, Sadie has her hand on MY ARM! Luke thought wildly. He was trying not to hyperventilate but remain calm. *SADIE WAS TOUCHING HIM! Don't freak out, man,* he thought to himself. "Um, sure, no problem Sadie," he managed to croak.

After Sadie left Luke ran to the window and watched her walk down Main Street and turn the corner onto South Road. He sighed. A whole morning with Sadie, and more to come! He already couldn't wait to see her again.

When Sadie got home she went straight to her room. Her aunt was in the yard digging. She was spending a lot of time collecting and preparing herbs lately. Sadie sat at her little desk and skimmed through the psych books, but in the end they weren't much help. She didn't feel like she had a psychological condition. It was more, spiritual. The spell book she'd look at later. What could it possibly contain that would help her?

Sadie spent the next few days in the library with Luke helping her. During the summer he worked mornings in the library during the week. Miss Liz loved him because he shelved books faster than anyone she had ever met. He also had read practically everything in there, so he knew where everything was and could make great recommendations. Luke certainly knew where to look to get the information she needed. They searched for other sources like medical papers, articles, obscure magazines, even documentaries, but the research was going slowly. They were looking at general topics because Sadie didn't really want to tell him exactly what she was looking for and why.

She returned all the books because they were dead ends.

"Sadie, this would go a lot faster if you would be a bit more specific," Luke said to her after three days of helping her search for information. He despaired when Sadie only looked at him coldly and left.

The next day she was back in the library. "I apologize for my behaviour yesterday, Luke," Sadie said, "and I do appreciate all your assistance." She was still frosty, but the biting cold manner was gone. Luke was cheered by the breakthrough.

She looked at Luke. She wanted to tell him about all of it, but she couldn't. It was ridiculous, even crazy what she was going through. But... she'd trust him with one part, just the normal stuff. Then, with uncharacteristic fluster (she rubbed her hands through her hair), she blurted out, "I want to investigate the circumstances around the Kellar burning and the hex," she confided to him.

Luke looked at her, perplexed. "Okay." Understanding dawned. "That's it? That's the big secret?"

Sadie's eyes drew together in displeasure. She leaned towards him and put her hands on his desk. The room seemed to darken and Luke instinctively backed away from her. She looked directly at him. "There is a stigma in this town regarding the witch, Willow Kellar," she said softly and coldly. "My aunt and uncle claim there is no relation to avoid unpleasantness, but there is no doubt that I am a direct descendant." Her icy violet eyes narrowed. "I've never told anyone my lineage, nor do I plan to claim her as my ancestress. I have enough problems with the girls in this town without them thinking I have delusions of grandeur regarding my heritage, despite the fact that being related to that witch would not fill me with pride." She waited for him to say something.

Luke smiled, breaking the dark mood that had settled over the library. Once again the sun was shining and birds were chirping. "That is so...COOL!" he said with glee.

Sadie stared at him, surprised. "We're supposed to be mortal enemies," she said loudly.

Liz, who was in the children's section helping a little girl, turned to look at them—interest lighting her face.

Luke dragged Sadie to Liz's office and shut the door. He took Sadie's hands in his. His were warm, hers were like ice. He searched her tight face. This admission had been hard for her, but he wasn't sure why. "Sadie, lots of people are fascinated with our town's history. It's not an unusual topic to look up here."

"That may be true, but I'm not just any person, Luke."

Luke stared at her. "Very true. Alright, not a problem. Since it bothers you, I won't tell anyone about what we're doing, Sadie. I'll help you search the archives, okay?"

Sadie nodded, looking slightly mollified as she stared at their clasped hands before she removed hers.

"And let's be clear," Luke said firmly, "WE are not mortal enemies," he said, taking her hands again and bending towards her. "*Willow and Jacob* may have been, but Luke and Sadie are *not*." He was whispering fiercely in her ear. His face was so close his cheek brushed hers. If she turned her head even the slightest bit their mouths would touch. She didn't move but Luke...

"Hey!" Liz banged on the door. "No need to whisper! I can't hear, out here, locked out of *my* office," she yelled.

"She's noisy for a librarian," Sadie commented quietly as she pulled away.

Luke sighed. "She sure is."

They agreed to meet the following day to inspect the archives. When Sadie arrived, Luke took her to the library's basement and told her where to look. "The Kellar witch trial took place on June 21, 1595," Luke volunteered helpfully.

"Oh, I know the date," Sadie said quietly, looking around her. The basement was dark and dusty and packed with...junk.

"The boxes are usually organized by year, but since this is the fifteen hundreds, you need to find the boxes from that century. I'm not sure how much stuff we have from that time."

"Shouldn't documents like that be in a museum or something?" Sadie asked, moving through the shelves and starting to check dates.

"It is likely that all the valuable books were removed, or put into private collections, but it can't hurt to check. Sometimes important things are missed. I'll look for any historical records upstairs. What you need is a firsthand account or some diaries to rifle through," Luke mused. He stared at Sadie. She was dressed in a knee-length black cotton dress, buttoned to her neck. She looked so fragile. Her white skin was almost blue under the basement lighting.

"Luke!" Liz bellowed from above.

"Whoops, gotta go. I shall return," he said and bolted upstairs.

Sadie had been down there for hours when Luke finished his shift and came back. The archives weren't in the computer yet but luckily they were neatly arranged by century and decade. She found five boxes shoved at the back of one of the upper shelves labeled fifteen hundreds. She was absorbed with the contents of one box and was working through the documents. She had Luke get the other four down for her. He obliged, but before she could move on to a second box, Luke stopped her and insisted Sadie take a break and have some lunch. It was early afternoon and he was starving. It looked as if Sadie could use a meal as well. She was so thin.

He dragged her, protesting, over to The Fry Diner for lunch. At the counter he rubbed his hands together while Sadie stood by quietly, clearly uncomfortable. "What do you want?" he asked as he scanned the menu.

"Water," she said. Her chin was up and her hands were clasped tightly behind her back.

Luke looked at Sadie then abruptly took her hand and walked out of the diner yelling, "be back Fred." Sadie, taken by surprise, did not have time to react and had to skip to keep up with him.

Outside the diner Luke looked at her disapprovingly. "You want *water*? That's it? Are you anorexic? Bulimic? You haven't eaten anything all morning. No one can go that long and not be hungry. You need to eat food." His eyes swept her thin frame.

Sadie looked at Luke coldly and hissed at him, "I don't have to eat if I don't want to." She tilted her chin up with pride as she said it, "and you're making a scene!" People were staring. They were generating a lot of interest these days.

Luke took a step back and considered her. In a split second he knew what her problem was. Her dress had no pockets and she had not come to the library with a purse. *I'm such an idiot,* he thought to himself. Money was never a problem for a Barrington. They were rich. He thought fast.

"Sadie, you need my help, and I'm willing to help you in any way I can. But I'm a teenager, a growing boy. I need constant sustenance, and I don't like to eat alone. So, you will do me the honour of joining me for lunch," he said in his sternest voice.

"That's how you invite me to lunch?" Sadie asked, coldly.

Startled, yet pleased, he smiled as charmingly as he could. "I'm starving," Luke wheedled, praying his puppy dog eyes would work as he blinked at her. "Would you please have lunch with me?" He fluttered his eyelashes at her.

He got a small smile out of her. "I have nothing to offer you in return," Sadie said a little stiffly. "As one of the librarians it's your job to help me. Lunch is not included."

"You do repay me, Sadie, with the utter pleasure of your company," Luke said with a grin. "You are the prettiest girl in town. Everyone will be jealous of me."

Sadie laughed spontaneously and was startled by her reaction. She hadn't laughed in...what...months? Luke's outrageous behaviour was wearing her down.

"Seriously Sadie, it's not a big deal unless you make it one. Let's eat, okay?"

"Fine, yes...thank you. I accept." Sadie inclined her head and Luke dragged her into the diner before she could change her mind.

When they got back to the library later after feasting on cheeseburgers and fries, their research led them to a book that was constantly referenced in different documents dealing with Willow Kellar.

"There's no detail. They just keep referring to Dame Parquhar's '*Book of Record*' for information," Sadie said to Luke. "If we want to know anything, we need to look there." So they went upstairs to see if the book could be located.

Luke was typing away on the computer, searching the other libraries in the area to see if the book still existed. Sadie felt full and sleepy. She was sitting in one of the eighteenth century red velvet chairs scattered around the library. She had pulled it close to where Luke was working. It was quiet and warm in the library this afternoon. The air conditioning was on but it wasn't so strong that it made the place cold. Sadie looked around and a red haze surrounded everything. She could smell burning and hear a woman's voice calling her name from far away, "Sadie..." she whispered...and then laughter.

"Sadie, you alright?" Luke asked. He had turned around when she had not responded to his question to find her staring blankly into space. He got the distinct impression she had been completely absent for a moment there. He touched her arm.

Sadie looked at Luke, slightly disoriented. The smell of burning was gone. "Did you smell burning?" she asked, looking around.

Luke sniffed the air. "Nope."

"Oh," she said lamely. She focused her attention on the computer screen. "Did you find anything?"

Luke stared at her briefly before turning back to the screen. Sadie had fidgeted. Not a good sign.

"I've requested Dame Parquhar's *'Book of Record.'* It's in Superstition's library. I had to search rare books. Normally they don't lend this book out. We would have to go to Superstition to look at it there under the librarian's watchful eye."

"But?" Sadie asked. She knew there was a catch.

"Well, I'm a Barrington, so I get special privileges."

"Thank you," Sadie said sincerely.

They worked companionably through the next week, going through the old documents together in the afternoons after Luke finished his shift. They chatted about many different things. Luke was easy to talk to, and he made her very comfortable, so it was easy for her to open up a little.

Sadie felt a big change happen inside her. After their first, uninterrupted afternoon together, she couldn't wait to get to the library every day. Talking with Luke, and having his undivided attention and company, was thrilling. He was a great companion. She felt close to him immediately and she cherished the feeling. She hadn't had one incident where she missed time, and she was feeling much more confident.

Luke was absolutely thrilled by Sadie's presence. He waited in breathless excitement every day for the library door to open and admit her. He guarded his time with her jealously, despite his mother's attempts to get him home in the afternoons.

"What is so interesting about being in a dark library? It's summer! I really don't see why I have the pool prepared at all when my family doesn't use it…" she could be heard muttering.

The following weekend, the books on possession and rituals arrived from Superstition with Gabriel, one of Luke's older brothers who was living there temporarily. Dame Parquhar's "*Book of Record*" wasn't in the stack.

When Luke asked, Gabriel only shrugged. "These are the only ones the librarian dumped on me. I'm sure your request hadn't arrived by snail mail yet from Limerick," he said dryly. "Trust me, Luke, Superstition's librarian is one organized and scary woman. She doesn't forget *anything*, and I believe she actually has eyes on the back of her head," he said, shuddering.

On Monday, Luke called Sadie to let her know that some of the books she wanted had arrived.

Sadie answered on the first ring. "I'll get them today," she said hurriedly, almost in a whisper.

"Okay," Luke whispered back, and then wondered why he was whispering.

At the Kellar farmhouse, Sadie brushed her hair and put on her white dress, which she had just washed and ironed. She had been up since dawn feeling restless and out of sorts. Her aunt had been up too, cooking something that was making the house hot and steamy. The smell was making her nauseous, and now she had butterflies in her stomach because she was going to see Luke. She just didn't feel like herself today.

Sadie thought about Luke as she headed downstairs to let her aunt know she was leaving. After years of suppressing feelings of affection and attraction to him, spending time with him had eaten away at her resolve to be indifferent. She dreamed about him. She felt longing for him. He was everything she had always thought he would be. Imagine! A Barrington—but such a sweet one!

She found her aunt in the living room. Liora was sitting in the middle of the pentagram that was permanently etched in iron on the living room floor. She had flickering black candles set in each directional. Behind her the hearth was lit, and hanging from cast iron rods was a black cauldron with bubbling liquid in the middle. It was that concoction giving off the steamy, earthy smell. Not an unusual sight, but it was a bit early. She stepped into the room.

"Sadie," her aunt said in a hard voice.

Alarm bells went off in Sadie's head. She tried to back out of the room but found that she couldn't move. She looked in horror at her aunt but her aunt's eyes were unfocused. She was just sitting there swaying and chanting. It wasn't Liora who had said her name. Sadie could now sense another presence. It was circling the room at a very fast rate. The curtains swayed as it roared past. The china cabinet started to shake and the crystal and china started to rattle. Sadie was thoroughly terrified. The entity began to laugh in a mocking and cruel way as it started to circle Sadie. Sadie's skin began to prickle with intense fear and she opened her mouth to scream just before she blacked out.

At the library, Luke was waiting for Sadie with a feeling of excitement running through him. He had missed her over the weekend. They did not move in the same social circles, so when they were out of school, he didn't get to see her at all. He actually wasn't sure whether Sadie had a social circle, or friends. Certainly not a boyfriend. *Maybe she did,* he mused. How does a girl that pretty not have a boyfriend? Just because *he* wasn't involved in her life, doesn't mean another boy wasn't. The thought made him unhappy, and a little jealous. *Luke,* he thought to himself, *you've been mooning over this girl since you were five, and have been more than a little crazy about her for two years now. It's time to do something about it.* As he worked he wondered what she thought of him. Every time the door opened his head snapped to see if it was Sadie. He wished his computer faced the doorway.

"You're going to get whiplash on the left side of your neck if you keep doing that," Liz smirked. They were working side by side. Luke was entering the new books after Liz coded them with the library's numbering system.

"What? Oh, yeah…uh, well, I'm waiting for Sadie Kellar," he mumbled. "She's coming to get some books," Luke said with a faint blush.

"Really?" Liz said loudly, staring at Luke with great interest and a big grin on her face.

Luke groaned, *here we go,* he thought to himself. But today was Luke's lucky day, or so he thought. A small boy tugging at Liz's skirt saved him.

"Miss Liz, can you help me find me a book on monster trucks?" he asked shyly. "My daddy wants a new car and told mommy it was going to be a man car this time no matter what she says," he said decisively. "I agree, so I'm helping him out."

Liz smiled and took the little man's hand and headed into the children's non-fiction section.

"Thank you God," Luke prayed silently. He already had enough interference in his life with his mother.

The door opened and Luke's head turned involuntarily once again. He was disappointed. It wasn't Sadie. He was about to turn back to his work when as the door slowly swung closed, he got a glimpse of long black hair and a white dress drifting by on the sidewalk. Luke's heart leapt. Sadie! But she was walking by. Why wasn't she coming in? Curious to see if it was actually her, Luke got up and walked outside and stood in the library's entranceway. He shielded his eyes from the sun and looked. It was Sadie all right. He knew that form and that white dress better than anything. But something was wrong. Very wrong. She wasn't acting anything like the Sadie he had known for years.

She was drifting along the street, moving lithely and gracefully through the people. It was a quiet Monday morning and most of the merchants were outside their shops on the sidewalk chatting with each other and enjoying the sun. A lot of them were boys he knew. Many of the businesses in Barrington County could trace their roots back to when Barrington was first founded. The Smiths at one time had a smithy, which they converted into a hardware store more than a century ago. The Farmers still had a farm but also ran the local grocery store. There were a few families like that. Most of them had a boy or a girl to work in their shop during the summer. Luke scanned the street. Yep, he knew everyone.

Sadie had always kept her distance. No boy, or girl, could actually say they were friends with her. Luke heard the typical boy's locker room comments about the local girls, including Sadie, but never heard that any of the guys actually pursued her and asked her out or dated her.

Sadie was not acting distant right now. As she moved past the different shops she stopped to chat briefly with a few of the guys from school. She seemed to be…glowing. Her skin was as white as winter snow. She was laughing and touching their faces. On some of them she kissed her fingers and placed them on their foreheads. She was quick and she worked her way around Town Circle, as if she were dancing in a circle with an invisible partner. From here, Luke could see that the guys were charmed by her as if she had cast a spell and everyone was trapped in it. They were smiling and laughing, trying to grab her arm or the tail of the bow at the back of her dress. She just danced out of their reach and made her way around. Luke was stunned. He couldn't believe what he was seeing. What on earth was Sadie doing?

Sadie ended up back at the library after making the tour of Town Circle. Luke stared as she drifted up the steps to him and smiled. His initial perception was correct. Sadie was glowing. Her lips were bright red, like rubies, and her violet eyes a deep, shining purple. Her long, gorgeous black hair was thick and straight and luxurious. It looked alive as it swayed behind her. The cheekbones of her face were prominent and when she smiled, her teeth were blindingly white. She kissed her fingers and touched his forehead before he realized what she was doing. He looked in her face and felt something click into place inside him, something that had been waiting to be woken up. He looked closely at Sadie and could see two people, a double image. Sadie was there, but so was someone else.

Luke's brain tried to process what it was seeing. Sadie's eyes narrowed, but the smile never left her face.

"The *Seer*," said Sadie, looking up at Luke and reaching up to touch his face.

Luke was terrified. He wanted to back away but he couldn't move. He felt evil all around him, and he was trying not to hyperventilate with fright.

Sadie snatched her hand back and stepped away from him. Luke could see the struggle between the two beings. Sadie bared her teeth and looked at Luke. "She fights hard in your presence. I bid thee farewell for now, Barrington," she managed to threaten ominously before Sadie's eyes rolled into the back of her head and she crumpled. Luke caught her and held her close. She smelled very good, like lavender. The glowing features were dimming and Sadie began to look more like herself. Luke, however, was wheezing and was finding it hard to breathe as he stood there holding her. Sadie opened her eyes and pushed him away from her. She took one look at him and pushed him into the cool dimness of the library and made him sit in one of the large red velvet chairs by the door. She was obviously disoriented, but she had enough wits to force his head to his knees and instruct him to breathe.

"You have to relax, Luke," Sadie said calmly.

Her mind was racing. How on earth did she get here? The last thing she remembered was whispering with Luke on the phone. Sadie was scared. She'd lost time again and now Luke had seen her. What had she been doing? She wanted to ask him, but she didn't want him to know something was wrong. What was she going to do now? She had no one to talk to who wouldn't think she was crazy. Was she going crazy?

Luke's breathing was returning to normal. She shook her head as he wheezed. She had always liked Luke Barrington and she didn't want him to get hurt. She was in agony, and she didn't know what to do.

"Sorry," he said in a muffled voice, speaking through his knees and trying hard to hide his embarrassment. "My heart races really fast sometimes, and I'm tall, so this is what happens..." He tried to laugh but he couldn't. Something strange had happened to Sadie, something terrible, and he was terrified for her. "Sadie, do you know what happened? I saw something...well, someone, actually, and she spoke to me. It wasn't you." Luke raised his head to look at her, but Sadie was already gone. "Ah, crap," he said, putting his head back down.

Sadie ran home. Her heart was pounding and she was scared. She now knew for sure that she was not mentally ill with multiple personality disorder, or anything normal like that. She knew without a doubt that she was being haunted and possessed involuntarily. She wasn't sure why, but she suspected by whom. She needed to speak to her aunt.

When she got home her aunt was in the kitchen preparing a soup. Sadie stopped in the middle of the room. It was very warm and steamy and it smelled strange. It was a spice or an herb she had never smelled before. Sadie stood there and found she was getting a bit dizzy.

"What's the matter with you, child?" Sadie's aunt asked, peering at her from the stove where she was slowly stirring the bubbling mixture. Sadie felt queer. She felt as if she were floating. Sadie smacked herself on the forehead to ground herself and backed out of the kitchen. She'd try and talk to her aunt later.

"I'm going to lie down," Sadie said to her aunt. "I'm not feeling well." Suddenly she felt so exhausted that she could barely keep her eyes open.

"Okay, dearie," her aunt said placidly, turning back to the stove and her stirring.

Sadie went back to her room, changed into her pajamas, and curled up in bed with her stuffed cat Blackie. She slept the whole day and didn't even wake up for dinner.

Luke finished his shift at the library and headed home. He didn't live far—the manor was right behind the library so he cut through the forest in the back and was immediately on Barrington grounds.

Barrington Manor, along with the town's church, St. Thomas of All Angels, took up almost one half of the South East Residential Quad in Barrington. Barrington was broken up into four residential quads with Town Circle in the center. Only four roads lead into Barrington, and they came from each cardinal direction and intersected with Town Circle, which acted like a roundabout. The quads were ringed by trees, so no matter which road you took in or out of Barrington, the residents' homes were not visible. The idea was to give the inhabitants the sensation of living in the forest, and at the same time, to provide them with a modicum of privacy during the Harvest Festival when thousands of strangers rolled into town.

After the tree line the lawn rolled smooth and green up to the manor, which was situated on a slight rise. The lawn was currently occupied by two little boys playing killer croquet. It was their way of turning a "sissy" game into one suitable for the male gender. Basically, while you try and hit your ball, any of your opponents can tackle you or distract you in any way. Even throwing rocks was acceptable, but not burrs. Those were not allowed.

"Wanna play, Luke?" they asked as they rolled on the ground wrestling each other. They were the youngest Crofts, Eddie and Zach, aged five and holy terrors. Luke looked at the grass stains on their clothes and the dirt on their faces and grinned.

"Pretty rough game you've got going there," Luke said. "Not sure if I feel like getting beaten up today."

The boys stood up, brushing themselves off. Both were beaming and red in the face. "We'll go easy on ya, Luke."

Luke laughed. "I'll pass. I'm going to go for a swim. How's Dean? I haven't heard from him in a few days."

The boys' expressions changed instantly to disgust and Zach said, "he's not here. He's on vacation with Nathalie. He's changed, Luke," the boy confided.

His brother nodded. "He's useless now. He just moons over Nathalie. She's nice and all, but she's a *girl*. Ew."

"Yeah, ew, and he won't play with us any more," Zach added. "All he thinks about is kissing."

"He's been macuslated!" Eddie said.

Oh boy. Who thinks this? Luke considered how to respond. "That would be 'emasculated,' and therefore, untrue," Luke said sternly.

"I knew that was the wrong word," Zach whispered fiercely to Eddie.

Luke smiled and his expression softened. "Look guys, as boys get older, their thoughts turn to girls and kissing."

It was the wrong thing to say. The boys were horrified.

Then Eddie brightened up and piped in, looking at his brother.

"Zach, you do kiss Ben."

"Yeah, but Ben's a dog, not a girl."

"Yeah," Eddie said, unhappy again.

Luke stifled his laughter at their logic and considered the two boys who now looked bereft. Eddie was scuffing his shoe and attempting to murder a small dandelion. Dean was their adored big brother, so his preoccupation with Nathalie must really be bothering them. As his best friend, Luke knew all about Dean's love for Nathalie. Sometimes that was all Dean talked about.

Luke had come home hoping to catch his dad alone, but if the Croft boys were outside and not in the pool, there was likely a town council meeting going on and he'd have to wait until after dinner to catch his dad alone anyway.

"Okay, one game of killer croquet. But no kicking me in the package when I'm down, like you did last time!"

The boys were wild with happiness. "Okay Luke!" they yelled as they got him a croquet mallet and a ball. "You first!"

Luke groaned as he took aim while the little boys plotted.

An hour later Luke limped into the house, and after depositing the two squirming little monsters in front of a plate of cookies and a jug of milk, he found his father in the main salon humming and mixing cocktails for the council members.

Luke smiled and punched his dad in the arm. "Are you sure you're supposed to be drinking during working hours dad?"

John Barrington smiled at his son and added an olive into each martini glass with a flourish. "Luke, no one's going to be driving, and council meetings are a lot friendlier when everyone's had a bit of liquid sunshine, so bottom's up. He he." He was still humming.

"You could have an accident in the pool," Luke reminded him and wondered how many drinks of "liquid sunshine" they'd already had. The town council consisted of most of the businessmen in Barrington, who were fairly affluent. Their parties were legendary.

"Nah, we're all old and out of shape. We only wade in the shallow end like children."

Luke laughed. "Oh, well, nothing to worry about then." He hesitated and then continued. "I need to talk to you later, once you're done your meeting. I saw something strange today and I thought I was going a little crazy. Happens to geniuses I heard," Luke said worriedly.

John Barrington had stopped humming. He looked at his son quizzically. "What did you see?"

Luke started to feel stupid. "You know what, it's nothing dad," he said, turning away, but his father grabbed his arm in a vice grip. Luke looked back.

His father's face was serious. "Give me a brief summary."

"I thought I saw... a ghost? Two people in one? A double image? A person superimposed on another? I don't know what I saw. I couldn't understand what I was seeing. Do we have a history of mental illness in our family? Am I too smart??" Luke tried to laugh, but it was weak.

John Barrington relaxed his grip and said casually, "nah, no mental illness. Could have been the heat, Luke. It does funny things to our senses and perceptions. After dinner we'll talk about it in more detail and see what we should do." And with that his father was gone with his tray of drinks.

Luke headed upstairs and found he was exhausted. He lay on his bed and slept until dinner.

The town council usually met once a month, and during the summer months, met in the luxurious Barrington home.

John Barrington brought the drinks out by the pool. The men were standing in the shallow end with water up to their waists, lounging by the side and chatting. A couple of them had cigars lit and were puffing away contentedly.

"Don't get any ash in the pool, Eric."

"Don't be such a woman, John."

"It's Claire you'll have to answer to," John said with a grin.

"Ah, well, who the hell needs that," Eric Sweet mumbled and moved his cigar to the side of the pool.

John passed out the drinks and tossed his back before he spoke. "Noah found information on the windmill in The Circle's '*Book of Record*.'"

"According to the book, the windmill was designed to be a warning to the town. It only spins in the presence of pure evil," Noah informed them.

Eric snorted. "Maybe my wife walked by it," he said with a laugh.

Noah Baker looked at him with disbelief. "Man, you have the sweetest wife..."

Eric raised his eyebrows.

"Er, no pun intended," he said with a laugh.

Eric gave him the finger.

"Boys, boys...can we please take this seriously? Something is wrong. There is no physical way that windmill can be working, and it has been spinning for weeks."

"John, the men who compiled this book believed lightening came from God when he was angry. They believed in magic and witchcraft. We know that none of that is true. Therefore, there has to be a reasonable explanation for this," Daniel Smith said dryly.

John shook his head. "They weren't perfect, and they didn't have the knowledge we have now, but they *were* smart. They knew things that have now been lost in time. They saw *something*. Why did they spend so much time, and detail, on this record then? We need to trust that the warnings they recorded for our benefit are true. The windmill was one of them, and I quote from Jacob's diary:

'The spinning of the windmill signifies the gravest danger. The lives of your families are in great perile. Do not hesitate as we dide! Acte! Marke the barnes with the sigils of containmente and destroy the evil...'"

Eric interrupted. "Paint the barns? Isn't that a bit premature? I saw the sigils and they look like graffiti. The festival is starting in a few days. All we need is to have mad old Heimler publish an article accusing the council of having the crazies because of symbols we vandalized our own barns with. Thousands of visitors are about to pass through. Do we need them to think we're nuts? I vote no. A windmill is just a windmill."

"We're taking advice from men over four hundred years dead," Bill Farmer added.

John stayed quiet. He didn't mention his chat with Luke. He didn't mention that he had seen other signs, signs that Jacob Barrington wrote about in his diaries. Thank God Jacob had been literate. Only one other diary existed to support The Circle's book, and that was Dame Parquhar's *'Book of Record.'* He needed more time to look into this. His council wasn't convinced with the information they had.

"It just seems so impossible," Eric Sweet said grumpily.

"Vote then," John ordered gruffly.

Only Noah Baker was with him. The rest weren't. The motion didn't pass. The barns would stay as is. John had a terrible feeling in the pit of his stomach that they would pay for their disbelief.

A few days later, Sadie showed up at the library as soon as it opened. Luke was working with Liz. She was telling Luke a story and he was laughing at her wild gestures. He looked relaxed, considering what had happened Monday. His hair was sticking up in places as if he had run his hands through it constantly all morning, and he was wearing worn jeans with a soft blue tee shirt the colour of his eyes. It said "BOOKS MAKE YOU SMRT" in white lettering.

Adorable, Sadie thought sadly to herself. She observed their camaraderie and felt a frisson of jealousy. Everyone loved Luke, even her, the ice witch. He was fun and easygoing, unlike her—completely opposite to her, in fact. She wasn't easy going or friendly, and despite the ache in her heart at what she was about to do, she was going ahead with it. No point in wishing for what she couldn't have, especially after her frightening and embarrassing episode.

Luke had always been in her life but just out of reach. When he was young he had been such a sweet and happy boy, and when those bullies had started picking on him…well, she had stepped in knowing even then that she was different and could scare the hell out of them. With happiness not being a constant in Sadie's life, even at that tender age, she wasn't about to allow a bunch of idiot bullies to tamper with a perfect example of happiness. Luke represented that possibility to her, and Sadie had looked for that in him every day since.

The problem now was that her feelings for him had changed over the last few weeks. Well, not changed, bloomed. What she had locked inside her had escaped. She was hopelessly infatuated with the tall, sweet, gawky, smart kid.

In school he always acknowledged her, and in the last couple of years, she often felt his eyes follow her. Interest? Possibly. She was… striking. The mirror showed her that. But a crush? Love? Not possible. She was too cold, too silent, and too distant. Strange. Nobody loved her. She was a Kellar. "Witch," they called her behind her back…those mean girls…the same ones who draped themselves around the loveable Luke Barrington. How could such a warm and happy boy like that love a cold, graceless girl like her? It was time to cut ties with him before she was distracted by a broken heart, even though she suspected it was already too late.

Sadie was despondent and decided to leave. She would speak to Luke later. She was still upset over what had happened earlier in the week. Although she very much wanted to confide in Luke, she observed that he seemed very happy without her. She was feeling very sorry for herself and this was completely out of character for her. Spending time with Luke was turning her into a big emotional mess. A mooner! On top of that, she was going crazy. Disgusted with herself, Sadie turned to go at the same time Luke glanced behind him and saw her.

"Sadie!" Luke cried happily, jumping up and stumbling towards her, his chair spinning away wildly.

"For God's sake, Barrington, be careful!" Liz yelled, hands in the air, before she turned and headed to her office.

His face grew serious when he saw the expression on her face. "What's the matter?" he asked her, taking a chance and putting his hands on her shoulders. "You okay? I missed you. What happened on Monday, anyway? You disappeared so fast." He looked into her cold face, not realizing the tumult of emotions raging around inside her behind her calm exterior.

"Look Luke, it's not your concern," she responded coldly, stepping back and away from his warm hands. *He had been so nice to her,* she thought to herself. *He doesn't deserve this,* but she couldn't thaw her manner or she'd cry, and that was not going to happen. "I've just come to tell you that my research is done and to thank you for all your assistance. We're done. Have a nice summer."

Luke was dumbfounded. He looked at Sadie's cold, tight face in shock. "Sadie, something happened to you. You were not yourself. I could see it plain as day." He bent towards her. "It was like you were possessed," he whispered. "I *spoke* to her. You had no idea she was there, afterwards."

Oh, this is bad. I didn't know that. "I have no idea what you're talking about, Luke, so just forget it. Okay?" Sadie said with heat and fear. She tilted her chin up with pride, and so she could look Luke in the eye. Sadie now knew that her aunt's strange behaviour and her missing time were linked. It probably wasn't safe for Luke to even be around her, and she panicked a bit at the thought.

"Whoa, now Sadie," Luke said easily, taking her icy, clammy hands in his. The thought of spending another summer without her was unbearable. Impossible. He'd tasted heaven. He was addicted. "I'm here for you. I want to help. We can figure this out together," he said softly, and a bit desperately.

How she wanted to believe that. How she wanted him to help her figure this out and not do it alone. Always on her own. Her sadness grew. She choked on her next words. "Just leave me alone, Luke," Sadie said in a final tone, jerking her hands out of his large warm ones. She turned to leave. "This isn't your problem, it's MINE."

"But Sadie..." Luke's voice faded as the door swung closed behind her. She could hear the pain in it as she took off running. She couldn't bear to see the hurt look on his face.

Luke was crushed. He started to wheeze with agitation and bent over to catch his breath.

"Girl problems, Barrington?" Liz asked casually, leaning against the reference desk and watching as the door swung closed. "Couldn't help but overhear."

"What? Oh, no...no. We were working on a project and now it's over," Luke said, his voice tight with loss.

"Yep, it's what I thought. Girl trouble," Liz said knowingly, nodding her head. "The signs are obvious. She ran away. You're hurt."

Luke just rubbed his face.

A kid came with a book. Liz whipped her head around and stared at him. He froze like a deer in headlights. "Make like magic and disappear, okay honey?" Liz said in her sweetest voice. "Come back in five minutes, 'kay?" Wide-eyed, the kid backed away and disappeared into the children's section.

"You know you have to go after her, don't you?" Liz said, putting her hand on his shoulder. "I saw the look on her face. That girl's just as awkward at expressing herself to you as you are to her. If we were all like you two, the earth wouldn't have people. Don't be a chicken shit, Barrington."

Luke looked at Liz doubtfully. It was one thing to have Sadie seek him out; it was another thing to pursue her. It was a daunting task, but Liz looked very smug at the moment, and strangely, Luke knew she was right. His resolve firmed. He was going to go to the Kellar residence tonight and insist Sadie talk to him, even though it was a scary prospect.

Liz was walking away and Luke ran after her. "Wait, Liz, can you tell me about the look on her face?" he asked desperately.

Liz just laughed. Boys were so dense.

"Next!" she yelled into the children's section.

After wolfing down his supper and *nearly* offending his mother with his table manners, Luke headed to Sadie's house. She only lived a few streets over from him. Luke had biked by the Kellar home hundreds of times. This would be the first time he actually stopped.

It was a large, white, two-story clapboard farmhouse with a wraparound porch. Even the low light of dusk couldn't hide the obvious fact that the house was badly in need of repair. The paint was chipping and the yard was overgrown and full of weeds. The tree at the front of the house was dying, and its branches looked skeletal in the fading light. Luke looked at it curiously and shivered. It had been healthy in the spring and now it was just creepy.

Luke's stomach churned with nerves. He took a moment to take a few deep breaths. Sadie had him in a constant state of emotional turmoil. *I'm not complaining, God,* he thought to himself. Better this than just dreaming about having her in his life. Straightening, he squared his shoulders and marched up the stone walkway. He knocked on the front door and waited. The porch light went on and Sadie's aunt opened the door. Her normal welcoming frown turned into a scowl when she saw who it was.

When Luke saw her expression, he recoiled.

"You are not welcome here, *boy*," she said in a low and menacing voice. "Barringtons are not welcome on Kellar land."

Luke was shocked. Her black eyes were staring at him with venom and she appeared to be baring her teeth, which were crooked and yellow. No one had ever been this mean to him before.

"Are you soft in the head boy?" Liora Kellar hissed at Luke. "Begone," she said and started to close the door.

"I'm here to see Sadie," Luke blurted out futilely as the door slammed in his face.

Luke stood in the doorway. He had the creeps. All of a sudden the house seemed to personify malevolence itself. Luke wanted to back away and go home. Everything about the Kellar property was the antithesis to his sunny personality. Luke kicked himself mentally.

Don't be a chicken shit, Barrington, he thought to himself. *Get your girl and talk to her.*

Luke turned and walked down the stone path, quickly cutting left and heading to the rear. He scanned the back of the house and immediately knew which window was Sadie's. It was the only one with white, perfectly ironed curtains. There were candles flickering in her room casting shadows on the walls. Luke looked around for some stones to throw at her window to get her attention.

The stones made cracking sounds against the glass. Sadie was lying miserably in her bed. Her eyes were wet. She couldn't get rid of the image of the stricken youth, with the soft blond hair and brilliant blue eyes, she had left at the library. He probably thought she was a crazy witch. *Witch, ha!* She thought, turning on her side.

Sadie ignored the first few cracking sounds but when they continued, she got up listlessly to investigate. In the yard she saw Luke waving his arms like an idiot. Sadie was shocked, having just been daydreaming about him, and blinked a few times to make sure she wasn't hallucinating. Nope, it was Luke waving his arms like he was on fire.

Sadie's heart started to pound. *Luke is here,* she thought weakly. She opened her window and climbed out, hanging onto the trellis running up the back of the house to her window. Her arms were shaky with nerves and she could hear Luke squeak with fear as she hung suspended two stories up. She clambered down easily and hopped onto the grass.

Luke ran to her and grabbed her. "ARE YOU CRAZY?? YOU COULD HAVE KILLED YOURSELF!" Luke yelled in a whisper, shaking Sadie. Fear had wiped away any inhibitions Luke may have had about touching his ice queen.

Sadie looked wildly towards her house and dragged Luke to the concealing shelter of some trees bordering her property before responding in kind. "ME?" she hissed. "I'M THE CRAZY ONE? WHO'S THE BARRINGTON ON KELLAR LAND, SNEAKING AROUND? MY AUNT IS JUST LOOKING FOR ONE GOOD REASON TO SHOOT ANY BARRINGTON, AND TRESPASSING IS AS GOOD AN EXCUSE AS ANY!" she whispered fiercely. Despite her initial joy at seeing Luke in her yard, she was spitting angry. He had taken a big risk. "I told you I don't want your help, Luke, so what the HELL are you doing here?"

Luke stepped back and looked at Sadie. Her eyes were red, and her face showed signs of crying, yet she was still stunning. Luke thought of how alone she was, and how despite everything, was still strong. Luke stepped forward and gathered Sadie into his arms. She was thin and frail, like a bird, and shivering with reaction.

"I'm here, Sadie, because I'm kind of nuts about you," Luke said quietly. She wasn't resisting his embrace, but she was still stiff against him. She wasn't used to being hugged.

"The thought of spending the summer without you is agonizing. *Please* don't shut me out," Luke whispered into her hair. "*Please*... I can't take it. I just can't take it anymore."

Sadie hesitated, but only for a brief second before happiness flooded her. One afternoon crying in her room had changed everything. She couldn't resist him. She didn't want to. *This was Luke,* she thought before she wrapped her arms around him and they stood together, hugging each other tightly. Wild joy and excitement filled Sadie as she put her head against his chest. She could hear his heart beating as wildly as hers.

"I'm not exactly sure what's going on—" he began.

"It's complicated," she interrupted.

"That may be, Sadie, but you can trust me," Luke said earnestly, tilting her head up and cupping her face with his hands.

Sadie smiled. "I know," she said softly, breathlessly, as she looked into his adorable face. He didn't disappoint her. He bent slowly and Luke Barrington kissed Sadie Kellar. His mouth was warm and sweet against hers, and she wrapped her arms around his neck to pull him closer as he crushed her body to his.

A few hours later Sadie sneaked back into her room with Luke whispering encouragement and helping her to climb the trellis into her bedroom. She remembered it being a lot easier when she was younger. She waved goodbye as she watched Luke disappear into the night, and hugged herself with happiness.

Behind her house ran Stone Creek, a small rivulet that ran the length of the furthest edge of the east quads. Small bridges had been built at regular intervals to span the little river. Each bridge was lit with a single lantern in the center and was very romantic in the moonlight. Beyond the bridges, on the other side, were the woods. She and Luke had walked to one of the small bridges close to her house and crossed it into the woods. They had complete privacy. After years of suppressed longing, Luke just wanted to kiss and couldn't get enough of her. He held her to him tightly and only released her mouth a few times to moan and nuzzle her neck before his lips and tongue found hers again. He wanted to devour her. She had laughingly tried to control him at first; pulling away and making him take a breath, but she gave that up quickly. She didn't want to be out of his arms either.

When they eventually agreed it was time to go home, he told her what Liz had said about the expression on her face in the library. "That's what gave me the courage to come and see you tonight, Sadie," Luke said while kissing her neck passionately. She'd have to thank Liz for that.

Sadie's room seemed small and stifling after drifting through the trees with Luke. She was too keyed up to sleep. She'd just spent hours kissing Luke Barrington. Her! A Kellar! Making out with a Barrington! Their ancestors were probably rolling in their graves. She felt flushed and out of control. Her skin was buzzing and her hair was floating away from her head as if she were full of static electricity. It was so unlike her. She felt loved, and it was amazing.

Over the next few weeks Sadie spent her time exclusively with Luke. Most days she waited in the library while Luke worked, reading de Rochefort's book on possession that he had acquired for her. It had been translated from the French by a mediocre translator, so she often needed his help to decipher meaning in some of the paragraphs. After she had confided in him, they discussed what Luke had seen and decided that if it was indeed a supernatural event, it was most likely a case of possession. That's where the signs pointed. Fortunately, she hadn't had one episode since she and Luke started seeing each other. Luke kept her with him as much as possible, hoping his presence would protect her somehow. Sadie was so absorbed with Luke and the feelings that spiraled through her with his presence (and his mouth and hands), she *almost* forgot her problem.

Luke was ecstatic with his new girlfriend. He would often stare at her while she read quietly, causing many a book borrower to have to clear their throat to get his attention.

"Mooning, infatuation, obsession," is what Liz called it. "Don't get creepy, Barrington. No one likes someone slobbering all over them."

Sadie had hugged Liz in thanks and she had just laughed. "He's a good boy," Liz said with much affection. "He deserves a nice, pretty girl like you. Now maybe he'll pay attention to what he's doing…or maybe not."

Liz may be right, but it was hard for him to control his obsessive staring. Sadie was gorgeous with her long black hair, striking features, and quiet manner. A goddess sitting in a red velvet chair. At times she would look up with her usual cold and indifferent expression on her lovely face, but when she saw him, it would melt into a breathtaking smile, and he'd get light headed. *Soon she'll be soft and warm in my arms,* he thought to himself, *and I'm going to…*

"Do your shelving, lover boy," Liz would say in passing, smacking him softly on the back of the head and bringing him back to reality.

Sadie would just smile and continue reading.

Their afternoons were spent swimming or walking in the Barrington woods so they could have some privacy. The Barrington pool always seemed to contain the Croft's five-year old twins who teased Luke and Sadie mercilessly, chanting "Luke and Sadie, sitting in a tree, K-I-S-S-I-N-G" only to be thrown in the pool by both Luke and Sadie to the boys' extreme, screaming at the top of their lungs, delight. Her participation in their punishment put Sadie firmly in their good books, which was a very hard place for a girl to get to.

The twin terrors were not wrong to sing that song. Luke and Sadie spent a lot of time kissing. There was something about the summer nights that made them ache to be close to each other. Sadie even dreamed about being in Luke's arms when they were apart, although she was very strict about where he put his hands when his arms were wrapped around her. "Luke…" she would warn when his hands would stray from her waist.

"I can't help it," he would groan. "You're delicious."

And Sadie would laugh as he held her tight and showered her with kisses.

Luke was lucky. He found out that Sadie had grown up with absolutely no physical affection from her aunt and uncle. Not one hug or kiss from either of them. She was not used to being touched in any manner whatsoever, but around Luke she felt so cherished she spontaneously responded with unrestrained affection. In private, of course.

While Luke was with Sadie, she stopped losing time, and having Luke as a constant companion was a balm to Sadie's lonely existence. She had grown up alone and never had any friends. Her aunt Liora had forbidden it.

"You are too good for them folk, Sadie," she would say.

But she never felt lucky at all.

Sadie was not often home anymore, but she did not want her aunt to get suspicious, so she was very careful not to act any different in front of her. Since Luke was not welcome to call or visit the Kellar residence, he had gotten her a cell phone so that they could keep in touch. At first Sadie had refused.

"I can't pay for this and I don't feel right taking this from you," she had said firmly, handing it back to Luke when he tried to give it to her.

"Sadie, think about it. I can't call your house. The standing order is to shoot me on sight. I doubt you'll be able to call me whenever you feel like it on your aunt's line. What are you going to do? Walk over to the manor every time you want to talk to me? To the library? What about if I need you? Do I have to risk my life with your aunt and ring the doorbell, or better yet, get caught sneaking around the back of your house?"

Sadie just stared at him.

"Suppose Liora has the Sheriff arrest me and put me in jail? I'm too weak to do time," Luke wheedled, looking at her with his sweet eyes. "Not to mention my poor mother..."

Sadie laughed at that, and took the phone. If nothing else, Sadie was very practical. Luke had been counting on that.

Hannah

Hannah Farmer had always been good friends with Luke Barrington. Her father was on the town council so she had often visited the manor, and she and Luke had grown up together. Their friendship was casual and easygoing. Luke was fun and great to talk to. He was down to earth, unlike his brothers who tended to be a bit dark and mysterious, and a bit frightening in Hannah's opinion. Hannah and Luke had spent a lot more time together than usual this year. With her editing the school newspaper and Luke doing yearbook, they often collaborated on both publications. By mid-year Hannah was completely in love with Luke. She wrote his initials over her books and spent a lot of her time daydreaming about what she would do if she ever got him alone. The frustrating thing was that he didn't seem to notice.

Hannah had tried casually pumping his best friend, Dean Croft, for information. They were sitting at the picnic tables during lunch period a few weeks before school broke for the summer, so she gave it a shot. "Luke is such a cutie. I'm surprised he's not dating anyone."

Dean had shrugged carelessly. "Luke likes everyone. Never mentioned a specific girl…" Dean trailed off. Hannah looked and saw Nathalie Parker waving and heading toward them.

Well, well, well… Hannah thought… *his best friend. Now we know the specific girl Dean likes.*

Nathalie was attractive, with long brown hair and green eyes. She had just the right number of freckles to make her slender face pretty but not spotty. She had a wide smile and was gorgeous when she was tanned. And she was nice! Everyone loved Nathalie, even Hannah.

Nathalie kissed Dean on the forehead before sitting down and unpacking her lunch, not even noticing that Dean had practically fainted with pleasure.

Hannah smiled and turned to quiz Nathalie. She was a straight shooter, smart and forthright. If anyone would answer her question honestly, it would be her, and she'd be discreet about it.

"Nat, why do you think Luke is not dating anyone? Dean and I were just discussing what a cutie he is."

Nathalie looked at Hannah briefly before answering. Hannah squirmed a bit, but then Nathalie nodded and answered.

"Well, my first guess is that no one seems to have caught his attention," she answered truthfully.

Phew, Hannah thought to herself. *No love interest.*

"Or, maybe the person he likes is so secret he never lets on. Luke is friendly but very private," Nathalie said thoughtfully.

"I never thought of that." Hannah said truthfully. "Thanks Nathalie."

"Sure," she said easily, smiling. She unwrapped her sandwich and automatically gave half of it to Dean, who ate it in two bites.

"Hungry?" Nathalie had laughed, turning back to her food.

"Oh yeah," Dean had said, staring at Nathalie with a very hungry expression.

Hannah had shivered and excused herself. She hoped Luke would look at her like that one day. In fact, she would ensure that he did.

Hannah's summer job was to write local articles for The Barrington Bugle, mostly once the fair commenced in August, but also during the summer to publish announcements about the fair and ensure the townsfolk were ready for the three months of chaos that is the Barrington Harvest Festival. Hannah had called up the hotels in Limerick to get a pulse on what their occupancy rates were from August to the end of October, and most hotels were fully booked for the three months in question. The job was fun, and Hannah loved being a reporter. She also loved the fact that the newspaper office was only a few buildings down from the library, so she saw Luke constantly. At least she had until lately.

In the last few weeks he had been preoccupied and unavailable. When Hannah had asked Liz, she had been noncommittal. "He's helping someone with a research project," she had responded vaguely.

Then Hannah had seen Luke across the square attempting to cajole Sadie Kellar into The Fry Diner. She couldn't hear what they were saying but she saw Sadie laugh and then saw Luke grab her hand and pull her into the restaurant. Hannah had stood outside the newspaper office, still as a statue, while a small sick feeling developed in her stomach. *Sadie Kellar? Sadie? The Ice Witch? The cold, unfeeling girl that spoke to no one? Impossible.* Hannah's thoughts rioted around her head. *Impossible that sweet Luke could like her. She was incapable of love. She never even smiled. But she had laughed...*

Hannah was in agony. She wanted to race over to the diner and see what was happening, but she didn't.

Impossible, she thought to herself again, taking calming breaths and rationalizing with herself. *Everyone laughs around Luke.* But still, a niggle of doubt wormed into her heart. *Why are they having lunch together?*

A few days later she was feeling better. She had seen Luke a few times in the evenings and on the weekend. He seemed like his normal self and didn't seem to be talking about anything, or anyone, special.

Hannah was standing outside The Bugle's offices when she saw Sadie Kellar turn the corner into Town Circle from South Road. She stood rooted in place as Sadie swept by the library and headed towards her. Sadie looked different. Rather than her pale self she seemed radiant. Her pale skin seemed whiter and her lips were as red as blood. Her long black hair shimmered and twisted down her back as if it were alive. Her purple eyes were glowing. Actually, all of Sadie seemed to be glowing somehow. She was utterly dazzling.

Sadie passed by Hannah and reached out to brush the hair from Hannah's forehead before she could react. Startled Hannah stepped back, but Sadie just laughed and kept going. Sadie had whispered something under her breath but for the life of her, Hannah had no idea what it meant. It didn't sound like English. She watched Sadie make her way around Town Circle and end up back in front of the library where Luke had been standing, watching her. Hannah observed the two of them with a sinking feeling. Sadie was looking at Luke very familiarly, but Luke was frowning. *Possessiveness and jealousy,* Hannah thought to herself. Those were the emotions on Luke's face. *Her Luke.* He was obviously not happy with what he had just seen. Hannah had a growing suspicion that something was going on between the two of them, especially when Sadie fell into his arms and then they both went into the library together.

Jealousy and anger rolled through her. Luke obviously felt *something* for the little tramp. Hannah looked around and noticed that Sadie's behaviour had caused quite a stir. At that moment the editor of The Barrington Bugle appeared, looking around him.

"What's all the commotion about?" he asked Hannah curiously. Hannah could almost see the reporter in him sensing some sort of story. If he had been a rat, his nose and whiskers would be twitching.

"Sadie Kellar just, well, danced her way around Town Circle and flirted with just about everyone," *including me,* she thought angrily to herself.

"Really? A Kellar did that? Well, that's very interesting, especially since they're such a cold bunch." He turned to look at Hannah. "Why don't you write a piece on young Miss Sadie. They say her ancestor, Willow, was irresistible. Perhaps she's feeling the same way? Coming out of her shell, eh?" He chortled and rubbed his hands together. "Interview her. It would be a good attraction piece for the festival."

But Hannah had another idea. Instead, she wrote a short letter to the editor, and started her campaign to get Luke back and turn the town against Sadie.

THE BARRINGTON BUGLE – THURSDAY, JULY 25
Letters to the Editor

Dear Editor,

Earlier this week I watched Sadie Kellar prance around Town Circle, flirt with (and touch) all the boys and cause quite a stir during an otherwise normal and quiet Monday morning.

Sadie may be related to the witch who brought shame and fear to this town, but that doesn't mean her "celebrity status" gives her the right to act like that. Who does she

think she is? It was inappropriate and embarrassing to watch. Where are her guardians? Her behaviour was just shameless.
-*Anonymous*

THE BARRINGTON BUGLE - SUNDAY, JULY 28
Letters to the Editor

Dear Ed,
In response to Anonymous' comments about Sadie Kellar in Thursday's paper, we just have one response. Sadie Kellar's HOT. She can dance the circle anytime she wants.
-*The Shop Boys*

Hannah grit her teeth as she read the paper. Unbelievable! Always thinking with their dicks. This wasn't over.

Sadie's reaction to the letter was more fear and embarrassment than anger. "Who would write this? Why does anyone care about what I do?" she asked Luke. She was fretting because she couldn't remember the events of the day. She already knew of the "circle dance" from Luke, who had filled her in. *What else did I do?*

Luke was perplexed himself and had no answer, only a theory.

After the response from the Shop Boys, printed a few days later, Sadie and Luke agreed to go with his theory. "Obviously a *very* jealous girlfriend."

Bethiah

Beth entered the small apartment she was living in over Clara's shop in Barrington's Town Circle. She was arriving from her day job at the candy factory where she worked. It was a summer student job and according to the townsfolk of Barrington, that's all she was. But Beth was much more than that.

She locked the door behind her and walked to the living room window, which overlooked Town Circle. From her vantage point she could see most of the circle. It was dusk and everyone was going about his or her own business. The lanterns positioned in front of the shops, around the circle and in between the trees of Center Park had flickered on. The town seemed to be shrouded in a soft luminous radiance. *Pretty town,* she mused to herself. The town had changed a lot since the last time she'd seen it. She longed to find a man to wander the park with. It was a very romantic setting, and it had been a long time since she'd been courted. Now that she was settled, it was time to remedy that. Beth's necklace began to glow. It started to get warm with the insistent pulse that powered it.

She ignored the call momentarily while her thoughts ran back to the day's events. Her frustration rose when she thought of Nathalie. A rival, she thought with dislike, and something like glee. It had been a long time since she'd faced a challenge like this. And Dean…she definitely liked him. Tall, muscular, well built. Pale, but darkly handsome in a vulnerable yet strong way…what's not to like? *And he's a Croft,* she thought. Destroy her rival by stealing her best friend… This could work out beautifully.

Her necklace glowed brighter and hotter, sending a shock into her chest. Beth sighed and turned from the window to the center of the room. It wasn't large and contained only an old sofa along the back wall. The other wall contained a chair and a long table. In the center of the room the space was bare except for a round carpet placed in the middle. Beth quickly rolled up the carpet and moved it to the side to expose a five-pointed star she had chalked into the wood. On the table near the chair were five black candles, partially burned. She put one at each point of the star and lit them. She sat in the center and took off her necklace, holding it between her hands. She chanted a string of words and the amulet grew extremely hot before seeming to crack open. Light blazed forth from its center, and from the light stepped a being.

"Hello Bethiah," the demon said casually, looking down at the seated girl. He was over nine feet tall. Muscle rippled throughout his body. His skin was a scorched red ocher. His eyes were yellow and slitted, the pupil running vertically like a cat's. He had black horns on his head and he exuded cold evil. Beth shivered. Even though Dannerlich was not fully corporeal, even in a semi-solid state he was terrifying. He could still hurt her, and she knew that he wanted to. Like any predator, it was in his eyes every time he looked at her. The desire to rip off her limbs and tear the flesh from her body while he listened to her scream emanated from him. Just for fun, for the hell of it. Thankfully, he needed her. She was safe, for now.

"Nice of you to answer my call so promptly," Dannerlich said, checking his nails for dirt.

Beth froze. Danner did not have much patience.

"I'm sorry, my lord Danner," she said submissively, bending forward until her forehead touched the floor. "I was late getting back from the factory..."

"Yes, yes." Danner said, waving his hand dismissively. He seemed bored. "I want an update."

"I found a Croft," she said proudly.

"Well, there are plenty to choose from, it would appear," Danner said dryly.

"Oh, well..."

"What about the witch?"

"No Kellar works at the factory."

Danner looked at her impatiently. "*Really*?" he said sarcastically. "What wonderful detective work you've accomplished—NOT." Danner sighed theatrically and rolled his eyes. "No decent Kellar would work at a candy factory, unless she planned to poison it. Anyway, meeting the descendant is not going to help you at this point. She's completely clueless, and her power has not manifested yet. You need to meet the one who cast the curse. Willow is here. I can feel her. Even now her power grows exponentially. Her transformation was almost complete before they captured her and put her to death, so she is not just a ghost. She's a powerful entity to be reckoned with. Soon she will be strong enough."

Danner stood in a thoughtful pose before putting his hands behind his back and quizzing Beth. "Did you find the Lore Keeper?"

"Not yet."

"You must, and soon," he said impatiently.

"Why? What is so important about her?" Beth asked petulantly.

"Or him," Danner corrected. "For this curse to be set in motion, the players and their roles need to be the same. We have accomplished that. The Lore Keeper notices things, you know, connects the dots. That's part of the gift. It was the Lore Keeper who blew the whistle on Willow in 1595."

"I see."

"Do you see, Beth? Do you? Because this is important. The Lore Keeper is usually pretty smart. She works with The Seer and will work against you to ruin our plans. We can't let that happen."

"You keep saying 'she.'"

"That's because *she* was originally a *she*," Danner said with exasperation.

"Have you acquired the name of the original Lore Keeper?" Beth asked. "The last name would help pinpoint her."

"It's Dame N something. I don't have it yet. Just find her and contain her," he said, irritation lacing his tones.

Yeah, yeah. Beth decided to switch topics. "What about The Seer?"

"Like I told you when I sent you here, the Seer is one of the Barrington boys. It was Jacob Barrington who verified the facts for the townsfolk and supported the Lore Keeper's story. The gift will have been passed down the Barrington line as well. Stay away from them. With Willow back, the power will manifest itself and you'll be exposed."

"Too bad. There are like, seven boys or something, and I heard they're handsome."

Danner snorted. "I see your penchant for men has stood the test of time. Don't you worry, my sweet witch, I'll send you someone to play with. In the meantime, no fooling around, not with those boys anyway. I've given you a beautiful body. Use it wisely since the last owner couldn't."

Oh, I will, Beth said, looking in the mirror behind her.

Danner laughed. "So vain... now what of the spell we need?"

"I have it."

"Do you have Elanah's book?" Danner asked. When Beth glanced at him, interest and anger warred in his face. There was history there.

Beth shook her head. "No. It was too big to steal. There was no way I could get it out of the library. That librarian has eyes on the back of her head. I copied the spells I needed, and a few others, but I had to leave the book itself. I hid it in the shelves, but when I went back, it was gone. I've tested a few of her spells and hexes, and they work perfectly."

Danner's face tightened with anger. "Yes, I imagine they do."

"Well, if the heirs to the gifts are in this town, I'll find them," Beth said confidently.

"You'd better," Danner said softly, touching Beth's forehead with a red finger.

Beth felt pain bloom and spread through her whole body. She screamed, and the other consciousness in her head shrieked as well.

"This isn't a vacation in the future, Beth. You're here to work. Get me the HELL out of this prison. You succeed and I will grant you any wish. If you fail, I'll turn you inside out and laugh while you writhe in agony."

A moment later Danner was gone and the amulet was closed.

Beth fell to her side and put her sweaty head on the wood floor. Danner's presence had cooled the room to the point that the floor was cold to the touch.

I won't fail, Beth thought to herself. *I can't.*

The Harvest Festival

Every year all of Barrington's townsfolk came out to the festival grounds to help set up. The young boys were particularly busy setting up booths and hauling items. Dean and Luke were no exception. John Barrington had them nailing booths together and stringing lights for three days.

"Some summer vacation," Luke grumbled. Normally good-natured, all this work had kept him away from Sadie from morning 'till night, making him irritable, especially when all he could do at night was drop into an exhausted sleep because of all the physical labour. He hadn't seen her in two days. She'd come to visit him at the site a couple of times, but it wasn't enough for him. The absence of her presence, and physical contact with her, was hard. He was suffering through withdrawal. He worked harder.

Dean silently agreed. It was backbreaking work, and he hadn't seen Nathalie much either. She was taking advantage of his absence to spend some time with her girlfriends.

The boys had caught up after being separated for a couple of weeks. Best friends since the cradle, they told each other everything. Dean told Luke about the change in his relationship with Nathalie.

"Finally," Luke had laughed, punching Dean in the arm. "You can stop mooning like a lovesick character in one of Shakespeare's plays and stop talking about your feelings. For God's sake man, we're guys!"

"And you're such a nerd Luke... Shakespeare's plays..." Dean had laughed.

Luke reciprocated with news of his relationship with Sadie, but leaving out all the odd happenings.

"Good for you man," Dean had replied. "It would be nice to get to know her. We'll double date and have the girls get to know each other."

The boys had just been sent back to the stable to help the gentleman who would be running a horseback riding activity for the fair. He was new to town and not like anyone they'd ever met before.

Wayman had an overwhelming presence. Tall, big, black hair, he was capable and confident. What they loved about him was his seeming mischievousness.

"Hello boys," Wayman greeted them as they arrived. He was shoeing one of the horses, working in a rhythmical and systematic way. It was hypnotizing to watch Wayman work.

"Hey Wayman," they said in unison, staring at him. Time seemed to slow down in the barn. The noise of the festival's set up activities faded away and became muted. You could hear the buzzing of the flies and smell the hay and sunshine as the warm summer wind blew through the stable. Days of physical activity took its toll. The boys felt themselves grow sleepy.

"Have a seat for a few minutes while I finish up. The barn's pretty much done. We just need to put up the signs and set up an admissions line. Then we'll set up my quarters in the top corner of the hayloft."

The boys sat on bales of hay stacked against one of the barn's walls. It was so peaceful.

"You sleeping here?" Luke asked, concerned. Now was fine but come September and October, the nights got pretty cool.

"Yep."

"I'm sure we can find you other lodging," Luke said. "You could stay with us," he said sleepily.

"No need to worry about that, Luke," Wayman said with a laugh as he hammered the shoe onto the horse and then shooed her into the padlocked field to graze. "The barn has everything I need. Plus, I think my lady will be more comfortable out here. More private, if you know what I mean." Wayman winked and smiled his white, cheeky smile.

Now that the boys had girlfriends, they knew exactly what he meant. They all laughed together and eventually got back to work, both boys wondering who the woman was who had caught Wayman's eye, and what she looked like.

August

Thursday, August 1
The Fairgrounds

The Barrington Harvest Festival opened with the usual flood of people on August first. Dean and Nathalie met Luke and Sadie outside the fairgrounds at dusk. Nathalie and Sadie smiled at each other. It was a good start. Nathalie had always felt a bit sorry for Sadie. In this town witches were anathema, and being a Kellar branded you instantly. Even though no one believed in witches anymore, the town's famous history kept the fear and suspicion alive in every person's subconscious. Sadie was gorgeous when she didn't smile and stunning when she did. Her face glowed with happiness as she stood beside Luke with her small hand wrapped in his big one.

Sadie was just as pleased as Nathalie. She had never had a girlfriend before, and she had always respected Nathalie. She was a nice girl who never took sides. She was practical and friendly with everyone. Dean had his arm around her and they seemed delighted with each other.

They walked through the fairgrounds, chatting and looking at the different booths. Nathalie smiled and nudged Dean as they watched Luke try to win Sadie a big, stuffed pig. He tried to sink the basketball, but it wasn't working.

"This is painful," Dean said, "and embarrassing."

"I swear, Sadie. I can play basketball. Ask Dean!" Luke wailed as his third shot bounced out of the game stall.

Sadie just smiled. "Sure, Luke."

"Dude, you *know* it's rigged," Dean yelled laughingly.

The stall owner gave Dean a dirty look.

"Just buy it for her," Nathalie suggested.

"What! Where's the chivalry in that?" Luke protested. It cost a lot of money, but he eventually won the pig.

They arrived at the huge food area, where you could get a variety of things to eat. The smell of hotdogs, popcorn, and deep fried things wafted through the air. A large, square bake table full of goods from The Royal Crust Bakery dominated it. It was doing brisk business and they watched as the sales girls rushed around bagging pastry. Off to the side was a booth representing the candy factory. Beth was serving drinks from a huge brown barrel with a tap screwed into it.

Nathalie was astonished. "Dean, did you know Shaemus was planning a booth this year?"

"Nope," he said curiously, looking in the direction Nathalie was pointing in.

"It's some sort of chocolate drink."

The sign over the barrel said:

Limerick Candy Factory
Presents...
O'Malley's Chocolate Coffee Liquor!
Try some FREE!

Dean and Nathalie looked at each other and walked over. Luke and Sadie drifted over to the bake table. "We'll be right with you. I'm hungry," Luke announced.

As they approached, Beth watched Nathalie in an unfriendly manner before looking at Dean and giving him her most dazzling smile. She was wearing a slim-fitting white dress that left nothing to the imagination. The thin material accentuated her slenderness and gave off the appearance of fragility. Her long, wavy blond hair was free and cascaded down her back. The dress was cut low in the front and she radiated sexuality. There were a lot of men standing around the booth looking at her in a hungry sort of way. Nathalie checked Dean's expression and then was mad at herself for doing that. He was just smiling back at her in his usual Dean friendly way.

Beth turned and got them each a cup of the chocolate liquor. "Drink up," Beth said cheerily, although her laugh seemed forced. Beth was looking back at the bake table. They sipped their drinks while Nathalie quizzed her.

"I didn't know Shaemus was planning a booth," Nathalie said casually.

"I'm *sure* he don't, er, *doesn't* share all his plans with you, Nathalie." Beth replied with arched eyebrows.

"Hmmmph," Nathalie replied, finishing her drink. It was surprisingly good. She looked at Beth with feigned disinterest. "Well, then. Thanks for the drink, Beth. See you tomorrow."

Luke and Sadie had joined them. Beth offered Luke a cup and he took it with glee. Sadie was looking at Beth with a slight frown, and Beth's eyes kept sliding to Sadie. When she saw Sadie assessing her, she took a step back and turned her back on them.

"This is delicious," Luke said to Sadie, licking his lips.

Sadie just gave hers to Luke, who gulped it down.

They turned to leave. Beth touched Sadie's arm as she passed by, but then seemed to think better of it. Startled, Sadie glanced at her, but Beth had already turned away and was pouring more samples for other customers, and Luke tugged her away.

"That girl was behaving strangely," Sadie said thoughtfully.

"What girl?" Luke asked. He hadn't even noticed Beth.

"Oh, it's nothing. Never mind."

The fairgrounds closed at nine o'clock and then most visitors headed to Barrington Town Circle, the center of town, to have a drink and listen to music or do some dancing. Town Circle had dancing until eleven o'clock. The town band played Thursday, Friday, and Saturday nights while the festival was open, culminating in the largest dance of the year at Halloween.

The two couples headed to the dining area to have a drink and do some dancing. Dancing took place in and around the covered Rotunda, in front of the band. The circular white structure was beautifully decorated with twinkle lights and white flowers. Many couples were already dancing and Nathalie noticed that a few of the single men were bowing and asking the single ladies to dance. A few married ones were doing the same.

Even she was feeling carefree tonight. It looked like they all were.

They all watched in astonishment as their school principal, Linus Green, asked Miss Kathy, a grade eleven math teacher, to dance. The band was playing old swing music and they watched as the couple got on the floor and began to dance, and laugh.

"Well, that's interesting," Nathalie said, taking Dean's hand.

"Yeah. Isn't he married?" Dean asked with a frown.

The four of them weaved their way through the tables surrounding The Rotunda and found an empty one. A waiter materialized out of nowhere. "Can I get you folks anything?" They all ordered coffees and sat back to enjoy the music and festive atmosphere.

Nathalie looked around and everyone seemed a bit glassy eyed. *It's hard work to get the fair set up,* she thought to herself. She grabbed Dean and dragged him, protesting, to the dance floor. "Swing me around!" Nathalie shouted over the music. Dean laughed and grabbed her, twirling her around until she was dizzy. They didn't know the steps, but spinning your partner around seemed to be a big part of it, so they just did that. Nathalie laughed when she stumbled and he caught her, holding her close. The band started to play a slow song and Dean tightened his grip.

She noticed that Luke and Sadie were on the dance floor as well, to the shock of the town gossips that were gawking. A Kellar and a Barrington dancing together! *Ooooh! That sight alone will make history,* Nathalie thought, and wondered how many nosey camera phone owners were taking pictures.

Dean turned her chin, smiling at her, and she forgot about everyone else. They danced two songs together during which time Dean pressed himself against her and discreetly kissed the side of her neck. She was flushed and tingling. She couldn't wait for the private "good night" portion of their evening. Their time alone had been short but sizzling since they returned from the beach.

The slow songs ended and Nathalie looked around in embarrassment, but no one seemed to notice them. Everyone was smiling and laughing at their partners. Some of the men were bowing to the ladies, who were flushed with pleasure. Many linked arms and walked back to their tables. A few of them slipped away into the private trees of the park.

Sadie and Luke were hugging and laughing. The sight was so intimate that Nathalie looked away. Dean smiled and kissed her on the mouth. They headed back to their table to sit down. Sadie and Luke came and drank their coffees quickly and then rose to leave.

"It's been great, guys, but it is time for me to take Sadie home," Luke said with a smile and a slight bow. Sadie's white skin got a bit pink but she got up in her usual dignified manner.

"Goodnight Dean, Nathalie," she said formally. After a brief hesitation she smiled at Nathalie a bit shyly. "I hope we'll see each other again soon."

Luke and Sadie held hands as they left, crossing the street and cutting through the narrow alley beside the library. Nathalie and

Dean watched as Luke swept Sadie up into his arms and bent his head to kiss her as they disappeared into the dark passage.

"Wow, he's...besotted," Nathalie said. She turned to look at Dean who was staring at her and twirling her hair around his finger. He pulled her close and kissed her. Nathalie looked around to see if anyone was watching, but no one was paying any attention to them. Too much laughing and revelry was going on. Town Circle was wild with activity.

"I understand besotted. So..." Dean whispered into her ear, kissing the side of Nathalie's neck. "Do you want to go somewhere quiet and make out?"

"Oh yeah," Nathalie whispered back.

Hannah watched numbly as Luke danced with Sadie and then took her in his arms. She had spent the evening at The Rotunda taking notes of the opening day and interviewing different people to get their impression of the fair for The Barrington Bugle. When they left together and she saw Luke pick Sadie up and kiss her, Hannah's heart exploded with fury. The sheer intimacy between them was almost illicit to see publicly. *How dare she?* She raged. *How dare she steal Luke from me?* Hannah was beyond furious. She had to do something about it, but what? God, she wanted to kill Sadie Kellar.

Friday, August 2
Limerick Candy Factory

The next day Dean came into work in his dark blue suit. *He's just gorgeous,* Nathalie thought as he approached her with a big smile. They couldn't kiss in the office so they just stared at each other. Even though they had spent hours the evening before moaning together (as Nathalie liked to put it), she never had enough. Dean's mouth was like a drug.

He smiled down at her. "How would you like to go horseback riding with me? Wayman tells me that Monday is very slow right after work so we can take a couple of horses for a few hours. Is it a date?"

Nathalie loved horses. "You are such a sweetheart! Absolutely, Mr. Croft, it's a date!"

"Then I shall take my leave to make the arrangements, Miss Parker." Dean bowed and kissed her hand while Nathalie laughed, and then he was gone to see his clients.

Beth seethed as she watched Dean and Nathalie together. Her feelings for the tall, handsome youth had grown into a full-blown obsessive crush. She hated Nathalie Parker more and more every day. She would enjoy hurting that girl.

Sunday, August 4
The Kellar Residence

The bells tolled and the faithful walked, shuffled or stumbled (depending on what they did the previous night) to the large stone structure called St. Thomas of All Angels, which was Barrington's Catholic Church. It wasn't a large church, but it was big enough to accommodate most of the visitors coming to the fair and wishing to celebrate Sunday mass.

Sadie heard the bells and groaned. The call to the faithful happened every Sunday morning at nine o'clock. Normally Sadie had been up for hours, but not today. She and Luke had gone out again, the night before, with Nathalie and Dean to have supper in Town Circle and dance the night away. Luke had walked her home and had climbed the trellis into her room once she had said goodnight to her aunt and uncle. They had curled up together whispering, giggling, and kissing. It was three in the morning when Luke had left, despite her protests. "My aunt never checks on me or comes in," Sadie had told him, kissing his neck and holding him tighter. "So there's no danger."

Luke had crushed her to him, kissed her soundly, and let her go. He had hopped out of her bed and grabbed his jacket. "It's not your aunt I'm worried about, Sadie. It's my mother." Luke had shivered. "She's got a sixth sense and eyes at the back of her head. Trust me, if I'm not back soon, I'm toast." Luke had climbed down the trellis, bowed and blown her a kiss before disappearing around the house.

Now however, Sadie's head was pounding and she felt light-headed. She smelled burning and was so sweaty she had soaked through her sheets. She swung her legs out of bed and swayed as she stood up. The house was hot and steamy. Her aunt must be cooking on the hearth again. She could hear her aunt humming…or was it chanting? Sadie couldn't tell through the pounding in her head. Showering was her only goal. Maybe that would help.

Sadie left her room and stumbled to the bathroom. She closed the door and put her hands on the sink to steady herself. She looked into the mirror above the sink and saw a sweaty girl with tangled black hair, but a second later she was blinking at a new image. In the mirror was an incredibly beautiful girl that looked like Sadie but wasn't. She was smiling, but in a cruel way, and her icy violet eyes were cold and evil.

"Well, this won't do," the girl said before Sadie blacked out.

The Barrington Estate

Luke was dreaming. He was watching Sadie sleep, nestled in her cozy bed with her cat Blackie. The sight was peaceful, but then the dream changed.

A spot appeared above the bed. It was black and spreading wider at an incredible rate. It floated right over Sadie, rippling and churning. It looked like oil or tar. Luke felt terrible fear.

The mass formed into the shape of a woman with long black hair wearing a long black dress. Her arms were outstretched as her form undulated above the sleeping girl.

Luke instantly understood what was going to happen. "Sadie!" Luke screamed. "My God, Sadie! Wake up!" He struggled to move, to do anything to change what was about to happen, but all he could do was watch helplessly.

The entity turned to look at him. Her eyes were white with black pupils. Her mouth was black against the deathly white skin of her face, and her lips were cracked and scabbed. Long cuts here and there marred the skin of her cheeks, leaving black slashes around her face. She was a living nightmare. Suddenly she rushed him, her mouth opening in a silent scream and Luke woke up in bed drenched with sweat. In terror, he reached for his phone.

Please answer please answer please answer, Luke prayed desperately as the phone rang and rang... and went to voicemail.

Luke tried calling Sadie all day with no luck. "Damn," he said uneasily, fear churning in his stomach as he stood on the terraced deck at the back of Barrington Manor and looked in the direction of her house.

Relax... she's probably out and forgot her phone, he thought, trying to reassure himself. *But she hadn't said she had plans,* he worried. He really needed to know she was all right and do something *normal* with her. He wanted her to come for a swim—it was shelteringly hot today, and he needed to know she was okay.

Town Circle

Hannah and her parents sat at a table in front of The Rotunda having breakfast. They did this most Sundays after mass, and it was especially nice during The Harvest Festival. For the next three months visitors and townspeople could enjoy meals from The Fry Diner or Joe's Java Coffee House outside, and during the evenings (after noon, that is), the local pub, The Witch and the Broomstick, ran beer and other drinks to festival revelers. The Curtis brothers owned the establishments. They hired extra waiters, cooks, and other assorted staff to manage the demand of the outdoor dining area and the long hours the festival required. The only restaurant that didn't cater outdoors was The Spells and Stars Restaurant. It was too exclusive and too expensive, and the owner was a snob. It did brisk business anyway.

Hannah was moody, and her parents' attempts to cheer her up were not working. *Why not me?* She wondered, rolling her sausages around her plate and picking at her pancakes. *Why Sadie and not me?* Hannah scanned the square and sighed. She didn't see any of her friends this morning. She needed a distraction. She needed someone to talk to. She needed to get rid of Sadie Kellar.

A flash of white caught her eye. She looked and saw Sadie Kellar appear at the corner of East Road beside the post office. She was alone, Hannah was relieved to see. Hannah watched her cross the street and cut through the restaurant area. She appeared to be glowing, the same way she glowed the day she danced around Town Circle feeling everyone up. It didn't even look as if she were walking; she seemed to be flowing.

It was hard to describe, but suddenly Hannah was scared. The back of her neck was prickling. As if sensing a watcher, Sadie stopped. She turned her head and looked straight at Hannah, who casually moved her glance to her meal and resumed eating even though she felt queasy. In that brief second Hannah could sense malevolence, a terrible violent evil emanating from Sadie. Sadie frowned and Hannah knew that whatever that thing was, it did not appreciate being stared at.

Sadie turned and continued, crossed the opposite street and disappeared down West Road. As Hannah's terror faded it was slowly replaced with an evil glee. Wait until she told Luke.

Town Circle—The Hair Haven and Nail Nook Salon

Hannah wasn't the only one who had witnessed Sadie's odd behaviour. After church Nathalie had headed to The Hair Haven and Nail Nook Salon for her monthly manicure. She had noticed Sadie while she waited for her nails to dry. She stood inside the shop and watched Sadie pause and then continue. Nathalie had the creeps. She'd just spent the better part of two days with Sadie, yet whoever that girl was, it wasn't the girl she'd been spending time with. Whatever that thing was, it was evil.

"You okay, honey?" Helen Haven, the owner and proprietor of the beauty salon, had asked. She was looking at Nathalie curiously.

Nathalie turned, her eyes round and innocent. "I'm just fine, Helen," she said in an airy way. "I just thought I saw my Dean."

"Oh, he's a cutie, honey. You hold on to that one," she said bustling away. Her husband, Burt, owned the two On Your Way In/Out Gas Station & Corner Stores positioned at the edge of town on the North and South roads. He was also the barber, but he only did that on weekends. They had been married since they were seventeen. He was bald, drove motorcycles, and had more tattoos than you could count—a complete contrast to the perfectly coiffed and proper Helen. Yet, they'd been together for twenty-three years and were still going strong. Nathalie loved that about them.

"He's a big, ole teddy bear," Helen always told everyone. "But don't tell him I said that."

Nathalie turned and watched Sadie disappear down West Road. What on earth was she up to?

Town Circle—The Apartment above Clara's Crafts & Crystals

Bethiah woke up with a start at the furious pounding at her front door. *For shit's sake, it's only eleven in the morning,* she thought angrily. "I'm coming, I'm coming," she yelled, pulling on a faded blue flower-print wrap over her nightgown.

She opened the door and a hot breeze blew in. She took a step back when she saw who it was.

Willow smirked and lifted an eyebrow. "May I come in?"

"Of course," she said breathlessly, *your majesty* she added in her head.

"My name is Willow Kellar. My hostess is...asleep for the moment." She stepped in and the door slammed shut by itself.

Bethiah was in awe. Where she came from, Willow Kellar was legendary, someone to be revered. Many witch coven leaders aspired to achieve what Willow had, even though she had been denied final transformation because of a lynch mob. Bethiah could sense that Willow, while not yet at full power, was still an extremely powerful witch. She would have to be respectful.

Willow proceeded into the room and stood in the exact center of the pentagram hidden under the rug. She turned to Beth, her face unsmiling and serious. "I have been in communication with Dannerlich. As we agreed, he is going to help me and I have agreed to free him in return."

Beth nodded.

"Do you have the item?" Willow asked quietly.

"Y...y...yes," she stammered. "I prepared it exactly as I was instructed by Danner, and it's exactly where I left it. I checked."

"Excellent," Willow smiled. "I am very pleased with you."

Beth turned beet red with pleasure.

Willow looked around and headed to the table where Beth worked her magic. She touched the herbs and fingered the lace and ribbons while she spoke. "Sadie is very powerful. Her power is still dormant except for flashes here and there, but it awakens. I can feel the essence of it growing aware and strong. Once she's reached her full potential my residence in this body will be permanent and I will be unstoppable." She turned to face Beth. "In the meantime, do not underestimate her. Everything must be ready when she reaches full power."

"Absolutely," Beth said, nodding her head in a fawning manner.

"I can see we are going to get along just fine," Willow said softly, smiling at Beth. "Just one more task for today. Here is what we need to do."

The Barrington Estate

"I swear, Luke, it was *her*," Hannah was telling him. They were sitting on the back terrace with a jug of lemonade, compliments of Luke's mother, Claire.

"That girl's on drugs and up to no good," Hannah said earnestly.

Luke looked at her warily. "Did you see something strange?"

"What do you mean?"

Luke fretted inside. "Well, what makes you say she's on drugs?"

"Her expression was *vicious* when she looked at me. Do you think she's jealous because we're friends?"

Luke looked askance at her. "What?"

"Never mind. Anyway, she was glowing and flowing—" God, she hated herself for rhyming. "I'll bet she was in withdrawal or something and going to, you know, score some more…what, blow? Stuff? Really, Luke, I don't know how else to describe it. I'm a reporter. I notice things."

Luke's heart plummeted to his feet and his stomach bubbled with anxiety. He had hoped and prayed that his original hallucination on the library steps was just that, a hallucination, but now the dream vision… It just confirmed that what he saw a few weeks ago *was* real. *Damn.* Something was happening to Sadie right now. Hannah had no reason to lie. She was like a sister to him.

Luke kept trying Sadie's cell. She never answered.

He fretted.

The Farmer's Field

Willow and Beth spent the whole day preparing the spells to mark the houses of the damned. They were ready. All they needed to do was complete the ritual sacrifice and mark the houses with blood.

It was pitch-black in the Farmer's field. The sacrificial animal had been chosen. They had isolated the small milking cow at the farthest end of the paddock near the woods. The other animals lowed and bleated restlessly at the evil that had infiltrated their ranks. Willow's presence terrified them. Willow held up the silver dagger. It glinted in the weak moonlight. Her eyes glowed as she chanted the spell that would bind the cow's lifeblood to her. Beth placed an unfired earthenware bowl, filled with a small pile of rocks scored with hex marks, on the ground underneath the cow's neck and held the animal still with a length of rope. With one swift motion the knife arced and Willow slit the cow's throat, spraying blood. The cow collapsed, making a gurgling sound. Beth swiftly nudged the bowl near the spurting artery and collected the crimson liquid. Kneeling, Willow cut out the cow's eyes. Her white dress was completely splattered with blood. Chanting, she took the eyes and buried them at her feet.

"Why are you doing that?" Beth asked curiously. While she had killed birds and chickens before to aid her spell casting, she'd never butchered an animal this big. Then again, she wasn't as powerful as Willow Kellar.

"So they will not reveal what they have seen."

"That can be done?" Beth asked interestedly.

"With the right spell."

The blood had stopped pumping. The bowl was filled with the cow's hot blood and there was a metallic smell to the air. The crimson liquid completely covered the stones. Willow placed her hand above the bowl and the liquid bubbled briefly before settling down. She dipped her fingers in and smeared blood on her eyelids, and then did the same to Beth.

"We must quickly mark the homes with the death sigil, starting with the Farmers. One rock must be buried at the doorstep of every home. The blood over your eyes symbolizes blindness. We will pass unseen this night."

Beth was awed. "You paint, I'll dig," Beth said, taking the bowl of stones and heading to the Farmer's house.

Monday, August 5
The Kellar Residence

In the small hours of the morning, Willow arrived home. Liora was waiting for her.

"Bury the dress," she said brusquely, peeling it off and flinging it at her. "I want to bathe, and I don't have much time."

Sadie woke up with a migraine a few hours later. It felt like little men knocking with hammers on her skull. She moaned and put her hands to her head. Her headache was still there. She must have fallen asleep again. Wait a second...what the? Her hair was damp. She didn't remember taking a shower.

The cell phone by her bed was flashing. She picked it up. Forty missed calls? All the calls were from Luke, of course.

She called him and he picked up immediately. He was frantic.

"Sadie, where have you been? I've been going crazy with worry! I tried to reach you all day yesterday but you didn't answer your phone. Didn't I tell you never to leave home without it?"

Sadie's mind was trying to process what Luke was saying. Yesterday? They were together all yesterday. "Calm down, Luke," Sadie said coolly. "What are you talking about? You just left my room a few hours ago," she whispered, rubbing her pounding head. "I wasn't feeling well and I must have gone back to bed."

There was silence at the other end.

"Luke? Hello? Are you still there?"

He sighed. "Sadie, my love. What day is it today?"

"It's Sunday morning, maybe afternoon."

"No, beloved. It's not. It's Monday."

Sadie was shocked. Monday? That was just not possible. She slept a whole day away? No, she knew that she hadn't been sleeping. A pounding head and sore muscles... She had lost time, and she had no idea what she had been doing in the meantime.

"Come-over-right-now," Luke said tightly. "Do you hear me, Sadie? Right now," he said and hung up. Frightened, Sadie flung on her black dress and headed to her window. Her aunt must have heard her get up.

"Sadie?" she yelled from below.

She didn't answer. She shimmied down the trellis and bolted to the Barrington mansion.

The Barrington Estate

Sadie and Luke walked calmly enough through the entrance way and up the grand staircase. Luke's suite of rooms was in the west corridor of the house. Once they reached his room and shut the door he grabbed her and held her so tight she thought her ribs were going to snap. He nuzzled her hair and kissed her neck before kissing her thoroughly on the mouth.

"I was so scared," he told her softly.

"Are you sure I wasn't just at home..."

"I'm sure. Hannah saw you passing through Town Circle yesterday morning. She was with her parents having breakfast. She thinks you're on drugs!"

Sadie didn't remember any of it. They spent the next few hours pacing Luke's room and talking. Well, Luke paced. Sadie sat quietly on his bed.

"What is the last thing you remember?"

"I had a headache...that's it. When I woke up this morning I had the same terrible headache, which is why I thought it was the same day." Surprisingly, despite all the stress, the headache was gone.

Luke questioned her closely and went over what Hannah had seen, but they were no closer to determining what she had done yesterday, or with whom. Nothing triggered a memory.

Luke laughed sheepishly. "I hoped that we wouldn't go through this again—that your missing time and me talking to...that being... had been a fluke...a product of my imagination."

"Mine too?" Sadie said dryly.

"Yeah, kinda."

They were now curled up on his bed, exhausted. Sadie was scared. Was she mentally ill or had she been possessed again? Why couldn't she remember anything?

Luke was holding her tightly and was kissing whatever part of her he could grab while they talked. After the panic and stress of Sadie's disappearance yesterday, he had no intention of letting her go.

Luke's physical affection had an overwhelming effect on Sadie. His warm mouth against hers made her body flush. It was quiet in his room. Dusk had fallen and the room was dim in the twilight. Sadie wrapped her arms tightly around Luke's neck and pulled him on top of her and they kissed feverishly. Luke pressed her into the bed while her hands frantically pulled up his shirt and roamed over the skin of his back and then into his jeans, sliding over his butt and hip to the front of his body. Luke gasped as Sadie touched him. She was wild. He had unbuttoned her dress, unclipped her bra and put his mouth over her breast. She hadn't stopped him. Instead, Sadie moaned at the sensations generated from Luke's tongue rolling her nipple in his mouth and sucking. Pleasure bloomed in her belly. It was exquisite. His mouth was hot and wet, and when he switched sides, her nipple stiffened in the cool air before he continued fondling it with his hand.

"God, Sadie, you are so beautiful," he groaned. She was still stroking him and he was like rock. He returned his mouth to hers. They were consumed with passion. Sadie was on fire. Luke lifted her dress and started tugging off her panties. *Yes,* she thought frantically, wiggling her hips to help.

All of a sudden they heard talking in the hallway outside his door, and they froze. John Barrington was talking with his wife.

"Blood on the houses? Is there a dead animal?"

"Yes, Bill Farmer says one of his cows was slaughtered and mutilated last night. They cut out it's eyes." Claire Barrington sounded disgusted.

"Did we get pictures of the sigils?"

"Yes, Sheriff Holt has a picture of each marking in his file. They're all the same as the one on our house."

"Claire, get a list of the families that were marked and make sure no one speaks to the press. I have no doubt Xander is sniffing around at this very moment..."

Their voices trailed off as they continued down the hallway.

Luke and Sadie clung to each other. Passion gone, their bodies now crushed tightly together for comfort.

"Oh no, Luke..." Sadie whispered in horror.

"Don't panic," Luke whispered back. "You don't know for sure that you were involved in this." He loved her so much and he wanted to reassure her, but he knew. Somehow he knew, deep in his bones, that Sadie had been responsible for the terrible events of last night.

"I need to go home and check my wardrobe. If I killed a cow and painted the town bloody, I must have been pretty dirty after that."

Sadie called Luke when she got home. "My white dress is missing," she said miserably. "Hannah said I was wearing white yesterday, right?"

"Yep," Luke said hollowly.

"My aunt claims she doesn't know where it is. She says I'M careless. ME. I'm sure she got rid of it. It explains why my hair was wet this morning."

In the end they agreed that they needed help. Sadie was at a loss but Luke was determined to get to the bottom of this.

"I say we confide in Dean and Nathalie," Luke said quietly.

"Is that really necessary, Luke? It may not even be safe."

"Think Sadie. I can't go over and check on you. I'm not allowed on your property! We need a few extra sets of eyes. You need a girlfriend who can visit at will. We need help! I have no idea what else to do."

"They'll think we're crazy," Sadie said. She really liked the two of them. "I just made some friends," she said sadly.

"I'm willing to take that chance," Luke said. "I've been friends with both of them for years. They may think we're crazy at first, but they'll help anyway. That's what friends do, Sadie."

"Okay," Sadie said resignedly.

The Fairgrounds

When Monday afternoon rolled around, and the promised horse ride, Nathalie was not speaking with Dean. They walked through the busy fairgrounds stiffly. Dean was upset. This was their first ride together and they were supposed to be holding hands and cuddling, not walking as if they didn't know each other. Damn Beth. She had taken him by surprise today by flinging herself at him and giving him a hug in greeting. He instinctively put his arms up to push her away, but not before he had felt Beth's hand pass over his butt and give it a little squeeze. The whole situation had looked very intimate, and that's when he knew Nathalie was behind them, watching. What he had not seen was the sly smile Beth had given Nathalie, nor did Nathalie allow him to explain.

Now... silence.

Dean was uncomfortable. This was a new Nathalie, and he didn't know what to do. He didn't want to fight with her. He wanted to touch her... constantly. In his opinion, they didn't get the chance to do it often enough. Didn't she realize how much he loved her?

Nathalie was mad even though she *knew* it was unreasonable to be mad at Dean. Beth was proving to be trouble, and for some reason, she had decided that it would be *Nathalie's* life she would ruin. Arrrgh, she wanted to scream. Nathalie stole a quick glance at Dean. He looked defeated. They got to the riding stall and stopped, not sure what to do and not looking at each other.

"Hey, Dean!" A young man called from the dimness of the stable. At least Nathalie thought he was young. She wasn't sure once she got a look at him. "And you must be Nathalie! Are you ready for your ride?" The man smiled easily at them and Nathalie felt a buzzing in her head. He was dazzlingly tall with broad shoulders and large hands with tapered fingers. His teeth were blindingly white as he smiled. The contrast with his black beard was startling. His black hair was wavy and longish, reaching to his shoulders and his eyes were a glowing green, like grass after the rain.

"Yes," Nathalie replied, a bit dazed.

"The name's Wayman," he said, observing the two of them and noting the tension. "Come on in," he invited, turning his back and leading them into the barn area where the horses were kept. Dean followed behind. The barn was strangely quiet after the noise of the fair.

"I have the perfect horses for you," Wayman said. "Their names are Pleasure and Pain. They're twins." He laughed lightly as he led them out and started saddling them. Nathalie watched him work. She felt odd, like time had stopped. He worked quietly and confidently, his large muscles flexing as he lifted the saddles and belted them on. Nathalie could feel heat emanating from his body and she flushed with pleasure as she watched him run his hands over the horses to make sure everything was in place. Nathalie felt aroused. This man had an overwhelming... presence.

Wayman gave her another wide, dazzling smile. She blushed and thanked God that he couldn't read her mind. He nodded to Dean and patted Pleasure. Dean nodded in response and vaulted onto the horse.

Wayman patted Pain and Nathalie approached hesitantly. The horse looked back at her with big brown eyes and snorted. He didn't seem that friendly. Wayman laughed again and put his warm hands around Nathalie's waist and helped her up. He rubbed Pain's nose and whispered in his ear. She prayed he was telling him to be good.

"The horses know what to do and where to go," he said, looking out onto the trail that lead from the barn into the woods surrounding the fairgrounds. The trail should take you about an hour. Once you hit the clearing you're half way. The trail meanders back here after that. No one else out there but you two right now." Wayman slapped Pleasure's rump and she took the lead.

The horses walked slowly and methodically on the path. Once Nathalie and Dean hit the forest it was a new world. Nathalie watched as Dean's body swayed gently in time with his horse. He was wearing a tight white tee that outlined his muscles visibly. He was beautiful, like a Greek god, and she couldn't touch him. It was her fault of course, because she was mad, but she didn't know how to fix it. The heat wasn't helping her mood. It was hot and humid and she was sticky. The bees were buzzing in the long grass beside the horse trail along with millions of other grass bugs that were singing their little hearts out. Other than the insect symphony it was eerily quiet and the silence stretched. After a time she could see a small clearing ahead, ringed by trees, and knew their ride was half over. When they reached the clearing they found a beautiful shady area where you could rest. The sounds of the town were faint and the horses stood idly, eating grass and swishing their tails, waiting for instructions. Nathalie and Dean waited at the clearing, not speaking. Nathalie fidgeted and fought with her pride. Dean was looking at her, obviously with no plans to move unless she said something.

Nathalie opened her mouth to apologize when suddenly they heard a sharp whistle and a laugh. Startled, Pain snorted and bucked violently. Taken completely by surprise, Nathalie yelled and tried to keep her seat but was flung off her horse. She hit the ground with a giant "OOOF!"

"Nathalie!" Dean shouted in a panic, vaulting off his horse and crouching beside her. She was sitting up and wincing at the pain in her back.

"My God, Nathalie, you okay honey?" Dean asked, frantically checking her arms and legs for breaks.

Nathalie swatted his hands away. "I'm fine, you silly Boy Scout," she said teasingly, smiling up at him. "I think I broke my ass and lost my dignity somewhere in the grass."

Dean laughed, and just like that their fight was over.

"Sorry," Nathalie said sincerely, looking at his beloved face.

Dean grinned. "Don't worry about it. I'm just glad to have my sweet girl back. Leave grouchy at home next time, will you? Like I tried to explain to you before, she just *threw* herself at me and took me by surprise."

"I know," Nathalie said, looking down, ashamed. "I just felt so jealous and I couldn't get past it."

"It's weird," Dean mused, sitting beside her. "Beth looks as pretty and as pure as a spring flower, but there's something very wrong with that girl. She is having a negative effect on pretty much everyone. Ill will emanates from her."

Nathalie nodded and stood up, rubbing her behind ruefully. "I don't suppose you can catch my horse?" she asked Dean, eyeing Pain speculatively. Pain was eating grass, but one wild eyeball was watching the two humans. He moved away two steps and continued eating.

Dean didn't look too positive. "Here Pain," he called soothingly, badly mimicking the voice Wayman used to get the horses to listen. Pain snorted and tossed his mane. Then he let out a steaming pile of poop.

"That, my darling, is your answer," said Dean. "Anyway, he's probably too spooked to ride now," Dean said knowingly. "Wayman said horses are sensitive creatures."

"Did he now?" she teased. "What else did *Wayman* say?"

"I think he would say that you should just ride with me," Dean said in a businesslike manner, patting the top of Pleasure's saddle.

"Er, you want me to ride with you in the same saddle?" Nathalie inquired. The saddle looked kind of small, and she was in no way, petite. Dean was a big boy at over six feet tall with a gorgeous, and well rounded, behind. "I don't think we'll fit."

"Sure we will. It's only a couple of miles, Nathalie," Dean said soothingly. He grinned at her and patted the saddle again.

Nathalie felt herself flush as she watched her boyfriend try and coax her over. They were the same pleasurable feelings she experienced around the undeniably appealing and virile Wayman. Unbridled lust. She smiled at the pun.

He reached out his hand and Nathalie stepped forward and took it. She stared up at him. His beautiful chocolate eyes were warm with laughter and... something else. He pulled her towards him and pressed her against him. His body was warm. He smiled at her and turned her around, putting his hands on her waist while her foot went in the stirrup and he lifted her up. He was behind her in a flash and Pleasure started forward.

Nathalie was trying to get comfortable in the saddle. Dean was so close that Nathalie was almost sitting in his lap. He shifted her slightly so that she was, in fact, sitting in his lap. It was a very comfortable position once she leaned into his chest so she didn't strain her back. Nathalie was acutely aware that her behind was resting firmly on Dean's private parts, and because the movement of Pleasure's body caused Nathalie to bounce around a little, it was causing a reaction of its own. Dean whistled for Pain to follow and then ran his hands down her arms and twined his fingers with hers. In this position they were locked together on the meandering horse.

"Am I squishing you, Dean? Do you want me to move?" Nathalie asked mischievously, wiggling her bum a little.

"No," he said in a hoarse voice, tightening his arms around her, "but you can keep doing that." Nathalie laughed.

They were under a spell of heat and silence in the woods. It was peaceful with the bees buzzing and the crickets singing. Dean tightened his grip and bent his head to softly kiss the back of Nathalie's neck and then the side. She could feel his lips and the shadow of his beard against her skin as his face rasped softly against her. Dean continued to kiss her softly, first on one side then the other.

Nathalie's heart was racing. She was panting and couldn't seem to catch her breath. She tilted her head and shifted her hips to the side so she could kiss him. They looked at each other briefly before Dean bent his head and obliged. His lips were full, hot and wet against her mouth. He kissed her thoroughly, sucking her lips one at a time, sliding his tongue over them before slipping it into her mouth. Nathalie moaned with pleasure as their tongues met. Dean freed one of his hands and was sliding it under Nathalie's shirt and into the front of her shorts, which he had unbuttoned and unzipped without her noticing. Nathalie put her arms around Dean's neck and kissed him fervently, holding his hot wet mouth to hers tightly as her body responded with intense pleasure to his busy hand. Nathalie was breathless and panting against Dean's mouth. Something wild was building inside her. She was writhing in Dean's lap and her squirming was making Dean moan.

She was sweaty and hot and she felt like she was burning up. Dean grabbed her tightly and lifted her up a bit, crushing her against him and allowing two of his fingers to slip inside her. Nathalie jerked and made soft moaning sounds as Dean continued his finger play. Then her body shuddered with pleasure. Dean groaned and bit her neck.

When they arrived back at the barn, everything was in order. Wayman lifted an eyebrow when he saw the two of them on one horse with Pain following defiantly.

"I take it he didn't behave like I asked him to?" Wayman asked with slight concern.

Nathalie opened her mouth to speak but Dean cut in smoothly before she could, "he was fine. He just got a bit spooked, that's all. You should give him a treat or something," Dean said, patting Pain on the neck as the horse tried to bite him and step on his foot.

Nathalie flushed. She had rebuttoned her shorts and run her fingers through her hair after their passionate riding session. However, Dean had continued to kiss her and rub his hands over her body until they were almost in sight of the barn. She hoped her bra was straight. She had been too languid and bemused the latter part of the ride to notice anything but his hands and mouth. He *had* straightened it, she remembered now because she had protested when he had done it.

"These are for my viewing only," he had said firmly.

"Let's ride again," Nathalie had suggested and Dean had laughed.

"I'd love to, but I'm babysitting tonight. I've got to get home. You could come..." he said suggestively.

"Nathalie?" Wayman interrupted her reverie with a booming laugh. "Did you enjoy your ride?"

"You have no idea."

Dean made a strangled, choking sound.

"Then I'll see you again," Wayman said.

"You'll see us tomorrow," Nathalie said decisively, taking Dean's hand, and they headed to the Croft's.

THE BARRINGTON BUGLE - MONDAY, AUGUST 5
SPECIAL LATE ADDITION

Blood Bath In Barrington!
By X. Agerate

With the rush of visitors visiting our fair town, crime and unspeakable acts have begun! In the dark of Sunday night, one of Bill Farmer's cows was brutally murdered and drained of blood.

"Ole Bess was alive when I hit the sack," the farmer said angrily.

As many of you know, Mr. Farmer has a farm on West Road and is also the owner of Farmer's Groceries & Goods, which includes an Rx Counter run by David Croft, our local pharmacist.

To make matters worse, it seems that the houses of some of our local citizens were defaced with blood.

"I woke up and there was blood all over my front steps and some sort of kid's drawing over the door. I stepped in it when I was leaving for my shop," claims Eric Sweet, owner of Ye Ole Sweete Shoppe in Barrington, as well as a member of the town council. "It was disgusting. I was gagging as I watched my wife clean it up."

Do we need a town watch? Are we safe in our beds? Good questions for our privileged town council.

The Croft Residence

One person did take an interest in the family homes that had been marked with blood, and only because her boyfriend's home was one of them.

Nathalie was curled up with Dean in the Croft's backyard. "I can't believe you didn't notice blood dripping off your house this morning!"

"What! It was early when I left, and I was half asleep," Dean said in his defense. They had picked up a Bugle newssheet on their way home from Wayman's stables. "Mom called to tell me, but then you were mad at me..."

They were watching his baby brothers while his parents were out. They had arrived late for dinner and found Jo Croft at her wits end. "Your father had to go out suddenly and I'm late for my book meeting. Dean, Nathalie, thank you for watching Eddie and Zach for me," she had said as she left.

At the moment, the boys were trying to knock out each other's teeth with rocks.

"Aren't you going to do something about that, Dean?" Nathalie asked with concern. One of the boys was getting mad. She couldn't tell which one he was.

"Nah. They're going to lose those teeth anyway," Dean said carelessly, setting Nathalie more firmly on his lap.

Nathalie laughed in exasperation and smacked his hands.

"I heard there's a secret council meeting," Dean said lazily, rubbing his hand along her leg. The boys looked at Dean with disgust.

Nathalie snorted. "Some secret. How did you find out?"

"Luke told me this afternoon."

"Oh," Nathalie said without much interest as she watched one of the boys trying to lift a large boulder. "Why is it so secret?"

"I don't know, but I think it's to talk about the vandalism."

"Were a lot of homes hit?" Nathalie asked. Interest stirred inside her... and a sense of foreboding. Her skin was prickling and she felt strange, almost excited. Something was going on.

"Not sure. I know that the Barrington mansion was one of them. The Bugle wanted to publish a list but it got squashed, according to Luke."

Squashed? Nathalie's senses were definitely tingling. "Really? Why?" she asked curiously.

"I don't know. Mrs. B. asked mom and dad to refuse to allow Heimler to put their names in the paper. Apparently she doesn't want the locals or visitors spooked in any way."

"Can you do that? Freedom of the press and all that..."

"Apparently you can in Barrington," he snorted. "It's just vandalism by bored, idiot kids. It's just like our reporter to exaggerate and our town council to take extreme measures."

"Nobody saw anything?" Nathalie asked with disbelief.

"Nope, apparently not. We didn't, and there are lots of us."

"Do you think Luke could get a copy of that list?" Nathalie asked. She was now burning with curiosity to see who was on it.

"Luke? Probably."

"Can you ask him for me?"

"Sure can, baby," Dean said nuzzling her neck.

The boys stopped their rough housing to stare at them in horror. Nathalie watched as they dropped their rocks and started picking up clumps of earth. They'd obviously had enough public displays of affection for one day.

Uh oh. "Danger!" Nathalie yelled as she vaulted off Dean's lap just before he was pummeled with dirt.

The Barrington Estate

The town council held an emergency meeting at Barrington Manor late Monday night. Only the council members knew of the meeting. This was to keep any nosey townspeople from butting in.

"I can't believe Heimler allowed Xander to publish that shit," claimed Eric Sweet, tossing back his bourbon and signaling for another. "If I'd known that he'd sensationalize it, I wouldn't have spoken to him."

John Barrington was annoyed. "What did you think would happen, Eric? This is *Xander* we're talking about here. Why would you even speak to him? You two hate each other."

"Ah, it just looks like a prank by a bunch of bored kids," said Noah Baker. "Why are you all so worried?"

"It *would* have looked like a prank if that idiot Xander hadn't blown things out of proportion," Eric said with irritation. "*'Blood Bath in Barrington,'* what a byline! You'd think there was a massacre or something," he snorted and then looked guiltily at Bill Farmer. "Sorry about your cow, man."

Bill just nodded.

"Only certain families were targeted—*town council families*. Claire put together a list." John Barrington's wife was extremely resourceful and efficient.

"So the cursed families have been marked," Bill Farmer said slowly.

"So it would appear," John agreed. "Except for one family, the Crofts. They were marked, but I'm not sure why."

"I heard Heimler wants to publish the names of the families," Daniel Smith said worriedly.

"That's not going to happen. Claire has spoken to all the parties in question and they've told Heimler to keep their names out of the paper."

"Except for Eric's," Daniel reminded them snidely. Eric gave him the finger.

"Heimler must have been mad," Noah said with a smile.

"If he was, he didn't show Claire," John said with a satisfied smile. "He wouldn't dare."

They all laughed and nodded.

"That won't stop any gossip," Eric said gloomily. Ye Ole Sweete Shoppe was a gossip haven for the town's youth, particularly girls. He shuddered.

Daniel eyed John. "That Kellar girl is involved somehow. She has to be. We'll need to keep an eye on her, John."

"I've got that base covered. My son Luke is dating her."

"Anyone else picking up on this? Local folklore fanatics playing connect-the-hex dots?" Daniel asked.

Eric snorted. "Are you kidding? I can't believe it myself. The only one who would believe this is Xander, and he's a fool. This is the twenty-first century for God's sake!" he said angrily.

Noah was the voice of reason. "Without The Circle's book or Jacob's diary there's no way to connect the dots. The true nature of the windmill has never been common knowledge, the blood markings look like vandalism..."

John cleared his throat. "So...the question now is, do we paint the barns?"

"This is ridiculous," Eric said with exasperation. "We're grown men! Now we believe in witches and fairytales?"

"It does seem like an old wives' tale," Daniel said dubiously. "What can paint and a symbol do?"

"The Circle's book says otherwise," John replied, shaking his head. "Remember, they thought the curse would come true *in their lifetime.* They prepared for it. These sigils are part of the town's defense."

"Defense against what? A ghost?" Daniel said incredulously.

"Why don't you just explain what the symbols do," Noah suggested calmly.

John nodded and took out the book. He held it gently. "Apparently, the spell is some sort of seal," John said, paging through the old journal. "Ah, here..." he muttered.

"The spelle must be caste through the sigils painted on the red barns to seale the town's energie and bind the evil one to his cage."

"If it actually works...I can't believe I'm talking about this. I feel like a teenage girl," Eric said sulkily.

"Eric, stop your bellyaching," Bill said mildly.

"I don't agree with doing this," he said.

"Perhaps we need a few more signs before we take that step," Noah said cautiously.

"Even though we have a dead cow and blood markings?" John pointed out.

"I agree with the boys," said Daniel. "It's just too unbelievable."

John was uneasy, but this was a democracy. "I disagree, but majority rules. We wait," John affirmed. "Meeting adjourned."

Tuesday, August 6

Nathalie's Journal – Entry for Tuesday, August 6

Dean and I didn't end up riding today. Dean was sent to a client with an urgent order and wouldn't be back until evening, so I spent the day working quietly at my desk. Unfortunately, Beth was in and she was in a *rotten* mood. I encountered her in the bathroom midmorning. Beth was furiously brushing her hair and it was wispy and flyaway, the static making it stick to her forehead and face. Her normal pale face was flushed pink. She called *me* an "amoral slut," and the astonishment on my face was evident as the crazy person picked up all her hair and put it *in her pocket,* even though there was a perfectly good garbage nearby. I could only stare at her in outrage as she flounced out of the washroom. At first I wondered if she had been in the woods yesterday, spying on me and Dean, but that just isn't possible. I mean, even she's not that creepy. Is she? I tried to find her later to confront her, but she had disappeared for the day.

After dinner I walked to the fairgrounds to look around. I hadn't had the chance to check out all the stalls yet. The regular tables were there. Clara had her crystals and crafts table. She waved at me as I walked by. I was tempted to stop and ask her what she knew about Beth, but I didn't want to bother her. Clara was busy so I made a note to catch her another time to talk about her tenant, and suggest eviction!

There are a lot of strange, new vendors this year. One stall had gorgeous glowing gems and stones that seemed to be filled with an inner fire. They came in all colours and sizes. Another stall was filled with different vials claiming to be love potions or cures for different things like warts or spots. *Spots*… and I thought about my freckles for an instant, but then, nah.

I had moved to the next stall filled with colourful scarves edged with tiny silver bells when I saw Sadie Kellar walk by the vial stall and stop. The girl running the stall was tall and very lithe with beautiful white gold hair, pale skin, and large green eyes—obviously not from around here. She nodded respectfully at Sadie who was frowning slightly as she looked at the merchandise. She touched a couple of the vials, inclined her head once to the girl, and then moved on. She didn't see me at the scarf stall. The girl looked at her like she'd seen a ghost. It was such an odd reaction. I was going to shout out to Sadie, but something stopped me. I don't know why but I didn't feel it was a good time to stop her. The same negative feelings I had experienced last Sunday, as I watched Sadie from the salon, overwhelmed me.

Good thing because just then I saw Ella, Dean's younger sister, arrive at the stall. She looked around and then paid for what I'm pretty sure was a love potion, if the red heart on the vial was any indication. Sadie forgotten, I raised my eyebrows in curiosity and drifted over.

"Hey Ella," I said casually. "The stuff here is pretty neat, huh?"

"What?" She looked startled. "Oh, hey Nathalie. Yeah, yeah, great stuff. Very different from other years." Ella was casually putting her purchase in her pocket. I didn't let her get away with it.

"What did you buy?" I asked her interestedly.

Ella sighed. She never got away with anything while I was around even though she tried very hard.

"I just bought a potion," she whispered defensively, her face red.

"REALLY? What kind of potion?" I asked expectantly, staring at the front pocket of her shirt.

"Purchases *are* confidential, you know," the shop girl said, butting in.

I ignored her.

Ella scowled and lowered her voice even more. "It's just a silly love potion," she hissed.

"A what??" I exclaimed loudly. The din at the fair was unbelievable. Ella was mortified and looked around to see who had heard. The girl at the stall looked at me disapprovingly and "tsked."

"Oh, mind your own business," I grumbled to her.

"You should too," Ella said stubbornly. I pulled Ella away from the stall girl's now interested expression and prying ears.

"Ella, I'm like your sister, so I'm not going to mind my own business," I said sternly. "So who's it for?"

"Not telling."

"Come on!"

"No!"

Oh for God's sake... "Fine! But hear me out. You realize love isn't real unless it's given freely, right?"

"What? Bollocks," Ella snorted.

Did I hear that right? "What?"

"Sorry, bullshit."

I frowned at her. "Watch your language, young lady."

Ella's eyebrows went up a bit at that. "I am not talking about this with you."

"Look, you can't *force* someone to fall in love with you. They have to use their own free will and choose. Haven't you read *'The Chaser'* by John Collier in school yet??" I thought they had. It was a great short story, and it was used by our ninth grade English teacher to illustrate the negative effects of obsession to Barrington teens—not that anyone paid any attention. Case in point right in front of me.

Ella's face was set. "Trust me, I won't need five thousand dollars later. Anyway, it's worth a try. Not all of us are lucky enough to have, well, our love...love us back, like Dean loves you."

My heart stopped for a brief second and I flushed. Dean *loves* me. "True, but it took me a while to figure it out. He didn't *force* me. It was much more fun the other way, even for *him*!"

"HE doesn't see me that way!" she wailed. "To him I'm just another boy."

Now I knew who the potion was for.

"Things change, Ella. Maybe you've never given him any idea you like him more than a *best friend*." I smiled at her happily. "Look at what happened with me and Dean. Give that a try first before you POISON HIM," I said loudly, putting my arm around her and squeezing.

"I heard that!" the stall girl yelled. "It's not poison!"

Ella didn't look completely convinced, but I knew she would think about it more before doing anything stupid.

"I'll wait a bit, but I don't think it's the same with me and Max. Dean has loved you since the day he met you. Nothing has changed recently, at least not for him." Ella then turned and disappeared into the crowd, leaving me pondering her words.

Dean loved me. He's always loved me. I loved him too but only recently realized it in the romantic sense. How did he stand it? The uncertainty? I could have dated other boys. I'm obviously not that observant.

I brought myself back to earth and headed to the potions stall. The girl looked at me balefully.

"Did you know the black haired girl that went by your stall about ten minutes ago?" I asked curiously.

"None of your business," she said with a satisfied smirk.

I obviously burned that bridge.

Thinking about Dean and lost in thought I drifted through the fair. I passed Wayman's stall and saw he was busy with a bunch of excited kids in thrall over the horses. He seemed larger than life as he lifted up the small kids with his huge hands. I noticed that Pain was not trying to bite *them*. He must save that endearing trait for Dean alone.

It was getting dark and the fairgrounds were lit up with lanterns that were strung from stall to stall. Behind the stalls, in the woods surrounding the fairgrounds, white twinkle lights had been strung through the trees, making the whole area magical and romantic. I wished Dean were here with me, holding my hand, so we could enjoy this together.

I was passing by an herb and amulet stall when the woman at the stall called to me. She knew my name. I stopped and looked at her curiously. I didn't know her, but she was smiling in such a friendly and welcoming way that I was drawn to her immediately.

"I'm sorry, do I know you?" I asked her shyly. I didn't really know what to say. She was breathtakingly beautiful in an unusual and intimidating way. She was tall with the lean muscularness of a female Amazon warrior from the myths. Her hair was a long wavy white-blond that reached her hips. High cheekbones and a pixie chin framed eyes that were an icy blue, but not cold. Right now they were warm and interested as they looked at me.

"Sorry to startle you," she smiled. I could swear she was glowing in some way. Must be the lanterns. "Wayman told me your name."

I blushed a little at that and tried to act nonchalant, not because Wayman remembered me, but because the memory of me and Dean on his horse had leaped into my mind. She was smiling at me and told me her name was Taline. She sold herbs and special jewelry.

Taline has a very interesting stall. It's shaped like a miniature stable, about six feet wide and eight feet deep. The back wall is built like a bookshelf and in each nook are glowing stones that flickered different colours. They were all different shapes; stars, hearts and moons in gorgeous shades of red, green, and yellows. She had them in all sizes, like small pendants for necklaces or bracelets that were all piled together in baskets that overflowed. She had all types of jewelry; brooches, earrings, and bracelets. The bigger stones had been made into figurines; fairies, toadstools, and beautiful flowers. Their colours blended together so well they almost looked real. They were all stunning. At the front of the stall was a table filled with jars of herbs, spices, and dried flowers.

"Aren't you dating the tall, handsome young man with the dark hair and really pale skin? His name is Dean, isn't it?" she asked casually as she wrapped twine around a bunch of herbs that looked like parsley, in preparation for drying.

"Yes, he's my boyfriend," I told her proudly. (I still get a thrill saying that.)

Taline smiled. "Love is a wonderful thing," she said lightly, looking towards the stable where Wayman was tossing little kids into the hay. I could see Pleasure bumping into him playfully as he did so. I had to laugh, and so did Taline.

She looked back at me again. "It can also be destructive. There are many types of love, and not all of them are the giving type. It's a very powerful emotion that should not be underestimated."

"So I'm discovering," I murmured, my eyes taking in all the merchandise she had for sale. "So, what are all these herbs for?" I asked, looking at the array of beautifully decorated jars and tied bunches.

"Herbs have different, and multiple, uses," Taline explained. "You cook with some," she said and pointed to the parsley she had wrapped into a tidy bunch, "but combined with other herbs and things, they can also be used to invoke spells of protection, healing, love, and things like that."

"Spells?" I thought that was weird—another person talking about spells and magic, like Beth.

"Yes, well, if you know the lore of it," Taline said simply, her hands moving to another bunch of plants I couldn't identify.

I took a better look at her and noticed that she was very much like Wayman in that she was different from the Barrington townsfolk. Taller, unearthly beautiful, with a kind of glow around her. I noticed there were a lot of folks like that at the fair this year. I felt as if something wasn't exactly right, but I wasn't getting any threatening feelings from her. In fact, it was the opposite. I felt safe, like she would protect me if anything were to try and attack.

"Is this 'lore' something you learned from your mom?" I asked her, fingering a bunch of dried flowers that were labeled hoar's bane and smelled like skunk.

"Yes," she said simply.

"I would have thought 'spell casting' would be a lost art," I said casually. *Especially since it isn't real,* I thought.

"For the most part it is, but it's also not something you advertise, especially in a witch hunters' town," she said wryly.

I laughed. "Is that what outsiders think we are?"

"For the most part."

"Where do you come from?" I asked her.

"From far away," she said with a sigh and turned to the back of her stall and began rummaging through a basket with different necklace charms in it. She selected one, took it out, and threaded two leather cords through the loops at the top. She brought the pendant over and placed it in the palm of her hand to show it to me. It wasn't one pendant but two, intertwined so skillfully it looked like one whole piece. It was an amber heart, but cut in relief in the middle were a man and a woman so intertwined that from a certain angle, they looked like one person. It was beautiful.

"A gift for you and your handsome young man," Taline said, placing the pendant in my hand and closing my fingers over it. "It comes apart. He wears one piece and you wear the other, symbolizing that you carry his heart and he carries yours."

"So, he wears the female figurine?" I asked and then realized what a stupid question that was. I carefully clicked the figures apart. They started to look lonely. Cool!

Taline laughed. "Yes, you big goose. The female figure represents you." She laughed again and shook her head. She pointed to the male figurine. You wear him near your heart. The cord is adjustable," she said, showing me how to lengthen and shorten the leather.

In my delight I didn't really think about the value of the item she had handed me. "I can't take this," I said, coming to my senses. The amber was flawless and the figures so perfectly sculpted, the labour alone to shape this must have been extensive. "It's priceless!"

"Nothing's priceless. It's just stone," Taline said.

"Still..."

"You can accept it and you will," Taline said firmly, closing my fingers around it.

"Can I do something to repay you?" I asked. I really wanted the pendant. It was warm in my hand and the figures seemed to be writhing in an effort to be one again. I opened my fingers and snapped them back together and a sense of calmness returned. They were us, Dean and me, struggling to be alone together. I flushed at my one-track mind. Luckily I could blame the August heat for my red face.

Taline looked at me speculatively. "You know, it gets pretty busy here. I'd love to have some help with the herbs. At the same time, I could teach you the herb lore I know." She pointed behind her and I could see a huge barrel of wild plants ready for sorting and drying.

"Well, sure," I said happily. "I'd love to."

After chatting with Taline for a bit, I walked over to the huge bake table set up by the Baker family. They run the main bakery in town, The Royal Crust, where the town buys their bread. Living in a small town was interesting. Because of the bakery, Mr. Farmer, the grocer, did not sell bread or sweets from outside of Barrington, only products you couldn't buy at the bakery.

Sometimes, when Barringtoners came back from traveling and wanted Bill Farmer to stock a new item in his store, he would. "We can't make it? You think people would like this? Okay, I'll stock it," he would say, nodding his head and inspecting the item. We loved him.

Ye Ole Sweet Shoppe, our local candy store, and Farmer's Grocery only stocked candy from the Limerick Candy Factory up the road. The candy store made all their fancy chocolate confections with the factory's chocolate. The original Mayor, Jacob Barrington, the man who built the town and gave it his name, made it clear that we would only thrive if we supported each other, and so we do. The town's merchants supported each other exclusively.

The Harvest Festival is organized by the town of Barrington every year. Anyone can set up a personal stall, and for Barringtoners, it's free. The Bakers set up a huge table every year filled with the most incredible pastry. This is when they make the bulk of their annual income. With people camping and traveling to visit the fair, breads, muffins, cookies, and pies are in high demand to feed families wandering the fairgrounds. Joe's Java Coffee House sets up a coffee table nearby, as well as The Fry Diner, who sells sandwiches and other fried things. They do brisk business. Only The Witch and the Broomstick

Pub is not allowed a stall at the fair. Alcohol was limited to Town Circle or the pub itself.

One of my girlfriends, Tess Smith, always helps the Bakers with their table at the fair every year. The Bakers have two boys that lack the bakery gene, so they switch kids with the Smiths. Reginald Baker helps at The Hammer & Anvil Hardware Store while Tess Smith helps at The Royal Crust. For three months it's round the clock for Tess, so I don't get to see her much during the summer. She works the bake table during the day and she bakes at night. I would have insisted on her taking a break and having a coffee with me today, but I didn't see her. I looked at the baked goods and I realized that I was extremely hungry.

There was an older lady running the bake table very efficiently. She was dressed in a very peculiar way, with a long grey dress with buttons from her neck to her feet that belted at the waist and had long, white, billowy sleeves. She wore a frilly white apron tied at the back in a pretty bow with a white lacy cap on her head. She was short and plump with pretty blond curls and rosy red apple cheeks. She looked like a throwback from the old days.

"Och, can I help ya lassie?" she asked me, smiling. She had a pleasant accent I couldn't place. I stared at her and was sure her blue eyes were twinkling at me, and I was getting a strange sense of déjà vu, as if I knew her.

"Why, yes," I said, shaking my head to clear it.

"What's your name, child?" she asked. She was staring at me, her expression suddenly very curious.

"Oh, my name's Nathalie. Nathalie Parker," I responded. I looked at the bake table to see if I could find my favorite cookies. "What's yours?" I asked.

"You can call me Nettie… a Parker, eh?"

"Do you know my parents?" I asked her curiously. I had never seen her before, so she couldn't live in Barrington.

"In a way I know everyone here," she said quietly, looking around her. She turned her eyes back to me. "Try these," she said, handing me a cookie. I bit into it. It was wonderful, spicy with a tart lemon icing.

"This is delicious!" I exclaimed, taking a bag of them. "They taste like my grandmother's!"

"An old family recipe," she said, waving her hand and looking at me. "So, are you married, dearie?"

I choked on my cookie and looked at her, shocked. "Married? I'm only *seventeen*!" I told her in a high voice.

"Och, so no children." She seemed disappointed.

Whaaaaat??? I thought to myself. I looked at her in disbelief. "No, of course not."

"Do you have a sweetheart?" she asked hopefully.

"Why, yes I do," I responded. She sure was nosey, but her face was so sweet and loving I couldn't help answering her questions.

She nodded happily. "That's good," she said. "Love is power. What's your young man's name?"

"Dean. Dean Croft."

"A Croft…well, that's unfortunate," she mumbled under her breath.

"Unfortunate?" I asked, now wondering if she was crazy.

"What? Och, no dearie. Not what I meant, not at all. I just knew a family of Crofts years ago…unlucky family, but that's neither here nor there." She bustled around the bake table, straightening things up.

"Where do you come from?" I asked her. I was curious now. Croft was not a unique name and there were probably Crofts everywhere, but it seemed personal to her.

"I'm from a long time away," she told me. "I'm here to help with the fair. Baking is my specialty."

She had odd expressions. It must have taken her a while to get here. "He's very sweet, my Dean, and extremely adorable."

She nodded in agreement. "My Crofts were too." She stopped and wrapped a pie and handed it to me. "Take a pie for your family, honey."

"Thank you," I said, taking the pie, "but it's not necessary—" My cell phone rang and I answered it. It was my mom.

"Hi sweetie, it's time to come home for dinner. You're dad's barbequing."

"Ugh," I said into the receiver.

"Be nice, Nat. Oh, and pick up a pie for dessert."

In the end, it was a strange, yet interesting, day.

The Fairgrounds

Much later Taline was closing down her stall for the night. It had been a busy day. She looked towards the stable and saw Wayman settling the horses for the night. He whistled while he brushed them, running his long fingered hands over their bellies and shanks. Taline shivered. She wondered what kind of night she was going to have with those hands. She hoped it would be a long one.

She looked over to see Nettie packing up the bake table. Not much left. Nettie's baking was hugely popular and was already gaining quite a reputation. The baking stall had a large silver fridge with electrical and water lines running to it, used to store the remains of the day's efforts, which would be sold the next day for half price. "Amazing, this silver box," Nettie said with awe, patting the fridge.

Taline laughed. "So, Nettie," she said casually as she walked over, sitting herself on one of the tables and kicking her long, slender legs back and forth. "The meeting with your descendent went remarkably well, considering. Of all the questions you could have asked her, you decided to freak her out and ask her about marriage and teen pregnancy." Taline had a huge smile on her face. "Interesting tactic."

Nettie *hmmmphed* and looked at Taline, narrowing her eyes. "Look here dearie, seventeen is a perfectly respectable age to be wed and havin' a child. How was I supposed to know that things had changed so much? I was married with my Henry at sixteen and had my Nathan at seventeen. What is she waiting for? She said she had a beau."

Taline sniffed. "Nettie, a seventeen year old today is like a ten year old in your time, *without* the sense of responsibility. They're babies on hormones."

"Perhaps... but you all seem like babies to me." Nettie sighed and looked around. "What am I doing here Taline? How is this possible?"

"I have no idea, Nettie. That's what Wayman's trying to figure out."

Town Circle—The Apartment above Clara's Crafts & Crystals

Beth slammed the door to her little apartment and threw her purse across the room where it smashed against the wall. She was furious. She was losing to her rival. She never lost. Never, ever. She'd chosen Dean and she was determined to have a little fun with him. She wasn't about to allow some mousy-haired blotchy-faced brunette get in her way.

Danner had visited last night and congratulated Beth on a task well done. Marking the families was a big step in their plan.

Then he had smiled slyly and informed her of Dean and Nathalie's ride in the woods. "He's getting so *handsy*...on a horse, no less!" he had said delightedly, describing the encounter in detail. "They are progressing way beyond kissing," he had taunted her, sliding an ocher finger down her face. "If you want any action from that pale meat bag you're going to have to step it up a bit, sister." His touch had been painful, but not as painful as his words that picked at her obsessive crush, making it bleed, and making her angry.

"Mind you, if he's too much of a challenge for you, I still plan to keep my promise to send you a distraction." He laughed as he left.

Today, Nathalie's face had revealed everything, and while she hated to admit that Danner was right, he was. She was a witch, and a powerful one at that. Men were pathetically weak when it came to temptation and sex. No male had ever stood against her before. She had always taken what she wanted. What was holding her back now? She had Elanah's spells.

She walked straight to the long table overflowing with different dried herbs, plants and flowers, which were all tied in bunches with twine. From her pocket she took out a tissue containing a single black eyelash—*to identify him.* Working quickly, she collected the rest of the items she needed; she chose a small white rose—*to attract him*, she cut a lock of her hair and selected a pink ribbon—*to bind and enslave him to HER;* she lit a white candle—*to seal the hex.*

She chanted a preparation spell as she worked. *"Prepare to receive, that which I make, I invoke thee, my spell to take, prepare to receive, that which I make, I invoke thee, my spell to take..."* She twined the ribbon around the rose, the eyelash, her hair and sealed it with wax from the white candle.

The words were a litany as she put the bundle into a crudely stitched hemp bag and took it to the sink where she sprinkled it with running water, using the energy from the earth to activate the magic of the bag. No more trips to streams for her. She took the damp bag and her candle and sat in the center of the pentagram in the middle of the room. The candle flickered as she held the bag tightly and closed her eyes, chanting the spell to bind the hex to the items.

"Master of Chaos, I submit to thee, by thy power divine, make him mine."

The bag flared brightly and then became mute. It was pulsing and glowing faintly in Beth's hands. The glow would not be visible to human eyes unless they were told it was there. Only those with power would be able to see it, but she didn't know anyone with those skills in this time, at least anyone who worked at the candy factory. It was liberating to know that those with the craft, and the ability to interfere, had died out.

Tomorrow, Dean Croft, you are mine. Beth laughed with delight.

Wednesday, August 7
Limerick Candy Factory

Beth hid the hex bag under Dean's desk at the back near the wall. She watched silently from a nearby cube as he arrived at his desk. He was humming and drinking a coffee from Joe's Java Coffee House. He was so beautiful. She admired the shape of his back in his tailored shirt and his dark hair curling at the nape of his neck. He was simply delicious. He sat down at his computer and turned it on, opened his notebook and started checking his voicemail. Then he frowned and rubbed his forehead. Beth smiled. He stopped moving and stared at his screen. This is what she'd been waiting for.

She drifted over to his desk. She had dressed very carefully this morning. Her black dress was tight and showed her slim figure off to great advantage. Her hair was a golden mass of scented waves. Dean stood up when he saw her and shook his head in confusion. She stood very close to him, looking up into his chocolate brown eyes. She put her hand on his arm and smiled, inviting him to hold her. She could see the internal struggle in his eyes as confusion warred with sparking interest as the spell wrapped around him and took hold. He took a deep breath and tried to step back, but he had caught her scent. Instead he gathered her in his arms and pressed her against him. He put his face in her hair and breathed in. She smelled like sunshine and grass after it was mowed. His favorite smells. So familiar...

She laughed. They could never resist.

Nathalie came by looking for Dean. She wanted to thank him for the coffee he had left for her. She stopped when she saw the scene at his desk and looked at Beth and Dean with horror. *Again? Seriously?* He can't think she was okay with this even if Beth did throw herself at him.

Angry and exasperated, Nathalie marched over. "What on earth is going on here?" she asked furiously.

Dean looked at Nathalie and for a split second his desire for her was so strong he ached and instinctively pulled away from Beth... but then the feeling went away. He looked at her with irritation. "Go away, Nathalie. We're busy."

Nathalie was dumbfounded.

Beth twisted in Dean's arms to look at Nathalie triumphantly and gave a throaty laugh while she ran her hands over Dean's firm behind. "Yes, BUG. Disappear...before I squash you," she said meanly.

Nathalie looked around and realized that no one was paying attention, or cared, that Dean and Beth were behaving inappropriately. *What is going on here?* Nathalie wondered frantically. She took a deep breath. No one was looking, and she'd had enough.

"I don't think so," Nathalie said, grabbing a fistful of Beth's hair and yanking her out of Dean's arms. Beth screeched in pain and outrage as she stumbled back. When she regained her balance she flew at Nathalie in a fury, trying to rake Nathalie's face with her long, red nails. Nathalie slapped her hands away.

"Keep those talons away from me, witch," she said firmly. Nathalie grabbed Dean's hand and tried to pull him away, but he hesitated and stumbled. When he righted himself he seemed confused and absent. Nathalie turned and grabbed Beth instead, but Beth just laughed and yanked her arm away. She was unnaturally strong for such a slight girl.

"Tough luck, BUG. Sweet Dean has decided that he doesn't want a cow for a girlfriend," she hissed viciously.

"Look, you scrawny little tramp. Don't you dare touch him again!" Nathalie yelled, all her hurt and anger boiling up, and to her shock, sent her fist flying right into Beth's mouth.

Beth crumpled. Blood spurted from her lips and mouth and dripped down her chin. Nathalie was shocked at what she had done. She'd never hit anyone before. What on earth was wrong with her? She was crazed!

But Beth just sat there and smiled, her teeth and lips covered in blood. Dean bent to help her up. They had finally drawn a crowd. "You're in big trouble, Parker," she said with vicious satisfaction.

"This isn't over," Nathalie said. She took one last worried look at Dean and went to find Shaemus O'Malley. He'd put a stop to all this craziness. She looked behind her and Beth was just staring at her, a vicious glint in her eyes. Dean stood there rubbing his head, but his arm was around her shoulders and hers was around his waist. For the first time Nathalie noticed that Dean seemed to shimmer. No…more like he was covered with static. She turned and ran to Shaemus' office.

When she got there, he was out. "Is he coming back today?" Nathalie asked his assistant desperately.

"Who knows?" Kelly said, sipping her coffee. "I understand he spends his nights dancing and drinking these days…not that he's invited *me*," she muttered. "Nor has he shown up for work in the last few weeks. But, he's the boss, right? He can do whatever he wants…"

"Oh." Nathalie was crushed. She wanted some adult help.

"Sorry, Nathalie. I'll tell him you stopped by, *if* he decides to stop by," she said bitterly.

"Er, well, thank you. That would be appreciated." Nathalie rushed on, "Are you okay, Kelly?" she asked. "You seem a little…tense."

"More like scorned," she mumbled. "Nah, I'm fine, Nathalie. Just fine. Nothing some Irish whisky and a gun wouldn't solve…a few shots of each should do the trick," she said loudly, slamming her desk drawers and smashing her keyboard with her fingers.

Nathalie backed out of the office and left. She prayed Kelly was just kidding.

Nathalie avoided Dean for the rest of the day, but she watched in agony as Dean and Beth had lunch together. Beth was nursing a swollen mouth, but not even that made Nathalie feel better. After work she watched the new couple walk down East Road together towards Town Circle, holding hands. He was obviously walking her home. Nathalie was overwhelmed with hurt. She stood there frozen, throat sore from swallowing unshed tears as pain and fury rolled in her chest. She didn't know what on earth was going on. What was she going to do?

Town Circle

Luke was heading to meet Sadie at The Rotunda for a quick dinner when he saw Dean holding hands with a strange girl that was *not* Nathalie. He looked at them in shock. *What on earth is going on here?* he wondered as he raced towards them.

"Dean! Hey Dean, wait up!" Luke yelled across the square.

Dean stopped and looked at Luke with irritation. Beth was frowning. Luke looked at Dean with surprise and disapproval. He ignored the girl.

"Dean, may I have a word with you, in PRIVATE," Luke said firmly. He had barely glanced at Beth because he was so focused on Dean, but she had quickly turned her back on him.

"Not now Luke," Dean said, turning away.

Luke grabbed Dean's arm. "I think RIGHT NOW is the perfect time," Luke said through clenched teeth, staring at his buddy. "Would you excuse us, Miss...?"

"Lacey. Bethiah Lacey," she said stiffly, turning to look at him.

"Ah, Miss Lacey. I need to borrow my friend. Perhaps he could meet you later?" *Or never,* Luke thought, glancing at her and giving her his most fake, yet charming, Barrington worthy smile. He had a moment of disorientation when he looked in her face, but he dismissed it as his eyes travelled to her split lip and then back to stare at Dean.

Beth didn't argue. She was desperate to be gone. She was in the presence of *The Seer*. Willow had warned her to stay away from Luke Barrington at all costs. The longer she stayed in his presence, the more likely his gift would manifest and expose her. Thank the stars he was distracted. She could feel his power. She yanked her hand out of Dean's.

"No problem," she said hurriedly and nodded nervously. "I'll meet you at my place later, Dean," she said as she bolted away.

Luke didn't waste any time. "What the hell are you doing, you stupid idiot!" Luke shouted at Dean. Sadie had spotted them and was heading over. Good, maybe she could scare some sense into him.

"What are you talking about?" Dean asked stupidly, rubbing his head.

"Holding hands with a new girl while you're dating Nathalie? The girl you've waited for since you were, what, born? Are you mental?" Luke yelled.

"She's not new. That's Beth," Dean said vacantly.

Sadie had arrived and raised her eyebrows at the pitch of Luke's voice. She looked at Dean and her eyes widened with surprise.

"I don't care who she is. She's not Nathalie!" Luke yelled.

"Beth's my girlfriend, now, and I lo—" he hesitated and blinked. "Just mind your own damn business, Luke Barrington," Dean said angrily.

"I don't get it. What's wrong with you? I'm your best friend," Luke said in a very frustrated voice. "I don't understand what you think you're doing? I'm trying to help you!"

"Like I said, it's none of your business," Dean said. His eyes drifted towards the North West Quad, and Nathalie's house. He looked confused.

Sadie put her hand on Luke's arm and squeezed, pulling him back to whisper to him. "You'll not reach him right now, Luke," she said, frowning at Dean with narrowed eyes. "Let him go."

Luke took a breath. "Are you going to basketball?" he asked Dean roughly.

"Why wouldn't I?" Dean replied curtly, and turning on his heel, headed towards home.

Luke stood there dumbfounded for a few minutes before he spoke. "Sadie, what just happened?" he asked in shock.

Sadie watched Dean speculatively as he crossed Town Circle and headed towards home. "If I wasn't going through my own odd happenings, I may never have believed it was possible."

"What? What was possible?"

"That boy's been hexed."

"With what?" Luke asked with agitation.

"A binding spell of some kind, it looks like. Why else would he be obsessed with a stranger?"

"Well, he does know her. That's the 'Beth' he and Nathalie have been talking about. They work together. She picks on Nathalie, actually. My God, I wonder if she knows? She's going to be devastated, if she isn't already," Luke fretted. "Do we tell her?"

"It's rivalry. Stealing a boyfriend or a lover is a very strategic way to destroy a rival. Love makes people crazy. It distracts them. They forget everything else, as *I* am personally beginning to learn..." Sadie mused and Luke watched her think. She drew her eyebrows into a small frown. "I'm absolutely sure Nathalie knows."

I distract her, he thought, pleased. *How did I ever think she was cold? I can't believe I used to be afraid of her. What a doll...*

"You're staring at me again," Sadie said matter of factly, taking Luke's arm and heading towards the Barrington Estate.

"I thought we were going to eat..." Luke looked back at the tables longingly. "We should call Nat."

"I need to do some research on this phenomenon of Dean's. I will also find Nathalie and check up on her. We have some time. Dean is going home. This is *very* distressing," Sadie said sadly. "I don't know what I'd do..." She looked at Luke's precious face. "Since we have some time before you head out to basketball, I thought we could smooch in the woods for a bit. I want to hold you right now," she said softly, taking his hand.

Luke's heart began to pound and he looked at Sadie with great interest, all thoughts of food forgotten.

Sadie glanced at him and smiled. She shook her head.

"You're better than food, baby."

That was a great compliment from Luke. "Thank you," Sadie said softly.

The Barrington School Gym

Luke was late getting to basketball so when he arrived they had already picked teams. He was not on Dean's, and he wasn't happy about it. He hadn't wanted to come in the end. He and Sadie had lain pressed together on a blanket they had hidden in the woods for their "alone time." What started as playful smooching turned serious very quickly. They had kissed deeply for over an hour. She was like a drug with her hot wet mouth. He had crushed her to him and groaned at her softness as their bodies slid against each other. Sadie had been flushed and panting and even she didn't want to stop, but they did it for Nathalie and Dean. He'd had to force himself from her and take a cold shower before donning his basketball shorts to avoid embarrassing himself. Sadie had just laughed at his dilemma as she drifted away through the trees towards home.

They ran around the gym and Dean ignored Luke. They bumped into each other a few times but Dean avoided looking or speaking to him. He was physically there but strangely absent. He didn't talk to anyone, not even the new guy they secretly admired. This guy never missed a shot and could jump higher than anyone. They attempted to make friends with him, and tried not to fawn all over him. He was friendly, but he always disappeared right after they finished playing.

After the game, Dean left quickly and Luke just let him go. As he was walking home Sadie phoned.

"Hi gorgeous," Luke said warmly.

"Hello, Luke," Sadie said in her cool voice.

Luke smiled. This was the girl who had been wrapped in his arms, sighing with pleasure a few hours ago, *but you couldn't tell by her voice,* Luke thought with a laugh.

"I looked through Elanah's spell book and found a section on hexes. It looks as if Beth might have made up a hex for Dean."

A hex? Now this was something out of the twilight zone. Luke shook his head. "Sadie, are you sure? A hex, really? It looks more like a love spell. God, what am I saying?"

"Spells can be good. Hexes never are. She's compelling him. Witchcraft is real, Luke. You've seen it yourself, and he's showing all the signs. Did he pay any attention to you?"

"No..."

"The hex will get stronger. Right now he's going through his regular motions, but shortly he'll lose interest in regular things. Today he's attentive but showing some confusion because his mind is fighting it. Tomorrow he'll be a bit more obsessed... until he becomes mindless to anything but her."

"How do we stop it?"

"We find the source of the hex and we destroy it."

"Oh my God," Luke's voice trailed off.

"We have to find it, and soon, Luke. There is a point of no return when this type of spell works on a person for a while. Binding spells are slavery spells and fall on the dark side of the spectrum. This is the dangerous part when fooling around with magic. Soon he won't be reasonable anymore, and even if we destroy the spell, Dean will be irrevocably changed. According to my source, it may even drive him to suicide."

"Your source?" Luke asked curiously.

There was silence on the line.

"Sadie?"

She sighed. "The hex is in Elanah's book, but she copied it from another witch. That witch was Willow Kellar. The identical hex, and notes on its effects, are in Willow's spell book. It's actually more of a grimoire. It's here, in the house. I found it, even though Liora tried to hide it. Willow *was* the master of male manipulation. She used men to get what she wanted."

"And you touched it??" Luke was aghast. "It's evil!"

"I took precautions when handling it."

"Do you think Beth..."

"Luke, we found Elanah's book with all the other books in the library, remember? Maybe Beth was the one reading it."

"It's possible. The rare books are available for anyone to read, but Liz is very careful when giving them out, and getting them back."

"Anything could have happened. It's not a nice spell, Luke. If Elanah copied it from Willow, they may have been working together."

"Great... did you reach Nathalie?"

"No, her mom says she went out, so I've been focusing on research."

"I'll see if I can find her. Do you want me to come over so we can talk about all this?" Luke asked hopefully, his mind shifting to earlier in the evening.

Sadie laughed. "My aunt was cleaning her shotgun today. Best you stay on Barrington property tonight."

Luke ached to hold her again. He seemed to have a one-track mind these days. He was a walking bag of hormones. "Okay, I guess," he said, pouting.

"Call me if you find Nathalie," Sadie said coolly. "'Bye darling," and Sadie hung up.

Darling! Wellllll... Luke grinned and biked to the fair. With Sadie helping they'd figure this out.

He knew where Nathalie would be—at the fair, keeping an eye on Beth. He found her watching Wayman giving kids horse rides.

Nathalie was devastated, but was holding it together in public. She seemed relieved to see him, "but if I have a minute alone, I'm going to lose it," she said sadly.

They had a quick conversation and Luke told her what Sadie had observed and what she thought was happening.

Nathalie was surprisingly receptive. "There was a weird mist around him, but it could have been my tears. Oh, I don't know," Nathalie said in a shaky voice.

Luke put his arm around her. "I'm sorry Nathalie. Sadie said it'll be an object, like a bag or a sachet. I can get into Dean's room..."

"Don't bother. The only place it can be is at the candy factory. The Croft household is like a bus station—there's no way anyone can sneak in the place. Plus, he left me a coffee on my desk this morning, so he was fine when he got in." Nathalie rubbed her eyes. "I'll look around his desk and see if I can spot anything out of the ordinary."

Luke was quiet for a moment. "You okay, Nat? You're taking this crazy idea very well."

She didn't answer right away. "No, Luke, I'm not okay," she said. He could hear the ache in her voice and sense the unshed tears. "I want to shake him and slap her, but I've got to believe something completely out of the ordinary is going on because it's not possible that Dean would do this. It's just not possible..." Nathalie's voice trailed off.

Nathalie had just been by to see Taline, who had frowned at hearing what happened. "So you didn't give Dean the amulet?"

"I didn't really have a chance, and I was waiting for the perfect time."

Taline had sighed. "Strange times, Nathalie," she said, looking around at the fairgoers. "It would have been better if he had gotten it sooner rather than later, but no matter. We'll figure this out."

"It's just a necklace, isn't it?" Nathalie had asked, looking at her curiously.

Taline just looked at Nathalie before adding, "I just saw Dean walking through the fairgrounds towards Beth's chocolate stall. I have to agree, he really isn't himself. He didn't say hello or stop at the stable," Taline had said. "It's not like him at all."

"The chocolate stall?" Nathalie said despondently.

Taline smiled grimly. "Don't worry. I'll get Wayman to grab him before he does anything stupid."

But Wayman had a barn full of excited children, as Nathalie had been observing.

"Luke, can you..."

"Sure, I'll go cause a ruckus."

Nathalie was grateful. She didn't want *them* to see her and humiliate her in public. She didn't want to give *them* the satisfaction of seeing her upset. Wayman looked at her worriedly from the barn, but he was stuck.

Luke turned to leave, but she remembered something. "Oh, by the way, I asked Dean to ask you, but I'm sure he didn't get around to it. Can you get me a list of the families who were vandalized on Sunday night?"

Luke hesitated for a moment, worry over Sadie's possible involvement setting off alarm bells in his head. "I think so. Why?"

"I'm just curious since Dean's family was one of the houses."

"Sure."

"And how's Sadie?"

"Oh Nathalie, she's awesome!" Luke gushed with true obsessive enthusiasm but then stopped and there was an awkward silence.

"Oh, for God's sake, Luke! I still care about other things! Anyway, I'm glad you finally got the girl you love...you big nerd."

Luke grabbed her and hugged her tightly. "Me too, Nat. Have faith," Luke said before disappearing into the crowd.

She watched Luke go and thought about what he'd said. Why wasn't she surprised? Disbelieving? Hexes and spells in modern day Barrington? That was Barrington history, not reality. Yet... something clicked inside her. The idea wasn't farfetched. It seemed... believable, normal. Something was going on in this town. She'd never seen so many strangers at the fair, so many odd people selling odd things. The blood markings... now a hex... all at the same time. It was weird.

Thursday, August 8
Factory & Fairgrounds

The next morning Nathalie arrived at the candy factory hours before anyone else. She searched Dean's desk everywhere but couldn't find anything out of the ordinary. She left a message for the receptionist that she'd be late, and when she knew Taline would be there, she headed to the fairgrounds to find her.

Taline looked at Nathalie and smiled, giving her a hug. "Great timing! I just finished setting up and was about to go grab a coffee and a piece of Nettie's berry pie at the bake table."

It was still very early. The sun was casting dappled shadows around the grounds and it was muggy. It was going to be a hot day.

"Did you find anything?" she asked softly.

"No. I couldn't find anything odd at his desk," Nathalie confided desperately as they walked towards the eating area. She had updated Taline last night after speaking with Luke.

"Couldn't hurt to check it out, sweetie," Taline said matter of factly.

Nettie was busy bustling around the bake tables. Nathalie knew Nettie had been up since the crack of dawn, baking and preparing for today's fair. There had been a record number of people visiting and buying her baked goods. She was a hit and the town's bakery was making a fortune. Nathalie felt her heart jerk when Nettie looked at her with her beaming smile, dressed in her sweet white apron. She just loved that woman.

"Hello lassies!" she yelled. She looked at Taline and then Nathalie. She reached to touch Nathalie's cheek and frowned slightly. "Something the matter, little one?"

She was so observant. Nothing got by her. "Just a little heart trouble, Nettie," Nathalie said sadly.

"Ah, trouble with your young man," she said, nodding.

Nathalie bowed her head. She was aching. Did she still have a young man? She didn't want to know what happened last night between Dean and Beth, and she didn't want to see them at the office.

"Yes, very suddenly and completely out of character," Taline said, with a significant look at Nettie. She took her pie, which Nettie had sliced into large pieces and put onto plates for them, and handed the other one to Nathalie.

"Sometimes things aren't as they seem, child," Nettie mused, a worried look on her face. Then she looked sharply at Taline, who shrugged helplessly.

"I certainly hope so," Nathalie said, eating her pie.

Limerick Candy Factory

After breakfast Nathalie headed back to work. By lunchtime Dean hadn't come to see her, and she was angry. She walked to the window and could see Beth and Dean holding hands and heading to the woods for a walk. She clenched her teeth and balled her fists as anguish stabbed her heart. She wanted to hurt Beth.

"Tough break," Emma said quietly, appearing beside Nathalie. Irritated, Nathalie glanced at her and was shocked.

"Emma, you look terrible!" She really did. Her hair wasn't brushed, her makeup was smudged, and her clothes were crumpled. She had dark circles around her eyes.

"Slept under a tree in Town Circle last night. I think I passed out." Emma laughed. "I can't really remember."

Nathalie was aghast. "You slept outside? Emma, you could have been hurt!" She looked around. "Why on earth didn't your boss send you home? You're in no condition to work. Doesn't she mind that—" She stopped before she put her foot in her mouth. Emma was looking at her and blinking sleepily. What was she going to say? *Doesn't your boss mind that you look like a rumpled street-walking bum and smell like an old shoe?*

Emma smiled. "She's not in. We were together last night. I think she went home with Pete Donovan."

Nathalie looked at her in astonishment. *Eww!* "Go home Emma," Nathalie said sternly. "If anyone asks, I'll tell them you took a sick day."

Although somehow she didn't think anyone would ask. Emma nodded and tottered off.

Nathalie heard her name being called. When she turned she saw Nettie holding a big bag of food. It smelled delicious as she sped over and put it on Nathalie's desk. Nathalie wanted to cry. What a wonderful gesture. Nathalie noticed that a few of her coworkers had drifted over, attracted by the smell. They all looked a little worse for wear. *It must have been some party last night,* Nathalie thought.

They eyed her bag hungrily, but Nettie drove them back. "Touch this bag and ye all shall suffer my wrath! I can promise you that," she said threateningly with a wink at Nathalie. They shot her mean looks and dispersed. There certainly wasn't going to be a lot of work done today. Where was Shaemus?

Nettie glanced outside, *tsked,* and pulled Nathalie away from the window. "You eat, honey. Then I thought I'd take a gander at your young man's desk and see if I can spot anything odd-like."

Nathalie ate while Nettie exclaimed over all the "interesting baubles" on Nathalie's desk.

"That's a stapler," Nathalie said with a laugh as Nettie picked it up and stared at it.

"What does it do?"

"It staples paper together!" Nathalie exclaimed.

"Well, no need to set your britches on fire. Show me how to use it."

With mild disbelief, Nathalie stapled some paper together.

"My, that's just genius. Gotta love human ingenuity."

Nathalie laughed and finished her sandwich. "You are so funny Nettie."

"What? I'm a baker and a scribe. I'm no administrator. These instruments are new to me."

"Oh, well, when you put it that way..." Nathalie had finished her soup and sandwich. Just a brownie left, but Nathalie was getting anxious. "I'll eat the brownie later. Let's search Dean's desk before he gets back."

They walked through the halls and Nathalie peeked to make sure Dean wasn't there. No one was there. It was completely deserted. Nettie walked to his cube and searched to no avail.

"Something is here, child. I can sense it in my bones. But I can't see it. You need someone with the sight."

"The sight?"

"Someone with the touch of magic." Nettie was looking at Dean's desk and nodding to herself.

Nathalie was still trying to wrap her head around what Nettie was saying. "Nettie, what are you talking about? Magic doesn't exist. It can't. It's impossible!"

"Then explain to me what is happening to your beau? Nothing's impossible, Nathalie."

"Well..." Nathalie spluttered. "There has to be a logical explanation for this. Maybe she's slipping him some sort of drug, or has hypnotized him, or is playing mind games... I don't know! OH, THIS IS JUST RIDICULOUS!" she fumed.

"What's ridiculous?" Beth asked, startling Nathalie almost out of her skin. She and Dean had come back from their walk. They were holding hands and Nathalie's heart filled with pain inside her. Beth's mouth looked like a painful, swollen mass with her split lip, Nathalie noticed with satisfaction. *At least that will limit any kissing,* she thought desperately.

Nettie cut in smoothly when she saw Nathalie was speechless. "Oh, we were just looking for Dean. I insisted on seeing her young man, even though she tried to tell me some silly story that they were no longer a courtin'. Well, bless me; it would appear that she is telling the truth." Nettie looked at Beth with a vacant, innocent expression. She frowned as she looked down at their clasped hands.

"That's right, old lady," Beth said with a sneer.

"Let's just go," Nathalie said in an agonized voice and pulled on Nettie's arm, but she didn't budge. Nettie was looking at Beth warningly.

"You'd better watch your tone with me, girlie. You have no idea who you're dealing with."

Beth took a step back, looking shocked.

Nettie looked at Dean. "Well, let me just say shame on you, young man," she said. She looked right into his face. Dean frowned in confusion and then the expression on his face smoothed out, and he didn't say anything.

Beth had regained her confidence and Nathalie heard her laugh as she dragged Dean away, but Nettie had a satisfied look on her face.

"What, Nettie? Tell me," Nathalie begged.

"That boy is bewitched, Nathalie. I've seen it before. You need to find that hex and destroy it."

Nathalie sighed. "Nettie..."

Nettie stopped her and took her arm. "You listen to me, lass. There are forces at work here that you don't understand, but that doesn't mean they don't exist." Nettie put her hands on Nathalie shoulders. "Your young man is in great peril. You need help. The right help."

"Well, I don't know anyone..."

"You know that Kellar girl."

"Sadie? Oh my God, Nettie, those witch stories are so mean," Nathalie said in horror.

Nettie shook her head. "The truth is not mean, child. It is merely the truth. That girl is a witch. It is her heritage. It is in her blood and her power is rising. You need her help. She'll be able to see what you and I can't."

"I..."

"Trust me, child. I *have* seen this before. The results are heartbreaking. She *can* help you."

They had reached the reception area. Nathalie noticed that Nettie didn't have a visitor's badge. "How did you get in, Nettie?"

"Right now, Nathalie, nobody is watching. I just walked right in."

After Nettie left Nathalie headed back to her desk. She had a fluttery feeling in her stomach. She realized it was fear. When she got there her chocolate brownie was gone. Whoever ate it left the paper bag on the floor. *Unbelievable,* she thought to herself and realized that many unbelievable things were happening. She picked up the phone and called Luke. He answered after the first ring.

"So?"

"I can't find anything. Neither could Nettie, but apparently I may not be able to."

"Nettie was there?"

"Yeah, she brought me lunch and suggested I may need some help from a professional...er...a gifted person."

Luke sighed in resignation. "Do you have a pen? I'm going to give you Sadie's cell phone number."

At full dark Sadie and Nathalie met on East Road outside the candy factory. It was completely deserted and very dark. From the back you could barely see Sadie. Her black dress and hair blended with the night. She was merely an undulating shadow. When Sadie saw Nathalie she nodded and followed her to the main door. Nathalie flashed her pass and opened it, motioning for Sadie to precede her. Sadie slipped in and Nathalie followed. She felt awkward. Asking Sadie had been difficult because she tried not to use words relating to witches, especially since she was not sure how Sadie felt about these types of things, being a Kellar and all.

Sadie had set her straight right away and been reassuring. "No point in beating around the bush. I'm a witch and can probably help you. Anyway, I'm the one who figured it out in the first place and looked up the hex after I saw Dean's demeanor."

"I really appreciate this," Nathalie whispered in the dark as they headed towards the elevator.

"Not at all," Sadie said quietly. She had a melodious and cultured voice. Her white skin glowed in the darkness and the dark made it seem as if she was floating.

"I know this must seem crazy..." Nathalie said.

Sadie waved her hand to stop her. "Nathalie, I'm a Kellar. I've been surrounded by witchcraft my whole life. I've read through Willow's grimoire. Her spells worked. To assume a sort of...supernatural power doesn't exist is just foolish." Sadie shook her head and frowned. "People have become lax. They think everything that happened during the witch trials was due to ignorance and mass hysteria of the people. Now we're 'enlightened.' But some of it was real. What Willow did to those children to gain power was real. Her hex is real." Sadie stopped and was thoughtful for a moment.

Nathalie was awed. Sadie spoke with such conviction. She didn't feel silly anymore.

They entered the elevator and got off on the second floor. Sadie automatically turned left. "There is definitely something here, Nathalie," she said quietly. "I can feel it emitting tendrils of power." Sadie turned the corner and walked right to Dean's cube. She immediately bent down and crawled underneath his desk and within seconds held a small brown bag in her hands.

"How did you know that was there? I looked everywhere, even under his desk. That was not there this morning," Nathalie said with surprise.

"Oh, it was there, but you couldn't see it. The person who made this hid it from plain sight. Part of the hex acts on you and tells your mind to ignore it, otherwise, it would be very easily discovered."

"How can you see it?" Nathalie asked, fascinated.

"I don't have plain sight," Sadie said simply.

Nathalie looked at the little sachet in horror. "So how come I can see it now?"

Sadie smiled. "I think it has to do with the fact that I'm holding it. Your mind kind of acknowledges its presence. Either that or my hands neutralize it. But if I put it on Dean's desk, you won't be able to see it anymore because I'm no longer interfering with the spell." Sadie put the little bag down and Nathalie could still see it. But once she blinked it disappeared.

"It's gone!"

"That's because your brain has lost track of it."

"Oh," Nathalie breathed. She was even more awed of Sadie now. "Why isn't anyone else affected?"

Sadie picked up the sachet and peered at it. "I suspect that some part of Dean is wrapped up in this little bundle. Perhaps some of his hair...she needs something from him to bind the spell to him and him alone."

"So...I'm guessing she's bound something of her so he would fixate on her."

"Exactly," Sadie said, pleased. "It's very simple."

"Why would she do this?" Nathalie asked. She was amazed and angry at Beth's audacity. What was the point? What was this girl trying to do? You can't force someone to love you!

"That's an important question, Nathalie. If it's just because she likes him and wants him for herself, that's one thing. It's obvious that he's completely besotted with you and some girls can't handle the rejection. She can't steal him from you by normal means, so she tries another way. She may just be a silly rival."

Nathalie blushed. Dean *was* besotted with her, and she with him. The pain of losing that was enraging.

"But if she has another purpose, that's what you need to be wary of." Sadie looked at Nathalie with a very serious expression on her face. "This witch is very powerful, Nathalie. This spell is simple, effective, and ruthless. It's one of Willow's, and it's power is growing. While Dean was obviously struggling against its call yesterday, his desire or inclination to do that will wane each passing day as the spell grows stronger, and the longer he stays in close proximity to it." She stared at Nathalie. "She didn't care about the consequences, Nathalie. Never forget that. It says something about her."

"I won't," Nathalie whispered. "So what do we do with it now?"

"We destroy it."

"How?"

"We have to take it apart and neutralize the hex."

"Can't we just incinerate it?" Nathalie thought of Peterson The Pyro and the sachet he had burned in her garbage can after her spider hallucination. Now she knew that Beth had been involved.

"Unfortunately, no, not this one. Whatever part of Dean she used has to be extricated and rendered useless for him to be free. Otherwise, there may be dangerous magical backlash. He's very tightly bound. I wouldn't take a chance."

"What about Beth?"

"The moment we start the ritual to destroy the hex, she'll know."

"What about now? Does she know what we're doing right now?" Nathalie worried. She didn't want anything to interfere with her freeing Dean.

"No. Dean may feel a lessening of the insistent demand of the hex, but not Beth."

"Assuming they're not together right now," Nathalie said with a crack in her voice.

Sadie smiled smugly. "Don't you worry, Nathalie. The worst that's happened is that Dean has been holding hands with a strange girl. Luke has been haunting his footsteps these last two days. And if you take into consideration the split lip you gave her... trust me, our Beth has not had any luck in the romance department."

"Dean probably isn't too happy about that."

Sadie shrugged. "He's being compelled. Other emotions pale to that call. If he is angry, he doesn't stay that way for long. Luke is working around it."

The girls left the candy factory and headed to Sadie's house. They went around to the back. Bordering the Kellar property was Stone Creek, which flowed behind all the houses on Sadie's street.

"Go to the water. I'm going to get the things I need to break the hex. I'll be out in a moment." Sadie headed to the back door and let herself into the kitchen and disappeared from sight. Nathalie headed to the bank of the creek. After a few trips, Sadie was satisfied she had everything. Her cell phone rang.

Sadie fumbled with the phone and Nathalie smiled. She obviously endured technology for Luke alone.

She glanced at Nathalie quickly and then turned when she answered. "Hi Luke," she whispered. Nathalie could only hear one side of the conversation, but got the gist of it quickly. "Yes, we found the hex... no, there's no danger... this IS my area of expertise, LUKE, if you would remember... he's being difficult? Well, of course he is. He's being compelled...lie to him...by the creek...there's no need...fine, we'll wait...no, we don't need coffees!" Sadie hissed and hung up.

Nathalie laughed. "Luke never changes."

Sadie grinned ruefully. "Luke is Luke, and he's insisting we wait for him. He's bringing Dean."

Nathalie felt a flutter in her stomach. She knew it wasn't his fault but she was still angry with him for being too weak to resist being compelled. Two days of hell. She wanted to punch him and kiss him at the same time.

Sadie looked at Nathalie in her assessing type of way. "Let's sit," Sadie said. She got a thick horsehair blanket from the Kellar's rusty shed and placed it on the ground. It was peaceful near the creek in the dark. The gurgling water was soothing and the wind through the trees made the leaves rustle around them.

The girls sat and Sadie settled herself before putting a hand on Nathalie's arm. Nathalie started to cry, heart wrenching sobs that rocked her body. Sadie scooted over and put her arms around her and let her sob.

When Nathalie was finished Sadie started to speak softly...as if she were crooning to a child. Nathalie sighed as she listened to Sadie's soft voice drift around her like the wind. "Cry Nathalie, get it all out, but don't hold any anger in your heart towards him," she whispered. Sadie's voice danced and echoed in Nathalie's head as she spoke. "Being compelled is like mental rape. The call takes you, wraps around you, sings to you, and you *must* obey. It is the master, Nathalie, and no human can withstand its power with their will alone."

Sadie paused, and then continued, "Willow used this hex on many men she wanted to use and then destroy. They went on to do horrible things for her. They stole children... They suffered terrible shame and indignities after she dumped them. A lot of the shame was because they still wanted her so badly. One of her lovers killed himself because he realized all hope was gone and that there was no escape." Sadie's voice trailed off. "No one knew about her spells and hexes. Willow was so powerful she was able to hide many things from the townspeople's sight. They just thought she was amoral. Only the town scribe knew, and Willow suspected she did, but it was dangerous to stick your nose in Willow's business, so the scribe bided her time until the time was right...and the rest is history. I have Willow's journal. She wrote it all down. I am a direct descendant of her line. I will free your Dean for you. I won't let another girl use Willow's evil magic to destroy more lives."

The two girls hugged. "Thank you Sadie," Nathalie said tearfully.

Sadie just took her hand. "I ache for you, Nathalie. If it were Luke, I don't know what I would do. I finally have him. He's mine, and I love him so much..."

Nathalie listened quietly as Sadie confided in her first girlfriend. "You are so lucky, Nathalie. Dean has always been in your life. I had to watch Luke from afar, not allowing myself to even consider whether it would ever be possible. If someone were to interfere and make Luke do something against his will... I'd kill them."

Nathalie nodded. Sadie wasn't kidding.

The boys arrived in a breathless, muddled heap. They had biked from the Croft's where Luke had been babysitting Dean, who had been babysitting his little brothers.

Dean was angry because the boys had slammed the door in Beth's face when she had come calling. Nathalie may monopolize their adored older brother's attention, and be a girl—two strikes against her—but they were loyal.

"Go away!" they had screamed.

"I'll get you, you little brats," she had hissed meanly as they stuck out their tongues.

"What's going on?" Luke had asked, coming to the door and looking outside, but Beth had already gone.

"She gave PMS to Dean," Eddie said angrily. "That's why he's been such an *asshole* the last few days."

Zach gasped at the bad word and both boys covered their mouths and giggled with the badness of saying it out loud.

Luke just looked puzzled. "What exactly is PMS in your world?" he asked the excited little monsters. He wasn't sure he wanted to know.

Zach rolled his eyes. "Pre Mental Syndrome. You know. Makes you crazy."

"Dean musta caught it from *her*, since he's been such an ass—" Eddie started, but Luke cut him off.

"Okay, enough with the 'ass' talk."

They had left as soon as Dean's parents had come home.

The girls jumped up and Luke grabbed Sadie, kissing her soundly on the mouth. Dean's expression was puzzled and angry. He just stood back, unmoving. Nathalie didn't move. She just looked at his blank face in anguish.

"You said Beth was here," Dean said accusingly.

Luke frowned. "She'll be here in a minute," he lied.

Sadie took one look at Dean and lit the pillar candles she had brought out of the house and handed them out. She was standing beside a special burner filled with coals. They were red hot. "Everyone sit down, around the brazier. At the cardinal points would be best. Place the candle in front of you."

Luke grabbed Dean and sat him down at the east cardinal and took north. Nathalie took west and Sadie sat south. They placed their candles and looked at Sadie expectantly. She took out the sachet and dangled it over the coals. She threw some herbs into the brazier and they burned like paper, emitting a thick smoke and a sickly sweet smell. Dean was staring intently at the bag. The area they were sitting in was strangely still, and the four of them breathed in the smoke.

"It smells like weed," Luke whispered.

"It is 'weed.' It's good for more than smoking. This plant relaxes all things."

"Are we going to get stoned?" Luke asked curiously, but Sadie shushed him.

Nathalie was getting dizzy. She could see the wind was still blowing through the trees but she couldn't feel it. There was no wind in the circle. All she could smell was smoke from the brazier. Dean's eyes were closed and he slumped forward as Sadie chanted strange words. She wove her hands around the sachet and it fell away. It looked as if it was floating. Wax melted. A pink ribbon unraveled and a dried flower fell into the burning brazier. Still chanting, Sadie dropped the ribbon and some hair attached to it, which burned instantly, giving off a terrible smell. At that moment a rush of wind roared through the circle. Dean opened his eyes briefly before they rolled back into his head and he lost consciousness, falling backwards onto the grass.

"Dean!" Nathalie screamed as she scrambled to kneel beside him. His normal pale complexion was chalky white in the darkness. Her hands fluttered above him. She didn't know what to do. Sadie and Luke knelt beside him, looking at him with concern. Dean's eyes fluttered and Nathalie fell on top of him, crying.

"Is it over?" he asked in a croak before he started to cry. He wrapped his arms around Nathalie and buried his face in her neck as they held each other tightly on the grass. Dean was whispering "I'm sorry, Nathalie. I'm so sorry. Sorry sorry..." while Nathalie shushed him and kissed him all over his face and wiped away his tears and her own.

Luke put his hand on his friend and waited for the emotions to subside. Sadie sat quietly beside him. Within a few minutes Dean and Nathalie had calmed down and sat up. Dean held Nathalie tightly and wouldn't let her go.

"How long?" Dean asked.

"Two days."

Dean looked relieved. "It felt much longer than that. I was completely powerless. It was as if someone else was controlling what I said and did."

Sadie interrupted. "You're very lucky, Dean. The spell would have only gotten stronger and stronger, and eventually driven you insane, maybe even to the point of suicide."

Dean looked horrified. "Are you kidding me?"

"According to Willow's grimoire, only a powerful witch can stop the hex, but it has to be caught in time. You can't force someone to love you, so eventually a hex like this will go wrong. One of her victims killed himself. The rest were still enthralled... but I don't have a record of what happened to them after she was burned."

Nathalie spoke, "so, we don't know for sure if they ever escape if the hex isn't broken. There aren't many precedents, only what Willow has written and recorded."

"So now we know Beth's a witch," Luke said quietly. It seemed surreal.

Nathalie basked in the warmth of Dean's big arms around her. "What I want to know is why she's here, in Barrington. What does she want?"

"That is definitely something we need to find out," Sadie said decisively, "but one thing's for sure, she's here to make trouble."

The Parker Residence

Later, Dean walked Nathalie home. They slipped around the back to the dark porch and the concealing darkness of the woods ringing Nathalie's house. Dean gathered her into his arms and kissed her passionately as if he'd been starved for affection for years. Nathalie wrapped her arms tightly around his neck and held his warm mouth to hers fiercely. When they broke their kiss Nathalie was limp, leaning against the back of the house while Dean rained kisses on her neck and face.

"I love you so much, Nathalie," he whispered in her ear. "There's no girl for me but you. Never, ever."

Nathalie moaned. "I love you too, Dean," she managed to say before he took her mouth again and crushed her to him.

Town Circle—The Apartment above Clara's Crafts & Crystals

Beth woke with a start. She knew her hex was broken. Where the edges of it used to pulse in her mind was now blankness, a yawning emptiness. She screeched in anger, pounding her bed with her fists.

She tossed the bedcovers aside and scrambled out of bed. The hex hadn't even had a chance to reach full potency. She should have had a fully-fledged lover by week's end. She dressed quickly and raced to the candy factory. Not caring who saw her, she flashed her pass and ran inside. At Dean's desk she could see right away that it was gone. In a fury she ran to Nathalie's desk. She wanted to hurt the bitch and smash all her pretty things. Beth reached for Nathalie's coffee cup but found herself distracted by the desk's nameplate. N. PARKER... it reminded her of something she had recently handled. Beth gasped as it hit her.

Upon returning home Beth invoked the amulet at her neck and it began to burn. She whirled around to find Danner in her room.

He smiled. His terrifying countenance pleased for once. "Hello Beth. You must have good news if you're calling me at this time of the night."

Beth was exultant. "I found the Lore Keeper! The spelling of the Parquhar name has changed over the centuries to plain old 'Parker' but the same blood runs through her veins." Her face was twisted with anger and hate at the mention of Nathalie's heritage.

Danner mocked her a little. "Oh, such bitterness over a young man slated TO DIE." He emphasized the last two words. "Tsk tsk." He waved his hand carelessly. "In the end, it's good news. He'll keep her busy. Affairs of the heart consume you puny humans. We need Miss Parker distracted."

Beth's face tightened with anger.

Danner only laughed. "I knew your spell had been destroyed. I could feel the echoes of Kellar magic in my prison. Too bad the Kellar descendent in this time plays for the other team." Danner sighed. "No matter."

"I'm going to kill her," Beth said venomously.

Within the blink of an eye Danner was right in front of Beth. He reached for her and she gasped as pain bloomed where his ocher hands touched her. "You'll do no such thing," he hissed ominously. "With all your mean games and silly hexes, I think you're forgetting the real reason you're here. I let you have your fun, but you're forgetting about ME."

Beth was gasping with pain.

"You're with me, aren't you Beth?" he asked softly, before his voice turned hard. "Find another plaything for now. I promised to send you one, and I did. He's on his way. But right now there is no room for vengeance or romance. Only me. Just ME. Only I matter. I saved you. I own you. You belong to me. Do you understand or do I need to teach you a lesson, witch?"

Beth's breath came in short bursts. "No Danner," she gasped, "no lesson necessary."

"Good," he said quietly, and then he was gone.

Saturday, August 9

Nathalie's Journal – Entry for Saturday, August 9

Today Dean and I sat on my back porch, swinging on the swing while the wind whistled around the house. It was dark. We had turned off all the lights at the back of the house so that the only light came from the glowing fairy lights wrapped around the porch railing. After a late dinner we had gone for a walk and were now relaxing under the stars. Dean had his fingers twined with mine and his thumb was rubbing the inside of my hand. We were looking at what stars we could see with the dark clouds scudding across the night sky. It was a full moon and very romantic.

I could feel Taline's pendant as it rested between my breasts, warm and heavy, a comfortable weight. I pulled it out and over my head and detangled my hand from Dean's so I could take the figures apart. He looked at me curiously, his big chocolate eyes and ridiculously long lashes staring at me with their "I want to touch you look." Dean and I have spent *a lot* of time kissing and holding each other following his enslavement by that nutbag. We were frantic for it. When we were apart we ached. We both agreed it was crazy, but since we were having fun... why not?

I got up and slapped him on the side of the leg to make him scootch to the middle of the swing. He smiled lazily as he moved his adorable butt over and invited me to sit on him. I smiled and sat on his lap facing him and wrapped my legs around his hips.

"That's interesting," he murmured as he wrapped his arms around my hips to keep me firmly in place. At first I thought the swing was going to protest and eject us, but we managed to balance very well.

"I have something for you," I told him. I showed him the pendant. In the dim light the male and female shapes appeared to be writhing together.

"Are they having sex?" Dean asked curiously, staring at the small figurines intently. We looked at each other and laughed.

"It's just the light!" I exclaimed. I broke them apart and put the female pendant around his neck.

"Will you wear it?" I asked him. My heart was pounding, but I continued on determinedly, fiddling with the cord so I wouldn't have to look at his face. "It's one heart split in two, see? I want to give you my heart to keep safe, and if you want, I'll keep your heart safe with me." I adjusted the cord so the female was at the exact position of his heart and put my hand over it. I looked up and Dean's beautiful brown eyes were dark, mysterious pools. He tightened one of his hands on my hip while the other caressed its way up the soft skin of my back underneath my shirt. He didn't say anything but pressed me close to him, bringing our mouths together.

His mouth was warm. He kissed me slowly and languorously, sliding his tongue along my lips before slipping it into my mouth. I could feel the blood rushing to my face as I slid my tongue against his. My body became flushed as I wrapped my arms tightly around his neck, running my hands through his hair. I could feel Dean was very aroused and I pushed myself against him until he moaned. The kiss deepened to the point where I didn't know where my body ended and his began. We were making out feverishly. My hands were running all over his body and his over mine. Reason came flooding back when I remembered we were outside on the porch. I broke the kiss and leaned back, panting heavily. He looked feverish and agonized.

"Do you want to go up to my room?" I invited softly. It was a big step, but I didn't care. I wanted him, only him, right now. No more waiting. I was going nuts.

"Yes," he said, grinding his hips against me. I groaned and covered my mouth with my hand. "Yes to both things," he said softly. "I'd be honoured to wear your heart close to mine, and, well, I've always trusted you with mine."

I looked at him; my body was tingling and demanding total, private alone time with him. I nodded and slid off his lap. Holding hands we snuck into the house and crept upstairs to my room. Luckily my parents were both dozing in front of the TV and didn't see us come in. We slipped into my bedroom and locked the door. The next second I was in his arms and the next few hours were... heaven. We gave each other hot, wet kisses. We took off our clothing piece by piece. Dean kissed every part of my body that he uncovered, and I did the same. By the time Dean slipped off my underwear and his, my body was screaming for him. We fell back on my bed, his heavy body a wonderful weight on mine as he slid inside me. We held each other tightly and kissed mindlessly as he thrust and thrust. We muffled our moans of pleasure against each other's mouths, and we did it again and again and again.

Later Dean and I lay together, our limbs entwined, while he inspected the two figurines, clicking them together and then pulling them apart.

"This is really cool, Nat. They lock together via their arms and their *private parts*," he whispered.

I giggled, looking at the figurines as Dean clicked them together.

"It's so intimate, the action I mean. Yet you can't really see anything but the arms hugging when they're together. See, the man has a small penis and the woman has a place for it. That's how they lock together. It's brilliant," he said in amazement, fingering the amulet.

Dean fell asleep but I was still too keyed up. I looked at his clothes, tangled with mine, with something like awe. Dean was actually *naked* in my bed. I couldn't believe how lucky I was, and how beautiful he is. I ran my hand over the side of his body and his hip. *He's so warm.*

Dean sneaked out just before dawn. "Are your parents going to notice?" I asked him sleepily as he got dressed to leave.

"Nah, they don't really keep track of things like that. With six of us to manage, they're usually dead asleep by ten o'clock." He kissed me goodbye and I fell back asleep.

What an incredible night!

Sunday, August 10
The Fairgrounds

After church Dean had to help his parents with his siblings in the morning, so Nathalie wandered over to the fairgrounds to help Taline. She was very curious about the amulet Taline had given her, especially considering the peculiar way it locked together. She thought about last night and blushed. The power of suggestion? It was strange; she just didn't feel like herself lately. All she thought about was kissing, being in love, and now, having sex with her gorgeous boyfriend. She felt flushed and excited all the time. She couldn't stop thinking about Dean and how crazy she was about him. The thought of seeing him, and his beautiful brown eyes, made her breathless. Nathalie shook her head. What on earth was wrong with her? Teenage hormones? She shuddered. If so, they had her in thrall.

The fair was already teeming with people. Nathalie walked by Taline's stall but she was busy chatting with a couple of women about herbs, and there were many customers looking at her amulets and charms, so she decided to look around the fairgrounds a bit and come back later when Taline wasn't so busy.

She headed to the stables to say hello to Wayman but was halted by someone whispering her name. Despite the noise and the bustle, the voice was clear. Nathalie stopped beside a small covered alleyway that lay between the last stall and the stables. Despite the sunshine, the alley was shrouded in gloom. A figure stood there, unmoving. It beckoned to her, calling her familiarly. "Nathalie… Nathalie Parker," it whispered. Nathalie felt disoriented. It's voice, soft and deep, compelled her closer. She started to feel scared before reassurance enveloped her. She stepped into the gloom.

The being was huge, at least nine feet tall. It looked almost solid. It's face was like something out of a nightmare. It had glowing yellow eyes, and when it grinned, she saw it's mouth was filled with long, shark-like teeth. A quick glance just below eye-level confirmed it was male. He was naked, and aroused. She knew she should be screaming in terror, but she felt such a lassitude… the sounds of the fair had completely faded away.

"Well, well," he rumbled. "You're a hard one to pin down." He studied her for a few moments before he spoke. "So you're the lost piece of the puzzle. The whistle blower. The squealer. You know, no one likes a tattletale."

Nathalie's thoughts were fuzzy even though her heart had started to pound in terror. *What on earth was this thing? What was he talking about?*

He continued. "Let me introduce myself. My name is Danner. I'm stuck in a terrible, terrible, terrible cage and I've been there for a very, VERY, VERY long time. I really want to get out." He laughed and Nathalie wanted to cringe, but she couldn't move. *He's insane!* she thought wildly.

"The worst? I'm so *bored*," he said carelessly. "I have a friend who wants me to hurt you a little, you know, as a favour. Normally, I don't do favours, but because I'm bored, I just might," he said with a horrific grin.

Hurt me? In the middle of the fair? Nathalie thought, and then realized there was no one else around. No one was looking.

"I need you to stay out of my business," he said calmly, stepping forward. He reached out an unusually long arm and brushed her arm from shoulder to wrist. His fingers were long with black pointed claws instead of nails. Pain bloomed and spread, following the path of his hand. Nathalie wanted to scream in agony but she was frozen and couldn't move away from the hideous and terrifying being.

"Nathalie?" She could hear Wayman calling her name from the stable. His voice sounded distant even though he couldn't be more than five feet away from her.

Danner frowned. "Darn. I wanted to break your fingers, but our time is being cut short. What a pity." He passed his hand over her face. "Forget me little mortal…but not my wish…stay out of my business, or I'll be back to skin you alive," he whispered as he tossed her a coin. It hit the dirt at her feet. He chanted as he faded, "find a penny pick it up, chances are you'll have bad luck…"

"Nathalie?" She turned towards Wayman's voice at the end of the alley. He was glowing. She swayed for a moment before crumpling to the ground. "Nathalie!" Wayman's deep voice boomed as he charged in and swept her up into his powerful arms. So strong…his body was warm and hard like steel. His soft shirt rubbed against Nathalie's cheek as he carried her to the stables and lay her down on some loose hay. Taline rushed in.

"You found her! Thank heaven! I saw her disappear and then the horses started going berserk! You could hear them across the fairgrounds. What happened?"

Wayman was inspecting Nathalie for injuries, running his hands over her arms and legs, checking for breaks. *This is what the horses feel,* Nathalie thought, and she laughed. Wayman looked at her with a small frown. He wasn't glowing anymore. Instead, Nathalie could sense a blackness rolling through him.

He scowled. "I saw her heading over and then I felt a presence. Someone I haven't felt for years. Then the horses went crazy just as she disappeared. After a couple of minutes I called for her and found her in the alley. No broken bones, but her arm is burned."

Taline bent down and put her thumbs on Nathalie's temples. Her eyes were still a bit glazed. "Nathalie, honey, do you remember who you were talking too?"

Nathalie shook her head. She had a flash of yellow eyes but it faded in an instant, like a dream. "Did I pass out? How did I get here? I don't remember," she said groggily.

Taline and Wayman looked at each other with concern.

"No, you had an encounter with a ... being of some sort," Wayman said softly.

Nathalie looked at Wayman with confusion. "What are you talking about?"

Taline shrugged, and shooting Wayman a glance, helped Nathalie to her feet. "Why don't you head home?" she suggested mildly. "I think the heat's getting to you."

Nathalie nodded. "Must be. I was heading here but I don't remember arriving." Now she wasn't feeling that well.

She said goodbye and they watched as Nathalie weaved her way through the crowd and disappeared.

"What is it, Wayman?" Taline said curiously. "What, or who, did you sense?"

"I felt Dannerlich's presence today, Taline. For the first time in, oh, I don't know how many centuries ... I felt superstitious. I think Danner's back, and he's up to something." Wayman knocked on wood.

The Parker Residence

Nathalie went home to take a nap. As she took off her shorts, a coin in her pocket fell out and rolled onto her bedroom floor.

How did that get there? she wondered.

She reached for it and when she touched it, a demon's image roared into her mind. Nathalie screamed in terror, flinging the penny away from her where it hit the wall and rolled back onto the floor. Shaking, she ran to the phone to call Dean, but by the time she reached for the receiver, she had become calm. *Why was she calling Dean? He's busy today, and she wanted to nap.* She was tired from her late night.

She looked down at the penny on the floor glinting in the sun and wondered where she got it from as she lay across her bed. She didn't know of any country that minted the hideous face of a demon on its one-cent piece. Maybe it's Roman...

I'll get it later, Nathalie thought before falling asleep.

The Croft Residence

Dean was wrestling with his little brothers when Luke showed up in the Croft's backyard. One of the twins launched himself at Luke and a small scuffle ensued, ending with the little boy sitting on Luke's back, rubbing his face in the dirt and making the victory sign. Dean smirked, and grabbing both squirming boys under his arms, walked to the end of the yard and dropped them in their wading pool, clothes and all. They were thrilled and immediately started a water war with each other. Dean laughed as he headed back.

"You okay, Luke?"

"Yeah," Luke snorted as he brushed dirt and grass off his body. "He took me by surprise. Those two brats have been at my house practically all summer. I'm used to it, although you'd think I'd be better prepared. I used to be my older brothers' plaything, too. That was more painful." Luke grinned and sprawled on the grass. Dean sat down beside him and there was silence. They had been friends for so long that Dean knew right away Luke needed to talk.

"What's up man?" Dean asked quietly. Did he want to talk about what had happened a few days ago? Destroying the hex had been pretty intense. Dean was still a bit in awe of Sadie.

"I have a problem."

"Okay."

"I think I'm in over my head."

"Is it Sadie? She's a nice girl, Luke—" Dean started, but Luke interrupted.

"Yes, it's Sadie, but it's not what you think." Luke sighed. "This is going to sound unbelievable."

"I have to say that I believe in more things these days. That happens when a modern, sexy guy like me meets an obsessed witch who creates an actual working hex..."

Luke laughed. "Having gone through what we did last week makes this easier to bring up, actually." Luke frowned and rubbed his eyes. He looked tired. "Sadie has been, er, missing time periodically since the end of June.

"Missing time? Explain."

He did. "She comes back to herself and doesn't know what she's done, where she's been, or who she's been with. Sometimes she doesn't know where she is."

"Whoa, that's wild."

"Yeah, we thought it was maybe split personality or something."

Dean made a groaning sound. "But...it's not."

"No." Luke pushed on. He explained what he'd seen on the library steps and in his dream. "So it's a mess. I'm seeing things when I'm awake. I'm dreaming things that come true. In the end..." he took a deep breath, "the current *theory* is that Sadie is being haunted and possessed by her ancestor, Willow Kellar."

Silence.

"*The* Willow Kellar?" Dean asked.

"Yes."

"The 'I hex you,' burned at the stake Willow from hundreds of years ago?"

Luke sighed. "Yes."

"Wait, I thought they weren't related to *that* Kellar. You know, that her last name, especially in this town, was merely...unfortunate."

"That was a lie to spare Sadie persecution as a child. She is actually Willow's direct descendant."

"Great. Hold on," Dean said as he got up and went into the house. He came back out with two beers and handed one to Luke.

"You can't drink those!" the twins yelled from their little pool.

"Yeah, you're underarms!" Eddie yelled bravely.

"That's 'underage' you dink!" Zach whispered furiously to his brother, and then yelled, "we're gonna tell!"

Dean glanced at the wet little monsters standing in their pool quivering with excitement. He shrugged and drank his beer. "So much for me taking you to the fair, tonight. Can't go if I'm grounded."

The boys frowned and huddled, turning their backs on the older boys. Dean snickered and Luke smiled. They really were the most conniving little brats. They put their arms around each other as they conferred. After it turned into a shoving match and a brief water fight, they had reached a decision.

"We see nothing," they said with dignity and continued on with their playing.

Luke laughed. His mood lightened and he opened his beer. With the sun shining nothing seemed ominous.

Dean raised his eyebrows. "You weren't going to drink that before they gave you permission, were you? Do those little guys intimidate you, buddy?"

"Yes. Yes they do. I've spent the better part of the summer *defending* myself from their tall tales to my mother! They're reputation ruiners with those sweet, innocent faces. Only Sadie can keep them in line. They squirm in front of her."

"They're pretty good with Nathalie too," he said with pride, thinking about what they had done to Beth. They drank in silence for a few minutes. "Some news, man. Does Sadie know you're telling me this?"

"Yes. She's actually worried about me, and after what Beth did to you... well, we need to band together. We need help."

"Did you talk to your dad?"

"I tried, but he's distracted." Luke was very close to his dad. "He's absorbed with the council these days, with the vandalism... and the windmill. He's obsessed with the windmill. Like I said, something strange is going on."

"Right, about the vandalism... can you get a list of the families for me? Nathalie really wants it."

"Already done." Luke reached behind him and handed Dean a piece of paper from his back pocket. "One of the reasons I came over. Nathalie asked while you were under Beth's influence. I was sure Nathalie would be here." Dean was looking at the list and Luke glanced at it. "I had to copy it fast since my mother hid it for some reason."

"Really? I wonder why," Dean mused, folding it and putting it in his pocket. "Okay, back to our conversation. For argument's sake, how do you know it's Willow Kellar and not just some random ghost?"

Luke shrugged. "I'm *not* sure. But I saw her... the ghost. She's female, gorgeous like Sadie... her aunt seems to be involved, so it has to be family related. Why else pick Sadie?"

"You pick Sadie because she has power and she's not like us regular humans."

Luke was thoughtful. “Okay, then why not pick Beth? We know she’s a witch.”

Dean shrugged, “I don’t know. Maybe Sadie’s more powerful.”

Luke shook his head. “I’ve thought this through. There’s a reason ... an attraction to Sadie, and I think it’s familial. It is premeditated. I got that sense from my dream. Sadie’s the target.”

Dean shook his head and snorted in amazement. He made the sign of the cross and felt his amulet. It made him think about Nathalie, and last night. What a night. Remembered pleasure made him smile. “This is messed up. You should get Sadie an amulet from Taline.”

“Who’s Taline?”

“Wayman’s girl. You haven’t met her?”

“Not yet. She sells amulets?”

“Yeah, all kinds. They’re cool. Apparently, this necklace would have protected me from Beth, or at least lessened the hex. Tell her what you need and she’ll find something to help.”

Luke looked dubious. “Is she a witch?”

“No more than Wayman’s a warlock. I’m not sure how, but they have special abilities. Trust me, go see Taline.”

“Can I see yours?”

“Sure,” Dean said, pulling it out of his shirt.

Luke looked at it. “Doesn’t seem particularly remarkable.”

Dean smiled. “Oh, it’s remarkable all right. You should see it when it’s with it’s mate. Apart, well, it looks kind of ordinary, but I think that’s the point. Nothing flashy, nothing to attract anyone’s attention.”

“Let me see what Sadie says.”

“Good idea. So what can I do to help? I’d do anything for you, buddy.”

Luke was at a loss. “I don’t really know. I can’t always be with her, and her aunt will shoot me if I go near their place. I’d like to have Nat help me keep an eye on her.”

“Sure. We’ll do whatever you need.”

The Fairgrounds

Luke hung out a bit longer and when he left he called Sadie and they agreed to meet at the fairgrounds. It was early evening and the sun was beginning to set. It was beautiful. The breeze smelled of ripe grass and sunshine. They met on the North Road right outside the entrance. Sadie’s long black hair shone. Her figure was thin in the severe black dress. Excitement flared up inside him as he watched her approach. *So cold and beautiful,* he laughed to himself. His girlfriend. His. *Mine.* The moment she was close enough he pulled her into his arms and wrapped himself around her. He felt her arms tighten around him. People milled by, laughing and talking. She stepped back and he stole a quick kiss. Someone whistled and Sadie smiled self-consciously.

"I may have a solution to your problem," Luke said, his voice full of hope. Sadie wasn't so confident.

"Really?" she said coolly, putting her hand in Luke's and walking into the fair. She knew that things were rarely that simple, but she didn't say anything.

They made their way through the booths. They passed the bake table and Beth's small drink stand. She was doing brisk business, but she looked up when Sadie approached. The girls stared at each other in passing, both with steely glints in their eyes. Beth's was anger; Sadie's was a warning. Beth dropped her eyes first and continued to serve her boisterous customers. There was a long lineup for her chocolate liquor.

Luke glanced back. "It wasn't that good," he muttered. "It barely tastes like chocolate. I don't understand the fascination."

"You loved it the first time," Sadie said.

"Yeah, but I've had it since, and it's not the same. Maybe she's tainted my memory of it." Luke looked at Beth with dislike.

Sadie looked back at the line. She knew many of the people waiting for their free sample. A lot of them were men, and Beth was a pretty thing. She hadn't tried the concoction herself, but she wasn't about to drink anything made by that girl.

They reached Taline's booth. It was beautiful in the fading light. The glow of the gems cast gentle light over the stall making it look mysterious. The bundles of herbs gave off a variety of comforting smells. Sadie looked at the goods and was pleasantly surprised. Some of the plants were very rare and hard to gather in large quantities. She wondered how Taline had gotten a hold of them.

Taline herself was a breathtaking woman. Tall and slender with long silvery hair, she was an image out of a fairytale, but without the wings. The old legends of The Fairy Folk...if they existed, Taline represented what Sadie imagined they looked like, and for a moment Sadie saw impossible beauty in a white ageless face before her vision righted itself. Taline smiled, her pale, but human, skin tinged slightly pink from the sun.

"Can I help you?" she asked. She looked at Sadie and inclined her head. Sadie returned the gesture.

Luke put his arm around Sadie and drew her close. He didn't know what to say that didn't sound absolutely crazy, and talking crazy to this creature was not something he wanted to do. All his old gawkiness came flooding back. Sadie looked at Luke and rolled her eyes at his awkwardness. Taline was now smiling. Sadie smiled back and stuck out her hand.

"My name is Sadie Kellar," she said simply, looking right into Taline's icy blue eyes. "I am looking for a protective charm. An amulet to prevent..." and here Sadie hesitated slightly before she continued, "to protect my person from unwanted... well... attention from a malevolent being."

Luke just nodded and pulled her closer to him. Taline noticed the protectiveness of the boy, and the innocence of their affection tugged at her.

"My best friend, Dean, said you may be able to help," he managed to squeak out. He coughed and his voice resumed its normal timbre. "My name's Luke Barrington. I know Wayman."

Taline laughed. "He mentioned you." She looked at Sadie. "Why don't you explain to me exactly what's happening and I'll see if I can help?"

They did, together. Luke described what he had experienced in Town Circle and seen in his dream. Sadie explained the missing time and her fear that she had been involved with the blood markings, but she couldn't remember.

Taline looked at Sadie with concern and dawning understanding.

They looked at her with such hope. She hated to burst their bubble, but she didn't have a choice. "I can't help you with exactly what you need right now, Sadie. I don't have a charm or an amulet that prevents possession."

Sadie stared at her with burning eyes, disappointment spreading over her face.

"The problem is that you have power in your own right that is in flux. It's manifesting, so at times you can do things, and at times you can't. Not only that, it will just destroy anything on your person that radiates magic that's not, well, your own because you haven't learned to control it yet."

Sadie's face had gone tight and cold. She tilted her chin up. "I don't want this!" she blurted out with frustration. "I want to be left alone! I don't want Luke hurt or in danger because of me. I just want to be normal!" She stamped her foot.

Luke was shocked. He'd never seen Sadie have a fit in public, or ever, for that matter.

Taline looked at her with ageless eyes. "I'm sorry Sadie. What you *want* is irrelevant, honey," she said sympathetically. "You aren't normal. You have great power. If you don't learn to control it, someone else will, and may be trying to already. What you need to do is face your heritage and turn it to your advantage, and not the other way around." Taline considered Sadie. The sheer strength and determination of the girl was palpable, but a glimmer of fear showed in her eyes for a brief second before it was gone.

She's so young. Taline took a basket from one of the shelves and rooted through it while she talked. "This isn't the 1590s where the townspeople will burn a woman on suspicion of witchcraft, Sadie, a situation your ancestor manipulated her way though. The 'age of enlightenment' has come and gone. People are unbelievers. They don't even see what's right in front of them." She looked up. "Now they seek out the mystical. People want love spells and to have their palms read. People with abilities hide them now so they won't be harassed or used, and not because they'll be put to death. It's a different time."

"Being different is hard," Sadie said sadly.

Luke looked at her with concern. "You're not different! You're unique and…and beautiful beyond belief," he said adoringly, tightening his arm around her.

Sadie smiled at him. "Okay, I have one fan. Yet, you have to admit, sometimes you're afraid of me."

"*For you,*" Luke corrected firmly. "The rest is *excitement,*" Luke said, wiggling his eyebrows.

Taline looked at Luke curiously. "Sorry, what did you say your last name was?"

"Barrington. Lucas James Barrington."

"Oh," she said frowning and turned to Sadie. "Unfortunately, I don't have a charm or an amulet that your power wouldn't just burn. As I explained, your power is possessive and will destroy another's magic."

Luke's shoulders slumped and Sadie put her head against him to reassure him.

"But, I may have another way around the problem," Taline said. She continued to sift through the basket and found what she was looking for. Taline threaded a stone onto a leather thong. It was perfectly round and white with a hole in the middle. It was a rock that had been shaped to look like a donut with wire twined around it for decoration. Taline closed the stone in her hand and a blue light emanated for a split second. She smiled and handed the necklace to Luke. He took it and placed it around Sadie's neck.

"Great, now lie to her," Taline said with a smile.

Luke was startled and Sadie looked up from inspecting the pendant.

"What?" he asked.

"The stone detects lies. Lie to her and see if the stone reacts. The iron circling the stone will get hot." Taline nodded in encouragement.

Sadie lifted her eyebrows with a slight smirk. "Yes, lie to me, Luke."

"Uh, okay, er..." Luke grinned. "Sadie, you are the ugliest girl I've ever seen." The stone started to glow. Sadie looked down, startled. Luke continued, "I am only dating you because there are no trolls in this town for you to take as a mate and I feel really sorry for you." Sadie yelped as the stone heated up.

"It's hot!" Sadie exclaimed. Luke reached to touch the stone and pulled his hand back as if stung.

Taline nodded. "When someone lies to you, the stone will glow and get hot. Small lies, small glow. The bigger the lie, the hotter and brighter the stone will get."

"But those were outrageous lies!"

"A lie is a lie," Taline said simply.

"Good, I wasn't sure he was lying," Sadie said with a straight face. Taline laughed but Luke looked worried.

"Sadie, honey, I was only..."

"Oh, I know you big goof," Sadie said smiling as Luke hugged her.

"Don't take it off. It will help you determine friend from foe," Taline said.

"So why doesn't my 'magic' just burn this rock to dust?"

"I don't think your magic can detect lies, so the rock isn't doing something your magic would consider a threat."

"Glow necklaces!!" a kid screamed, dragging his harried mother to Taline's table. "I want, I want!" he yelled. The mother looked at

Taline. "Do you have anything to shut him up?" she asked, obviously at the end of her rope.

Taline smiled. "I just might," she said to the woman and pulled out another basket of stones.

"Good luck," Taline said with a small wave as Luke and Sadie left. As they exited the fairgrounds, Dean was coming in with his little brothers.

"Hello monsters," Luke said to the two excited boys. They could barely contain themselves as their gaze flitted from one place to the next. They were like little jumping beans, quivering in place.

"Whoa little dudes," Dean said. He looked at Luke and gave Sadie a quick hug hello. "Did you find what you were looking for?"

"Not exactly," Luke admitted, "but Taline did help us. Let's meet in the library tomorrow night, after supper. We can use Liz's office and chat. Where's Nathalie?"

Dean frowned. "She's not here? She's supposed to be helping in Taline's stall."

"We didn't see her," Sadie said.

"That's strange," he started, but then the boys started to jump up and down and scream. "Horsie! Oh my God Dean a HORSE! Oh GEEZ! LOOK AT IT POOP! IT'S TAKING A SHIT RIGHT IN FRONT OF US!" The boys were ecstatic, but Dean was obviously embarrassed as many heads turned in their direction at the boys' outbursts. The boys just stood in awe, staring at the huge steaming pile of fresh poop, totally fascinated. A calculating look appeared on their faces. Dean's eyebrows rose in alarm.

"Don't even *think* about it you little brats," he said severely.

"Whaaaat??" they said together, the picture of innocence. Their hands in their pockets. A woman passed by and smiled, "what little sweethearts," she said as she walked away.

Luke looked pained. "Good luck with that," he said to his pal and then chuckled. He grabbed Sadie's hand and they headed towards Town Circle.

Dean grabbed the boys' hands and pulled them into the fairgrounds, away from the horse poop. "Any sign of trouble and we're going home, got it?"

"Sure, Dean, sure, sure," they said, eyes huge as they looked around. They played a couple of games and Dean got them some cotton candy. Wayman let them sit on Pleasure and they squealed in delight. Wayman laughed and swung them around. He looked at

Dean, who was watching from his seat on a bale of hay. "You should visit Taline," he said casually.

"Alright," Dean said, getting up to leave.

"He's so big," the boys said to Dean as they left the stable.

"He's a good guy," Dean said absently, looking ahead to Taline's stall and hoping for a glimpse of Nathalie.

"Yes," they agreed.

Taline smiled at the boys and gave them each a little rock necklace. "For protection," she said. "Don't take them off!"

The boys looked at her with round eyes. "You're big for a girl," Eddie said in awe.

"And kinda shiny," said his brother.

Taline laughed. "Ah, such sweet talkers! You are great little guys!" she said, ruffling their hair. They both blushed and scuffed their running shoes in the dirt, suddenly shy. They held their necklaces tightly.

"Taline, where's Nathalie?"

She looked worried. "She's at home. There was an...incident this morning." Dean looked alarmed. "Don't worry. She's fine, but we can't talk about it here...too many strange ears. Wayman is looking into it. We're hoping to have a bit more information tomorrow."

Dean told her about meeting Luke and Sadie in the library tomorrow evening.

"After that, come here. We'll meet in the stable. There are some things you need to know," she said mysteriously.

Dean felt apprehension curl in his gut, and curiosity.

Taline smiled at the boys. "Have a good time, little ones."

The boys were showing signs of their usual boisterousness and were impatient to leave. They whispered and then bowed in unison. "Good evening, beautiful one," they said with great flair.

Taline laughed in delight and inclined her head to them. Dean looked stunned.

"Where did you learn that?" he asked as they walked off.

"Television," they said.

"The chicks love rivalry," Eddie said smugly.

"It's *chivalry*," Zach hissed furiously.

Dean just snorted.

At the bake table Nettie gave each boy a huge cookie, but shooed Dean away when he tried to pay for them. "I have a soft spot for little Crofts," she said. She looked at the boys eating and talking and sighed. "Crofts were always the sweetest looking children." She looked at Dean, "but I'll bet these two have the devil in them."

Dean laughed. "They sure do, but since they've stolen everyone's hearts, they get away with murder."

Nettie's face crumpled at the word. "You keep those boys safe, Dean Croft," she said sternly.

"Yes m'am," he said with a slight bow and a chivalrous smile of his own.

It became apparent it was time to go home. The boys had started slapping each other, which meant it was bedtime, and Dean wanted to see Nathalie. Uneasiness sat within him. Something had happened to her today. He needed to make sure she was okay. Why hadn't she called him this afternoon?

As he left, it was impossible to avoid Beth, who was manning her little stand. She looked up when he walked by and she called his name. Dean gritted his teeth. It had to be that exact moment her stall was free of customers.

"Dean, can I speak to you for a moment?" she asked. Beth was a beauty. Her long blond hair lay in soft crinkled waves to a slender waist she emphasized with tight fitting dresses. Her pale skin and blue eyes practically glowed. She was a catch, but not for him. He was already hopelessly in love.

"It'll have to be quick," he said tonelessly. "I have to get my brothers to bed." The boys had halted and were looking at Beth with unfriendly expressions. *Uh oh,* Dean thought to himself.

She looked at them with narrowed eyes. "Well, hello little ones," she said, bending down to look at them. She appeared to be sizing them up as if they were dinner. Both boys took a step back, but didn't say anything. Dean gave silent thanks. Sometimes you just never knew what would come out of their mouths.

"Well, aren't you the sweetest little things," Beth said sarcastically. "Do you want some chocolate?" She rummaged around in her little stall and produced two chocolate bars. The boys looked at each other in silent communication and accepted the proffered candy. "Enjoy," she said evilly. Beth turned to look at Dean.

"There seems to be a *grave misunderstanding* around what happened last week," she said softly. Her blue eyes looked at Dean earnestly. If he had never seen the hateful glares she'd directed at Nathalie, and lived through a hex she'd created, it would have been easy for him to believe she was the simple, sweet person she pretended to be. But he knew, with all his heart, that while her outside was beautiful, her soul was black. There was something very wrong with this girl.

"I do admire you so," she continued. "I realize now that your friendliness towards me was just kindness and not an interest in courting," she said indulgently.

Dean bristled. *Courting? Ha.* She made it seem as if he had led her on when he had made it very clear that his only interest was Nathalie. No, she had violated him and he was still angry about that. Furious. But he also knew that letting her know how he felt was dangerous. Beth was vindictive and spiteful. He didn't want to take a chance that she'd do something to Nathalie.

"It's water under the bridge," Dean said affably, but his eyes remained cold. Beth sighed as he nodded and walked off with the little boys.

Such a handsome man. Such cute little boys. She smirked. What a pity. If she couldn't have him, then no one could, and she'd take the two brats along with him. She turned and smiled at a tall youth waiting for his free drink. She smiled at him and he smiled back. "Aren't you the Baker boy?" she asked flirtatiously, batting her eyelashes at him and wiggling her bottom as she poured.

"Why yes I am. Name's Reg," the boy leered, staring at her ass.

"Nice to meet you," she replied demurely. *You're mine tonight.*

Town Circle

Luke and Sadie walked through The Rotunda. The place was wild with dancing and drinking. "I've never seen anything like this," Luke said, laughing.

"Neither have I," Sadie replied as they joined in, letting the music move their feet. They felt happy after seeing Taline. Now they had *something* to help them.

They ate and then walked hand in hand through one of the circle's paths towards the outer sidewalk. It was pretty on the paths at night, and each path was different. This one was called *Lantern Way* because it had small glowing streetlights shaped like old-time gas lanterns lighting the path, making the tree and bush lined walk a romantic place to stroll. For lovers looking for some privacy to steal quiet moments together, all the paths had openings to grassy resting areas popular during the day.

As Luke and Sadie walked through holding hands, leaving the noise of the revelers behind, the soft sighs and sounds of passionate couples drifted around them. The wooded areas were full of people having "private" moments. At one turn they were startled by the sounds of heavy breathing, a zipper opening and an ensuing groan.

Shocked, Sadie glanced at Luke, and while she couldn't exactly tell by the lantern light, she suspected he was a bit flushed. She suppressed an embarrassed giggle as Luke pulled her and they ran through the clandestine path as fast as they could.

When they reached Barrington property they headed to their secret place. Luke pulled her into his arms and put his mouth against hers, and they made their own lovers sounds.

The Parker Residence

After dumping the boys in their beds and chatting with his parents for a few minutes, Dean headed to Nathalie's house. He took his bike and pedaled as fast as he could.

When he arrived the Parker residence was quiet. All residences in Barrington were nestled in the trees. Nathalie's yard was surrounded by huge maples and firs, and all that could be seen of the surrounding houses to the sides were twinkling outside lights. The residential quads were magical at night, the streets lit only by hanging lanterns in the trees. Built in the valley at the base of the Spire Mountains, Barrington land rose gently from the town's center, creating a town shaped like a bowl. The north quad Nathalie lived in was hillier than the flatter south quads, so homes were at slightly different levels, each higher than the next as you moved west. The effect at night was a stacked fairyland. It was beautiful. Nathalie lived at the base of the hill. Her family had a breathtaking view of the neighbourhood.

He walked to the front porch and knocked on the door. It was just past nine, so he was sure Nathalie's parents were still up. When there was no answer he rang the doorbell. He heard a shout and then saw Nathalie through the glass, coming down the stairs. She opened the door and pulled Dean inside. She slammed the door behind him and launched herself into his arms. Dean held her closely. She smelled like roses. He loved roses. Her face was pinched and pale. He kissed her forehead softly and looked at her. "What happened? I thought you were at the fair but Taline tells me you didn't stay."

Nathalie nodded. There was fear in her eyes. "I met a demon, Dean."

He was still for a moment. "What?" he said incredulously.

"I swear to God, I met a demon at the fair today." Nathalie shuddered. "He said his name was Danner." Her eyes widened. "I have proof!" she said. Dean followed as Nathalie raced upstairs. She bolted into her room and stopped in the middle. She pointed and Dean bent down to look at the object of interest. It was some sort of penny.

"Don't touch it!" Nathalie said, backing away. "It roared at me."

Dean looked at her. She didn't look crazed, just stunned.

"Why didn't you call me sooner?" he asked angrily as he stood up. He was frightened and trying to get his confused thoughts together. "Tell me exactly what happened."

She told him what she remembered. "Then, when I got home I fell asleep. I was so muddled afterwards, I actually forgot. He told me to forget, but I remember! I remembered when I put on my amulet!" She shrugged. "I know I didn't dream it. Wayman rescued me. Without the amulet I only have a sense of fear. He did something to me to make my memory fade."

"You took off your amulet? After what happened with Beth? ARE YOU NUTS?" Dean roared. He was looming over her, bristling and fierce, the horror of his experience in his face as well as terror for her. *That being could have taken her and murdered her, and no one would have been the wiser,* he thought to himself in a panic.

"I'm sorry. I wasn't thinking," she said earnestly, giving him a hug.

Dean shook his head. "Okay, let's test your theory. Take the amulet off."

"What?" Nathalie said, clutching it to her.

"Take it off. I'm here. I'll remind you." He shook his amulet at her. "Let's see if your theory holds water."

Nathalie took the amulet off and put it on her bed. A look of disorientation crossed her features briefly as she looked around her room. Then she wrapped her arms around him and kissed him, slipping her hands under his tee-shirt onto his back. *Wow, that was fast.* He kissed her back and was tempted to worry about the demon thing later, but then he shook his head. "Nathalie, why do you think we're up here?"

"To fool around?" Nathalie said, kissing his neck and rubbing him. "Why else would we be in my room these days?" Dean groaned and put her away from him. Nathalie laughed. "Don't worry! My dad told me he was taking my mom on a 'date' tonight. Nick is at a friend's."

Dean looked at her in astonishment. "We were just talking about a demon. Try and remember, Nathalie."

"What ARE you talking about, Dean?" she asked, stepping away from him and crossing her arms across her chest.

This demon's kung-fu is strong... Dean thought as he walked over and picked up the odd penny. It got hot in his hand but there was no other reaction. No roaring. He inspected it carefully. It wasn't a penny but some sort of ancient coin. He noticed that his amulet was getting hot. He grabbed a Kleenex from the box on Nathalie's desk and wrapped the coin in it tightly. His amulet cooled off. *The coin needs skin contact,* he thought to himself and filed the information away.

Nathalie was smiling. "Find a penny pick it up..." she frowned. "Wait, do you get good luck or bad? I don't remember the jingle. You can keep the penny," she said uneasily as he wrapped it.

Dean frowned. "Put your amulet on," he said quietly, "it's on the bed." Nathalie scooped it up and placed it over her head. Her eyes widened.

"Oh my God, Dean...I remember!" Nathalie grabbed her keys and headed out the door. "We have to speak to Taline and Wayman and find out what happened!"

He grabbed her as she swept by. "And we will speak to them, tomorrow. The fair is closed and Town Circle is nothing but madness and mayhem. You won't find them this evening," Dean said.

"What does this mean?" Nathalie was terrified.

"I don't know. There's a lot of weird shit going on." He told her about his conversation with Luke and their meeting at the library tomorrow. "It looks as if they're not the only ones that need help at this point. After that Taline wants us to meet her and Wayman at the stables. They're looking into something themselves."

Nathalie stood by her window and looked out at the twinkling lights of her neighborhood. "Do you think he'll come back tonight?"

"If he does, we'll meet him together," Dean said, stripping off his clothes and climbing into Nathalie's bed. Nathalie's body flushed as Dean's intention became clear as it rose from under the sheet. She turned off the light and peeled off her own clothes. Moonlight pooled onto the bed from the window as she slipped under the covers and into Dean's arms. He was hot and his body warmed her chilled one. The breeze coming through the window was cool with the smell of summer. His arms circled around her and he held her close as they slid their bodies against each other. Dean lay on top of her as he kissed her and pushed her legs apart so he could press himself against her.

"We have to do something to keep busy while we wait, and this is our new and fun activity," he said lightly before focusing his attention on her and kissing her deeply, rolling his tongue with hers while his arms tightened around her and his hips moved against her with pleasurable friction. She wrapped her arms around his neck and her legs around his hips and as he thrust into her, her cries of intense pleasure filled the room.

Later they lay together, giving each other soft kisses. Thankfully, no demon appeared. They heard Nathalie's parents arrive home sometime in the early hours of the morning, sounding like drunken teenagers.

Now it was Dean's turn to head home. Dean touched the amulet lying between her breasts then gave them both a kiss before kissing her mouth in a soft goodbye.

"Don't take this off for any reason," Dean said, playing with it and then taking his and clicking it together with hers.

"That's kind of erotic," Nathalie said sleepily. He unclicked them.

"Yeah, it's pretty cool."

She palmed the amulet. "If I miss you I'll rub it's little penis," she said in a naughty voice, "or I can rub your big one…" she said reaching down under the sheet. Nathalie licked her lips.

Dean stared, his body reacting. The urge to plunge his body mindlessly into hers flooded him. He couldn't seem to get enough. He had tried leaving an hour ago but he had been drawn back to bed when Nathalie had tousled her hair and spread her legs in wide-open invitation. That action and the view had done him in. He had accepted and they had rolled around for another half an hour, but now he had to leave before his parents came searching for him. But his body was on fire, again, and he didn't want to go. He watched as she slid the sheet off their bodies. The sight of her hand rubbing him made him even harder. He pressed her back, his big body crushing hers. He held her hips steady and just pushed himself into her ready body over and over again. She moaned with satisfaction as he pumped his hips. He was sucking her tongue and her lips. She was using her hands to push him deeper.

"Dean" she whispered against his mouth, "don't stop," she said as she lost herself to pleasure. Dean slid inside her a few more times before he shuddered and groaned, his hips slamming against her. They made out wildly, tongues tangling together.

"I could eat you," she said, kissing him again. "I *love* sex," Nathalie breathed. "Why did we wait so long?"

Dean laughed against her mouth before getting up to get dressed. He pulled on his shorts and shirt and watched as she lay there, pouting, her naked limbs pale against the sheets.

The bed felt cold without the warmth of his body. "Stay," she said softly.

He smiled as he looked at her. His best friend. His lover. His goddess. Nathalie…the girl he'd loved his whole life. He knelt beside her and took her hands in his. He kissed them feverishly. "I love you Nathalie Parker. Thank you for sharing yourself with me. It has been an incredible pleasure to be with you. Now get some sleep!" He stood, and with a gallant bow, the idea stolen from his little brothers, he snuck out of her room. He had to leave now or Mr. Parker would be loading his gun.

"What a god," Nathalie thought. She stretched luxuriously and fell into a deep sleep, all thoughts of the demon forgotten.

Instead, she dreamt of a windmill. Barrington's windmill, the historical construct protected from destruction by Barrington County law…innocuous in it's ordinariness as it waited in a field…now alive and spinning…warning the townsfolk to beware…warning them that they were in grave peril.

Nathalie woke up sweating.

Monday, August 12
Barrington Library

The four met at the library late in the afternoon. They clustered together in Liz's small office. Sadie had picked up hot coffee from Joe's. They added cream and sugar and Luke cleaned everything up. "Liz is kinda fussy," he explained.

Dean yawned.

"You look tired," Luke commented. "You're so pale I can see the veins in your eyelids." Dean's face got a little red.

Nathalie glanced at Luke. "He slept over to protect me from a demon and then put in a full day's work," she said seriously.

"You slept over?" Luke asked with interest and a twinge of envy. Dean waggled his eyebrows.

Sadie frowned at Luke before turning her stare to Nathalie. "A *demon*? Are you sure?" she asked.

"Yes... no, yes... He certainly *looked* like a demon. I don't know what else to call him." Nathalie described her encounter. Dean pulled the wrapped coin from his jeans and laid it on the librarian's desk. Nathalie and Dean took a step back while Sadie unwrapped it and peered at it closely.

"It looks like a penny..." Luke said, reaching for it.

"Don't touch it!" Sadie said sharply. She waved her hand over it and shook her head. "Well, well, well," she said angrily, rewrapping it and putting it into the pocket of her dress. She looked at the group. "This 'penny' is a demon talisman. It's not money. It just looks that way so people will pick it up. It's *extremely* dangerous."

"Why would anyone pick up a penny?" Luke asked.

"Rich boy," Dean muttered, but agreed. "I'd pick up a one or two dollar coin, but not a penny."

Sadie turned and tweaked the nose of her wealthy boyfriend. "It's made of gold. If you saw something gold on the ground, you'd have a look."

"Seriously, though, Luke has a point. It looks like a penny and no one picks up pennies anymore," Dean said.

Nathalie shrugged. "People used to pick up pennies all the time. They weren't always practically worthless."

Luke offered his opinion. "Very true. A penny used to buy a lot more than it does now, like a loaf of bread or a bag of sweets. Anyone would have picked one up. If this demon thinks people still pick up pennies—maybe he doesn't realize how much times have changed, which would mean that he hasn't mingled in human society for a while."

"I'm convinced," Dean said.

Luke's argument made Nathalie think. "He's definitely trapped somewhere. He said he was bored. When he threatened me he seemed... at the end of his rope."

"If he is trapped, then it's very possible his memory of society is very old," Sadie agreed.

"Or, he had a bunch of coins printed up and wants to use his stock," Dean quipped.

"I don't know... the coin looks rare and is made of gold. I'd pick it up," Nathalie said, not entirely convinced.

"Can't hurt to investigate when a penny was actually valuable," Luke said, sitting at Liz's computer and typing away.

Sadie looked at Dean. "Did you touch the coin?"

"Yep. It got hot, so it was doing *something,* but I wasn't affected because of my amulet." Dean took it out from under his shirt. "Nathalie warned me. It roared at her when she touched it, but she didn't have her amulet on at the time."

Sadie looked at Dean's amulet with great interest. "It grew hot countering great power. The demon talisman is invoked simply by touching it. It calls the demon to you so it can compel you to do its bidding. Taline's work is quite remarkable," she said softly, as if confirming something for herself.

"It's bidding?" Dean said skeptically.

"Yes. Whatever it wants or needs done," Sadie said seriously.

Nathalie looked scared. "Why didn't he come to me in my room?"

Sadie thought for a second. "I don't think the demon always has to respond. After all, it's *his* calling card. He's not being forced. Plus, he'd already 'handled' you that day. I think he ignored it."

Dean seemed to be struggling with the concept.

"You remember the hex you just battled? Your torment and agony? Your *helplessness*?" Sadie asked pointedly.

"Yeah," Dean said in a low voice.

"Beth's *human*. She needs something tangible to cast a hex, like a spelled hemp bag. Tangible things can be found and destroyed. We were *lucky*. But imagine a being so evil, so purely self-serving it doesn't care about anything but itself. To it humans are like cattle; we're just slaves. You are there to serve its every whim. His power comes from himself, so if you're enslaved, the only way to end the torment is to kill it or yourself. That's it. It can't be reasoned with. It doesn't care, it doesn't feel, and it doesn't love. Those concepts don't mean anything to it. It *revels* in the suffering of others and in the chaos it creates. It hates unendingly and unreasonably. It would make you suffer, and everyone you love suffer... likely at *your* hand."

The room was quiet. They were all looking at Sadie, appalled.

"And that's his nice side," she said gravely. She looked at Nathalie. "When you were telling us about your encounter, you said you didn't remember at first."

"Only once I put my amulet back on. I wasn't wearing it that morning. The memories flooded back, but when I take it off, it's like I was dreaming. Hanging on to those memories is like hanging on to a dream when you wake up. It's almost impossible."

"Beings like that use forgetfulness to use people. Their victims forget, take the blame, and can be used again. It's a part of them, the forget spell. It's their protection—a way for them to hide from prying eyes. The victim doesn't remember anything and can't explain their actions, or more importantly, expose them."

Luke piped in. "It could also be the brain's way of coping with the supernatural. Otherwise insanity may set in if a person can't accept what they've seen or what's happened. There are many cases of unexplained violence and insanity in otherwise normal men and women committed to insane asylums or sanitariums. I've read tons of books on the phenomenon. It's horrible."

"That's terrible," Nathalie said uneasily.

"Sometimes the forget spell doesn't work," Sadie said quietly, "in very special people. Those are the ones who go crazy 'claiming' to have seen the devil and done his bidding."

"We need to hide the talisman," Dean said worriedly. "Bury it in the woods."

"No, we need to destroy it. I'm not sure if it will give off a call... you know, attract someone with a weak mind to dig it up. We'll give it to Taline and Wayman," Sadie said determinedly, "they'll know how to get rid of it. We need to warn them because there *will* be more. It's no coincidence that this demon is here, now."

"Won't we be putting them in danger?" Dean asked.

Sadie smiled slightly, "I have no doubt they can handle themselves," she said vaguely. She turned to Nathalie. "Did he say his name?"

Nathalie nodded. "He said his name was Danner."

Sadie looked disappointed. "That's probably not his name, or at least, not his full name. I was hoping his pride would nudge him to announce it, especially if he thought you were an unbelieving mortal."

"Why does knowing his name help?" Luke asked.

"In the past people were so superstitious they kept journals of the interesting folk, or 'evil' beings, they met. With his name, we could possibly have found some information on him. But he's not taking any chances. He knows to have his full name is to have power over him."

Nathalie looked interested. "Are you saying there is possibly a book about him somewhere? That someone may have written about him?"

"Absolutely, my family has many demon reference books."

There was silence at that. What a childhood, demon study instead of Sesame Street.

"Why would he allow himself to be recorded?" Nathalie asked curiously.

"Pride cometh before a fall, Nathalie. These creatures are extremely vain. They expect humanity to worship them in all their terrifying glory. I'm quite certain it had at least *one* mindless slave in thrall who was writing about him in a journal or a 'tome' as they used to call them."

"Maybe we should look for something like that," Nathalie said, looking worried. "He told me to stay out of his business. What business? I had no idea what he was talking about!"

"You said he wanted to break your fingers, but as a favour for whom?" Sadie wondered.

"Well, if we could find his tome maybe it will tell us what his business is."

"My searches on prices and pennies are not turning up anything concrete on the internet," Luke said. "I'll do a tome search in the library database."

"You think a demon's tome would be shelved near romance or fantasy in the fiction section?" Dean asked dryly.

"You never know," said Luke.

"Describe again how he appeared to you, Nathalie," Sadie requested.

"He wasn't completely solid, but he could touch me. He burned my arm. It was very painful," she said, rubbing her arm.

"Any marks?" Sadie asked as Nathalie pulled up her sleeve.

"Oh, well, no actually..." she said confused as she checked her arms. "There were some yesterday. Wayman said I was hurt."

Sadie shook her head. "You can feel pain but he doesn't leave any lasting marks, so he's not corporeal. It's all mental. It's just in your head. But in a situation like that you wouldn't have been able to tell."

"Did he say anything about where he was?" Dean asked.

"No, he just uttered a saying about the penny he tossed, but not the normal one. He twisted it to suit himself," Nathalie laughed tonelessly.

"Repeat it," Sadie said.

"Find a penny, pick it up, and you'll be sure to have bad luck," Nathalie said.

"No kidding," Luke said. "A superstition. That's interesting."

"That's *gay*—for a demon," Dean said derisively.

"You're right. That is silly. But it explains the gold pennies. That must be his tell," Sadie said calmly.

They all looked at her with confusion. "His what?"

Sadie sighed. "Every demon has an… MO I guess you'd call it. A modus operandi. A peculiarity, a type of style. You know a fire demon because he spouts fire and burns things down, or a storm demon because he causes storms when he's around, etc. That's how humans told demons apart, by their different specialties or types of natures, which could be determined by how the demon impacted the people, or society, around them. Every demon is different."

"But most normal people can't see or remember them," Luke said.

"True, *normal* being the operative word. But witches can, and the special people impervious to the forget spell that we talked about before, or a demon's human thrall."

"This is getting stranger and creepier," Dean said nervously.

"So, witches had contact with demons along with special people," Nathalie said.

"Yes. Willow had contact with a demon, and she knew how to call them. It's the blackest magic, and to get that knowledge was very difficult since much of it died with the druids. She wrote about it in her diary."

"So, I'm not special," Nathalie said in a relieved voice.

Sadie laughed. "Now how do I answer that? No, not special to demons. Special only to your friends and family."

Dean took her hand. "You're special to me, baby."

"Do you have the invocation spell to call a demon?" Luke asked Sadie, aghast.

"Of course I do. No one would believe it works these days, but I'll bet it actually does. Why do you think a witch's grimoire was secret and kept hidden? It contained very dangerous information, and in the wrong hands, well… Willow's grimoire is a *very* bad book," Sadie said, shuddering as she thought of some of the spells in it.

"That's awful," Nathalie said. "Why don't you destroy it?" she asked curiously.

"I can't," Sadie smiled cynically. "It won't let me. There's a self-preservation spell infused in the book. It can't be done."

"Willow was one devious witch," Dean remarked.

"Actually, it wasn't Willow who did it. It was another witch. She stole the book from Willow's home at the same time the townsfolk were sentencing Willow to die. That witch spelled it to protect the knowledge in it. She was the one who returned it to the Kellars to keep for the heir, along with Willow's diary."

"Wow, I wonder how you do that to a book?" Dean asked curiously.

You kidnap and murder a living person by performing a ritual that drains their blood onto the spelled vessel, a book in this case, and as the person dies, you chant your spell, and their life essence transfers to the now animate object. Self-preservation spell complete. Simple. Sadie thought in her head.

"I have no idea," she said out loud. Some things were better left as a witch family secret.

"Who was the witch?" Dean asked.

"Elanah Von Vixen," Sadie said.

Nathalie looked startled. "Really? Elanah Von Vixen was instrumental in helping the witch hunters root out witches in the history books I've been reading!"

"Self-preservation," Sadie said. "If you can't beat them, join them. I'm not sure who she was working for, but she was playing for both sides."

"Guys," Luke said with barely controlled excitement. "I think I found a tome! I remember seeing this when Sadie and I were doing research. It's called the '*Tome of Dannerlich*,' by Klaus Deitriche."

"Are you kidding?" Nathalie asked incredulously.

"No. It's in Superstition, but it's a reference book. You can't take it out. You have to read it there because it's in their special collection and it's over four hundred years old, and it's in German."

"Dannerlich? That's close enough to Danner for me. I have a reference book of demon types at home. I'll look him up and see if he's in there," Sadie said.

They all looked at her with odd expressions.

"Remind me again *why* you have books like that?" Luke asked with a slight frown at her.

Sadie frowned back. "We *are* a family of witches, Luke. They're heirlooms. The book is very old and very valuable. It's hand written and it actually has a lock on it. It lists different types of demons and provides a description of how to identify them. Some have markings; some have a peculiar effect on the people and places around them; some of them have special abilities. Danner seems superstitious, and superstitions had to come from somewhere. Someone at sometime suffered, oh I don't know, by having a black cat cross their path or by walking under a ladder. Maybe it was because he was around and, let's not forget, he's probably been around for thousands of years."

"Everyone has an accident now and then. It's not because of a ladder or a cat," Dean said disbelievingly.

Sadie gave him a wan smile. "True, but if a *whole town* of righteous, God-fearing, witch-hunting people were to experience the same phenomenon consistently, they would cry evil and hunt it down."

Nathalie spoke. "I agree. Superstition has got to be the stupidest name for a town I've ever heard of. They named it that for a reason, and that's one of the reasons Rain is out there. She's researching the origin of Superstition's name. Since she's there, I'll get her to find the book. Maybe she can have it photocopied and we can get it translated." She paused for a moment. "I'll also ask her if she's noticed anything unusual in that town and have her ask around to see if anyone knows how the town got its name. If Danner is or was there then someone at some point wrote about what was happening either in an official town record or in a personal diary."

"That's going to take a while since they work on a horse and buggy system," Luke said. He still hadn't received a few of his interlibrary requests.

Dean cleared his throat. "So…Sadie…how do you fit into all of this?"

Sadie was startled. She had forgotten about her own problems while helping Nathalie with hers.

"Luke mentioned that you had a problem and that you may need some help…" he trailed off.

Everyone looked at her expectantly.

Sadie sighed. "Nathalie has a demon and I seem to have a ghost or some sort of entity possessing me. It borrows my body to do things but I don't know what it does, or why."

Luke had stopped typing and beckoned for Sadie to come sit on his lap so he could hold her. She stood apart from the group for a split second with her chin lifted before she headed to Luke's lap.

"This is really not dignified," she said, embarrassed and sitting stiffly, but putting a slim arm around his neck. Luke just smiled, his eyes crinkling with pleasure.

"Things came to a head with the marked houses. I suspect that I participated in that ritual. I woke up the next morning with my hair wet and in my pajamas. I cannot locate my white dress. I am certain that my aunt is an accomplice in this but she won't talk about it. I'm certain she knows what's going on. Right now I'm playing dumb so I can continue to have my freedom."

"Maybe you were just dirty..." Dean offered, but when Nathalie snorted, and he took a really good look at Sadie's pristine person, he back tracked, "but that's impossible. I'll shut up now."

"My white dress is missing, which leads me to believe it wasn't salvageable, or it was damning evidence of some sort. I take meticulous care of my things." Sadie's voice cracked slightly. Luke cradled her and she rested her cheek against his. It was a touching sight. "I thought it was mental—a breakdown of sorts. I thought perhaps I was sick, or I had schizophrenia or something. But Luke..."

"She was possessed." Luke said. There was no doubt in his voice. "That thing, it, *she* spoke to me. I'm certain it was Willow Kellar because she looked like Sadie. I could see her overlaid over Sadie, like a double vision. Sadie struggled and overcame her and I caught her as she fainted on the library steps. There's nothing wrong with Sadie's mind. Her body is being invaded and controlled."

"She's getting stronger," Sadie said softly, twisting her black hair around her finger. "I realized that I started to feel her at the end of June. It was just whispering then. She was calling me from far away. Now I just lost a whole day and night where I don't remember anything."

Nathalie was thinking. "I saw you that Sunday, from Helen's. I had such a bad feeling... and had the same feeling when I saw you at the fair on Tuesday."

Startled, Sadie glanced at Luke. "The fair?"

He shrugged, surprised.

"I wasn't at the fair. I went to bed early with a migraine, so I didn't even know about that missing time," she said angrily.

Luke looked worried.

"I knew something was different," Nathalie exclaimed. "I was going to follow you but I got the feeling that it would not be a good idea."

"So we have demons, ghosts, and witches in Barrington," Dean said, listing them on his fingers. "Why now?"

Sadie shrugged. "Well, we've always had witches," and she smiled at that. But as for the rest... they were all at a loss.

"And the windmill," Nathalie added. "I had a dream about the windmill, and Luke says his father's been obsessing about it. Something's up with that."

"Let's go see Taline and Wayman," Dean said, grabbing Nathalie's hand and heading to the door. "We need help and Taline said they'd have some information for us by tonight. They helped Nathalie with some pretty weird shit, so I've no doubt they can help us with this."

The Fairgrounds

Ella Croft was back at the fair. So far she hadn't had the nerve to use the love potion she'd bought, but now she'd heard about something new. A lady was selling wishes. Wishes that came true. Ella was going to get one of her very own.

The fair was busy. It seemed much busier this year compared to last year. Mind you, she'd been smaller then and was only allowed to go to the fair with her parents or her older brother, so maybe she had missed the peak times. Distracted, she didn't see the big man barreling down on her. He was dressed in a black leather vest and pants, and when he brushed by her he knocked her over. He stopped to look down at her and all she could see was long wild black hair. At eye level, Ella could see that his fingernails were black and pointed. When she looked up at his face, his brown eyes glowed red as he stared at her intently. He seemed immense. He smelled the air and his tongue flicked out as if to test its taste. He licked his lips. His teeth were pointed like a shark's. Ella stared in fascinated horror before Nettie came along and exclaimed over her, shooing the man away with a dark look and a threatening "begone cur." He hissed at Nettie as he clomped off, glancing at Ella briefly before walking away, his heavy leather boots thumping the ground.

"My God, was he ever *ugly*," Ella said primly, dusting herself off. Nettie looked at her worriedly.

"Did it... er... did he touch you?"

"He bumped into me," Ella said, thankful for Nettie's interference but impatient to be off about her business. She had a date with a wish.

"So he didn't touch you, with his hands... on your skin?" she persisted.

Ella looked at Nettie distractedly. "Of course not...Why? Is he some sort of perv?" Ella asked breathlessly, her narrowed eyes darting in the direction the man had gone, illicit interest lighting her eyes.

Nettie's jaw dropped in surprise and then she snorted in disgust. "You are a silly girl," she said and walked away muttering, "imagine finding the likes of that interesting."

Ella shrugged. "See you at the bake table, Nets." She spied the stall she had come to visit. She checked her pocket and her money was still there, so she drifted over and waited until she caught the stall keeper's attention.

The woman was large—her hands, her belly, her shiny smile and red apple cheeks—everything. She wore a blue dress covered with a white apron and her hair was held back by a white kerchief. She reminded Ella of Nettie. "Can I help you, my sweet?" she asked Ella in a booming voice.

"I came to buy a wish," Ella said shyly, and quietly.

The woman laughed, and it was so happy and infectious that Ella laughed with her.

"Well, that I can do for you, poppet," she said kindly. She reached into the large pocket of her apron and handed Ella a small vial. Ella took it and at first couldn't see anything inside, but then in the light she saw it. It was an eyelash.

Of course! Ella felt glee and triumph as she held the vial to her chest and looked at the woman with shining eyes.

"I'll take it," she said in a whisper. "How much?"

The woman looked at her, her blue eyes crinkling in a smile at the expression on Ella's face. Her gaze was sharp and Ella felt something pass through her.

"For you, just a dollar, poppet."

A dollar! How lucky was she!!!

Ella handed the dollar over and thanked the lady again.

"Wish well," she said in parting before turning to help another customer.

The Croft Residence

Ella did wish. She ran to the woods behind her house, close enough to be safe, but far enough that her nosey twin brothers wouldn't find her and interrupt. She took the vial and pulled the stopper. Then carefully, very carefully, she knocked the eyelash out of the vial onto her hand. It was so little, and for a moment she wondered whose eyelash it was, but before the wind could whisk it out of her hand, she made her wish loudly to the listening wood.

"I wish for long hair to my bum!"

Within seconds Ella was twirling through the woods with her long hair flowing around her. She shrieked with glee! Who would have thought? It worked! Now it was time to put her plan into action!

The Fairgrounds

Dean, Nathalie, Luke, and Sadie had no luck catching Wayman or Taline. Both of them were surrounded by budding equestrians or interested shoppers. While Dean stopped to visit the horses, and Luke and Sadie browsed different stalls near Taline, Nathalie drifted over to see Nettie. The bake table was busy, but Nettie had everyone well in hand moving the goods. Fresh things came from the bakery every hour and everything sold. Nettie saw Nathalie and beamed with delight, her rosy apple cheeks red and her eyes twinkling. She wiped her hands on her apron and headed towards her. She leaned over and gave her a brief hug before reaching into her starched apron pocket and taking out an old fashioned book. She smiled at Nathalie and handed it to her.

"This is for you lassie," Nettie said fondly. "You remind me of me at your age."

"What's this?" Nathalie exclaimed with delight. It was beautiful. It was a book bound in soft brown leather the colour of a saddle with lighter tawny streaks of brown swirling throughout. It had a clasp and a small lock with keys dangling from the loop. It was a journal.

Nathalie was touched. "Thank you, Nettie," she exclaimed, popping the lock and opening it. The pages were lined, white and crisp and ready for words.

"When I was young I wrote things down and kept track of things in a journal. It helped me many times when I couldn't see things clearly. Helped me look for patterns. It's a good habit to get into," she said, patting Nathalie's arm. "Sometimes some people have the luck, or the misfortune, to witness things others don't. After what happened yesterday..." Nettie shrugged, "you strike me as one of those people."

"So you heard."

"Yes, lassie."

Nathalie rubbed her fingertips over the supple cover, turning the diary around in her hands. "I've just had a string of... well, odd luck. I've been in the wrong place at the wrong time, I guess."

Nettie harrumphed. "Nothing like coincidence to get the mind going, but my experience has been that there is no coincidence. Things happen for a reason. Sometimes when you write things down the patterns become apparent and you can act."

Dean joined them, smelling like horses. He had a goofy grin on his face. "I love horses," he said happily, rubbing his arm.

"Did you get bitten?" Nathalie asked as she took a look at the large red mark he was favouring. "What happened?"

Dean looked down at his arm. "This? Oh, it's nothing. Pain bit me, you know, like a love bite. Horses do that. I just love that fellow." He laughed softly then noticed the journal. "Hey, nice book, did you just buy it?" Dean asked as he reached for it.

Nathalie laughed at her adorable boyfriend. Even Nettie's face softened at Dean's simple cheer. "Such a sweet line," she said softly.

"But deluded about horses," Nathalie added dryly.

Luke and Sadie joined them. Sadie nodded at Nettie, who nodded back. Their conversation was over now that everyone had arrived. Nathalie was sure Nettie was trying to tell her something but she had no idea what. She was going to take her advice though. After yesterday, she was going to be more diligent about keeping track of what was going on around her.

Taline called and waved them over. "I'm going to close my stall for a bit. Meet me at Wayman's!" She put up a "back in five minutes" sign and headed to the stables.

Wayman was settling the horses for the evening. "There's nothing else scheduled and soon it's going to be too dark for a ride." He looked out at the mass of people at the fair. "I wouldn't trust any of them with my horses at this point." He smiled his big white smile, and again Nathalie felt a bit dazzled. "A lot of alcohol floating around."

They had no news. "We're still looking into it," Wayman said evasively, a twinge of frustration lacing his voice.

"If you're worried about the word 'demon,' we're way ahead of you," Sadie said.

"Our theory is that Nathalie met a demon named Danner," Luke said in a low voice.

Wayman looked relieved. He glanced at Taline, who nodded. "I would agree, even without having confirmed it. His full name is Dannerlich."

"His tome is in Superstition. We're going to ask Nathalie's sister Rain to research him for us."

Wayman frowned. "It is very important that Danner doesn't find out someone's snooping around. Keep Rain's work, and location, a secret or she could end up in grave danger."

"Keep your amulets on," Taline said sternly, handing one to Luke. "They'll protect you."

His was similar to Sadie's, but his stone was black. He put it around his neck.

"What does mine do?" he asked curiously, fingering the smooth stone and the iron filaments twisted around it.

Taline explained, "It's like Dean and Nathalie's. It'll protect you from…well, let's call them outside influences, spells and hexes. But this one also makes you difficult to see, if there's malicious intent. Their eyes will just slide over you."

"Cool," Luke said, pleased. He felt safer.

Wayman and Taline shooed them off. "We've got things to do, so bye bye."

The kids left.

"Wayman was keeping something from us," Nathalie noted as they walked away. When they looked back, Taline and Wayman were deep in conversation.

Sadie studied the pair. She could see their muted glow with her sight, but she didn't say anything to the other three. "I wouldn't worry. If they are keeping anything from us, I have no doubt it's for a good reason."

Luke agreed. Somehow he knew they could be trusted.

"I'm so tired of worrying. Nothing is as it should be. I just want to have some fun!" Dean exclaimed with a bit of frustration. So, they agreed to meet the following evening for dinner and dancing at The Rotunda.

As they passed Beth, who was still manning her busy little drink stand, they ignored her.

The Croft Residence

When Dean got home the twins were outside playing their version of "hide and seek" which was "hide or die." His mother was reading a book and hoping a trip to the clinic for stitches would not be in the cards that evening. His other two sisters were still at the fair with their dad. Only Ella was home, and he found her in the bathroom with a towel around her head. Dean stopped and stared at her suspiciously.

Ella gave him an interested, "are you looking at me?" stare.

"What did you do?" he asked, frowning and looking at the towel.

"Nothing," she said and smiled angelically. "Maybe I took a shower."

Dean snorted. "You're not even wet." He gasped. "Did you dye your hair?"

"No! Of course not! That's something mom would *notice*."

"Did you cut it?"

Ella hesitated.

"You did!"

"Didn't!" she said loudly, and then sighed. She took the towel off her head and her hair fell past her waist.

Dean gaped at her. "Wow, hair extensions. That's awesome!" Dean said, reaching over and touching her hair. "It feels so real."

"It is real."

His expression was disbelieving. "Can't be."

"Yep."

"Really. How?" he asked. It was impossible. Ella's hair was shoulder length this morning.

"An eyelash," she whispered conspiratorially.

"A WHAT?"

"I got a wishing eyelash at the fair... and I wished for long hair to my bum, and it worked!" Ella squeaked. She couldn't contain her excitement.

It took Dean a moment to grasp what she was saying. "That's impossible."

"Apparently not," Ella said, bouncing back to her room. "By the way, you smell."

"Yeah yeah. What are you going to tell mom?" he yelled towards her retreating back.

"Hair extensions!"

"Where? At the fair? You can't afford them at Helen's!"

"I know THAT," she said, indignantly.

"So which stall—?"

“The one beside the potion seller,” Ella said as she slammed her bedroom door.

Dean’s heart was pounding. Another superstition... wishing on an eyelash. He was shocked, but also excited. There was no way Ella was making this up. Why would she? She didn’t know what was going on with Nathalie and Sadie. Nathalie! He had to tell her *now*. He tried to call her with no luck, so he showered quickly and changed into fresh clothes. He biked over to Nathalie’s, and by the time he reached the Parker’s he was sweaty again.

It was almost dark but there were no lights on. He knocked on the Parker’s door but no one answered. He tried the door and found it unlocked. He walked in and heard the shower going. He locked the door behind him and vaulted up the stairs two at a time. “She never thinks about safety,” he grumbled. “Nathalie?” he yelled.

“Dean? In here!” she called back. Dean hesitated, but it was as if Nathalie could read his mind. “Don’t worry,” she yelled over the water, “my parents took Nick to the fair.”

Dean walked into the steamy bathroom and immediately began to sweat. It was hot in the little room. He peeked inside the shower and saw his beautiful girlfriend stretching in the shower, her skin heated pink and glistening with water. Nathalie looked back at him and smiled, and Dean’s body went into overdrive.

“Why don’t you get out of those clothes and come wash my back?” Nathalie asked invitingly, wiggling her round bottom at him, but Dean was already stripping. He stepped into the shower and pressed his front tightly to her back and slid his arms around her belly then lower down as he bent to kiss her neck. Nathalie shuddered with pleasure as his fingers stroked her. One of his arms came up and supported her breasts. She could feel his arousal pressing against her before he pushed it between her legs, rocking gently back and forth while she squeezed her thigh muscles tightly together. They were both moaning by the time Dean angled himself upward and pleasure changed to ecstasy.

After an hour of what seemed like wild gymnastics, first in the bathroom and then in Nathalie’s bedroom, they lay together sleepily in her jumbled bed sheets. They were chest to chest. Nathalie’s hands were kneading his butt cheeks while he held her and his free hand stroked her back. They were kissing softly. Their warm lips, swollen from their savage session earlier, were soft and their tongues slid against each other. Nathalie felt awesome cuddled up against him. He lived for these intimate moments with her. How things had changed since June when they were just friends and an hour like this would have only happened in his fevered dreams. First kissing and now lovers. This change had been an unstoppable force for the both of them. They say it's hormones, but he knew it was love. Those feelings took over everything and supplanted everything. They were everything. Nathalie felt the same way, and he knew it.

Something stirred at the back of his mind. Something he was supposed to tell Nathalie... but he couldn't remember. All that mattered was her skin, her smell, her heat. She was kissing him more insistently now. She wrapped her arms around his neck and was rubbing herself against him and making small satisfying sounds. Dean was flooded with desire and happiness that she wanted him so badly. He'd remember what he wanted to tell her later. Dean deepened his kiss and rolled on top of her.

Tuesday, August 13
The Fairgrounds

Nathalie and Dean walked hand in hand towards Town Circle after work. Dean had left his bike at Nathalie's so he'd have it after he walked her home. Hopefully by then her parents would be asleep and he could spend the night with his beautiful and naked girlfriend. He flushed and looked at Nathalie who smiled at him and lifted their joined hands to kiss his. If he didn't know she felt the same way he'd feel like a rutting animal. Dean swung her into his arms and held her tightly. They stayed like that for a few minutes, just enjoying each other's embrace before Reginald Baker biked by, hair neatly combed and dressed for an evening out.

"Get a room," he yelled, laughing.

"Go put your head in an oven you burnt loaf of bread," Dean yelled back. Reg barked a laugh and gave him the finger before turning on West Road to head to Town Circle.

"Oh, good one," Nathalie said, rolling her eyes.

"He *is* the baker's son, Nathalie," Dean said haughtily. "I was being pithy."

"I believe that's 'witty' my sweet," Nathalie said.

At the office today they had had a long talk about their relationship. There really wasn't much else to do. With Shaemus gone, the office had become party central. Beth hadn't turned up either. No one missed her.

"I feel different," she had happily confided in Dean. "I feel as if the time we spend alone together is magical. I feel out of control and excited all the time. I love it."

Dean felt it too, very strongly. When he wasn't with Nathalie she was all he thought about. "Yooo hooo," his mother had knocked on his head this morning at breakfast. "Anyone there?"

When they reached Town Circle things were in full swing. People were dancing in and around The Rotunda and many of the tables were full of people eating and drinking, but mostly drinking. Luke and Sadie were already there. They had secured a table for four sandwiched between a large group of rowdy, beer swilling men and a family with two screaming children.

"It's gonna be like eating at home," Dean said wryly, putting his arm around Nathalie and pressing her close.

They made their way towards their friends. Once they were seated there was a tense moment when a couple of beer guzzlers at the table beside them noticed Nathalie and Sadie, the two pretty girls at the table next to them. Dean frowned and stared warningly, and Luke followed, but it was Sadie's cold expression that deterred them. The other guys in the party noticed and distracted their friends with a comment about "plenty of warm, *friendly*, girls around." The tension died, but the four decided to switch tables.

Luckily, they found one close to one of the path entrances and the dance floor, so they had quiet behind them and fun in front. They placed drink orders and started to look through the menus.

The musicians were playing big band music again. The dancers were swinging each other around and laughing. Luke's toe was tapping. He knew how to swing. Heck, he knew every dance. His mother had made sure her sons were cultured. They could dance, sing, play an instrument and eat at a table like "civilized" gentlemen. She had put all her boys in charm school, run by hers truly, and they had turned out remarkably well, judging by his older brothers' great success with girls. The music pulled at Luke. He wanted to swing Sadie around and make her squeal with laughter. They had been apart in the afternoon because Sadie had things to do at home with her aunt. Luke had been bored. He had hoped they could spend some quality time together alone in the woods.

He watched as Sadie talked with Nathalie. She obviously enjoyed the attention of another girl, and Nathalie was the nicest person he knew. A wave of affection for Nathalie flowed through him at her kindness towards Sadie.

The waiter arrived, and after cheeseburgers and grilled chicken salads were ordered, Luke got up and swept a gallant bow to Sadie.

"May I have this dance, fair one? You must be a witch because I find myself enchanted by you," Luke asked in his most charming voice. He held out his hand and wiggled his eyebrows in a dashing manner.

Sadie laughed and put her hand in his. "I would be honoured, fair sir," she said before she was swept away. Luke twirled her around and the laughing couple melted into the crowd.

"I forgot what a great dancer he is," Nathalie mused, watching them as they moved gracefully to the beat of the music.

"I shall also sweep you off your feet, my fair lady," Dean said in a deep, chivalrous voice he called "the lady killer," "but alas, we must protect our small plot of land for which we have fought fiercely, not to mention your small feet from my overlarge ones!"

"Silly," Nathalie said over the table, twining her hands with his and reaching over to give him a soft kiss. They stared at each other. Love, desire, passion, trust, and a whole host of other emotions seemed to spiral between them. "Maybe there'll be slow dances," Nathalie said breathlessly.

"One can hope," Dean said, kissing her hands without breaking eye contact.

After a few songs, Luke and Sadie came back to the table. Before Sadie could sit he bent and kissed her hand like a true gallant before slipping his hand behind her head and planting a solid kiss on her mouth. For once Sadie just laughed as her besotted boyfriend seated her in her chair. Nathalie and Dean eyed each other. They understood.

"That was fun, Luke," Sadie said happily. "I had no idea you could dance like that!"

"I am a man of many talents, my beauty. But right now, I need food! Where on earth is our waiter?"

He appeared moments later. They dug in and talked about the success of the Barrington Harvest Festival. They studiously avoided the serious and confusing topics looming at the back of their minds. It seemed that they had made an unspoken agreement to just enjoy themselves tonight.

After they had finished eating it was finally dark enough that the fairy lights and the beautiful gas lanterns could cast their glow on Town Circle. The band started a slow tune and the heavy partiers went in search of alcohol. Couples came onto the dance floor and moved slowly together under the dim, twinkling lights. It was beautiful. Town Circle had been transformed into a fairyland. The boys grabbed the girls and they joined the group of dancers. A few of the couples were already kissing.

"The park's paths are going to be busy tonight," Dean whispered into Nathalie's ear. Luke and Sadie were completely wrapped up in each other. They were talking quietly as they swayed to the music with eyes for no one else but each other.

They danced a few dances before they noticed that the crowd around The Rotunda had grown large and boisterous. They were calling for music with energy! Nathalie could see that a couple of the beer table boys were already making out with some willing girls they had found. They were obviously drunk, but then most everyone was, Nathalie noticed.

"Time to go," Nathalie whispered in Dean's ear. "The party's gone to the next level." He agreed. Dean tapped Luke on the shoulder and they exited the dance floor just in time. The band struck up a rowdy tune and a wild crowd surged to the dance floor.

They watched in wonder at the partiers. The beer guzzlers who had been making out with the girls were performing lewd moves. Their hands were everywhere, but the girls didn't seem to mind.

"You know, my friend Emma slept in the park last week. She got so drunk that she couldn't remember what happened. She could have been hurt." Nathalie looked at the girls worriedly, but they didn't seem to have a care in the world.

Luke glanced around. "Where's the Sheriff in all this?" he asked quietly.

The four turned and chose one of the many lighted paths leading out from the center of Town Circle to the street. This path was called *Narnia* because it was lined with cedars and tall trees with lanterns dotting the way. Every ten feet an arch had been formed to allow access to the park greens and fountains. Now, however, the group did not stray from the path. It was obvious from the intermittent moaning and grunting noises coming from the archways that those dark green spaces were occupied by other types of lovers at the moment. They tried not to laugh out loud as they ran through the park. Part of it was shock, but the rest was... awe.

"I can't believe they're allowed to do that," Luke said, shocked.

"I agree," Nathalie said. "Why aren't Sheriff Holt and his men doing something about this?"

"Yeah, otherwise they should rename the path *Porn Alley*," Dean added.

When they hit Main Street things were back to normal. It was a bit disorienting after the adult atmosphere in the park. People thronged the streets with their families, chatting and enjoying the beautiful evening. They walked to Ye Ole Sweete Shoppe to get ice cream. It was teeming with parents and children despite the lateness of the hour. Licking their ice creams and enjoying the crowd, it was hard to reconcile the difference between the people on the lighted street and the ones in the park.

They parted ways after they finished their treats. Nathalie and Dean headed to the Parker residence so Dean could drop Nathalie off at home. Luke and Sadie headed to the Barrington Estate. Sadie had agreed to spend an hour with him before heading home, and Luke was desperate for that hour to start *now*.

Luke and Sadie strolled to the library in order to cut through the alley. Once in the alley Luke swept Sadie into his arms and ran into the enveloping darkness of the wood surrounding the manor.

From the park's edge two figures stood and watched Luke and Sadie with fury and disbelief. One of them was Sadie's aunt Liora. Liora was shaking with rage as she watched the Kellar heir, her own niece, kiss the Barrington murderer. A Barrington! A Kellar kissing a Barrington! She couldn't believe what she was seeing. Her claw like hands gripped the bag of herbs she had bought at the fair and her nails punctured the bag. She narrowed her eyes and swore they would both pay for this outrage.

The other observer was Hannah.

Hannah also felt rage roll through her. Rage and helpless jealousy as she witnessed the intimacy and love flowing between Sadie and Luke. She hated Sadie so much she could taste it. She wanted to hurt her. She wanted her dead.

The Barrington Estate

Oblivious to all of this, Sadie and Luke spent a blissful couple of hours in each other's arms. Luke and Sadie were twined together on their blanket. Through the haze of desire Sadie realized that she wanted Luke. She wanted all of him and was completely crazy about him, obsessed even. She couldn't get enough of his smile, his mouth, his hands, his body, anything. She wanted to strip herself, and him, and claim him as hers…feel the most private part of him joined with her, filling her, possessing her…but she hesitated. With her missing time, and being haunted and used, it was unfair to bind Luke even closer to her than he was now. She wanted that closeness desperately, but she needed to make sure she didn't follow in Willow's footsteps by using sex as a means to snare Luke and keep him close. For his protection, her desires had to be securely locked away for now.

Instead, she allowed him freer rein tonight because she couldn't help herself when he touched her. She let him open the front of her dress to touch her breasts. His tongue and sucking kisses had left her bra wet on both sides. Now they were kissing heavily and sighing softly. Her legs were spread apart and her dress was bunched around her hips. Although they were separated physically by the material of their clothes, Sadie could feel the hardness of Luke's body as he pressed and moved against her. She could hear him groaning as her hands, which she had slipped into the back of his jeans, squeezed and massaged his backside, pulling him closer.

Luke pulled away from her mouth and kissed her neck. He popped her bra open and put one of her small, perky breasts in his mouth and sucked, hard. Sadie arched as electricity shot to the core of her being. Luke's hot mouth took her other breast and repeated the procedure. It was as if he wanted to devour her. Consume her whole. It was thrilling. Sadie's body was wild with longing.

"Touch me, Luke," she whispered urgently. He did. He slid his tongue back into her mouth, and she was taken by a flush of heat. Shifting his weight slightly to the side Luke slid his hand down over her belly and into her panties. She was slippery and hot at the junction of her legs. He rubbed her there while he made love to her mouth, sliding and thrusting his tongue against hers. She moaned as his fingers slid back and forth between her legs and then into her body. She shuddered as he slid in and out in small movements, pushing his fist against her core and allowing the pressure to accentuate her release. Sadie slipped her hand over Luke's taut stomach and into the front of his jeans and stroked him. Luke moaned against her mouth as he came, the warmth of his orgasm spilling over her fingers.

Then she was back in his arms and they were kissing and holding each other fiercely. Love bloomed between them, filling their hearts and joining them together. Luke had grown up with a lot of love in his house, from his parents and siblings, but he had always been missing her. Sadie's love. Luke gave silent thanks that he had her. She was his, all his, and she loved him back.

Sadie was thankful too. After years of loneliness, and no love at all, she finally had Luke, a wonderful boy whose love suffused her being, and gave her the chance to return it in spades. Now that she knew how wonderful love for Luke felt, she knew she could never live without it again, never live without Luke.

Luke and Sadie kissed and whispered to each other for a bit longer before Luke sighed and made the decision to take her home. They had just gone through something so intimate it was hard to imagine being separated from her for a minute. Sadie smiled brilliantly at Luke. He smiled back and kissed her eyes and brushed the hair out of her face. Seeing Sadie Kellar disheveled, by his own hands no less, was extremely sexy. He straightened her up, including her delicates, which made her laugh because it tickled, and they headed to the Kellars. The moon was out and there was a slight breeze in the air. It was the perfect night for a walk. Luke kept his arm close around Sadie, and they walked in companionable silence.

When they reached the Kellar residence and headed around the back to make sure Sadie got into her bedroom okay, Luke instantly sensed something was wrong. Even Sadie had halted and was frowning. The air was charged with what felt like static electricity, the prickling sensation you get just before an electric shock. It was an unpleasant tingling along the skin and Luke rubbed his hands over his arms. He looked over and he could see some of Sadie's hair standing on end.

"Get out of here Luke," Sadie said abruptly. She had just noticed what he had failed to see when arriving in the backyard. Liora Keller was standing at the back, in the dark, and her fury was evident. She stood stiffly, her arms out to the sides with her fingers spread. Her eyes were wide and wild, and her gray hair stood out in a fuzzy tangle. The air seemed to buzz around her as she stared at Sadie.

"How dare you," she hissed at her niece. "Cavorting with a Barrington! The descendent of a murdering lynch mob family!" She was shaking with anger and little sparks of purple electricity seemed to emanate from her fingers. She turned to look at Luke who was staring at her in shock. He knew his family's history. The Kellar burning is what made Barrington famous. It was his ancestor that had condemned Willow Kellar to die.

"Aunt Liora..." Sadie began coldly, folding her arms in front of her.

But Liora wasn't listening. She continued to stare at Luke. Insane fury twisted her crone-like face. Luke frowned as she raised her right arm and pointed a finger at him. "Die Barrington bastard!" she screeched, saliva spitting out of her mouth. A jolt of power hit Luke right in the chest and sent him flying backwards. He fell into the grass with a thud, stunned and terrified. He couldn't take a breath. *Holy shit! What is going on here?* he wondered frantically, his thoughts racing. *What the hell just happened?*

Sadie was standing rigidly, an expression of shock on her face. Had her aunt actually tried to kill Luke? She glanced back and heard him groan, and when Sadie looked back her aunt was storming towards her. She grabbed Sadie by the arms and her nails bit cruelly into her skin.

"You stupid little bitch," she screamed, shaking Sadie violently, "you are ruining everything!" Sadie's head snapped back and she bit her tongue as her teeth clattered together. Her aunt was crazy!

"Liora!" Sadie shrieked in horror. "Control yourself!"

"I'd rather see you dead than with a Barrington!" Liora screeched back, slapping Sadie across the face and sending her sprawling.

Luke was stirring. *Don't move Luke,* Sadie prayed desperately as she slowly regained her feet. She was dazed and her aunt seemed to have superhuman strength. *Please don't move, sweetheart.* But it was too late. Liora had already seen him.

"I have enough power to stop the heart of one measly boy," she muttered to herself as she crossed the lawn to where Luke lay. He was still in shock and looked at her in horrified confusion as Liora laid her crackling hands on his chest. His eyes rolled back into his head and his body slumped.

Sadie watched fearfully, with her heart in her throat. *She's going to kill him,* she thought desperately. Panic and fury filled Sadie and time slowed... her aunt moved as if in slow motion and something cracked inside her, a vessel that had lain dormant within her for as long as she could remember. The vessel shattered and something escaped, something that every descendent of Willow Kellar inherited.

Power.

Sadie crackled with it. It crawled around her and hummed with a bluish-violet light. It arced between her spread fingers like little lightning bolts as she raised both her hands, palms up. "Stop," she whispered. Liora looked up and screamed in terror before she was flung back at least ten feet from Luke. Within the blink of an eye Sadie stood beside him. Her eyes were glowing purple. Her voice was deep and alien, as if many voices were combined to make hers. With her black hair and milk-white skin, she was a terrifying sight.

She looked at her aunt. "If you harm him I will kill you," the glowing Sadie being said. It wasn't a threat. It was a fact.

Liora's mouth worked, opening and closing like a fish as she scrabbled backwards on the grass. Sadie stared at her unblinkingly until she got up and raced awkwardly to the house, her old gray housedress wrinkled and full of grass stains.

Sadie looked at her hands with wonder and saw Luke staring at her with wide eyes before she fainted.

Liora fumbled at the back door and slammed it shut behind her once she was inside. She was breathing heavily and her face was red from exertion. After taking a few calming breaths to steady her breathing, Liora was back to normal and smiling with satisfaction. She laughed out loud. Boris slid into the room and watched her cackling without emotion.

"It's done!" Liora shrieked with glee and a hint of vindication. "Willow was right! Nothing unlocks power like desperation and fear. Nothing! Our vessel is complete!" Liora was so happy she was doing a small jig at the door.

Boris looked at Liora. "I don't think you know what you are dealing with, Liora. Sadie is not Willow."

"She's a Kellar and that's all that matters."

"Willow is using you."

"Of course she's using me, you idiot. That was the point! The only reason we were born, our only purpose was to bring about the fulfillment of Willow's hex if the heir was born and the timing was right. It's done. There's nothing else, Boris. There never was."

"But the preacher's line is incomplete. There are no more Browns. We've searched."

"Nothing to worry about," Liora said with finality, smoothing her frizzy hair back from her face.

"It's not possible," grumbled Boris.

"Oh yes, my dear cousin, it is. Willow has found herself a friend. A *very* powerful friend. Everything's going to change. It'll be the time of the witches soon." Liora laughed and rubbed her hands together. "Time to make an important call."

The Parker Residence

When Nathalie got home her father was still up. He waved cheerily at them from the front window and playfully made a shooting motion with his finger at Dean. Dean laughed nervously and only kissed Nathalie quickly before grabbing his bike.

"You're kidding me," Nathalie said with disbelief.

"You never know with fathers," Dean said with a grin. "I'll see you tomorrow, love." He pedaled off.

Nathalie laughed to herself as she went into the house. Her father was smiling like a Cheshire cat—very pleased with himself.

"I won't ask if you're pleased with yourself because I can see that YOU ARE," Nathalie huffed.

"I like that boy of yours," he said, rubbing his hands together like he did when he faced his barbeque. "He's respectful. That's my 'go away pesky boyfriend so I can have my daughter to myself' sign. He got it. Smart kid."

Nathalie snorted and flopped on one of the big comfy chairs in the living room. Her father was watching a horror movie on TV. It was an old monster story. People were running and screaming from something, and it was basically pandemonium on the screen. *Kind of like Town Circle this evening,* Nathalie thought to herself then wondered why she made the connection. Something wasn't right. Things seemed so…lawless.

She looked at her father. Despite his occasional (okay, daily) silliness, her father was her rock. He was the one person she depended on that she knew wouldn't let her down. She knew he loved her to the depths of his soul and would kill anyone who laid a hand on her or hurt her. Her daddy.

"Dad, have you been to Town Circle in the evening lately?"

"Me and your mom were there last night with Nick," he said, eyes on the TV.

"It's pretty wild. People were…*are* doing some, well, crazy things."

"Just blowing off steam, I'm sure. That's what weekends are for, honey." He didn't seem concerned.

"It's Tuesday, Dad. There was a lot of drinking and none of the Sheriff's men to be seen."

"Vacation, then. Lots of people want to have a good time when they visit. No one wants the police around ruining their fun," her father said, looking at her. "No law against drinking there, anyway."

"It just seemed so out of control," Nathalie said. A feeling of uneasiness haunted her.

"You've got to learn to *relax,* honey. Cut loose a little. A little partying never hurt anyone," and as if realizing what he'd just said, clarified, "if you're an adult, of course," he said firmly.

Nathalie's father's lack of concern was a bit of a concern. Today she had felt there was no adult supervision around at work or in Town Circle, and she missed that sense of security. The candy factory was a mess with Shaemus gone, but was the fair always this way? Had she been too young to notice before? She wasn't sure, but nobody seemed to care.

"I'm going to bed," she said with a yawn, getting up and giving her father a quick kiss on the top of his head.

"Goodnight sweetie," he said, his eyes trained on the TV.

The Croft Residence

When Dean arrived home everyone was in bed. There was a strip of light under Ella's door so he knocked softly and went in when she answered. As the eldest and closest in age they were the closest siblings. Only a couple of years separated them, and they got along well. Ella adored her older brother, and Dean appreciated his smart and practical sister. They were an unbeatable pair when they banded together. Ella was lying on her bed in an obviously grumpy mood.

"Uh oh," Dean said out loud, sitting on the edge of her bed. Her hair was still very long and Dean groaned inwardly. He had completely forgotten about the wishing eyelashes with Nathalie's incredibly hot body around. How could he have forgotten? This was important! And now it was too late to call. He made a note to tell her tomorrow *before* he allowed himself his first kiss of the day.

Ella sighed loudly, looking pointedly at her brother.

Pulled out of his reverie, he apologized. "Sorry, I got distracted."

"What, did I accidentally say your girlfriend's name causing you to daydream? I don't believe I said the 'N' word. I'm not that stupid," she grouched.

Dean grinned sheepishly. "I care, sweetie, I do. Tell me what happened."

"Nothing happened."

"Now don't be like that..."

"I'm not 'being like that.' Nothing happened. That's what happened."

Dean looked confused. "I'm trying to care here," he said carefully.

Ella rolled her eyes and sat up, flinging her long hair back. "I went back to the fair to get another wishing eyelash and this time it didn't work."

Dean felt relief rush through him. He hadn't realized how much stress he had been ignoring as his brain struggled to accept the idea that magic was real and that reality was not as he'd always expected. He couldn't put it plainer than that.

Dean looked at her. "Are you sure?"

"Absolutely."

"What did you wish for?"

"Not telling," she said mulishly.

"Maybe I can tell what went wrong if I knew what your wish was," he wheedled in his most sympathetic voice.

"No way in hell I'm telling, so forget it."

Ella could be a vault when she wanted to be. The trait had its pros and cons. Right now it was a con.

"Fine." Dean yawned and stretched. It was time for bed. He had to work the next day. "So you got a dud. Maybe your hair growth was a fluke."

Ella looked confused. "No, that worked," she mused.

Dean sighed. Back to square one.

"How's Nathalie?" Ella inquired.

Dean grinned foolishly. "She's awesome. An angel. Hey, I haven't seen Max in a while. How's he doing?"

Max was Luke's younger brother by a couple of years, the same age difference as Ella and Dean, and Ella's best friend.

"Oh, he's the same," Ella said in a disgruntled voice.

"Good, good. Well goodnight," Dean said tiredly as he got up to leave. He didn't notice the sad look on his sister's face.

Wednesday, August 14
The Limerick Candy Factory

When Nathalie arrived at the office the place was in complete disarray, starting with the receptionist, who was flirting with a handsome man in a suit instead of guarding the door. She didn't even glance at Nathalie when she walked by.

Hmmmph, Nathalie thought to herself. She headed upstairs to put her and Dean's lunch away, but there was no space in the fridge. It was full of beer. "Hmmmph," she said, loudly this time.

Nathalie went in search of Emma. Her friend always knew the office gossip these days, so Nathalie was sure she could give her the scoop. She found Emma asleep at her desk.

"Emma! Are you in your pajamas?!" Nathalie asked, horrified. It looked like one of those frilly baby doll styles and it didn't cover much.

"There was a big party here last night after the band stopped playing at The Rotunda. What day is it? Is it morning?" Emma jumped up in a panic. Nathalie was aghast. The girl didn't know what day it was and she smelled like a brewery.

"My God Emma, just go home," Nathalie said in a shocked voice.

Emma didn't respond. She just grabbed her purse and ran. Unfortunately it was open and things fell out of it in a trail behind her.

Beth glided by and stared at Nathalie in a knowing manner and smiled at her in a satisfied way. Nathalie was chilled. With her were two office girls who had become her permanent cronies, Lilith and Selena, both tall, willowy blondes. Nathalie had made a point to learn their names. *Know thy enemy.*

They were all carrying factory stock, boxes of chocolate and candy.

She looked at Nathalie and said the strangest thing. "You going to record this, Parker? You gonna write down every little thing you see?" she asked.

Nathalie was taken aback. "What? No, why would I?"

"You just seem the type." She shrugged. "A goody little two shoes."

"I might report you for stealing, though," Nathalie said primly.

"Go ahead," Beth said carelessly. The three of them assessed her, laughing softly before moving on.

"She's such a BITCH," Nathalie said decisively, "and a thief."

Dean ghosted up behind her. "I'm not sure what's going on here, Nathalie, but something's very wrong."

Nathalie nodded, taking a good look around her. Most everyone had shown up for work, but no one was actually working. "I don't understand what's happening here."

"The fridge is full of beer," Dean said quietly.

Nathalie lifted up their lunch bag. "I know," she said.

"Where's Mr. O'Malley?"

"I have no clue. I haven't seen him since I got back from vacation. I assumed he was on vacation, but now I'm not so sure. Kelly said he was partying, but I haven't seen him at The Rotunda. He's disappeared."

"Not much for me to do. I have orders to fill but all the stock is spoken for and the production line has stopped. The only thing coming out of this place is that chocolate drink."

No Wednesday candy day, Nathalie thought sadly.

"He's gone away before and this has never happened," Dean said with confusion as he watched a coworker playing on-line poker.

"What do we do now—?" Nathalie asked and then sputtered in astonishment as she watched the office manager, Bobby, walk by her with a box of printer paper, seemingly heading to his car.

"We maintain order," Dean said firmly as he ran to stop Bobby.

It ended up being a tough day for both of them. Beth and her girls roved around the office like a gang, picking on the less attractive office girls. Some of them cried and went home.

"This is getting old. This isn't high school you know!" Nathalie said in outrage to the office thugs. "This is a professional office!" Beth's cronies made rude gestures at Nathalie, but Beth just gave her a sly smile and made a small hand gesture towards Nathalie. To her surprise, her amulet heated up briefly. That witch! She'd tried to hex her!!

The men were no better. Dean broke up two poker games and forbid the use of the boardroom video conferencing equipment for daytime soap operas and sports. By early afternoon everyone was gone. Even Beth had left with her followers in tow. *Probably to the fair,* Nathalie thought. She had secured the keys to the office from the receptionist and had convinced a grumbling Bobby to disable the electronic passkey system.

"Sorry Bobby," Nathalie had said. "Things are a bit too out of control with Mr. O'Malley gone. You saw the office."

"Fine," he said. But he was obviously not pleased. Nathalie suspected that the fridge was filled with his beer for late night card games with his buddies. He only turned over his keys when Nathalie gently reminded him that he would be held responsible if anything should happen to the office."

"S'not my fault!" he had responded heatedly, slurring his words a little.

She had sighed inwardly at his boozy breath. *Unbelievable.* But Nathalie had looked at him with her newly created, wide-eyed and vapid "I understand" stare and had replied, "exactly, and it would hurt me *terribly* to see you blamed for someone else's *carelessness*." She pushed aside the urge to talk in a southern belle accent. She would have put her hand on his arm, but she didn't. He looked unwashed.

Dean just rolled his eyes with disgust as Bobby shuffled away. "He was very easy to manipulate," Dean said with a frown.

"Yes he was. That's a problem," Nathalie replied as she locked the front door to the office. It looked so barren with its empty parking lot in the middle of the afternoon.

"Why?" Dean asked curiously. Nathalie was smart and observant. She also made connections to things that were not obvious to others.

"He's the adult, Dean. He has the authority at this factory. If he doesn't care, and he can be manipulated by a teenager like me, that's a problem. We sneer at them but adults maintain order. Their maturity and experience is supposed to keep *us* in check. Sometimes their authority is the only thing protecting us from danger, and well, chaos." Nathalie looked worried.

Dean's face took on a worried look as well, but then his cell phone rang. He flipped it open and barked "yep" into it and within a few seconds was frowning. "We'll be right there."

Nathalie looked at him questioningly.

"It's Sadie. Luke wants us to come over immediately."

"Let's go," she said, taping up a sign that read CLOSED UNTIL FURTHER NOTICE. They crossed East Road and headed towards Barrington Manor.

The Barrington Estate

When they arrived, Luke answered the door before they could ring and rushed them upstairs to his room. It was actually a suite with a bedroom, a small sitting area and an on-suite bathroom. It looked like a mini-hotel room, but larger. The Barrington house had been built to house many people. Now it allowed each individual of the eight-person family to live in luxury.

Nathalie walked in and saw Sadie sitting on the couch in the sitting room. She looked very pale and sad. She was not her usual cool and composed self. Her hands were wringing a small handkerchief and her black dress was dirty and torn at the hem. Nathalie could tell instantly that she was very upset and on the verge of tears.

Nathalie looked at the boys, who were hovering just outside the door. Luke looked a little wild-eyed. "Help me," he mouthed.

"Guys, we need drinks and snacks. Both of you—go rustle something up. And don't come back too quickly," Nathalie said quietly. With obvious relief they scampered off down the hallway to the grand staircase and down into the kitchen.

Nathalie closed the door softly behind her and went quickly to the couch where Sadie mumbled a small "thank you" before bursting into tears.

Shocked, Nathalie sat beside her and hugged her tightly, letting her cry until she couldn't cry anymore. She had never seen Sadie break down—ever.

"You know, I've never had a friend," Sadie said in a small, muffled voice. "I've never had a boyfriend. I've never had any family or anyone I thought loved me even a little. I was used to it. I didn't feel much either." Sadie sat quietly for a moment and Nathalie watched Sadie overcome her fear of opening up and letting another person see inside her.

"Then there came Luke, like a freight train. You can't avoid him. He smacks right into you and worms his way into your affections, your heart, your life, and then you realize that you can't live without him anymore. You can't live without his love because it's such a wonderful thing. It warms you up and makes you want to live life to the fullest, and without love, life would be too bleak, too unbearable. You realize you are vulnerable and you wonder why you allowed it in the first place."

Nathalie was nodding. Her family and Dean were her weak spots. Sadie shifted away and sat closer to the edge of the couch so she could look at Nathalie. Despite the storm of tears, Sadie's beautiful face was like white porcelain without one red spot. Only her tear filled lashes showed otherwise. Beautiful even in misery.

"I tried to break up with Luke this morning," Sadie said quietly, looking away, her gaze drifting towards something in the middle of the room.

Nathalie gasped audibly. That's big. That must have been terrible for Luke.

Sadie nodded at Nathalie's gasp. "Needless to say, it did not go over very well."

"You obviously... decided against it," Nathalie said carefully.

Sadie smiled sardonically. "Oh, I wanted to. I was determined." She sighed. "I was wild in my room last night. I paced and cried and pulled my hair like a crazy person *agonizing* over what to do. I decided it was for his own good and protection…" Her voice trailed away. "But I couldn't do it," she said softly. "I'm weak now. His obvious anguish was like a sword in my own heart. So I didn't go through with it. Not only for him, but for me too. I'm selfish. I want him." She shrugged her shoulders.

Nathalie was now dying of curiosity. Something had happened last night that had obviously been some sort of threat to Luke. Something that had gotten out of control.

There was a soft tap at the door and Luke peeked in hesitantly. Sadie gave him a small nod and he raced into the room with a tray of hot chocolate while Dean followed with crackers, cheese and cookies. Nathalie realized that she was starving.

Luke forced a mug on Sadie and quickly made her a plate. "Eat, please," he said desperately and she complied by popping a cube of cheese into her mouth.

Dean had a mystified look on his face and Nathalie gave him a small shrug. Luke caught the exchange and sat down at Sadie's feet. He looked at Sadie and took a breath.

"Sadie's magic…power…whatever you want to call it, manifested itself last night," he said quietly.

Nathalie and Dean sat very still.

That's it, Dean thought resignedly, *I just can't dodge that bullet, can I.*

Nathalie shook her head to clear it.

"It's purple," Luke babbled.

"Okay," Nathalie said soothingly. "Purple. Why don't you start from the beginning?"

Luke told them about Liora Kellar's attack. "I couldn't reach Sadie this morning at all. She wasn't answering her cell. So I sneaked into the woods behind the Kellar house early this morning, and if I didn't see her, I was going to call Sheriff Holt and insist he search the Kellar house."

Luke was breathing heavily and Sadie looked at him with some concern.

"Luckily, Liora and Boris went out so I climbed the trellis at the back and saw her sleeping." Luke took a deep breath. "I tried to wake her up but she was so disoriented. I was sure Liora had drugged her! Then she tried to break up with me and told me to leave!" Luke's voice was agitated. "So I pleaded for her to come with me and she agreed, so here we are."

Dean raised his eyebrows in alarm and Nathalie put her hand on Sadie's. "So, what's the situation with your aunt?"

Sadie shrugged. "I'm not sure, exactly. After I fainted in the yard, Luke revived me and wanted to take me home with him, but I knew I couldn't come here. It's too much of an imposition."

Luke snorted. "You don't know my mother," he said with pride.

She smiled slightly as she continued, "Luke helped me to the door and Uncle Boris opened it. He made sure Luke was okay and then sent him home. He said it was dangerous for Luke to be here right now. At first Luke wouldn't leave, but Boris assured him I'd be just fine. After Luke left I walked into the kitchen and faced my aunt, who was sitting at the kitchen table as if nothing had happened. I told her never to threaten any of my friends ever again. She just *agreed,* and I went to bed." Sadie shrugged. "I was a bit feverish afterwards, but she was there, wiping my face with a cool cloth and taking care of me. She was happy! When she left, I started to pace. I think that's when shock set in. I was exhausted this morning when Luke found me."

"I don't trust her," Luke said with a frown. "Who threatens to kill you and then wipes sweat off your face? Liora's crazy! I'm missing something," Luke exclaimed, frustrated that he couldn't figure out what he was missing.

Sadie shrugged again. "Regardless, that's my aunt and my home, and I think that my aunt is slightly afraid of me. After I threatened her, Uncle Boris explained that Liora had been a bit stressed lately, and when she saw me in town with *that Barrington boy,* well..." she smiled wryly at Luke, "the shock sent her over the edge. It's just that the Barringtons have always been considered our mortal enemies. A famous feud, like Shakespeare's Capulets and Montagues. Instead of Romeo and Juliet we're Luke and Sadie." Sadie sighed. "Apparently she was regretful."

"So why break up with Luke?" Dean asked with innocent curiosity. He was stuffing his face with cookies. Nothing hurt his appetite.

Sadie shook her head and her face tightened. "I don't want Luke to get hurt."

"I'm not going to get hurt!" Luke said heatedly.

Sadie stared at Luke. "You don't understand. I can feel it, deep inside. Something is happening around me that I don't understand yet, but believe me, someone or something has a plan for me. If Willow is haunting me or controlling me, I'm quite sure her plan does not include having a Barrington for a boyfriend."

Luke made a sound of protest.

"You are always with me!" Sadie exclaimed. "Suppose you're there when I lose time? You could get hurt, even killed! I can't take that chance. I won't." Sadie's voice was laced with fear. "And now this power. Suppose it's used against you? I flung my aunt ten feet and it didn't take any effort."

Luke looked at his friends. "From what I saw last night, Sadie is extremely powerful. More powerful than Willow ever was, I'd wager. Definitely more powerful than her aunt."

"How can you tell?" Nathalie asked, surprised.

Luke squeezed himself on the couch and pulled Sadie close. "You can feel something like buzzing or static when Liora is using her power, like she doesn't have full control of it. It doesn't seem like she's powerful enough to harness it, you know...keep it near her, so it dissipates a bit creating that static electricity feeling. Our hair was standing on end. With Sadie, well..."

Everyone waited expectantly.

"Sadie just pulled energy towards her...no static or buzzing, just ropes of purple power and full control. Liora is nowhere near as powerful as her."

"Power that can kill in the wrong hands," Sadie added seriously. "I know that instinctively."

Ah, the crux of the matter. Nathalie thought. *With missing time, she's scared because she doesn't know what happens during that time.*

"You would never hurt Luke," Dean said reassuringly.

"I wouldn't. But that *thing* haunting me might," she said coldly. Her anger at being used was apparent.

"Willow," Luke said decisively.

"We never confirmed," Sadie said stubbornly.

"So let's confirm," Nathalie said. "Sadie, do you know of a way to communicate with this entity?" Nathalie asked curiously, looking at Sadie. "Do you have a...spell of some sort we can try?"

"Talk to a ghost?" Dean said with some skepticism. "Like a séance?"

"Exactly," Nathalie said with an admiring glance at Dean.

"It's Willow," Luke said brusquely. "I know it's her. It has to be. I'm not crazy. She spoke to me on the library steps. She didn't introduce herself, but she looks just like Sadie, and she's evil. Who else could it be?"

"Luke, I agree with you, but let's make sure. What's preventing us from solving anything is we continue to act like victims, pretending it's not happening and waiting in fear to see what's going to happen next. It's time to take control—record what we know and get answers for what we don't know." Nathalie took a determined breath. "The seemingly impossible or supernatural is actually true." Nathalie said decisively. "Luke witnessed Sadie when she was being possessed. No one else could see it, but Luke could. We need the name of that entity."

Luke nodded.

"I was hexed," Dean said quietly. The inability to control himself or make his own decisions during that time still gave him nightmares.

"That's right," Nathalie said with a frown. "I couldn't see the hex bag but Sadie could."

"And there's Nat's demon," Sadie said finally. "The one who likes superstitious jingles and leaves gold coins as calling cards. The one we almost forgot about."

"I wonder how many other beings we've encountered that we don't remember," Dean mused, thinking about the person who sold his sister the eyelash. "There are a lot of new and strange people visiting or participating at the fair." Dean told them about Ella's hair and her wishing eyelash.

Nathalie was shocked. "Are you serious? And you're just telling us now?"

"It slipped my mind!" Dean said sheepishly.

Luke looked doubtful. "Are you sure? Ella's smart. She's played a joke or two on you, buddy…"

"Nah, man. Her hair is real. I checked. Apparently the second eyelash didn't work for her though, so who knows."

"What concerns me is that Ella is playing with *magic*. Doesn't that strike you as odd? We may not be the only ones having strange experiences," Nathalie said.

"So all these odd things are happening now, and maybe not just to us," Luke pointed out. He had moved so that Sadie was settled firmly in his lap. He wrapped his arms around her tightly.

"When I was at Taline's stand, I asked her for a special stone that wouldn't let me forget things that happen to me." Sadie lifted her wrist and a blood red stone was lashed tightly against the underside of her wrist with some sort of woven, hemp cord. "I'm not sure if it will help when I lose time because I think my mind goes to sleep and doesn't record memories, but it will prevent me from forgetting any other 'special' beings I may meet."

"Maybe we should all get them," Luke suggested, taking Sadie's wrist and looking closely at the stone. "It's pulsing. Wow. It's beautiful."

"Yes, and very rare. It's a bloodstone. It matches your heartbeat. Taline lent me this one for now because of my problem."

Nathalie was frowning. "I never wrote my sister for information on the demon," Nathalie realized, angry with herself. "This is what I mean! We talk, it's important, but the urgency just, well, fades."

"We're distracted, even my dad," Luke said quietly. "He hasn't said anything, but he's become more secretive since the windmill started spinning and houses in town were marked with blood."

"Yes, and if you look at the list of families who were targeted, they're all on the town council, except for the Crofts. So why Dean's family? I did some checking. The only other tie all the families have is that they are all originals."

"Originals?" Sadie asked.

"The book I'm reading on Barrington County calls the first settler families 'originals,' but not *all* original families are on Mrs. Barrington's list," Nathalie said. "Only a select few, so I can't figure out what the connection is."

"Maybe there is no connection," Dean suggested. "Maybe it's random. Why is this so important to you, Nat?" Dean asked curiously.

"I'm not sure," Nathalie said, shaking her head. "The fact that the list wasn't circulated or published in the paper is significant. Claire Barrington doesn't pull strings like that unless it's important."

"We need to figure out what the link is," Sadie said.

"Maybe it's just wild behaviour. Nathalie and I closed the factory this afternoon. The place was nuts. Employees playing games and drinking beer. We've never seen this. Ever. It's crazy," Dean said.

Nathalie nodded. "I felt the same way last night observing the behaviour at The Rotunda. The town is wild every night with revelers, and there's absolutely no control. Even my dad was blasé about it."

There was general agreement.

"I think we've all had the same thoughts," Nathalie said, thinking back to her conversation with her dad. "So for argument's sake, if we boil it down we have a mysterious witch in town, a trapped demon threatening people and tossing around evil gold coins, the ghost (to be confirmed) of Willow Kellar haunting Sadie, and a town gone wild."

"Yay," Dean said under his breath.

Nathalie looked around at her friends. "Time to make a plan. Luke, please get me some writing paper and a pen before I forget again. I'll ask Rain to find Dannerlich's tome, or anything by that writer."

"Deitriche. The writer. His name is Klaus Deitriche," Luke supplied helpfully, along with paper and pen. "Nothing like the memory of a genius IQ," he said with a small self-deprecating laugh.

"I'm also going to need that coin. I'm sending it to Rain. The markings may be important."

Sadie was standing. "Right. I'll check the demon reference book at my house and get the coin. I've memorized his markings," she added.

Nathalie looked around at her friends. "No more ostrich behavior. Magic exists, witches exist, demons exist, ghosts exist and possession is possible. Any questions?"

"Nooooope," Dean said for all of them.

"We're going to figure this out. It's no coincidence that this is all happening at the same time. We just need to tie it all together."

Barrington County
Wednesday, August 14

Dear Rain,

Hi sweetie, hope you're doing well. We really need your help, so I'm going to jump right into it. Please, I need you to take this very seriously even though you may have a hard time believing what I'm about to write.

Things have gotten very strange in our town. The festival is wild this year. It's kind of worrisome because it seems to be a bit out of control and none of the adults are doing anything about it. Nothing bad has happened yet, so maybe I'm exaggerating, but it's still creepy. Some pretty strange folk have come to visit, and stayed.

I am working with some friends to figure out what's going on here and we need some books that are only available in Superstition's Library. In this envelope I've included a coin. It's a very special coin. It has been shrink wrapped so you can see the markings, but DO NOT, UNDER ANY CIRCUMSTANCES, touch it with your skin! It is coated with some sort of poison that will make you sick. I'll explain more about it when I see you next.

For now, we desperately need information on the being stamped on this coin. We believe he's a demon and that his name is Dannerlich. One side of the coin has the demon's face. On the other side the demon's symbol. Apparently there is a book in Superstition's library about him (according to the on-line catalogue). Sadie says it's probably a large tome (book with leather and buckles) with the demon's face or symbol etched on it. It will contain a record of the demon written by the humans or witches that knew him. See if it matches, if it does, we need to know his story. Right now Sadie was able to identify him as a bad luck demon that made superstitions come true. Considering the name of the town you're in, we suspect he was there at some point.

Sadie is also having a strange summer, to put it mildly. We've discovered Beth (the girl I complained to you about) is an actual witch. Now a demon and a ghost (I know, I need to explain but I don't have time)... we think this may all be tied together somehow.

I am also looking for the "Book of Record" by a Dame N. Parquhar. Luke and Sadie requested it from Superstition but it never came. We need that book! Can you look for it as well? It's going to be in rare books for sure. Steal it if you have to!

I need to post this right away, so I don't have time for more details in this letter. See if you can find the tome and anything else pertaining to the start of the three counties. I'm not sure Limerick is involved, but Superstition definitely is. Something significant happened around here in the last five hundred years, and we need to know what that is!

Your sister,

Nathalie

PS: Nick says hi.

PPS: Don't tell anyone except Gabriel what you're doing. It may be dangerous if the wrong person finds out what you're researching.

THE BARRINGTON BUGLE - WEDNESDAY, AUGUST 23

Barrington's Harvest Festival - A Smashing Success!

By Patrick O'Callaghan

The festival so far has been a smashing success! Despite the innocent vandalism proclaimed in the papers earlier this month by a sensationalist journalist, more visitors than ever before are streaming in for Barrington's Harvest Festival. New vendors have set up shop and a multitude of new and interesting trinkets and novelty items are for sale. One vendor is selling "wishes" in coloured vials, while another has jewelry made from glowing gems. For the men, designer weapons for display are laid out to view along with exclusively designed belts and shoes. Toymakers, from our own Toys, Trains & Merryment Toy Store, doll makers, and other crafters are there for the pleasure of your little ones.

As for food, no need to eat at home or the outlying hotels! Baker has outdone himself this year with his goods, Ye Ole Sweete Shoppe is represented in full force, and the Curtis brothers have Town Circle covered for good food and drink. For those romantic diners, the Spells & Stars Restaurant is still your best choice - but you'll need a reservation. Not to forget - the new chocolate drink that has become this festival's rage - produced by none other than Barrington's own Limerick Candy Factory run by Shaemus O'Malley. It isn't available for sale yet, according to the pretty servers, but it is free for anyone who wants a cup.

Who would have thought we could have shaken a coin from that old leprechaun Shaemus, eh? To top it all off, the legendary reveler has been unusually absent this year. Come out from under the shamrocks, Shaemus! Bottoms up and top o the mornin' to ya!

On the activities front, the riding barn has been a galloping success with the kids. Wayman's arrival in Barrington has been a godsend. His popularity has spurred a committee of town members to form a group to plan new and exciting activities for our guests. Surprisingly, one of those members is actually part of the town council - old Eric Sweet. (Finally doing something to earn that councilman salary. Don't think I don't remember that twenty bucks you still owe me, you old weasel.) The plan is to organize hiking excursions to Crystal Falls with lunch included, mock "witch hunts" through the woods, and a nightly staging of the Kellar Witch trial and hanging, among other things. The activities will be posted as they're organized, so don't forget to check The Bugle Bulletin Boards at the fair and around town.

THE BARRINGTON BUGLE - THURSDAY, AUGUST 24
LETTERS TO THE EDITOR

Issac:

I really must protest you allowing your reporters to broadcast their personal messages and gambling debts in the town's newspaper under the guise of an article. It's unprofessional and inappropriate. The paper's articles should report facts and not act as a vehicle for personal communication. It sends the wrong message to the visitors of our town. If O'Callaghan wants to go drinking with his buddy, or collect money he's due, he should just pick up the phone.
-Anonymous

Dear Anonymous:

He's your husband! Why don't you tell him yourself? Anyway, I kept in the personal comments because they were funny, but I'll take them out next time.
-Ed

Dear Editor:

In yesterday's article, "Barrington's Harvest Festival – A Smashing Success" O'Callaghan claims that the vandalism in the town was minor, but the families who ended up with blood splattered runes painted on their homes think otherwise. I know who did it. I know who viciously attacked these God fearing people. The apple doesn't fall far from the tree, and we have the direct descendant of the town's famous, murdering witch living here. She should be watched with suspicion. She should be run out of this town, or she should be burned.

-Anonymous

Thursday, August 24

The Barrington Bugle Newspaper Office

When Issac Heimler, editor of The Barrington Bugle, picked up the newssheet Thursday morning and saw the second letter, the one he *hadn't* approved, he read it with shaking hands.

"Who put this in?" he roared at his copy boy.

The boy looked confused. "I have no idea," he said.

"Ha!" Issac said with a laugh, "I love it! A witch hunt in Barrington…now THAT will sell papers!"

Hannah just smiled as she tidied her desk for the day. A witch hunt was a very good idea.

The Kellar Residence

Sadie was horrified when her aunt came home with the paper.

"Folks were eyeing me funny today. Some were plain rude and others were sympathetic, asking how I was. Those hypocrites…now I know why!" Liora said, tossing the two-page paper on the table.

Sadie was shaking with fury as she read the short but vicious letter.

"I don't understand," she said in a strained voice. "How can the paper just print that letter? Don't they edit hate mail? Don't they need proof to print claims like that?" *Did they have proof she didn't know about?* Sadie bit her lip. "The writer is suggesting the town *burn* me like they did during the witch trials! This is ludicrous."

Liora huffed. “Letters are people’s *opinions,* girl. Nobody named names, but the point is clear. They think they have the right to say whatever they want. Freedom of the press and all that. Bah! I’ve a mind to sue that old German coot for slander and threats against my family,” she muttered under her breath.

Sadie eyed her aunt. Hopefully, that’s all she would do. Now that she had witnessed her aunt’s power and her temper, she paid more attention to her outbursts. For herself, and her own power, she was careful never to use it. Not that using it was a problem. After that first incident when her power had manifested for the first time, Sadie had not been able to produce a repeat performance. She had no idea how to call it.

Liora snorted. “Bet your young lad’s mother won’t be too pleased at the scandal of you being tied to the vandalism,” she said, pleased.

“But as you said, aunt Liora,” Sadie replied coolly, “the anonymous writer never mentions names.”

Liora just grunted.

Boris, who was sitting at the table having tea, looked at Sadie seriously. “You need to figure out who wrote that, Sadie girl,” her uncle said after reading the offending paragraph. “You have an enemy, and this town has never been particularly friendly to Kellars in the past.”

“They don’t burn people anymore because of one person’s silly, *and completely outlandish,* declaration,” she whispered.

Boris frowned. “No, not if they’re in their right mind,” he said ominously.

And many people didn’t appear to be in their right mind, Sadie thought, and her hand rattled on her teacup. The more she read it, the angrier she got. What *would* Claire Barrington think when she read this? Luke was going to lose it if he thought someone was threatening her. The audacity of this person! She could feel power gather and crackle along her arms as fury filled her. She was losing control of her emotions, and her power was coming. Her teacup exploded and shock replaced anger as she stared at her hand uncomprehendingly. Her aunt and uncle shouted in surprise as the shards sprayed them. Her power started to fade. She needed some solitude to calm down. She needed to speak to Luke.

Sadie stood up and swayed.

“You okay girl?” her aunt asked in a peculiarly deep voice, as if from far away. Sadie felt odd. She turned and the most beautiful girl Sadie had ever seen was standing beside her. Her black dress looked strangely like hers, but it was longer and had more material flowing around the legs. Sadie was confused. Who was this beautiful girl? How did she appear so quickly? She was feeling woozy.

"I need to sit down," Sadie said, but her voice sounded far away.

"Yes, why don't you rest, my sweet. Liora, I need to borrow my granddaughter for a few hours." The girl smiled as she looked at Sadie, but it wasn't a nice smile, and Sadie could only gasp in horror when the woman's violet eyes turned white and she walked right into her. Sadie stopped moving abruptly. There was a brief struggle as Sadie's face changed expressions before she groaned and bent her head, rubbing it. When she looked up, her expression was calculating and cold.

"Hello, Willow," Liora said fawningly.

"Liora," she said shortly. "We have no time to waste. Sadie has grown much stronger. She should not have been this difficult to subdue," she said with irritation.

"She released her power..."

"Yes, I can feel it. It is not yet at full strength, but it will be in time for the ritual," Willow said, extending her arms and flexing her fingers. She drew power easily. Purple electricity rolled over her arms and fingers in waves.

"I've never seen power like hers—" Liora said with awe and a bit of fear.

"Yes, an inheritance building for centuries, and I will use all of it. It must be mastered if I am to transform and live in this body permanently when the time comes. Get my spell book, Liora. I need to start preparing immediately."

"Yes, Willow," Liora said as she ran to the basement.

Willow looked at Boris and inclined her head. He did the same.

When Sadie woke up she knew right away it was much later. She was aching and sweaty. She groaned as she sat up. She remembered everything and she stumbled to the mirror in her room and ripped off her dress to check her stomach. The faint markings of the pentacle enclosed in a circle that Willow had drawn on her belly had faded to thin white lines. Willow had tapped into her power and used it easily to burn the sigil onto her body.

Willow, Willow, Willow... I'm being possessed by my ancestor... Willow, Willow, Willow... confirmation... no denial possible... Willow Willow Willow... crazy terrifying evil murderous witch... she chanted mindlessly as she grabbed her cell phone and checked the time... she has a ritual she has to do soon… Sadie searched her memory… come on, come on, she thought to herself… a ritual on… arrrgh… she couldn't remember… she growled in frustration… it was a date she should know… it'll come to her.

It was three in the morning. She had missed over fifty calls, all from the same number, but because nothing good ever happens at this time of the morning, she didn't call Luke back.

Friday, August 30
The Barrington Estate

The four friends met at Barrington Manor an hour before midnight. The hoots and sounds of music and wild partying could be heard faintly from Town Circle. Nathalie and Dean had stayed on the lighted streets and pedaled their bikes furiously through town. It was Friday night, the second to last day of August.

After Sadie's last "missing time" incident a week ago, which they believe was triggered by the nasty letter published in the newspaper, they had decided to hold a séance. Now that Sadie had confirmed, without a doubt, that the evil spirit they were dealing with was, in fact, Willow Kellar, they planned to summon her, bind her, and destroy her. Sadie found the spells they needed in Elanah's spell book and had spent the last week studying the rituals and getting the items they would need to cast the spells. Some of the items were very difficult to acquire, so they gathered the moment they had everything they needed.

There was definitely something wrong with their town, and it was somewhat of a relief to realize that they weren't the only ones going through something strange. They believed Beth was involved, and that is was her publishing the hate mail about Sadie.

When Luke and his mother confronted Heimler about the letter, he claimed he never saw it before it was printed. It just *appeared* in the daily. They didn't believe him, of course. Heimler had no scruples about slander or invading people's privacy when it came to his publication. But, they had no proof, and as Heimler pointed out with a smile, no names were ever printed.

So, the fact that Beth was a witch and a stranger made her the prime suspect in Luke's eyes. Barrington County was fun-loving chaos, and this craziness had started shortly after *she* had arrived. She was bad news.

Not only that, Beth and her posse had set up two new drink booths; both in Town Circle to "meet demand" (she claimed), but these drinks had alcohol in them making them even more popular. Luke was surprised it was allowed, but Nathalie wasn't. Nothing surprised her anymore.

What Nathalie still couldn't fathom was why Beth put so much effort into these drink booths for nothing. The drinks were free. The candy factory certainly wasn't paying her for all her hours. With the factory shut down, no one was getting paid anymore. So what was she getting out of it?

Both Nathalie and Dean had stopped working the previous week. The business was at a halt with O'Malley missing, and people stopped coming to work. Nathalie had locked the doors and left a note for Shaemus, should he return. He hadn't yet. Dean had called all their clients to let them know that the factory was undergoing "renovations" to improve their assembly lines, and that as soon as they started production again their sales rep would be in touch. Any leftover stock had been hauled out and sold to Ye Ole Sweete Shoppe because Eric Sweet had demanded it.

"Drunken sot," Eric had muttered about Shaemus as he moved the inventory into his storeroom.

At the manor they crept into Luke's room. The furniture in his sitting area had been pushed aside to make a space for them to sit in a circle. Four fluffy pillows dotted the floor. Each one of them had brought a white pillar candle. Nathalie had gotten the herbs they needed from Taline, and Luke had procured a large, pewter brazier from his attic.

"Wow, what a beautiful antique," Nathalie whispered, putting her candle down beside her and sitting on one of the pillows."

"Believe it or not, it belonged to Jacob Barrington, the very man who condemned Willow to die."

"Because things can retain echoes of previous owners, we're hoping she'll sense her arch enemy and it will draw her to us more easily," Sadie said.

"Don't you need a pentacle for this?" Dean asked curiously. He had taken the suspension of disbelief very seriously. He had read up on séance rituals. He started with Ethan Graver's book, *Contacting the Dead*, but he quickly realized it was garbage, and the guy was "full of shit and had no idea what he was talking about."

Sadie had searched her aunt's library for Willow's grimoire without success. Elanah's book didn't have any information on séances. She found a secret stash of books in a huge locked wooden chest. Sadie found the key in her aunt's room, but it wouldn't open even after she unlocked it.

"It was magically sealed," she explained. Frustration and desperation had brought forth Sadie's power, destroying the magical seal instantly, and she was able to access the trunk's contents. Willow's grimoire was still missing, but one of the books in there was exactly what they were looking for. It was called, "*Séances: The Art of Calling The Dead*." It was handwritten, and the author was a witch named Hester.

"We're lucky it was preserved considering the witch hunters destroyed all books they considered 'of evil taint,'" Dean said as he read the book.

"It looks as if the Kellars hid books for witches," Sadie said.

"Or collected them," Luke added.

"Well, these women would have been executed if they had been found with them," Nathalie said, waiting for her turn to look at the section on séances, which was complete with instructions.

"So, is Elanah Von Vixen reliable?" Dean asked worriedly. "We haven't been able to compare her spells to any other witches. Suppose something goes horribly wrong?"

"From what I understand, she was almost as powerful as Willow, but not evil. She didn't consort with demons."

"Are you sure? Her book has some pretty awful spells," Nathalie said quietly.

"Well, it's the family's book, not just hers. I don't know much about her except that she worked with the witch hunters and was the one who went back to retrieve Willow's grimoire and her diary before the witch hunters could destroy them. She returned them to the Kellars."

In the end Hester's séance ritual looked viable, but two of the key "call" ingredients needed were fresh blood and earth from a graveyard.

"Do you think the blood needs to be hot and fresh?" Luke had asked, a bit sickened as he read through the ritual's ingredients.

"It doesn't say so," Sadie said calmly, "so we don't have to kill anything." In the end Sadie had gone to Bill Farmer and asked him for some blood so her aunt could make blood pudding. He had grimaced. *Gross,* he thought to himself. To him, the Kellars were strange folk, but so as not to show prejudice, he ordered blood for her from a butcher in Limerick. It had arrived this morning and they knew the ritual had to be tonight.

Luke had gotten the graveyard earth from Barrington's graveyard in Limerick. He convinced one of his older brothers to take him, but he didn't stay long. "Graveyards give me the creeps," he admitted to Sadie.

"The pentacle is under the carpet. I had to hide my artwork from my mother. For some reason I think she would object to me drawing, in chalk, on her wood floors, and the design leaves something to be desired," Luke said nervously.

"He did a perfect job," Sadie said quietly, taking her pillow. "Even though we can't see it, it's there, and it should protect us. The brazier is the vehicle of communication." There was a white circle of salt around it. "As long as the salt circle isn't broken, we'll be just fine. Does everyone have their supplies?"

Dean had gotten the vials of holy water from Father MacGunne and everyone had brought their own candle. "Remember, if things get dangerous, throw the holy water at her, or at yourself, but don't forget to use it if something goes wrong."

"It never works against vampires in movies," Dean said nervously, but Nathalie shushed him gently.

They lit their candles and Luke turned out the lights in the room. The room was dark and cool, protected from the August heat outside. The moon was out but not shining into the room, and the trees were black smudges through the windows. The four youngsters took deep, calming breaths, trying to quell their nerves and get to a meditative state.

Sadie's melodious voice was soft as she started to chant in Latin. The words were repetitive and after a few minutes began to blur together.

Nathalie was aware of Dean's deep breathing beside her. She felt as if she could hear his heart beat in time with hers. She opened her eyes and Sadie had lit the brazier. It burned steadily, giving off a pungent incense-like smell. The sweet smoke twisted its way around her, numbing her mind and making her sleepy. She felt herself fall asleep but was still awake. It was a weird sensation. Sadie was casting the summoning spell, and in her relaxed state her power came easily to her. It flowed through all of them, creating a circle. Nathalie could see the violet link and feel the warmth its presence generated.

"It's time," she called to them softly. She wasn't speaking in English or Latin, but another language, an old one, Nathalie realized, one they all understood.

Nathalie registered that Dean and Luke now had their eyes open. *Our conscious selves are asleep,* Nathalie thought fleetingly, *it's our unconscious selves that are participating in this ritual. Hester and Elanah didn't mention that in their books. I wonder what else they missed.*

Sadie called Willow. She cut her finger and put three drops of her blood onto the burning brazier. The pig blood had soaked the herbs and provided the initial call. Now Sadie used Kellar blood to draw her ancestor.

It worked, but it didn't.

It wasn't Willow who came.

A wild wind ripped through the room. A presence was manifesting itself over the brazier, a presence Nathalie had felt before. The flames in the brazier shot up. Nathalie was sure everyone would be burned in the inferno, but the heat didn't reach beyond the salt line.

Sadie frowned as the demon turned towards the source of power, and made a mocking inclination of his head. "Greetings to the Kellar heir," he hissed. "How may I be of assistance now that you have rudely pulled me from my resting place?"

"I did not summon thee," Sadie replied neutrally.

"*Thee* did. You called using blood, and I was the first to respond."

"I called one of my ancestors."

"Oooh, well, pardon me for crashing your family party, but here's a magic tip for you. Next time, only use your own blood, silly witch."

That wasn't in the books, either, Nathalie thought dimly.

"Why are you here? What is your connection to Willow Kellar?" Nathalie asked curiously. They had called Willow and he had appeared. She knew it was Danner even though he hadn't introduced himself.

"Why *hello,* puny human. I see that you remember me. Interesting! Is your gift getting stronger or has some one diddled with you magically?" The demon sighed. "I did tell you *not* to interfere, insignificant one. Don't say I didn't warn you." He adopted a thinking pose. "So, participating in this sham... and exposing our secret relationship... well that *does* constitute interfering," he said, and as fast as lightening, tried to grab Nathalie but his arm hit an invisible wall. He looked down and around. "Damn salt. I hate that stuff," he muttered irritably.

"Most witches forget to put it down. Oh well..." He smiled a terrible smile at Nathalie. "I guess you're safe, for now," he said ominously.

"Answer the question," Nathalie said.

"Why? You haven't compelled me." He looked unconcerned as he picked invisible dirt from underneath his nails.

"I *compel* you to answer any question put forth in this space," Sadie said formally.

"That doesn't *actually* work, but I'll play along. Very well," he huffed, but then he smiled. Nathalie realized that he was enjoying himself.

"Yes," he said, looking directly at her, "I am enjoying myself because it's *very* boring where I live. I love field trips."

"Answer the question," Luke said in a dead voice. His eyes were blazing a curious green.

"Look here people, everyone knows Willow. Her deeds are famous, and I admire her work."

Luke frowned. "Her work killing children for power? How admirable."

The demon's eyes flicked briefly to Luke before dismissing him. "That's what evil things do, *boy*."

"You are an abomination," Luke said in the same dead voice.

"Ah, now, now, Barrington. Sticks and stones, and all that," the demon said cheerfully.

"Are you in contact with Willow right now?" Nathalie asked, trying to focus his attention.

"Me? Oh, no," he laughed. "I'm here with you guys right now!" He looked around and fixed his gaze on Dean. "Take good care of that one, sweetheart. He's special."

"Why are you here?" Nathalie asked again in a far away voice.

"Seriously? You *called*. Hello! Well, anyway, it's been a slice, really, but I'm bored now. But let me leave you with a few presents. Give them out to your friends..." and with a laugh a shower of coins flew into the room, tinkling and rolling on the floor before disappearing. Danner was gone.

Everyone fell sideways to the carpet, completely drained. Luke was the first to recover. He dragged himself to his feet and went to his bedroom to grab the snack trays and thermoses of hot chocolate he had prepared earlier. They were all very grateful as they gobbled down the cookies, fruit, and cheese Luke had stashed.

"God, you're so smart, Luke," Dean said around a mouthful of food. He was attempting to wash it all down with a huge swallow of warm hot chocolate.

"It was Sadie's idea," Luke said simply, watching Sadie carefully to make sure she was eating. "Apparently when she was small she did a few rituals with her aunt and uncle and they always drained her."

What a different upbringing, Nathalie thought to herself as she looked at the pale girl.

"It didn't work," Sadie said. "We have to try again and do it right this time," she said a bit desperately. "Willow's still out there."

Luke gathered her in his arms and kissed her head. "We'll get her and destroy her."

"What's the point? He wouldn't answer any of our questions. We can't compel him; he's too powerful. What makes us so sure we can handle her? I'm just surprised we're not more terrified after what we just saw, and who we spoke to," Dean said worriedly, grabbing Nathalie and hugging her tight. "That demon really has it out for you."

Luke spoke up. "It has to do with our subconscious... it was awake during the ritual. It's treating the experience like a dream. That's why our fear is fading."

"I knew it," Nathalie said, getting up.

Dean let her go and spoke up, "I have to agree. I don't know about you guys, but the memory of this experience is fading fast. In a few minutes I won't remember any of it."

Nathalie went to her pack and took out the diary Nettie had given her. She opened it and scribbled furiously before she forgot anything. "I'm also noting that we need to be more careful when using blood. Elanah and Hester weren't very specific about that, or about the subconscious part."

Sadie sighed. "I suspect there is certain basic knowledge that witches taught each other, but didn't write down because everyone knew it. My problem is that I don't know all the rules, like how to use blood in a ritual properly." Sadie looked at Nathalie. "Do you know why he told you to take care of Dean, Nathalie? It's not good to have a demon aware of you. We are nothing but cattle to them. He's never met Dean before, so why did he say Dean was special?"

"Maybe he was joking? No wait, maybe he meant 'special' as in 'retarded' and sees me as a boy who licks bus windows and plays with his own poop," Dean said with an edge of hysteria in his voice.

"It could be a threat against me to watch my loved ones," Nathalie said, fear threading her voice. "He did warn me not to interfere."

"No," Luke said clearly. "He's interested in Dean, but he doesn't want him dead. That was obvious. He didn't lie, but he went around the question about collaborating with Willow. He answered the question truthfully, but it was overshadowed with an omission. We didn't ask the right questions. They were too general and we gave him room to skirt around the answer. And, we didn't use his full name. That would have made a difference, but it's a good thing we didn't. I think if he thought we knew his name we'd all be in big trouble. It's better this way for now."

They all looked at Luke with astonishment. He shrugged self-consciously. "What? I can see things that aren't there and sense... untruths. That's how I know my dad's worried about things. Sometimes he lies, and other times he just omits information or only partially answers my questions. It amounts to the same thing."

"At least we learned something with Luke being here," Nathalie remarked as she scribbled.

Sadie spoke up. "The only reason Willow is here is for revenge. Her curse is still pending after hundreds of years, and all the parts have aligned."

"And Danner is helping her," Luke said tiredly. "His comment about 'admiring her work' is bull."

"Yes, it's more than that," Nathalie said softly. "They're working together. We need to research what exactly happened the day Willow was executed. We need to understand who was there and the exact hex. We need to find out what happened with Danner and where he is. I hope Rain writes back soon.

"One last thing," Dean said, clearing his throat. "Before he left, Danner gave us a gold shower... where did all the coins go?"

Saturday, August 31
The Barrington Estate

It was the last day of August and the town council was meeting to discuss the happenings in the town, which had been party central for pretty much the whole month.

"Not a bad turnout. I've never seen so many people..."

"... having so much fun..." Eric finished with a laugh. He had stopped in Town Circle to pick up his special drink before coming to Barrington Manor. He just couldn't get enough of it. He spiked it, of course, but everyone knew that. They all loved it, except John. For some reason Barrington didn't drink it like everyone else. What a party-pooper.

Something isn't right, John thought worriedly as he watched his friends, who were also the town's leaders, laugh and drink. Despite the fact that they were the guardians of The Circle's knowledge of the hex, and by their heritage, responsible to act in defense and protection of the people of Barrington, they seemed out of control, like everyone else.

Earlier that evening, he and Luke had stood at the edge of Town Circle and watched the revelry. People were dancing and laughing, but it didn't seem like clean fun. There was an edge of madness to it. He watched as older members of the community acted like teenagers.

"Kinda weird," Luke had laughed, but the confusion in his voice was apparent.

"Just enjoying the last of summer's freedom," John had said to his son reassuringly, but he was lying. The partying and dancing when the festival opened was normal and continued as visitors came and went. However, this year visitors didn't seem to be leaving, and the number of people in the town was swelling. Even the townsfolk, whose excitement eventually died down and the thrill of the fair and the evening activities became more of a weekend thing, seemed to continue to be enthralled. He knew many of the people dancing and drinking in the square.

Only Noah Baker seemed grounded and concerned. Even the Sheriff had come by earlier to voice his concerns.

Noah walked over and nodded. "It's time John," he said quietly, looking at the other men with a slight frown. "According to The Circle's book, it's written:

'*... and under the influence of the witch, the town shalle become lawless and the people concerned unto themselves...*'"

"Jacob's diary corroborates. The signs are complete," Noah said with finality.

John nodded. "You're right. Paint the barns with the sigils to warn all who enter Barrington that we are hexed."

September

Tuesday, September 3
Barrington School Grounds

Despite the "university-like" party town evenings, supplies were bought, new clothes acquired, and school started like it did every year. Barrington's two schools were located right behind the restaurants in Town Circle, but separated by a small wood. The two school buildings were more like large houses than institutions. There were only about two hundred kids in Barrington to begin with, so classes were pretty small and were held in large drafty rooms with archaic desks. In each building there was a small teacher's lounge and a fairly large dining room where the kids ate their lunch when the weather was bad, although the older kids ate at the restaurants most days. Because the town was so small, the pub opened it's kitchen for lunch and allowed the teens to eat there, but most of them went to The Fry Diner or to Joe's Java Coffee House.

Both of the schoolhouses had entrances at the back into a small but perfectly designed gym where the kids could play basketball, floor hockey, or do gymnastics. The gym was free for use by the community in the evenings, so a third door at the back was for public use. Barrington had a lot of clubs and the town was generous when supplying equipment.

The school grounds were not extensive, but they were beautiful and picturesque like every other part of Barrington. At the front there was a small park for the little kids to play in and a field in the back for soccer and football. There were picnic tables interspersed in the small wood so the kids could eat and socialize outdoors.

The school area took up almost half the quad. The rest were houses, a rusty (but now working) windmill, and a red barn.

The elementary school kids were in a separate building from the high school students. This was to protect them from teenage "corruption" according to the principal, Mr. Linus Green. Not many of the kids liked him and called him "Sinus" or "Snot Green."

Little kids with bulging knapsacks and excited faces milled around the front of the "Little House" schoolhouse, which is what the elementary building was nicknamed. Barrington County Elementary School was just too much of a mouthful.

The "Big House," or Barrington County High School, was where you went starting in grade seven. It also was teeming with teens milling about the front and talking excitedly about their summer, and the festival, as they parked their bikes.

Nathalie stood at the edge of the wood and scanned the crowd. She saw Dean shepherding his twin brothers, who were starting kindergarten. His sisters were nowhere to be found.

Uh oh, Nathalie thought. *The two precocious ones don't look very happy.*

Dean saw her and waved. When he arrived he gave her one of his wide smiles and kissed her soundly on the mouth. Some of the older kids made comments and kissy noises. Nathalie just smiled. The little boys looked disgusted.

"I don't think you should do that in public," Zach said, scandalized and looking around.

"Yeah, you're in front of little kids!" Eddie piped in. "It's a bad sample!"

Zach frowned and whispered furiously to his brother, "it's 'example,' not 'sample,' Eddie!"

"Example!" Eddie yelled loudly.

"A little kissing never hurt anyone," Dean said easily.

At that moment a tall, pretty blonde lady stepped out of the Little House to check on her young charges. A bell clanged and she started motioning and calling the kids to come inside.

The boys looked at her with their mouths open. Dean smiled. "That, my boys, is Miss Linda. She's your kindergarten teacher."

The boys looked at each other and headed towards the steps. They looked very small with their huge knapsacks bulging with supplies. Dean started to follow, but they told him to go away. "We can handle this by ourselves," they said over their shoulders and made shooing motions. Dean and Nathalie watched as the boys climbed the stairs and introduced themselves to their teacher. She smiled when they held out their little hands to be shaken.

Nathalie looked at Dean with raised eyebrows.

"It's polite," Dean said, shrugging.

"If you could point us in the right direction to the kindergarten rooms, kind lady…" they asked in very charming voices.

"Why, *certainly*, young sirs," she responded formally and herded them in, giving Dean a small wave as she did so.

"Well, that went a lot easier than I thought it would," Dean said with mixed emotions, rubbing his chin and worrying a little. Nathalie put her hand in his and pulled him towards their building.

"They'll be just fine. They always are." As the two of them walked closer they could hear a conversation going on amongst some of the older kids.

"I'm telling you," Reggie Baker was saying loudly, "I watched the Sheriff paint those symbols on the red barns myself."

"I thought it was more vandalism," one of the girls said.

"All the same symbols, perfectly painted? Vandals wouldn't do that," a boy said loudly.

"If it was a gang symbol they would," she retorted hotly.

"What do you know about gangs," he sneered.

"Did you ask the Sheriff why he was doing it?" someone else in the crowd asked curiously.

"Yeah, but he told me that it was *none of my concern*," Reggie said, his face tightening with anger.

"I hate it when adults don't think we should know things," another girl said.

"I agree," Luke said quietly behind Dean and Nathalie. They turned and Luke was there holding Sadie's hand. Poor Sadie, she looked…uncomfortable, and Nathalie knew why. It was one thing to start dating someone in the summer. You spend a lot of time together with no observers or interference. It was another thing to announce it to the whole school. Sadie looked as cold and as perfectly pressed as usual in her high-necked black dress. Her violet eyes did not betray any uneasiness. The fact that she was trying to tug her hand out of Luke's did, but he had a death grip and wouldn't let go.

Nathalie smiled. *She's going to have to deal.*

Tess Smith stopped by to say "hi" and give everyone a hug. Nathalie hadn't seen Tess pretty much all summer. She watched as Tess stopped at Sadie, who tilted her chin up imperceptibly.

Tess smiled warmly at her. "Hey, Sadie," she said with a laugh, looking at Luke. "I guess we won't be going through another year of Luke mooning over you."

Luke blushed. "Jeez…I wasn't that obvious," he mumbled.

"He was," she said, punching him on the shoulder, and with a "see you later," Tess headed towards another group of kids.

Sadie smiled and looked at Luke adoringly. He seemed to stop breathing at her expression, so Dean helped out by smacking him on the top of the head to bring him back to earth.

"Okay, lover boy. What were you just talking about? 'Fess up."

"Oh, the barns, right." Luke lowered his voice. "I overheard my dad give Sheriff Holt the order to paint the barns. Those symbols mean something. They're supposed to be a warning for others not to come here."

Sadie nodded. "In the old days, everyone recognized them. The sigils indicate that the town is hexed or cursed in some way, and warn people from other towns to stay away."

"Judging by the turnout at the fair this past weekend, no one understands what they mean anymore," Dean said wryly.

"The Sheriff only painted them on Sunday," Sadie told him.

Luke licked his lips. "Sadie and I looked through the diary kept by Jacob Barrington—the one that belongs to my dad that no one is allowed near."

"Brave," Dean commented.

"We were desperate, trust me, but we didn't have it for long. We flipped through quickly and found the sigils carefully drawn, with scale measurements and an explanation of what to do. The barns are special. They were built to serve as warning beacons in case the hex Willow uttered was ever set in motion."

Sadie nodded. "This town was *very* carefully designed. The fact that there are only four roads into Barrington, each road following a cardinal point with a red barn at the entrance, was *deliberate*."

"We need the exact wording of that curse," Nathalie said quietly. "We need to understand what we're facing. Are we all going to die? Suffer a plague? Is the town going to blow up?"

"Jacob chronicles what happened to Willow, but we didn't have a chance to read it. Sadie and I stole the diary for an hour while my mom and dad were out, but it took us almost that long to find the sigils and read up on them. The book is hard to read, and we were lucky. My dad normally hides it, especially lately, but he left it out. Thankfully I was home," Luke said.

"The guy who read Edmund Spenser's '*The Faerie Queen*,' and then explained it to our English teacher, had a hard time with the language?" Nathalie said in disbelief.

"They couldn't spell for the life of them back then, at least not consistently, and the pages are very faded."

"How did people know they were hexed, anyway?" Dean asked curiously.

Sadie answered that one easily. "If a town had a string of bad luck, like a series of animal or infant deaths, curdled milk, drought…they would announce they'd been hexed and find a scapegoat. That usually meant a woman everyone was jealous of, whom they would accuse of witchcraft. She would be blamed for 'cursing' the town, and…well… we know what happens after that."

"Unbelievable, the innocents that died," Dean said.

"Mobs, mob-mentality, people become crazed with fear and lose their reason. Tragedies happen," Sadie said.

"Reminds me of that short story, '*The Lottery*,'" Nathalie added.

"Yeah, good story, but creepy," Luke agreed. "Anyway, the Sheriff painted the sigils, so the warning is there, but they missed a step. According to Jacob, for the sigils to actually protect the town, they need to be '*made active by means of magic*,'" he quoted.

Nathalie stared at Luke. "But they burned witches."

Luke shrugged. "Well, they didn't burn Elanah Von Vixen. Not only was she part of the witch hunters, she secretly helped Jacob with his spells. He *knew* she was a real witch because she set up the spell to activate the sigils once drawn."

"That's all fine and dandy, Luke, but your dad doesn't have a witch to help him in this century," Dean said, puzzled.

"No, he doesn't, but I do," Luke said proudly. "That's why, after school, Sadie and I are going to the red barn on East Road to activate the sigils and protect our town."

"I found the spell in Elanah's book. Maybe once it's activated it will keep Danner and Willow away from us," Sadie said quietly, her eyes haunted.

"That Elanah is a real enigma. Whose side was she on?" Nathalie wondered out loud, fascinated by the witch woman.

"Again, probably both," Sadie said. "At the time, what else could she do?"

The bell rang and the kids filed into school, unhappy to be leaving the warm and sunny September day. Barbara Farmer was their grade twelve teacher, and she frowned as her daughter Hannah slipped into the classroom a few minutes late.

Hannah does not look herself, Nathalie thought, and then felt a pang of guilt. She hadn't spent any time with her girlfriends this summer. She had no idea what was going on in their lives. Hannah looked at Nathalie unsmilingly, with a closed expression on her face. Nathalie felt a shiver of surprise. *What was up with her?* Luke's face lit up when he saw her and he gave Hannah a friendly punch on the shoulder, but she ignored him. His face crumpled a little. *Very strange,* Nathalie thought.

Getting back into a routine was tough. By lunch the class was desperate for a long break. As the kids streamed out of the Big House and headed to the restaurants or the picnic tables for lunch, Sadie, Luke, Dean, and Nathalie debated what to do.

Hannah tried to walk by them without saying anything, but Luke and Nathalie called her at the same time. She turned reluctantly towards the group and headed over. Hannah looked at Sadie with utter loathing for a split second before smoothing her expression into something more neutral.

Oh no, Nathalie thought to herself, remembering a conversation she'd had with Hannah before summer break. Luke didn't notice, but Sadie did. She stiffened and her gaze sharpened on Hannah. Luke was blabbing incessantly in his goofy, friendly way. Hannah was like a sister to him.

"Hi everyone," Hannah rushed, avoiding everyone's gaze. "I'll just say it…I'm not in the mood to be sociable right now. I've got a lot on my mind, you know…stuff I'm dealing with after the invasion at my farm." Her eyes flicked towards Sadie and then back to the ground. "I know you all care, but I just need a bit of space, okay?"

Before anyone could say anything, Hannah backed away and left, cutting through the wood towards Town Circle.

Luke was stunned. "What on earth!" he said with confusion laced with worry and was about to go after her when Sadie stopped him.

"Luke, leave her be. Sometimes being a good friend means giving someone the space to work things out. Call her tonight and see if she'll talk to you, but do not do anything public. You'll embarrass her."

Luke nodded. He looked at Sadie as she stood there quietly, her hand gently on his arm, the voice of reason. Jeez, he was so nuts about her. "Uh, Sadie, do you want to go have a picnic lunch in the woods?"

"What!" Dean said in surprise.

Sadie laughed. "No," she said decisively.

"It's a private joke, you blockhead," Nathalie said to Dean. "Try to keep up!"

They took their lunch things and found a quiet table in the trees. They got settled and Luke told them about the emergency council meeting that had been called for that evening.

"I'm going to that meeting. My plan is to hide in the room and listen."

"Hide where?" Dean asked around a mouthful of sandwich.

"I secretly cleared out the broom closet at the back of the room."

"There's a closet in there?"

"Exactly! Yes, but no one ever goes in it. No one remembers it's there."

"What happens if you get caught?" Dean asked curiously.

"If what we suspect is happening actually *is*, then my dad's anger certainly can't be worse. Anyway, it's for Sadie," he said worriedly, glancing at her. A small frown marked her brow but then smoothed away.

"More incidents," she told them. "Short time spans but more frequent, mainly in the evenings."

"Do you know what you end up doing?" Nathalie asked quietly.

"Willow practices using my power and casting spells, but I don't understand them," Sadie replied. "The good thing is I'm learning from her. I don't think she realizes I'm semi-awake now."

The gang mulled that over.

Sadie didn't tell them about Willow's plan for permanent residence. She didn't want to freak Luke out until she had to.

Town Circle–The Apartment above Clara's Crafts & Crystals

Hannah was relieved they hadn't stopped her. She could barely contain her hatred for Sadie Kellar. She wanted to rip the girl's throat out and watch her die slowly, writhing in agony and drenched in blood. She told them to stay away, and they'd better if they knew what was good for them.

Hannah cut through the wood and ended up in front of The Fry Diner. Kids were waiting in line to get food. She walked to West

Road, crossed, and headed to the back of Clara Innes' shop and climbed the stairs to the apartment above.

Beth was waiting for her, as agreed, but she wasn't alone. Hannah walked in and closed the door behind her but didn't advance into the room. The visitor was huge. A man at least six and a half feet tall, muscular and dressed in black leather pants and vest. He had a lot of chains looped around him. His long hair was wild and as black as night. He was extremely handsome in a disturbing way with sharp cheekbones and strangely glowing blue eyes. As he looked at Hannah he licked his lips and she could see pointed teeth. He rubbed himself as he stared and Hannah's eyes couldn't help drifting to the movement. He had large hands and long fingers with nails that were black and pointed. Hannah backed towards the door and pressed herself against it.

Beth looked at the man appraisingly. The front of his tight leather pants was bulging. Beth could see the tip of his manhood protruding out of the leather waistband. *He is BIG,* Beth thought in admiration. She hoped Hannah wasn't going to freak out. *Stupid high school kids.* The things she had to work with.

She walked towards Hannah. "Call Danner," she said.

"You call him," Hannah retorted in a terrified voice, in no mood to be bossed around.

Beth's eyes narrowed. "My way is painful, you little bitch. Call him!"

Not taking her eyes off the giant, Hannah reached into her pocket and took out Danner's coin. Within seconds of contact with her skin his presence was in the room. He looked around, bored.

"My Lord," Beth said in greeting, inclining her head.

Hannah just stared at the demon, and the being behind him, paralyzed with fear.

Danner looked behind him and laughed. "Why, hello Venius. You came. Thank you." The man just made a low growl and leaned against the far wall, watching.

Danner turned back to Beth and Hannah. "My pretty Hannah, good job on the letter, but you need to *keep* writing them, my little cow. Need some slander spread here. Time's a wastin'. Now that the town is a little bit more, er, suggestible, it's time to turn up the heat. You know, have some fun with lynch mobs and other exciting and murderous activities."

Hannah nodded and just continued to stare.

Danner tilted his head. "I want you to write about the dangers of the Kellars. I want the town in an ugly mood. The man controlling the printer is in my thrall so you won't have problems adding your letters."

He turned to Beth. "My beautiful witch, Bethiah…I want you to up the main ingredient in our elixir. Venius and his brother will help with the chaos part," Danner said, flicking his head at the being leaning on the wall.

"Heimler will figure it out," Hannah said fearfully, finally finding her voice.

Danner laughed. "Are you kidding? Heimler is in his *element*. No gold coin necessary for that one! He'll let it go a bit longer before he's forced to investigate, and only because he's being sued," Danner said nonchalantly. "Let me worry about those details." He looked at Hannah and frowned. "Your fear bores me." He waved his hand dismissively. "Go back to school little girl and do me proud. If you do, I'll grant you your heart's desire in the form of Luke Barrington. If you don't…"

Hannah's hand fumbled for the doorknob. She swung the door open and bolted.

Danner laughed. "Ah, teenagers in love! Such a powerful and obsessive emotion for them. I love it! It makes them so easy to manipulate!" Danner appeared delighted. He turned to Beth, "One other thing, Bethiah. Be a sweetie and take *good* care of my lieutenant for me. He's the gift I promised you. He's doing me a great favour by coming and deserves a little fun R&R while he's here…" Danner warned before he disappeared.

Beth looked at Venius. He was looking at her with interest now. The bulge at the front of his body was substantial. *God, he's enormous,* she thought with anticipation. She had never gotten over Dean's loss, and she was tired of high school boys. She walked towards him, opening her shirt at the same time. He hadn't moved from his place against the wall, but he was staring at her intently and had started rubbing himself again.

His tattooed arms are so hot, she thought, looking him over. She licked her lips and unfastened her bra, letting her breasts swing out in front of her. Her nipples tightened as the cool air hit them. His eyes widened and began to glow with lust as he inhaled her scent. Beth stopped in front of him and unbuttoned his leather vest. She put her hands on his stomach, allowing the edge of her palm to touch his protruding flesh. His skin was hot, almost burning.

He moved from the wall and herded her to the bedroom, using his big body to block any exits in case she was thinking of changing her mind. Beth started to pant with excitement at what was in store for her, once she saw what was in his pants as he stepped out of them. He was thick and long and ready. Faster than she would have thought possible, Venius pulled off the rest of her clothes and threw her backwards onto the bed. She bounced once before spreading her legs as wide as she could in open invitation. She gasped as he dropped his huge body on top of her and thrust inside her, his hips bunching powerfully. He used his weight to pin her down as he pumped back and forth, and he grunted as he slid in and out. Beth moaned in pleasure and pain underneath him as her body accommodated his size. He went faster as his pleasure built, and Beth came as he slammed his body into hers again and again. He roared when he orgasmed, almost bending her body in half with the force of his release before slumping on top of her. Within a few minutes Beth felt different, powerful. This being had given her something. When she looked up his eyes were a clear blue.

"What are you?" she asked wonderingly.

"Not human," he grunted evasively as he pulled himself out of her and stood up. He looked at her and his eyes held a hint of madness.

The other being inside Beth stirred and snatched the power Venius had unwittingly given them. "No!" Beth said desperately as she struggled briefly before disappearing.

Venius watched the tussle with interest. "I understand," he said to the new girl beneath him.

"Stay," she said. "Again."

He looked at her with cold surprise. "I will hurt you. I am not a gentle lover like your weak and puny males."

"Again," she said invitingly, lying back and stretching her naked body luxuriously. She sighed and ran a hand over her breasts and to the juncture of her legs. Venius could smell their essences mingled together. He bent down and put his face between her legs and worked her with his long tongue and fingers. She moaned and put her hands in his hair. His eyes began to glow again, like a predator.

"Again," she insisted.

He stayed, and he didn't hurt her too much.

Later, when Reggie showed up for their usual afternoon roll, Beth brushed him off. Today's session with Venius had lasted hours and nearly torn her in half, but she was angry because she only got to watch from the sidelines as her cohabitant enjoyed the large man the rest of the afternoon. Beth could sense the girl was pleased, and she fumed. Who knew she could be so strong? Her body was sore, and she hurt, but just the thought of Venius made her burn for more.

My turn next time, she thought spitefully.

No, was the answering response in her head. The power Venius had transmitted upon ejaculation was fading and Beth was back in control. Now she was no longer interested in the many high-school boys she entertained. Venius had made it clear that this body was for his use only. However, Beth understood Reg's infatuation with her, and how important that was going to be for her to use.

"I've got a busy night ahead of me," Beth said brusquely.

"You okay? You look a bit stiff," Reggie said with concern.

That's an understatement, Beth thought and then smiled. "Fell on my back."

"Why don't you get someone to cover for you at your booth tonight? You can take a hot bath and then I'll massage your back for you," he suggested slyly.

Beth sighed inside. "No one to cover," she said quickly. "Tonight may be a good time to see your friends," she suggested as she ushered him out the door and locked the apartment behind her.

Beth took off and left Reggie standing in a pool of disappointment. He walked down and headed to Town Circle. *Maybe some of my buds are around,* he thought morosely. He was about to cross to The Rotunda when a glimmer of gold caught his eye. It was a coin. He reached down and picked it up.

The Red Barn—East Road

Sadie and Luke stood before the enormous red barn down the street from the candy factory. The barn had always been there. The wood never rotted and the paint never faded. Luke had never thought about that before.

Sadie was staring at the sigil. It pulsed weakly. There was old magic pushing at it, wanting to activate it, but the catalyst needed hadn't been applied.

The catalyst was here now.

"What does Elanah tell you to do?" he asked, looking at the spell book Sadie was holding very carefully.

"Elanah already set the spell. It just needs a chant and a witch's touch. That's it. It's very simple, yet very powerful. She took care of all the complexity and ritual up front and made it easy to activate because she was sure they'd have to do it in an emergency situation. No time for ritual. She was a *very* smart witch. She must have been something else," Sadie said with a touch of awe. "Why couldn't *she* be my ancestor, and not some crazy, deranged, and murderous girl?"

"The age old question," Luke smiled wryly. "You can only pick your friends, not your family."

"Indeed," she said, studying the sigil. It was just a circle with a plus sign painted inside it.

It only took a second. Sadie chanted a string of words and touched the center of the sigil. Luke could see purple power flash by him as the barns were connected. Magical energy thrummed around the town in a circle.

"The barns make a circle; the four streets make a plus sign. I need to touch the center of The Rotunda to complete the seal," Sadie said.

Once they got to Town Circle the band was just starting to set up.

"Sorry, I'm just looking for my lost bracelet," Sadie lied as she walked to the center of the stage. The band shrugged and continued with what they were doing.

In the middle of the stage was the sigil. It was cast in iron and perfectly level with the floor. The Rotunda had been built around it. Sadie chanted the same string of words and touched the center of the miniature plus sign within a circle. Again, Luke could feel her power arc by him. The town seemed to hum. The band members didn't notice anything.

Luke was studying the sigil. "You know, I think the town spell was designed like a Celtic cross."

"So simple, yet so effective," Sadie said, impressed. "Smart witch."

The Kellar Residence

Later, Luke walked Sadie home. He stopped at the edge of the Kellar property and kissed her goodbye. He held her close and whispered to her. "I'll find out what's going on, Sadie, I promise. I'll call you as soon as my dad's meeting is finished." He looked up and saw Liora Kellar glaring at him from the front window. Sadie glanced back with a frown and the curtain twitched closed.

"Be careful, Luke." She kissed him softly on the mouth and drifted out of his arms. He watched until she was in the house before sprinting home to put his plan into action.

The Barrington Estate

Luke wolfed down his food at dinner while his mother looked at him with disapproval. "I didn't realize tonight was a free for all at the Barrington *trough*, Luke," Claire Barrington said frostily.

Luke looked up at his mother, his mouth full of food. He did a good job of swallowing without choking while his siblings looked on with amusement. His father hid a smile behind his napkin.

"Sorry, mom. Got a project to do. I need to get cracking."

John Barrington looked interested. "A project, already? On what?"

"Er, electricity," Luke lied.

Luke's mother snorted. "You could teach a class on what you know about electricity."

"I'm working with Dean," he said lamely.

"Oh, well that explains it," Claire said, as his father nodded, and they continued to eat. "But that doesn't excuse poor table manners, Luke."

"Sorry mom." *Poor Dean, they think he's an idiot.* "May I be excused?" Luke had cleaned his plate in five minutes flat.

She looked disapproving. "For homework, yes."

"Great, gotta go," Luke said, leaping out of his chair and grabbing his schoolbag.

"Be home by eleven o'clock or you're grounded," his father warned.

"Will do," he called as he sped out the front door…and snuck back in the house through one of the main salon windows, which he had left open for that purpose. He closed it quietly and could hear his family chatting in the dining room. Thank God the house was so big. Luke headed for the small broom closet at the back of the room. When the house had servants, this small space had been used for brooms and buckets to clean the main floor. Empty, there was enough space for a teenager to sit with a laptop and stretch out his legs and elbows. Luke had tossed a seat cushion from their outdoor patio set on the floor so his bum wouldn't kill him if he ended up in the closet for hours. The meeting was due to start at seven o'clock sharp and last for at least two hours. He should have plenty of time to report to the others before making his curfew.

Eventually the council members drifted in, greeting each other and chatting. Clinks of glasses and the sound of liquid being poured could be heard through the door. *Those men love their drinks,* Luke thought, shaking his head.

Once the rustling and moving around stopped, John Barrington called the meeting to order by reciting the traditional words of opening, "I call the Barrington County Council Meeting to order. We, the remaining five descendants of the original six, bound together by the shedding of blood, gather to protect our demesnes and the denizens living therein."

Shedding of blood? Luke shuddered.

"Hear hear," the men intoned.

"The Circle is convened. The room is magically sealed. No one can hear our conversation."

Magically sealed? Luke was surprised. *My dad knows magic?*

"Your boy is dating the Kellar girl," Eric Sweet said nastily, "won't it be tough on you if you have to kill his girlfriend?"

Luke froze in horror.

"We are not killing anyone," John Barrington said with a threat in his voice.

Whew!

"We did once," Eric snorted.

"It's one thing to kill a witch that had already murdered two children and was planning a third in order to transform into a powerful demon. It's another thing to kill an innocent human girl because her last name is Kellar," John Barrington said in outrage.

Bill Farmer cleared his throat. "My Hannah says that Sadie Kellar is a witch and that it was her that murdered my sweet cow." He wiped his eyes before he continued. "She says that Kellar girl has bewitched your boy Luke, and that he dances to her tune. Apparently Luke and Hannah were almost an item at the beginning of the summer, but the witch stole him."

Luke was shocked to his very core. *Me and Hannah an item? Stupid, stupid, stupid, unobservant, self-obsessed idiot!* Luke thought to himself furiously. He should have known. Still, why was Hannah lying? *She's supposed to be my friend!* he thought angrily. The broom closet started to feel tiny. He prayed he wouldn't start to hyperventilate.

"Well, she is one pretty girl," Eric said lasciviously.

John spoke harshly. "Watch it Eric. It was *your* ancestor who suffered under Willow Kellar's bewitchment. It has been a source of shame for your family for generations because Alaric bawled like a baby at her hanging. Do not make shameful comments like that here. It's beneath you," he said severely.

"Bah..." Eric said, waving his hand angrily.

Noah Baker spoke up. "I did some research from the last time we met. I'm not sure how the hex can be activated, John. Willow distinctly said, 'gather and die.' That would require a surviving heir of Father Joshua Brown, who according to Dame Parqhuar, presided over the attempted saving of her soul. He was one of the six."

Of course, Luke thought, *the hex! That's why Willow's here!* Luke was floored.

"So, what does that mean?" Daniel Smith asked. He was Noah's best friend and a "one word should sum it up" type of guy.

"I'm getting to that, Dan," Noah said patiently. "Jedidiah Brown was the last surviving child of Joshua's direct line. He died in 1860 of tuberculosis. He was only seventeen."

"Our kids are all seventeen," Bill said musingly.

"Wasn't Joshua a priest?" Eric said snidely. "I thought they weren't supposed to have 'relations' with women, and that they were unclean temptresses."

What an ass, Luke thought to himself.

"According to Jacob, Joshua was married in his teens and lost his wife during childbirth. He didn't want to remarry. He let his sister bring up his son so that he could pursue the priesthood. This was his promise to God if he would let the child live. Apparently, neither of them should have survived," Noah explained.

"Tough," Dan said sympathetically.

"Their loss is our gain," Eric said in his usual unsympathetic way. "Too bad about the family dying out, but that solves our problem."

"We're missing something," John said, shaking his head. "The hex is active, so it's safe to assume that maybe one of Joshua's descendents had a child out of wedlock who exists in this time, near here. Maybe we just don't know about it. There's no other explanation."

That is odd, Luke thought.

"So, you don't really have confirmation, yet you had Holt paint the barns without council approval," Eric tossed out accusingly.

"Yes, I did. It was my right as mayor and owner of Barrington County, and they're going to stay that way—at least until the festival is over on All Saints Day."

Owner? We own the whole county? Luke was shocked for the second time that night.

"It doesn't hurt to be cautious," Noah said quietly.

"Get confirmation, then, Eric. Your son's a computer nerd. See if James can follow the Brown's bloodline."

"Fine," Eric barked.

Lie, Luke thought to himself. He knew Eric was lying. He had no intention of asking James anything.

Luke heard sounds of shuffling and Eric's voice again, "But for now I'm going to The Rotunda for a drink. Who wants to join me?"

"I move to adjourn the meeting," Dan Smith announced.

"I second," said Bill Farmer.

"May we be excused, John?" Eric asked grouchily.

"Meeting adjourned," John said smoothly, releasing the containment spell. The men filed out, but his father didn't leave.

"John," it was his mother. "Sheriff Holt is here to see you."

Luke waited as the Sheriff walked in and closed the door behind him.

"Bit of a ruckus at The Rotunda yesterday," he said calmly. "Some huge tattooed leather dude rallied up a bunch of drunken idiots and hunted a man through the woods all the way to the lake. The man's a wreck. He says they kept screaming 'run skin bag' and were shooting at him from their horses with hunting rifles. He escaped by jumping into the lake. Apparently, the idiots had 'dates' and didn't want to get wet, so they left."

"Do you think they would have harmed him, or was it just macho games?"

"He claims the guy in leather would have done it," the Sheriff said uneasily.

John was shocked. Violence in his town…murder.

"I don't know, John, but I'm not taking any chances. I'm radioing up to Limerick for some additional staff until the festival's done. It's a bit much with just me, my deputy, and the unarmed neighborhood watch."

John asked the dreaded question. "Should we close the festival early this year, Holt?" It had never been done, but this type of thing had never happened before either. He had to consider the safety of the town.

"Number of vendors has swelled, and most folks are paid up until the end of October. Could have a mutiny," the Sheriff replied with a shrug.

"You're right. No need to panic. Do what you need to do, Sheriff," John said grimly.

After the Sheriff left, John shut the light and left the room. Luke burst out of the little cupboard. The small dark space had started giving him the creeps. He took great gulps of fresh air. He couldn't believe what he had just heard. He headed to the door and checked the hallway for adults before heading to his room to call Sadie.

Wednesday, September 4
Barrington School Grounds

The next day the four congregated around a picnic table under the trees far away from the crowds of kids milling around. Dean's little brothers were poking each other with sticks on the Little House's lawn.

Luke looked at them worriedly. "Shouldn't you break that up? One of them could lose an eye."

"Nah, it's inevitable anyway," Dean said casually. Luckily the kindergarten teacher came out and within seconds the boys looked angelic. All signs of the sticks were gone.

"See," Dean waved casually in their direction, "all taken care of."

Nathalie laughed and smacked the back of Dean's head. "Can we focus now?" she asked, drawing everyone's attention back to the matter at hand. Luke had big news, and she wanted to know what it was.

Luke explained how his father had sealed the room, how the council believed the Kellar hex had been activated, and then repeated the actual hex, verbatim.

"'Gather and die?' That's it?" Dean looked disappointed.

Luke snorted. "What? You want more? You want to add some codicils to make it interesting, like... in agony? With a disease?"

"Luke..." Sadie said, horrified.

Nathalie was determined to stay focused. "But you said they confirmed Jedidiah Brown's death in 1860. So if the curse is 'gather and die,' how can you do that without a Brown?"

"He was our age," Sadie said quietly. "Do you realize that every family on the town council has a child that's seventeen?" They all looked at her as she continued. "The town council is made up of five original families that founded Barrington. Not all original families, only five of them. Why? Why are they the lucky ones who run the town and get all the privileges? They are also the only families whose homes were marked with blood, except for the addition of the Crofts. No others. Why add the Crofts?"

Luke spoke slowly. "I remember…the families who eventually became part of the town council were set apart because they were the ones who saw justice prevail on the worst evil that ever affected the town."

"Willow's death. So, they were lauded by the townsfolk then?" Nathalie said.

"No, it's the other way around, actually," Luke explained. "The council was formed by the cursed. They banded together to take the steps needed to protect the town, and themselves. None of the other original families were involved, so I'm not sure why the Crofts are."

"Great," Dean mumbled.

"I looked in the book I bought on Barrington County. The families hexed by Willow aren't listed, so we don't have a confirmed list; however, we can hazard a pretty accurate guess who they were. Our town council plus the Browns."

Sadie nodded. "As confirmed by Mrs. Barrington's list. I looked up the blood marking. It's actually a death sigil. They're used by spells to call the victims. According to Elanah, the blood and the symbol together identify 'the called.' When the call comes, the victims go."

"Great," Dean said again, depressed.

"It makes sense that the family names are omitted," Luke said. "The less information people have, the less possible it is to bring all the parts together to activate the Kellar witch's legacy. It's strategic."

"I think I know how the hex was activated," Sadie interjected. "A couple of things I found out from my aunt last night. She said I was the first female born of the Kellar line since Willow. The rest were boys. So the presence of…well…*my presence* may have been a catalyst. I was brought back to Barrington County just before my first birthday. I do not know what happened to my mother or my father." Sadie sighed.

"I always wondered why your family returned to Barrington, especially considering the town's history and the fame of the Kellar name," Nathalie said curiously.

"I'm glad they did," Luke said with a grin, grabbing Sadie's hand and giving it a loud kiss.

Sadie's lips twitched. "Who knows for sure? I think it was because I was the first female born since Willow."

"I don't know why, but it never occurred to me that Willow had any children, but she must have," Luke said.

Sadie shrugged. "She did, but we have no records. Personal information on Willow or her heirs was hidden or deliberately destroyed. I know I'm descended directly from her, so her heirs were well protected since we've survived. But if I'm the first girl since Willow, then she had a son at some point."

"She was too young for kids. She was twenty-one when she *died*!" Dean exclaimed.

"I don't think that was considered young then," Nathalie mused. "All this havoc and terror from such a young girl. It's too bad. Much of what we know about Willow Kellar is through other people's perceptions and opinions of her. We have nothing from her perspective."

"Didn't she have a diary, Sadie?" Dean asked.

"Yes, she did. She was educated and could write," Sadie confirmed. "She also wrote her grimoire. Trust me, she had to have written that herself. Too bad her diary only records her last couple of years in Barrington. There's no information on her life before that. It may have helped us in some way."

"Anything she wrote would have been burned as a work of the devil. Don't forget 'The Rock.'"

The Rock was the place where the gallows had been lifted to hang and burn Willow Kellar for witchcraft, consorting with the devil, and murder. It was her final resting place as her body burned to ash. The Rock had been engraved with a warning, in Latin, to all those who would follow in her footsteps. It was a chilling monument left by their forebears. No grass grew around it.

Just recently a creepy visit to The Rock became part of the new "Witch-Hunt Excursion," organized by the Social Activities Director of Barrington. It involved participating in a witch hunt, trial, and mock hanging. It was hugely popular because it seemed so real. People returned terrified…and thrilled. The activity was fully booked until Halloween.

"So we have some holes," Dean said.

"Yes, like the dead line of the Browns," Luke reminded them. "We can't explain that."

"We need more information," Nathalie said worriedly. "The question now is…when? When do the signs stop and the action begin?"

Sadie frowned. "I should know this. I feel like I've seen the date, but I just can't remember."

After school, Luke and Sadie were headed home when they were intercepted by a band of school kids on bikes, led by Reg Baker. Reg was the town's loudmouth and was generally harmless, just very annoying in a braying donkey kind of way. Today was no exception.

"Hey, Sadie!" he yelled to the snickering accompaniment of the sycophant idiots around him. "The witch-hunt is a freaking blast! I think it would be even better if we were hunting an actual Kellar," he said, laughing harshly. "It would add a mind blowing level of reality to the game."

"Yeah, and I'd love to chase your ass through the woods, Kellar," said another boy, making lewd gestures at Sadie from his bike.

Luke was shocked and furious, and so was Sadie. She stood stock still, but he could feel power crackling in her hands where their fingers were entwined. Before anything could happen, the boys took off, hooting and yelling like the hooligans they were.

Nearby, Hannah stood in the shadows of an alley and watched, her fingers itching with a story.

The Kellar Residence

When Sadie got home she was still upset.

"It's just Reg," Luke had said soothingly, kissing her on the top of her head. "We all know he's got dough for brains."

Sadie had smiled weakly at his pun, but remained concerned. She had noticed that a few of the townsfolk had subtly made the symbol to ward off evil towards her, one of them being their principal. Hostility towards her family was rising.

Liora was sitting at the kitchen table when Sadie walked in. She took one look at Sadie and grunted. "What's your problem, girl? Did that Barrington scumbag dump you?"

Sadie frowned at her aunt. "No, of course not."

"You should dump him, then. He's not good enough for you," she muttered under her breath. She was drinking tea and the steam from the cup was giving off a peculiar odor.

"Aunt Liora…" Sadie warned.

"All right, all right girl, you made your point about the boy."

Sadie sat down at the table. Her aunt seemed different, almost dreamy. "What are you drinking?"

"It's a special tea for witches," she cackled.

Sadie's look bored into her. "For witches? Why do you say that? Are you being treated differently lately? That ridiculous hunt/show they are putting on... shouldn't we complain about the inappropriateness of it? It doesn't seem to take much to get people, well, riled up these days over silly things. The town feels different, like there's an edge of madness. I'm afraid they'll start believing all that nonsense they're spouting and actually come after us."

Liora looked at Sadie with her dreamy eyes. They were slate gray and moist. "It's not nonsense, you silly girl. We are witches."

"I know, but we're not dangerous."

"Who says, girl. You? *You're* not dangerous. It's embarrassing," she muttered.

Sadie's mouth firmed and she frowned. "What did you do, Aunt Liora? Have you been stirring things up?" she asked warningly.

She jumped as Liora's hand hit the table with a loud slap. "You better believe I have!" she yelled, spittle flying everywhere. "I stirred things up, I did! Make the sign of the devil at me! Ha! I cursed *all* of them! 'BOO!' I screamed at their kids on the street, and did they RUN!" Liora was laughing insanely. "We'll show them! Oh, we'll show ALL OF THEM! Our time is coming, Sadie girl, and there's no stopping it now."

Sadie sat frozen at the table. "When?" she asked quietly. Her heart was beating rapidly in her chest. But her aunt didn't answer her. She was still laughing and slapping her hand on the table. Sadie got up and saw her uncle in the kitchen doorway. She wasn't sure how long he'd been standing there.

"Look at the calendar," he mouthed. He was staring at Liora and frowning.

Of course. The calendar... the Witch's Calendar. The only calendar Liora cared about. Sadie drifted over to the wall where it was pinned. It was just one sheet of all the feasts, solstices, moons, and power cycles. Sadie looked closely. Summer solstice had passed in June. June 21. The next one was... Samhain, one of the times when a witch's power was at its peak. Otherwise known as All Hallows Eve or Halloween.

Sadie went to call Luke but she never made it.

The Fairgrounds

Wayman watched unsmilingly as Barrington's troupe of actors pranced around, exciting the crowd over what they were about to see—the capture of a witch! Her trial and JUSTICE! They spoke in old-fashioned terms, loading the eager show-goers onto the large hay wagon. Their clientele squeezed together and talked excitedly. *This is so wrong*, he thought to himself, but he didn't have a choice.

When Mrs. Throckmorton-Frosst had first approached him about having the "Witch-Hunt Excursion" leave from his stables using his hay wagon and horses, he had said no.

She had been taken aback and looked at him haughtily, jowls shaking above her pearls and pink suit.

"Whatever do you *mean*, my dear man? This is to increase the success of the festival! This show is already so popular that the excursion has already been booked solid through October, and it hasn't even started yet! It's only one show a night, and it occurs after you've closed the stalls for riding," she had blustered.

"My dear lady," he had said winningly, his white teeth spread in a wide grin that made Mrs. Throckmorton-Frosst fan herself. "I understand the success of the festival is key to the town's yearly earnings, however, you are proposing to stage the witch-hunt, trial, and execution of the ancestor of a *current* resident of the town; a resident that just so happens to be a friend of mine."

Mrs. Throckmorton-Frosst huffed. "I know very well that the Kellars are residents, but they have claimed no relationship to the witch, so the point is moot. Also, I'll have you know that this is a... historical reenactment! It's the history that made this town famous and people have the right to come for miles to be chilled and horrified by it!"

Wayman had disagreed and politely sent Mrs. Throckmorton-Frosst away in a huff. Unfortunately, she appeared later that day, like a bad penny, but with Eric Sweet in tow.

"Mr. Wayman..." she began—

"It's just Wayman," he said smiling at her. She fluttered a little. "Oh my," she muttered.

Eric rolled his eyes. "Look, 'just Wayman,'" he said condescendingly, looking around the stable with derision, "the activity WILL go on. The festival council has made their decision, and you'll abide by it."

Wayman's green eyes glowed as they met Eric's, and he seemed to flicker.

"Got it?" Eric asked disparagingly. He was fingering a gold coin and tossing it into the air nonchalantly. "Something wrong with your eyes?"

Wayman frowned. "No, and that's a bad penny my friend," he said casually, noticing the markings.

"Not planning on spending it," Eric said carelessly. "I think we're done here," he said, turning away to leave.

"It's not a good idea to reenact the terrible evil that has happened in a town. It could have serious repercussions," Wayman said warningly.

"Luckily we're not a superstitious bunch," Eric called back in a bored voice as he headed into the fair, and towards Beth's booth.

Mrs. Throckmorton-Frosst followed quickly. "The show will start the last Friday of August. The sets are being built right now Mr.…ah…Wayman."

He frowned at the memory and watched as the hay wagon lurched away. The show was hugely popular. The wagon was full to the brim every night. He turned to reenter the barn when he caught a flash of movement from the corner of his eye. He turned and watched grimly as a show straggler caught up to the wagon and hopped on. The people were tightly packed together, but they made space for the newcomer, seemingly unconsciously. The figure was wearing a black hooded cloak. The flash had come from the metal on the necklace she was wearing. He was startled to realize that she was staring at him. Her glowing violet eyes were narrowed and filled with fury and hatred. She knew he could see her and she bared her teeth at him just before the wagon disappeared into the woods.

Sadie. No, not Sadie. Someone else. Someone vicious.

"THAT'S what I was afraid of," Wayman whispered and sprinted to get Taline.

The Barrington Bugle Newspaper Office

Hannah laughed as she typed her letter to the editor. She wrote furiously to make tomorrow's edition.

THE BARRINGTON BUGLE - THURSDAY, SEPTEMBER 5
Letters to the Editor

Dear Editor:

Strange things are happening in Barrington that defy explanation! Many of our citizens have been having a run of bad luck. People have been walking under ladders and having accidents. Milk is curdling after one day, even in the refrigerator. People are picking up cursed pennies and are bewitched into doing evil things. A black cat crosses your path and something bad happens immediately afterwards! Don't forget, they are traditionally used as a witch's familiar. When will this town realize what's happening? We know who's behind this! Let's have a real witch hunt. Let's hunt the cause of our problems through the woods and make her confess to her witchcraft. Has she not bewitched the son of her mortal enemy? The son of our Mayor, the most powerful man in Barrington! If he were in his right mind, there is no way a Barrington would be dating a witch whose ancestor his family burned! No, he has been seduced by the devil's temptress. Beware before ruin comes to us all!

-Anonymous

THE BARRINGTON BUGLE - THURSDAY, SEPTEMBER 5
Special Late Afternoon Supplement

Witch Hunt Excursion Cursed! Spectators Almost Die After Trial!

By X. Agerate

It was a horrifying event for many who attended the witch-hunt excursion last night. According to organizers, after Willow is sentenced to die as a witch, the spectators (who play the jurors) are supposed to follow the Kellar witch (played by our own lovely Rose

Bane) to the gallows screaming "burn her!" Everything is done by torchlight and the hanging and the burning are, surprisingly, realistic. However, things took a strange turn when everyone in the crowd started suffocating or screaming they were on fire.

"It was unreal," said a gum cracking teen from Limerick, "but it was cool."

Not everyone found it exciting. "I felt chills the whole time during the trial, like icy fingers on my neck," said Ms. Bea Little, also from Limerick. "I noticed lots of people rubbing their necks. When we left the juror box and started to play our part, that's when I started to suffocate. It was terrifying."

Mr. Mike R. Phone claims he was on fire. "I swear I was on fire. I don't have any marks, but I was on fire. It really hurt and I dropped my beer. I never drop my beer."

According to Dr. Leo Tauran, a prominent Limerick psychic, he suspects the spectators were so psyched for what they were going to go through on the excursion that they all underwent what he calls a "communal psychic event." Tauran says this is common. "Even though the event isn't 'real' people develop mob mentality, which goes against today's societal norms, causing deep stress. This stress manifests itself physically through 'ghost pain,' like what was experienced during this communal event. They channeled Willow's agony."

During the panic and pandemonium, the gallows did catch on fire and burn to the ground. Luckily, new gallows were put up immediately, so the show will go on tonight.

Again, do we need to remind our visitors of the dangers of smoking in the woods?!

Thursday, September 5
Barrington School Grounds

Luke was frantic. Sadie was not in school and he couldn't reach her on her cell phone. She hadn't met him at their usual spot to walk to school together. He had waited as long as he could before he ran to school, hoping she'd be there.

"I'm sure she's fine," Nathalie said, but not before Luke caught the worried glance she darted at Dean. It was not like Sadie to be late, or to not call.

Luke agonized during morning classes. By lunch he was ready to explode with anxiety.

"Where are you going?" Dean yelled as Luke streaked by their usual lunch table.

"I'm going to the Kellar's to check on Sadie," he shouted.

Austin Baker was walking by as Luke ran past. He stopped by Dean and Nathalie's table. "Sadie was at the Witch-Hunt Excursion last night. I saw her getting on the hay wagon just as it was leaving," he commented before walking off.

"Last night?" Dean asked curiously. He turned to Nathalie. "I wonder why she didn't say anything to Luke?"

"Maybe it wasn't Sadie," Nathalie said meaningfully.

"Shit, that's not good."

The Kellar Residence

Luke arrived at the Kellar's farmhouse sweaty and out of breath. He ran to the front door and banged on it. Liora Kellar opened the door a crack, glaring at him. "What do you want, boy?" she asked him spitefully.

"Is Sadie home? Is she okay?" he asked fearfully, talking a step back as Liora started to grin, her yellow teeth rimmed with spittle. She looked crazy.

"Sadie is just fine, boy. Just a little under the weather. Go away." She slammed the door in his face.

Liora watched as Luke walked away slowly, glancing back like a wounded dog, worry written all over his face.

"Fool," Liora hissed.

"Is that the Barrington boy?" Sadie's voice asked from the kitchen. She was sitting at the table, but the cruel expression and the derision dripping from her voice instantly confirmed that the person speaking was not Sadie at all. "Luckily I'm getting stronger. I can hold her for longer periods now. Soon I won't need to gather my strength and wait for a weak moment to take her." Willow flexed her hands in front of her. "I can't tap her power completely yet, though power rolls through her like a lava storm waiting to erupt. Soon...soon I will be strong enough to use all of it. I touched it last night, and it was marvelous, incredible. Look what I achieved! People choking and burning—enjoying some of my last mortal sensations. I could have murdered them all!" Willow's face filled with fury. "Imagine, the Witch-Hunt Excursion!" she hissed. "Every last person who participated will feel my wrath and suffer what I suffered."

"You'll get your chance, Willow. Not long now," Liora said ingratiatingly, pouring tea.

"That boy is a nuisance. He's just like Jacob. You can't hide from the true sight of the Barringtons, Liora. You must keep him away from me."

"He already knows what's happening," Liora said, putting another cup of the fragrant tea in front of Willow. "Sadie has told that boy everything."

"That is fine, Liora, just keep *us* apart. When his emotions run strong, so do hers, and she's harder to manage." Willow pushed the tea away. "This won't help anymore. She awakens and she's strong. Soon! Prepare the way, Liora. My host and my refuge must be ready!" Willow said firmly before crumpling to the table.

Barrington School Grounds

When Luke got back to school, the kids accosted him. "Hey Barrington! Looks like your girlfriend's a jinx!"

Luke grabbed a paper from a passing student and started riffling through it.

"Look in the 'Letters to the Editor' section," Nathalie said quietly. Luke flipped to the page and read the small, mean letter. "Anonymous, again. What kind of person writes that?"

"And what is Heimler thinking, allowing that to be printed?" Nathalie asked angrily.

"Did you find Sadie?" Dean asked, putting a hand on his friend's shoulder.

"Liora says she's sick, but I think she's lying."

"Maybe she's upset about the paper..."

"Sadie only reads the paper at lunch or later. It's not delivered to her house, so she gets a copy on her way in."

"Oh, it's just that her episodes are triggered when she gets upset. At least she becomes more vulnerable..."

Tess came by and gave Nathalie a hug before turning to Luke. "I was just at the fairgrounds and Wayman gave me this for you," she said, handing him a note.

"Call me," she mimed to Nathalie as she walked away.

"What does it say?" Nathalie asked.

"He wants me to go and see him after school. He says...oh no... he saw Sadie last night too, and we need to talk."

"So Austin wasn't full of shit the little...shit," Dean muttered.

Nathalie smacked him. "He's not the ass, Dean, it's his brother. Don't take it out on him."

"Ass-ed-ness runs in families," Dean muttered.

"Excuse me, you three," a disdainful voice said behind their backs. They turned around to find the principal staring at them, his hands behind his back, and a look of inquiry on his face. The rest of the area was empty. "Perhaps you think the rules don't apply to you? Hmmm? Yes? The bell rang five minutes ago. Perhaps you would deign to join your fellow students for afternoon classes? Hmmm? You think?" Then he frowned. "March!" he barked at them.

Luke crumpled the note and put it in his pocket as the three of them hurried into the school.

The Fairgrounds

The afternoon seemed to take forever. Luke fidgeted until his English teacher asked in exasperation if he had ants in his pants. When the school bell rang, Luke dashed out of the school.

"Wait up, Luke!" Dean yelled, sprinting after him.

Nathalie stayed behind to make sure the twins were headed home with Ella before heading to the fair herself.

When she arrived the boys were talking with Wayman in the barn.

"Wayman, are you sure it was her? Why didn't you call me right away?" Luke asked.

"It was her all right, physically anyway." Wayman smiled in welcome at Nathalie as she walked in, and she got that peculiar buzzing in her head that she always experienced around him.

"And the reason I didn't call you is because the being possessing Sadie is evil. Murderously evil and furiously angry. Hate bleeds out of her. Sadie is one powerful witch, and that being would have murdered everyone at that show, including you. Especially you. However, it's obvious she has not fully tapped into Sadie's power. I'm telling you, I haven't seen a witch that powerful since…"

"Since?" Luke prompted, curious.

"Well, a really long time. When the witch hunters burned witches in the late fifteen hundreds, most of them weren't actually witches. Some were, of course, but they weren't the smart ones. The powerful ones hid and worked their magic under the cover of night. The arrogant ones were caught. The rest were just regular women, victims of jealousy, spite, and superstition mostly."

"Wayman, we've confirmed that Sadie is being possessed by her ancestor, Willow Kellar. We are also certain she's invoking her hex and trying to bring it about."

Wayman nodded, as if none of this was a surprise. "The signs are there. Taline and I thought the same thing."

Nathalie was curious about a couple of things. "How did you guess?"

"We're not from around here, honey," Taline said softly as she came up behind Nathalie and gave her a hug. "It takes a lot of energy to get us here from where we…live."

Dean looked confused, but Luke nodded. "I suspected as much," he said simply. "You're Fae, Faerie, what many call the old folk."

Wayman bowed. "Mr. Seer with the true sight."

"I'm confused," said Dean, putting a voice to his expression.

"We're not human, Dean. Mortals call us the Fae or Fairy Folk. To put is simply, we live in a different realm, but we can interact with people and live on earth," Taline said quietly.

"Oh God," Dean groaned.

"Our story's for another time," Wayman said firmly.

"So, what do I do about Sadie, Wayman?" Luke asked softly.

"Willow is still not strong enough to hold Sadie for long. Sadie is too powerful in her own right. What we don't want is for Willow to hurt Sadie while she's in control of the body…" Wayman hesitated.

"Are you saying I should stay away from her?" Luke asked in a tight voice.

Taline walked over and put her arm around his shoulders. "Luke, Willow Kellar hates you. It's not only because you can see her, and possibly interfere with her plans. Your ancestor executed her in a humiliating, terrifying, and painful way and ruined what she was trying to accomplish. There is no distinction for her between you and Jacob. You are a Barrington and she wants you dead."

Wayman looked towards the woods. The hay wagon was ready for the evening's festivities. "What you need to be aware of is that all of these events are generating an energy around Barrington that is growing exponentially. When your father painted the town barns, and Sadie invoked Elanah's ancient spell, she magically sealed the town and trapped the energy here. Without the spell, the energy would diffuse and spread to the other two counties."

"So?"

"The spell is designed to protect two towns—Limerick and Superstition. For some reason this was of paramount importance, controlling the energy of Willow's hex," Wayman said.

Nathalie was piecing the puzzle together. "Energy...the spell doesn't do anything for Barrington. I'll bet that the spell has to do with that demon, Dannerlich, who bothered me and left his calling cards around town."

"Yes, he's imprisoned in Superstition. We were able to confirm that before the barn spell was activated," Taline said, "but now our means of accessing information has been cut off, so we have to speculate, just like you."

"Internet's up," Dean said quizzically.

Taline laughed and looked at Dean affectionately. "It's not the Internet Dean."

Nathalie was thinking furiously. She watched as Nettie left the bake table and headed over to the barn.

"One of the towns is a red herring," Nathalie said decisively. "This spell only really needs to protect one town, the other one is just to throw us off. The town in danger from energy is Superstition."

Dean snorted. "They don't even have electricity now. Why would more power be a bad thing?"

"The question to ask is why does Superstition avoid electricity—one of the most incredible power sources of your time?" Nettie asked quietly. "When and why did they choose to live like that?"

Nathalie answered. "Because power is power...magical or electrical...energy in any form obviously has an effect, most likely negative if they refuse to use it. If they thought the hex would create great energies, they would want to protect Superstition from it."

"Protect what, though?" Luke asked.

Nathalie shrugged. "It has to do with Dannerlich. I know it does, but I don't know why."

"We need to find out when Superstition was founded, why there, and by whom. That, at least, will give us a time frame," Dean suggested.

Nathalie nodded. She hoped Rain would find some information that answered their questions.

Taline looked at Luke. "Now about Sadie…you're going to have to wait until she comes around and she's herself again," she said gently. Luke looked crushed.

"And be warned, lad. The witch's power will only grow stronger as the days get shorter and the year moves on to Samhain. That is a very powerful night for a witch. The veil is thin and evil is at its height, as will be her power," Nettie said ominously.

Dean shook his head. "I just don't get it. We've gone over the hex, the facts. The Browns don't have a living descendent of the line, so how can this be continuing?"

Nettie smiled grimly. "Never underestimate Willow Kellar, my boy. She always has means and a plan. Men would have killed for that slip of a girl."

Nathalie looked at Nettie strangely. "You always speak as if you knew her personally."

Nettie laughed. "Och, when you've lived with a story as long as I have, lassie, everything seems personal."

"So how does the demon fit into all this? Why is he here? What does he want?" Dean wondered.

No one had an answer, but Nathalie had a thought. "Well, we know he's trapped and very bored. I'll bet you Beth knows. I'll bet you Beth knows a lot more than she lets on."

"Maybe she picked up one of those coins…" Dean said, looking beyond the barn to where Beth was giving out her free drinks.

"Maybe she's *giving out* his coins," Wayman said meaningfully. "That would explain where Eric Sweet got the coin he was tossing in the air. From what I understand, he's one of her most faithful patrons and he frequents her booth regularly," he said with disgust.

"The guy's an ass," Luke said suddenly, remembering what Sweet had said about Sadie at the last town council meeting.

"Luke, let us know when Sadie calls you," Nathalie said abruptly. "I'm going to find Clara Innes. It seems to me that things started to go wrong when Bethiah came to town. I'm going to check when Beth arrived exactly, and how she's paying her rent now that the candy factory is closed."

"And that's the other question. Where is Shaemus?" Dean wondered out loud.

Wayman laughed. "He's Irish. The man ran. The Irish know what to do when strange comes to town. I'm sure he's in Limerick, and he hasn't been sober since July."

"Watch out, guys. Trust no one. You never know who's holding a gold coin these days," Taline warned.

Luke headed home and Nathalie made a beeline for Clara's little booth. She was in luck. Clara was there arguing with her favorite person, Father MacGunne.

"Hello, Father," Nathalie said respectfully.

"Why, hello Nathalie me darlin'," Father MacGunne replied with a smile and a twinkle in his eye.

"I don't think callin' her *darlin'* is proper for a priest to be sayin'," Clara said primly, her r's rolling from her thick Irish accent.

"And what on earth do you know about what's proper?" Father MacGunne said loudly. "You're a right heathen with those tarot cards and crystals!"

Clara snorted and Nathalie smiled. Father MacGunne winked at the two of them before heading out. "I'll leave you to your girl talk."

"An' I don't think winking is appropriate either!" Clara yelled after him. He just waved before disappearing in the afternoon crowd.

"I didn't mean to interrupt," Nathalie said shyly. She loved Clara and her shop. The woman herself was a gem.

"Och, it's no matter. He's no good for business anyway, always preachin' and starin' disapproval at me customers. What can I help you with love?"

"I wanted to talk to you about your tenant."

Clara was stringing crystals onto leather necklaces and hanging them up to display. She stopped to look at Nathalie. "My what, now?"

"Your tenant...boarder...the girl who's renting the apartment above your shop."

Clara looked at Nathalie as if she had grown a third eye. "Love, what are you talking about? I don't have a boarder, and I wouldn't rent my apartment...it's not permitted."

Right...strange Barrington law...no graveyards or hotels. No ghosts no strangers.

"Oh, my mistake. I was quite sure that she told me she was staying at your place."'

"Who, lassie?"

"Why..." Nathalie turned and pointed to Beth. "That girl over there."

Clara turned to look at Beth and frowned. "I don't believe we've met. I've only ever seen her here, at the fair. She certainly isn't renting my apartment."

"Oh." Nathalie was flustered. "I'm so sorry to have bothered you for nothing, Clara. My misunderstanding... how silly of me."

"Pay it no mind," Clara said easily. A client walked up and Clara waved as Nathalie walked off. She turned to look at Beth and found her smiling slyly at her. Nathalie just turned and headed home.

Town Circle—The Apartment above Clara's Crafts & Crystals

Nathalie's question had made Clara curious. She hadn't been up to her apartment since she bought her house the previous year. She took out her ring of keys as she climbed the metal stairs to her old place. *Brings back some good memories,* she thought as she searched for the one she needed. Clara found the key and opened the door.

Friday, September 6
Barrington School Grounds

That morning Sadie was waiting for Luke at their regular spot to walk together to school. When he saw her he sprinted towards her and wrapped her tightly in his arms. Her arms tightened around him and she sagged against him. She looked exhausted and felt so frail that he felt he could crush her as easily as a delicate bird. He kissed the top of her head. "What happened?" he whispered fearfully.

"Later, after school. We need to talk," she whispered.

"Okay," he whispered back.

They held hands as they walked along Town Circle to school.

Sadie looked pale and tired. "The date is Halloween. That's the day Willow plans to unleash the hex. For witches it's the festival of Samhain, a very powerful night for us. I can't believe I didn't think about it. To top it all off, the witches' calendar is hanging up in my kitchen." Sadie frowned. "I'm not myself, Luke. I'm usually smarter than that." A ghost of a smile crossed her face. "I have to be able to keep up with my genius boyfriend."

Luke laughed and after cutting through the alley beside Joe's Java, he danced her through the trees. They had so many worries, but Sadie was here, now, and all he wanted to do was kiss her, so he did.

Luke's lips were warm. She savored them and locked the memory away in her heart. She wanted more than a kiss. She wanted to devour him.

"We can skip school... go to our secret place," he whispered to her.

Sadie shook her head. "I need to make an appearance. Did you see the paper yesterday?"

Luke clutched his bag. "Yeah, that one anonymous writer who hates you is really getting under my skin. I just can't imagine what their motivation is."

"They're motivated by gold," Nathalie said meaningfully, waving the paper in the air as she walked towards them. "It's the demon's influence, like Mr. Sweet's bullying of Wayman. I'm sure the person who is writing those letters owns a gold coin."

"Then there's the event from Wednesday night..." Sadie said quietly.

Nathalie looked at her. "Was that..."

"Me," Sadie confirmed. "Well, not me, but I was physically there."

"Wayman saw you," Dean mentioned as he joined them.

Sadie turned to Luke. "The most important thing right now is finding out who is writing the hate mail. This ridiculous author is turning the town mean. Besides being accosted by Reg and the idiot squad, our home was defaced with excrement last night. 'Die witches' was written on our front door. The *last* thing we need right now is all this attention. Luke, Hannah works for the paper. Can you ask her if she knows who it is, or at least help us find out who it is?"

Luke looked uncertain. He hadn't told anyone about Hannah's lies because he had wanted to speak to her first in case her father had been exaggerating. But broaching this would be a good test. His expression changed to one of determination. *Let's see what kind of friend she really is.* "Absolutely, that's a great idea my sweet... and she's over there! Hannah! Wait up!" Luke yelled, yanking Sadie along behind him. Nathalie watched as Hannah turned slowly and reluctantly.

"Hannah! Just a quick question for you! We need your help!" Luke said in a non-threatening voice. Hannah looked at Sadie and their eyes met briefly before she turned and acknowledged Luke.

"I don't really have time..."

"It'll just take a minute," Luke said seriously. "The letters to the editor, do you have any idea who's writing those lies or why someone would want to hurt Sadie?"

Hannah's eyes flicked to Sadie quickly before she shrugged. "Sadie's name is never mentioned. Anyway, I don't know who the author is. It's probably just sensationalism to build interest in the town." She turned to go.

Lie! Luke thought to himself incredulously.

"Why does Heimler allow it?" Sadie asked pointedly.

"Ask Heimler," Hannah replied in an unfriendly voice.

Luke grabbed her arm to stop her from leaving. "We won't tell, Hannah," Luke said reassuringly.

She shrugged him off. "Sorry, I wish I could help," she muttered before she left.

"Lie!" he said out loud this time. "Some friend," he muttered, hurt from her betrayal in his voice.

"She was lying," Sadie said. She was clutching her necklace. It was hard to see in the sun, but it was hot and glowing.

"What? What was she lying about?" Nathalie asked, her voice tinged with dismay.

"Everything," Sadie said grimly. "She was lying about everything. She knows exactly what's happening at the paper."

Luke turned to go after her, but Nathalie stopped him. "Luke, leave her be. She's not going to be reasonable right now."

"Why not? Sadie's in trouble. Hannah's our friend and should help us. We'd help her."

Nathalie sighed audibly now. "Because she doesn't *want* to help *Sadie*, Luke," she said with emphasis.

He knew that. He just wished it wasn't true.

THE BARRINGTON BUGLE - SATURDAY, SEPTEMBER 7

LETTERS TO THE EDITOR

Dear Editor:

About Xander's article, "Witch Hunt Cursed." The only thing cursed around here is Xander's writing. "Dr." Leo Tauran is full of shit. This paper is going to Hell! Who on earth is allowing these retards to write in our newspaper? I'll tell you how stress is going to manifest for Tauran-it'll manifest as pain when I kick him in the ass for spouting all this crap.

-Dr. Lance Peabody

```
Dear Editor:
    Dr. Leo Tauran is wrong. An uninvited
guest was at the event that night and she
planned to kill everyone. She's just not
powerful enough yet. Beware…the witch grows
stronger every day. Get her before she gets
us. Burn her!
-Anonymous
```

Sunday, September 8
Town Circle

After church, Sadie met Luke, Nathalie and Dean to have breakfast at The Rotunda. They chatted as they ate, enjoying the weather. Before parting ways, the four agreed to rendezvous at the fair after supper.

Luke and Sadie went for a walk and looked forward to a day to themselves, *alone*. They walked hand in hand. It was beautiful outside, warm and sunny, the perfect late summer day.

They walked the paths in Town Circle Park, now lover free, and eventually came out across from Pages Bookstore. They crossed over to look in the window, but Luke didn't want to linger in town.

"Let's go to our spot," Luke said.

They walked slowly towards the Barrington Estate. The mood was somber. Luke kept looking at Sadie's face. It was set and determined. Luke sighed. *There's going to be a fight,* he thought to himself. Their talk on Friday had not gone well.

As they walked around, Luke began to notice that people were making signs to ward off evil, and muttering to themselves. They were looking at Sadie. Luke stopped in shock as an old lady spit onto the street in front of Joe's Java. He looked at Sadie and she was standing stiffly, her chin notched up a bit higher.

"Strega!" The old lady hissed. "Witch!"

"Are you kidding me?" Luke yelled as another man walked by and made the sign. "Are you all ignorant assholes?" he yelled in anger.

Sadie's face tightened. Luke never used language like that. He was changing for the worse… because of her. She wanted to cry.

People dropped their heads as they walked by. Joe Curtis came out of the coffee house. "Move along," he growled at a few of the gawkers. He looked at Luke. "No point in yelling in the street, Barrington. Ignorance is a disease that spreads even to smart people." He looked at Sadie. "You be careful now, Miss Kellar. The talk I'm hearing in the house is not very friendly. People aren't reasonable these days. That anonymous letter writer in the newspaper isn't helping, either."

A server came out with two coffees and some pastry to go. Joe handed them to Luke and Sadie and disappeared back into his establishment.

"See, Sadie, an act of kindness. Not everyone in this town is against you," Luke said encouragingly.

They picked up their pace until they were safely on the Barrington Estate. They headed to their spot where they laid out their blanket and sat down. Sadie spread herself out on the blanket and closed her eyes. Luke sipped his coffee and explored the bag of pastries. Eying her, he took out the largest one he could find. "Eat it," he commanded, pulling her up. "You're all bones, baby, and you need your strength to fight." She eyed the pastry dubiously, but took it.

They ate and drank their coffees, which were strangely fortifying. Eventually it was time to talk, again.

Sadie cleared her throat and brushed the crumbs off her dress. "We need to break up, Luke," she managed to say matter-of-factly even though her heart was breaking inside. Luke fell back onto the blanket and put his arm over his eyes. Sadie turned and lay on top of him. She kissed him softly and found herself suddenly underneath him, his heavy warmth pressing her against the ground as he kissed her. His mouth was warm and his tongue heavy as it slid against hers. Sadie moaned and tightened her arms around him. When he broke the kiss Sadie was panting. He burrowed his face into her neck and kissed her delicate, white skin.

"I know Willow hates me, Sadie. I know that my presence angers her because of what Jacob Barrington did to her. But I don't want us to be apart. I'm so afraid we'll never be together again," he whispered into her neck. "I love you. With you I'm complete. I don't want to be a half person anymore." He sounded so sad, and she could feel wet tears from his eyes roll down her neck.

Tears were leaking out of Sadie's eyes too, but she didn't relent.

"It's only until this is over, Luke. Willow thinks I'm dormant when she takes over now, but I'm not. I'm quiet, but I can see and feel what she does. Her emotions go beyond hate, Luke. Before she died she was using her magic to transform herself into a demon so she could have eternal life. She hates humanity like the fallen angels did. I've never felt anything that strong before. People hurt her and took her life from her, and this started way before Jacob Barrington came along and finished the job. She'll hurt you and me. Once she gets her way, she'll take my body permanently, but even that's temporary, I've just found out. Once she transforms she won't need a physical body anymore." Sadie sighed. "She has to see me as valuable and not just as a Barrington boy's girlfriend, and therefore someone to *despise*. She is so angry that my loyalty is with you—her own flesh and blood! The passage of time has no meaning to her, only achieving her goal. I need to placate her. She has to believe my allegiance is to her."

Luke was silent, but then he sat up, pulling Sadie with him. He wrapped his arms around her. "Wayman is worried about the same thing," he admitted quietly. "He believes Willow will hurt you because you've made a poor choice in boyfriends," Luke winced at that, "but really to strike at a Barrington to make one suffer."

"Things are going to get worse, with the townsfolk as well. There's a witch craze going on. It's not rational, like Joe said, but that's what's happening. People are starting to believe what we would normally consider nonsense. Of course, the irony is..."

"It's actually true?" Luke finished.

"Yes," Sadie said with a laugh.

"So, if this event is inevitable, this hex, then we need to change our tactics and do everything in our power to sabotage it and stop it."

"Exactly, so I'm going to spy on the other side, go deep under cover," Sadie said. "I'm sick of being used. I'm going to show her a thing or two, myself."

"So tonight..."

Sadie shook her head. "I won't be going. I suspect that once Willow is strong enough, she'll be able to access my knowledge and memories and use them against you. Better I know nothing from now on. I'm going to need to bury this conversation somewhere deep."

"So, just until Halloween..."

"Luke, you are the smartest boy I know. Nathalie is proving to be unusually perceptive. I have no doubt that together you two will figure this out. I'm expecting that All Saint's Day will be our first date after we destroy that witch."

Luke nodded. His face was bleak.

"I'm not gone yet, though," Sadie said as she pushed him back down on the blanket.

The Fairgrounds

Wayman and Taline watched from the stable as Beth distributed drinks and flirted with the men lined up for their free cup.

"There is something wrong with that girl," Wayman muttered. "I just can't put my finger on it."

"She has definitely been tampered with somehow. Damn this hex. Since it was put in motion, and the town sealed, I can't see. It's like I'm blind," Taline complained. "She must have a glamour."

"We couldn't see anything before," Wayman growled in frustration.

Taline shifted over, her long silvery hair swaying. She kissed Wayman on the neck, pressed her front to his back and wrapped her arms around his waist. She looked at Beth carefully. "I feel mortal."

Wayman just laughed.

Then something interesting happened.

"Hellooo," Wayman said in surprise as he watched a large, leather clad man elbow his way through Beth's line.

"Oh my God, Wayman, is that Venius?" Taline asked in shock, stepping out from behind Wayman to get a better look. "I thought he was banished."

"He was," Wayman said grimly. "I didn't know he had come through."

"Me neither. He's hard to miss. Where has he been?"

"Probably hiding in shadows . . . and hunting. I should have known when they reported it in the newspaper," Wayman said.

People were grumbling as Venius stopped and looked at Beth. He grabbed her arm and she laughed. "Take over for me," she yelled to one of the girls near her and she allowed herself to be dragged off.

"That can't be good," Wayman said. "Stay here."

Wayman followed the couple discreetly as they left the fairgrounds and entered the encircling woods. Wayman watched as Venius looked briefly at Beth before waving his hand in front of her face and giving her a kiss. Setting a human "no-see" spell around them, he set Beth against a tree, and lifting her skirt, started thrusting himself into her like a power drill. Beth moaned and wrapped her arms and legs around him while Venius grunted as he worked his hips. Within minutes she gasped and he roared, his eyes glowing blue as he ejaculated. She lay against him bonelessly, and they stayed like that for a few minutes before he withdrew and set her on her feet.

"Okay?" he asked in his guttural voice.

"Okay," she replied.

Venius took her in his arms and kissed her thoroughly before disappearing into the woods. Beth smiled for a brief minute and looked into the air, but before Wayman could check what she was looking at, Beth gave a frustrated "oooh!" and stomped angrily back to the fair.

Wayman was shocked. Intercourse, public or private, was something he was used to with his race, but a kiss? *Venius kissing?* Something was definitely up with that girl, and very wrong with Venius.

When he arrived back, Taline was waiting impatiently. "So?"

"She's pleasuring him..."

"Oh," Taline said losing interest. *Big deal.*

"But...he kissed her."

That got her attention. "WHAT? That's *impossible*! Venius is..."

"I know, but he just *made out* with her like a mortal teenager. He asked her if she was okay! I am completely freaked out myself, to use a human expression."

Taline spread her arms out and tilted her head back. Power rolled along her arms. "I think I just figured something out."

In the evening, when Dean and Nathalie arrived, Wayman had just watched the hay wagon head off for the Witch-Hunt Excursion. "Playing with fire," Wayman muttered.

Luke arrived without Sadie.

"What happened?" Dean asked

"Sadie and I broke up."

"What! Man, what's she thinking?" Dean asked angrily.

"It's the right decision," Nathalie said to Luke, with sympathy.

Luke nodded.

"The timing is wrong for both of you to be together in every way, publicly and privately," she added.

Wayman nodded his agreement and his eyes shone with approval as he looked at Luke.

Luke basked in the glow.

"It'll look like you deserted her, especially after all the press she's been getting. They'll call you 'Bastard Barrington,'" Dean said.

"I'll support that one hundred percent. Display her as the victim," Nathalie said. "Maybe she'll catch a break and finally get some empathy from this town."

A true friend, Luke thought, pleased. "That's a wonderful idea, Nat. Sadie will get some sympathy...let's hope this works in her favour. Right now she needs all the help she can get," he said worriedly, remembering the hate coming from the old woman. "It's only until Halloween," he added.

"So she confirmed the date," Wayman said.

"Yes, the date's important on the witches' calendar, and to Willow as well. She needs to be at the height of her power to pull this off."

"God, why do we have to wait? Just get it over with," Dean whined grouchily. The constant tension and worry was draining.

"The time has to be auspicious, young Mr. Croft," Nettie answered as she entered the barn with a plate of cookies.

"Sadie broke up with me," Luke said mournfully, reaching for the goodies.

"Smart lass," Nettie replied briskly, smacking his hand as he tried to take the plate.

Luke rubbed his hand and looked at her balefully.

"She has her part to play, and she's going to do it. You do yours," Nettie said sternly.

"What's mine? What help can I be?" Luke asked in despair, reaching and taking one cookie.

"You mean you don't know? Och, laddie, are ya dense? You see true, dontcha? Aren't you The Seer? Do you not have the gift of true sight as passed down from your ancestor, Jacob?"

"Er..." Question marks seemed to be popping out around Luke's head.

"Have you not seen Willow with Sadie plain as day?"

"Yes...funny that, I thought I was going crazy. You know, geniuses..."

"Pah! The rest of us just see Sadie, that's why no one suspects anything's wrong, least of all possession. You can see the other entity. Nothing is hidden from you. It's the gift of true sight, ye have."

Luke was thinking furiously. "She called me that, on the library steps. She called me The Seer."

Nettie nodded. "One of the reasons Willow hates you is because she can't get away with things under your nose. It was the same with Jacob. It was verra disorienting for him at the beginning, to be sure. He had the true sight. Good thing too as Willow had bewitched half the council to believe her..."

Again Nathalie looked at her strangely. Wayman caught the look and cleared his throat. "Well, enough with the history lesson, Nettie my dear."

"Och, of course, ahem. Didn't mean to bore... Just one more bit of history to clear up. The Seer always has a chronicler, a Lore Keeper. Not blessed with true sight of course, but one able to put the pieces of the puzzle together, and one who can't be bewitched. A strategist I believe you'd call it now."

"That's me," Nathalie said quietly. "We're a pair, just like Jacob and Dame Parqhuar were. Luke and I are paired." She knew it in her bones.

"As it should be. The curse is meant for revenge, so the circumstances have to be the same."

"Do you mean she's going to kill more children?"

"Och, no. She's marked her people for death. She has touched them all in some way, and marked their homes with blood."

"Sadie's dance around the square," Luke breathed as realization struck.

Nathalie was looking at Nettie suspiciously. "How do you know so much? You're a stranger."

"Hmmmph," was Nettie's reply.

"Well, to Barrington, anyway," Nathalie amended apologetically.

"As Wayman said, I have a knack for history, and keeping up with current events is not hard. Lots of talk around the ovens at the bakery... gossip at the fair. A daily newspaper full of interesting tidbits."

"Hmmmph," was Nathalie's reply.

"There's something else you should all be aware of," Taline said seriously. "Since the hex was set in motion, the town has changed."

"Yeah, I'll say," Dean replied.

"People are wild, and now they're getting violent," Luke said, looking toward the fair crowds.

"They're also more... how shall I say it... amorous?" Taline asked archly. Startled, they all turned red and she laughed. "I know this because Wayman just saw an emotionally dead being kiss a human girl."

"So?" Dean said curiously.

"Kissing is... very private for us. It's an act of love that means more than sex. Now, I don't want the details of your love lives, trust me. But Willow used sex as a means to an end. In the 1590's she would have been considered a scarlet woman and shunned."

"Aye, if it weren't for the powerful spell she had cast so people wouldn't pay attention to what she was doing."

"Except she couldn't fool the strategist in town. Am I right, Nettie?" Nathalie asked pointedly.

"My, you're a smart lassie, putting two and two together like that," Nettie said with round, innocent eyes.

Taline frowned at them for interrupting. "My point is, if people, and beings, who don't normally love are falling in love, then we can surmise that there's a foreign influence magnifying, even modifying, people's normal emotions. Love, passion, lust, jealousy, revenge... all these emotions will be very much enhanced with Willow's presence."

Wayman looked out over all the people milling around the fairgrounds. "And with the containment spell, the feelings will cycle back on themselves and mutate. Love, even more than hate, can drive incredible levels of violence. Crimes of passion are legendary."

"So, the love fest is for an evil purpose?" Dean countered.

Wayman smiled. "It's a distraction. People are so involved with their emotions they may forget important things, do reckless things, or worse. What's happening in Barrington is not natural. I just saw that with my own eyes." Wayman shuddered.

Nathalie spoke slowly. "So... no one's watching. Even our adults have been swept up in this magical frenzy."

Taline nodded. "And possibly powerless to help themselves. They are caught in the throes of whatever obsessions they have, like everyone else. What has been unleashed needs to run its course."

Dean groaned. "Another two months of this to endure."

Wayman agreed. "The next eight weeks will be painful. More painful than you can imagine. Be on your guard, everyone. We are trying to find out what Danner is getting out of this, and what his connection is to Willow. It's no coincidence this is all happening now. Beth *is* in league with him. She has been consorting with a mercenary we know follows a more, let's say, evil path."

Nathalie was staring at Beth. "I'm not surprised. She's been a bitch since she got here. Almost everything started when Beth arrived in Barrington. It seems to coincide exactly with when Willow started possessing Sadie."

"Och, well that's a good point, lassie. Tell me then, when did the windmill start to turn again?"

"The windmill?" Nathalie said, perplexed.

Nettie looked at Luke and hesitated, indecision showed on her face momentarily before it was gone. "The windmill is enchanted, lass. It won't turn unless there is resident evil. It was placed there by Jacob Barrington, who also oversaw the construction of the four barns. The windmill is turning, dearie. I noticed when I got to Barrington."

"That rust bucket is working?" Dean asked in amazement.

Nettie turned to Luke. "Your father knows about this. You need to be speaking to him, lad. As the Barrington heir, the records of Jacob Barrington would have been handed down to him, and now should be handed down to you. Your father is following the protocol set out by Jacob himself."

Nathalie looked at Nettie suspiciously.

Nettie was looking at Luke with concern. "You need to tell your father that you're The Seer, Luke, and he needs to give you Jacob Barrington's diary to read. It's probably not safe for you to be roaming around alone."

"Luke, is your dad around?" Dean asked.

"Nah. He's out playing cards somewhere, or so he says."

"What about your mom?"

Luke looked shocked. "You want to tell my mom? Are you crazy, dude? You want martial law instituted in the town?"

"Yeah, what was I thinking?" Dean muttered. "Never mind."

Wayman cut in. "Try and talk to your dad as soon as you can, Luke. It's getting close to supper time, so I suggest you all head home."

The gang nodded and turned to leave.

"And guys, take precautions to protect yourselves. Wear your amulets. Protect the other kids. You know things they don't. Make sure no one takes advantage of them. Act—lead, but don't panic anyone," Wayman said grimly, thinking of Venius. Because where there was Venius, his brother Clovis wasn't far behind. Clovis was bad news.

Nathalie headed out of the barn. "While I understand that the hex Willow put on us is having an interesting effect, I've noticed that some of us haven't degenerated as much as others have." Nathalie looked towards Beth's booth and Town Circle. "I think it's time I got a sample of Beth's little concoction and had it analyzed."

"That's a good idea. Have any of you had any?" Taline asked curiously.

"Only when she first opened, but not since," they said.

"Only Sadie never had any. I drank hers," Luke added.

Taline nodded. "Let us know what you find out."

Wayman stopped Luke. "Seer, do you see anything odd with Beth? Similar to what you see with Sadie and Willow?"

Luke looked startled, but thought back. "Not really, but I've never taken a really good look at her."

"Do that for me. Something's off with her."

"Absolutely, Wayman," Luke said, but when he passed by her booth, Beth was nowhere to be found.

The Barrington Estate

When Luke got home, his father wasn't there. He debated for a minute then called Sadie. He fidgeted in anguish while he waited for her to pick up the phone so he could hear her voice. She answered on the first ring.

"Luke, why are you calling me?" she whispered softly.

"I can't do this without you," he whispered back. "We were talking about the windmill..."

"Don't tell me anything!" she said anxiously.

"I won't...I won't...but we need to know when it started spinning. I'm guessing it happened around a major feast this summer."

"Luke, you could have looked this up yourself in two seconds," she said with amusement. She sighed. "The last major feast was the summer solstice. Look around June 21."

"I love you Sadie," Luke said in a heart-broken whisper.

"Luke, don't call me again," Sadie replied coldly before she hung up.

Luke searched and found the article by Xander. It was confirmed. Badness arrived in Barrington at the summer solstice.

THE BARRINGTON BUGLE - SUNDAY, JUNE 23

It's Alive! Eyesore On West Road Works After... Well, Never!

By X. Agerate

I have complained for years. Take it down! Take what down? The view from my house. The eyesore that can be seen from most homes in the South West Residential Quad (admittedly through the trees). The big, old, ugly, rusting windmill on West Road, that's what.

"Why is it still standing?" is a question I've asked the town council many times before they made a law forbidding me to ask it. Why? It doesn't work, not even under gale force winds! It has never worked.

Well today I have something new to report!

During the storm on Friday night, the rust bucket actually started spinning! Imagine my surprise! My incredulity! It screamed bloody murder when it started to turn, but there you have it. Now, there's only one problem. It doesn't stop spinning! EVER. Even without wind, the piece of junk spins! What kind of windmill does that? And it's still ugly! For the love of all that is holy, the rust bucket needs paint! This is a big HINT to the town council. PAINT!

Or better yet... Tear it down!

The Rock

Wayman and Taline were in the woods near the place they had arrived, which was very close to The Rock. They tried to communicate with their people but couldn't. No portal would open.

"Our way is lost," Taline cried in frustration.

Wayman held her close. "The way is never lost. There is just no door right now. We have a hex that has bound three worlds together, mortal, spiritual, and demon. To force a portal now will tear a veil somewhere between dimensions. We need to be patient and accept that we're stuck here until Halloween too."

Town Circle

"So far so good for a Friday night," Deputy Johnson said to the Sheriff as they patrolled around Town Circle, listening to the revelers at The Rotunda as they raised the proverbial roof. They didn't bother patrolling through the quiet pathways of Town Circle Park anymore. With only two armed law enforcement officers in Barrington, it wasn't worth dealing with people's anger at their perceived invasion of privacy.

"Whatever happened to renting a cheap motel?" the deputy asked irritably.

"There aren't any motels in Barrington, Johnson."

"Okay, but there are motels in Limerick. It's only a short drive away. Sheesh."

"Yeah, seeing someone else's 'Johnson' is not my idea of a good time either," the Sheriff said with a straight face.

"Oh, good one, Chief. *Funny*. Like I haven't heard that one a million times before," the deputy said dryly.

Funny or not, that's the way it was.

"When are reinforcements coming from Limerick?" the deputy asked.

"They've come and gone," the Sheriff said shortly.

"What are you talking about, Chief? I haven't seen any of the Limerick boys lately."

"That's because they didn't stop," the Sheriff replied. He had seen the Limerick police cars. Two squads. They drove right through town and didn't stop. Blank faces. That was what had scared the Sheriff. Their blank faces. He had tried to call Limerick after that but only got static. He gave up. There was no help coming.

"Johnson, we are on our own this year."

"Dang," he said worriedly, fingering his gun strap.

"You got that right."

Monday, September 9

Barrington School Grounds

The following week was tough. Sadie sat with Luke, Nathalie, and Dean that first lunch and chatted with them, but kept it friendly only. They did not talk about what was happening in Barrington or about the hex. For everyone's safety, they kept it light and neutral. Luke was in hell. He was having a hard time adjusting to their separation and stared at Sadie with great longing.

Sadie refused to acknowledge him, and Nathalie gave him shit.

"Do you think this is easy for her? Stop making it harder than it already is."

She didn't sit with them again.

The news of their breakup spread like wildfire. Everyone whispered and speculated. Hannah was ecstatic. She was sure her writing was having the intended effect and that Danner was making good on his promise. Kids were shunning Sadie, and Hannah fueled the fire.

"How dare she hurt a great guy like Luke!" she said to all the girls. They agreed wholeheartedly.

"It's because he's a Barrington and they're arch enemies."

"He's better off without her!"

"She's stupid if she didn't realize how lucky she was."

Luke tried to take the blame and told everyone that he broke up with her because he was embarrassed by all the negative press on Sadie in the newspaper. He told everyone that dating her was bad for the Barrington family image, so he'd had to dump her. Unfortunately, nobody was buying it. They wanted to hate Sadie. It was easy to do. Hate Luke? Impossible.

Sadie just tilted her chin higher. *Great, back to square one,* she thought with a bit of despair, but then stiffened her resolve. *But not for long.* She hissed at the next person who muttered under their breath about her. The girl jumped in fright and Sadie laughed. Time to have a little fun for once in her life.

Hannah approached Luke in a friendly manner for the first time since he started dating Sadie in the summer. Now that Nathalie had clarified things (she told him about her conversation with Hannah in June), he could see clearly that Hannah had a serious crush on him. She apologized for her behavior and asked if he would go to Joe's Java and have a coffee with her after school.

Luke wanted to say no. He wanted to hurt Hannah like she hurt Sadie. She had lied when she said she didn't know who the author of the hate mail was. But Sadie was right; it was not time for emotion or revenge. This girl had information, and he had every intention of getting it out of her. With his classic goofy smile, Luke said sure and made a date. Hannah smirked at Sadie as she walked by her, but Sadie was reassured when Luke winked at her. They knew what they were doing. They may have "broken up," but they were inextricably and irrevocably linked by love. He squeezed her hand briefly in passing, and she squeezed his back without thinking.

"No," Nathalie said quietly but firmly, coming between them and slapping Sadie's hand.

"Girls, no hitting," Dean said sternly as he walked into the school.

Sadie found an unexpected ally in Reg Baker, who sidled up to her after classes mid week.

"I heard you were flying solo now," Reg said suavely. Sadie looked at him coldly. "Such a pretty bird, to be all alone."

My gosh, can you get more pathetic than that? she wondered, staring at him.

"I've cut loose the girl I was seeing, so I'm a free man. Any chance you'd like to go on a date? Say Friday? The music and action at The Rotunda is just awesome." Beth had dumped him for some huge biker dude, and when he was about to protest and confront him, he thought better of it when the guy flexed his muscles and bared his pointy teeth.

Sadie looked at Reg with distaste, like he was a squirming bug under a microscope. He actually started to squirm a little at her silence, but then she decided to be polite. "Why, thank you Reg, for your kind offer. However, I'm very recently... single... and need a bit more than *three days* before going on a date. You understand, I hope."

"Absolutely, and with all the scandal with the newspaper and all, I guess you wouldn't want to tarnish my image either."

What an idiot. "Absolutely my first consideration," Sadie said sweetly.

Thursday, September 12
Barrington School Grounds

Thursday arrived with an altercation between two teachers. They had barricaded themselves in a classroom to engage in a shouting match, or screeching match, as Dean put it. Despite the closed door, the shouting could be heard along the whole second floor.

The principal was beside himself. "Let's all calm down, ladies, please. I'm sure it's all a misunderstanding," he said from outside the door. There was a crash and the sound of glass shattering. He looked wildly down the hall at the interested students milling about.

"Begone," he yelled at them irritably, flicking his fingers at them in a shooing motion. "Schools out for the day. LEAVE!"

Most kids didn't need to be told twice and bolted. Anyway, the classroom window was open, so the fight could still be heard from the yard outside, and even observed at times when the hair pulling passed in front of the windows, which was where the dismissed students congregated to continue listening to the show.

Everyone heard the gist of the conversation.

"Ewww...he's sleeping with both of them? That's vile!" Tess said loudly.

"Er, isn't our esteemed principal married?" Dean asked Nathalie.

"Yes," she said with disgust.

Eventually the Sheriff was called and asked to keep the situation quiet.

"Wouldn't want to upset the parents," Principal Green said with a straight face.

"Or your wife," the Sheriff said easily.

THE BARRINGTON BUGLE - FRIDAY, SEPTEMBER 13
SPECIAL MORNING EDITION

Barrington Principal Murdered During "Wild Hunt!"

By X. Agerate

Early this morning, Mr. Linus Green, principal of Barrington High School, was found murdered near Crystal Falls. According to a witness, he saw Principal Green being pursued through the forest by leather-clad men on horseback.

"Their eyes were glowing red and they were laughing while Green screamed in terror. I saw them. I heard him."

Unfortunately, the witness had already imbibed over a dozen beers. According to the Sheriff, his testimony is not reliable.

"I don't know what 'imb...imbribed' means, but I wasn't so drunk that I don't know when men are out hunting. A wild hunt by monsters is what it was. That man was fleeing in terror like an animal. T'weren't normal."

Unfortunately, the sot was the only witness who has come forward. A wild hunt? It sounds like a tale of terror in the early morning hours of a very unlucky Friday

```
the 13th, but the sad fact remains. Linus
Green's body will be transported to Limerick
and buried in the Barrington cemetery.
Information on the funeral arrangements will
come in tomorrow's paper.
   Anyone with information on Mrs. Green's
whereabouts should notify the Sheriff.
```

Saturday, September 14
The Parker Residence

Nathalie woke up on Saturday with a start. Her brother Nick was standing by her bed, staring at her. She rubbed her eyes and stared back at him. "I wish you wouldn't do that."

"Why? You're pretty when you sleep."

Nathalie loved her little brother. She tossed him on her bed and tickled him until he was screaming with laughter and tears were coming out of his eyes. She finally noticed the white envelope clenched in his little fist.

"What's this?" she asked, taking the letter from him.

"From Rainy," Nick said promptly. "It arrived yesterday but you didn't see it. I know you're waiting for a letter from her, so I brought it up."

Nathalie tousled his hair affectionately. "Thanks buddy."

"No problem," Nick said. "I'd better go eat my waffles." He padded out of the room and Nathalie ripped open the letter.

Superstition County
September 10

Dear Nathalie,

I got your letter and I wanted to come home right away. You scared the shit out of me! However, Gabe convinced me that helping you from here would be the best thing, especially since we found one of the books you are looking for. (I wanted to steal the book and bring it home, but the librarian here pats us down as we leave!) Gabe and I have been digging around Superstition's archives and found some interesting stuff. We found a book in a text we couldn't read. It didn't have a title on it, which is why I ignored it the first time. But after you sent me that strange coin, I realized that the book I discarded had the exact same symbol, a scythe with a stick of wood crossing it. The book is really old.

However, I think you might find this interesting. We took the book and Gabe scanned it onto his laptop and we ran it through a language translator we found on the Internet. It turns out that a crazy settler wrote this book in archaic German in the 1590's. If this book is true, Superstition was not a town then. It was actually a very remote place in the middle of nowhere where he and a group of settlers were given the sacred task of guarding a very special prison. He calls it the daemon's prison. Apparently a nearby town was plagued by bad luck and insanity. (We believe the town he's referring to is Limerick.) When the town's leaders figured out the source of the problem, they banished it here. He goes on to complain about "the new way of life" and warns about power constantly... but we're not sure of the context of that yet. The book was very worn, so that's all we've been able to translate so far. Surprisingly, Gabe is a good code cracker, and even though he doesn't know any German, he's been rather resourceful translating this thing on the computer.

This town is strange. At first I thought it was neat, but now I'm finding it a bit creepy. Any superstition you can think of happens here. The inhabitants knock on wood all the time saying, "Saints preserve us." They have rules about salt, they're careful of each other's shadows, they hang long coloured ribbon on their ladders so you don't walk under them, and they have no black cats, not one. Black cats are destroyed immediately when they're born.

This is so freaky—especially if it's happening in Barrington now. Please be careful, and keep an eye on Nick!

Love,

Rain

Monday, September 16
Barrington Police Station

The following week the school was closed for two days while the town mourned the principal's death. Rumour had it that the principal's wife had been having an affair with one of the leather clad hunters. When word got around to her of *his* affairs, she asked her lover to kill him. The papers cited it as a "crime of passion." Not surprisingly, Mrs. Green was nowhere to be found.

A string of animal deaths occurred during the week as well. Their carcasses were left at the church door. "Blasphemers!" Father MacGunne was quoted as yelling.

Nathalie tried to get a cup of Beth's "special drink," but Beth wouldn't allow it.

"Why do you want to try it now?" she asked suspiciously.

"Because I want to try it…now," Nathalie said lamely.

"No."

"But it's free!" Nathalie said, exasperated.

Beth smiled slyly. "Not to you."

Nathalie tried the other two stands at The Rotunda, but Beth's sycophant friends weren't buying it either. "No means NO Nathalie," they sneered.

In the end, Nathalie just took a cup from a man who put his down for a second to light a cigarette. She called Luke.

"I have a sample. Can your dad get it analyzed?"

"Sure, bring it over. I think the Sheriff can do it. He has some equipment in a small lab at the station.

In the end they had to enlist Dr. Peabody's help. "Of course I know how to use a mass spectrometer. What the hell do they teach you kids in school these days, anyway?"

Nathalie, Dean, and Luke looked at each other, but they had no answer to that.

"Shame on you, Sheriff. We learned this in grade three."

"Been a long time since grade three, Doc," the Sheriff said dryly.

"Hmmmph," he grumbled as he fiddled with the machine. Eventually they had some results, and the doctor whistled. "Well, well, well. It's really no wonder why everyone loves that hot cocktail."

"Why?" Nathalie crowded around to see. She was burning with curiosity.

"Because it's laced with narcotics and some sort of hallucinogen, although it's not a compound I've ever seen before."

Luke was stunned. "You mean to say that Beth has been *drugging* people for the last month and a half?"

The Sheriff cleared his throat. "Now hold on Luke. Innocent until proven guilty. There's no guarantee that she's aware of the contamination. After all, this is supposed to be Shaemus' contribution to the fair, and the man has been gone since July. She could be a victim in all this."

Nathalie didn't think that was likely, but she shook her head at Luke and Dean. *Leave it,* her expression said.

"So, what do we do now? She's giving away free drugs!" Luke said in outrage.

"Now that's a quandary," Dr. Peabody said, "and likely the reason she has regulars. They need a hit, a daily dose to keep going. Probably crave the stuff."

"There's always a huge lineup," Luke said.

"We'll shut it down," the Sheriff said, radioing his deputy.

"Whoa, now, hold on Sheriff," the doc warned. "Thing is about substance abuse, addiction involves painful withdrawal."

"Surely no one's that addicted..." Luke started.

"Narcotics are extremely addictive, and fast. I'm quite sure there are many people out there with a dependency now, all to varying degrees, of course."

"That would certainly explain the town's wild behavior," Nathalie said.

"They're all on drugs," Dean said with wonder.

"It certainly does explain the town's behaviour, proving my point. They've been feeling good, and rather uninhibited, for some time now."

"Spit it out, Doc," said the Sheriff. "What are we looking at here?"

"We can't just cut them off. We don't have the meds or the resources in Barrington to handle mass withdrawal from narcotics and whatever this hallucinogen is. People will become crazed, and there are a lot of people in Barrington right now."

"Crazier than they are now?" Dean asked with a laugh, remembering the sounds in Town Circle Park's bushes at night.

"Right now it's friendly crazy. Withdrawal is ugly crazy," the Doc said matter of factly.

"So, we have to keep the people of the town drugged until we can organize a town rehab clinic?" Nathalie asked, aghast.

"That pretty much sums it up," Dr. Peabody said with a grin.

"How long if my dad can pull some strings?"

"I'll need at least two weeks to get an outpatient clinic organized and some staff in from Limerick," the Doc said, getting ready to leave.

Oh my God, that's the end of September, Nathalie thought to herself.

"How long is rehab?" Dean asked curiously.

"About a month. It is not going to be pretty here for a while. Luke, I'm going to need to see your father."

"Get in line, we're all waiting to see him." Luke was frustrated. His father was so busy he'd been almost impossible to talk to all week. He wanted Jacob's diary!

"Wow, could timing for Danner and Willow be more perfect?" Dean whispered to Luke and Nathalie while the Sheriff and Dr. Peabody discussed next steps.

"Most adults out of commission. It's brilliant," Nathalie said with grudging admiration.

"Foiled by withdrawal. How unlucky can you get?" Luke muttered.

Nathalie frowned. "Their evil plan is unfolding perfectly. Nothing stands in their way. Who could have predicted this?"

Thursday, September 19
Barrington School Grounds

By the end of the week the tension in the air at the school was palpable.

"What the hell is going on with this town? It used to be the most boring place to live. Now, every day we have a death, human or animal, violence, murder, and betrayal. It's like a soap opera!" Dean complained.

The anonymous contributor to The Bugle pretty much blamed the troubles in the town on Sadie Kellar, claiming she used the blood from the murdered animals in rituals to curse the town.

The town certainly seemed cursed.

One student went so far as to throw a stone at Sadie as she arrived at school. It drew blood as it flew by and grazed her cheek. She narrowed her eyes as she looked at her tormentor. What they couldn't see, but what Luke clearly could as he bolted across the yard, was the roll of purple power along Sadie's skin as she prepared to retaliate. Luke beat her to the punch. He slammed into the kid and punched his lights out before Sadie could do anything incriminating. The girls hung back but the boys gathered around, their eyes filled with blood lust. Luckily, the other kid was out cold. A teacher appeared and the mob dispersed.

"Kellar, go see the nurse. Barrington, come with me." She marched Luke to the principal's office and closed the door. "Sit," she said, pushing him into a chair and then leaning against the principal's desk. "Nice punch. That kid's an asshole. Had it coming to him, but that's not the point," she said pointedly. "Look, I'm not going to write you up this time, but I'm going to warn you. The mood in the yard is ugly. Kids don't channel fear well, especially when they don't realize they're scared. They turn into real shit bags, bigger shit bags than they normally are, if that's even possible."

Luke was shocked at the teacher's language, but she just laughed. "A polite kid. Wow, but there's no time for that. I know you two broke up, but please ask Sadie to be careful. All this propaganda against the Kellars is making stupid even stupider."

"I will."

"Good boy," she nodded in approval then told him to get out.

Hannah was waiting for him as he left the office. Despite all his efforts during their coffee "date," and subsequent other small rendezvous with her, he had been unable to extract any information on the elusive hate mail writer. She normally had no problems confiding in him, but she wouldn't budge on this. He now suspected it was her.

"You okay?" she asked with concern. She linked her arm in his.

"Fine," Luke said abruptly. He wanted to pull his arm away from her but he restrained himself from being rude.

"Luke, I know you have a soft spot for Sadie, but she's only getting what she deserves."

Luke felt himself flush with anger as loyalty for Sadie reared up. "Why do you say that?" he asked through gritted teeth.

"Because she's a witch, and she's infecting the whole town. She's a disease, Luke, and she needs to be eradicated."

Luke was frozen. Did his friend Hannah, a girl he'd known since he was a baby, just suggest Sadie needs eradicating? What the hell was wrong with her? She was so twisted.

"I know you think I'm twisted, Luke," Hannah smiled, "but strange things are happening! Milk curdles, people getting bad luck after spilling salt or breaking a mirror. I've seen it!"

"That isn't Sadie's fault," Luke said tightly, controlling his anger with effort. He searched wildly for another reason other than "it's a demon."

"I know you're just trying to protect her," Hannah said soothingly, "but what other explanation is there?" Hannah stopped in front of the vending machine. "Do you want anything? My treat!"

"No," Luke said tersely. Hannah pulled out her change, and then he saw it. The gold coin with the demon's face. Danner's penny. "Where did you get that?" Luke asked Hannah as he reached for the coin.

"Why?" she asked suspiciously. Her good mood was gone. She closed her fingers over the coin.

He thought fast. "I've never see anything like it," Luke said winningly. "Is it a mule? Can I have a look?"

"No, I don't think that's a good idea," Hannah said, stuffing her change back in her pocket. *Not Luke,* she thought. She had to protect him. "Anyway, I'm only holding it for a friend."

Luke didn't push, but now he knew Hannah was compromised, and now he knew who the Sadie hater was. "Sure, Hannah, no problem."

Superstition County
September 14

Dear Nathalie,

I got the news of Mr. Green's murder. Both Gabe and I were shocked at what happened. I'm going to try to get to the cemetery to pay my respects. "Sinus" was a headache at times, but he did do right by me when I needed letters of recommendation to pursue my studies. I'm sorry he's gone and that he died in terror.

Gabe was able to translate more of the book. It has to be fiction, I mean, really, this is unbelievable. Get this—apparently this town guards the prison of a demon named Dannerlich. The lore goes that Dannerlich betrayed his demon brothers by using them to help him open some sort of portal from the demon realm to the mortal realm, which he escaped through, but didn't let them use. He wreaked havoc around here in the 1500s, using human fear and superstition, and watched as the people blamed and murdered each other (which they did—according to Klaus Deitriche, the author. Humans are laughably easy to manipulate). At the end of the century, one of the town leaders discovered Dannerlich's existence and set out to get rid of him, once and for all. Anyway, it took a group of five people—two powerful puritans, one witch, and two people they called old ones (or faerie—we're not sure what they are), to imprison him. Superstition was set up around the prison to guard it so that he wouldn't escape. The "way of life" Klaus was complaining about was instituted deliberately. Trust me, modernization will never come to Superstition while the demon is imprisoned here.

There is a catch. Nothing is foolproof, not even Dannerlich's cage. Like most things evil, he can be freed through a "calling of blood" in his name. From the language, Gabe says it can't be just a cut or a stab wound. It has to be a large act, like a murder. And, it wouldn't work with only a one-person sacrifice! To free an entity like Dannerlich from the prison he's in, it would have to be a bloodbath since it took some serious mojo just to banish him. Apparently blood multiplies power, so the more blood spilled, the more powerful the call, the easier it would be to break the locks and free him. I've stopped calling Klaus the crazy German. He was probably one of the five (unconfirmed), but it doesn't say who the other five were. Only the initials of the witch that participated were recorded—EVV if that helps you in any way.

Klaus also wrote extensively about Dannerlich's conquests. Apparently, he couldn't keep it in his pants, if you know what I mean. His ladies of choice were witches, and he had a lover IN BARRINGTON. Klaus did not know who it was, but I think we can all guess. Danner was finally banished in 1597, which is the founding year of Superstition.

I tried chatting up one of the local girls, her name is Penance (don't ask) and she says that Superstition has always been this way (odd—where Superstitions are true). She didn't realize it wasn't like that in other places!!! She wasn't particularly helpful until Gabe batted his long eyelashes at her. I think she likes him. It's kind of annoying. He gets invited to every girl's house for dinner. He claims it's his raven black hair, good looks and dashing personality. Ugh. Anyway, he asked her if she'd ever heard an old legend or story of a demon trapped in this town, perhaps named Danner or Dane? She said no, but unconsciously made the sign to ward off evil. I've since asked a few of the townspeople to see what they know of the history of Superstition, and no one knows or remembers anything much. It's nothing like Barrington, whose history is told and retold in every boring detail.

We found one more thing of interest, an actual, official, record of the Kellar burning in an old, dusty journal belonging to a... Dame N. Parquhar! The book you've been looking for! According to this, she was "appointed to writt, as scribe official of Barrington, the horrible deeds and the righteous sentencing of the Kellar witch who hath consorted with the devil, performing many misdeeds as proclaimed by the Mayor of Barrington, and so payeth with her life. May God have mercy on her soul." We took a quick look at the journal, but it's hard to read. Like Klaus's book, the writing has faded and the wording is archaic and hard to understand. Like I said before, no one could spell for shit!

As for the hex... Willow Kellar placed a hex on the families in Barrington that burned her at the stake in 1595. The hex is simple but brutal. Check the history book you got at the bookstore in the summer to see if the family names are listed. Now that it's no longer a secret to have your family's name associated as one of the witnesses, they may be printed somewhere since now it makes you famous! Shameful! Anyway, the list of "attendees," according to Dame Parquhar, was originally kept a secret, but she recorded them: Bakers, Browns, Farmers, Smiths, Sweetes, and of course, Barringtons.

I'm going to continue researching the demon. We'll let you know what we find out. I've enclosed Dame Parquhar's diary. I was able to smuggle that one out. Good luck with it.

Oh, and feed me some news on you and Dean! Finally, I mean really. I'm pretty much love starved over here and need a little bit of gossip! Gabe's telling me I'm nosey. He's the one who's nosey—always asking me questions about myself. You're my sister! Of course I'm nosey! What an as... donkey, and I don't care if he's a Barrington. I'm not telling him anything. I see him flirting with all the girls in town, and they're just mooning over him. It's disgusting! Although I have to admit, he's a great sleuth.

Love,

Rain

Hi Nathalie, it's Gabriel Barrington writing. Rain has no idea I've opened her letter before posting it and am adding in my note. However shameful that may be, I don't care. I'm desperate! I need some insight into your sister. Can you write me and tell me a bit about her? She's so secretive and stubborn! She won't listen to me (or anyone for that matter), and I'm afraid she's in danger. I did NOT read her letter to you (above), but I couldn't help noticing the last line. I am NOT flirting with all the girls. I've always gotten a lot of female attention and have had to spend my life managing them, especially now since we need information and Rain's about as popular here as electricity. Personally, I find females EXTREMELY ANNOYING AND THEY CONTINUE TO RUIN MY LIFE EVEN IN ANOTHER TOWN!!! Oh, except for you, of course. Please, help a brother out. If you decide to, please give your letter to Luke and he'll post it.

Much appreciated, Gabriel Barrington

PS: I'll pay anything. Name your price!

Nathalie's Journal—Entry for Friday, September 20

Everything clicked into place today after reading Rain's letter. Dannerlich is imprisoned and he wants out. To get out he needs energy to weaken his cage. To break the lock, he needs blood—a lot of it—hence his interest in helping Willow's hex come to fruition. I'm sure she doesn't care whose name the murders are called in, as long as there are murders.

It's a good thing the barn spell is protecting us all from Danner by cutting him off from the energy building in Barrington. I don't even want to think of what would have happened if Sadie hadn't activated that spell. Dannerlich's prison would be pretty weak by now, and I'm quite sure he would have followed through on his threat to break my fingers. Thankfully, he remains trapped. But if Willow is successful, and makes her blood call, all hell will break loose, literally.

At least I'll be dead, or will I?? The Parkers aren't on the list, but we're still involved. Lucky me.

Luke and Dean were not very surprised when I told them what Rain and Gabriel had found out from Danner's tome. I don't think anything can surprise us anymore.

Time to write some letters. There certainly seems to be some (lovers?) tension between Gabriel and Rain. Poor guy, Rain can be a tough nut to crack, and it's obvious he likes her. Like me and Dean, it may take her a bit longer to figure out what she's feeling. I think I'll be nosey for a change and do a little innocent interfering!

Barrington County
September 20

Dear Gabriel,

I got your note and have decided to take pity on you and help you out.

Rain is very independent and headstrong, so make sure you treat her like an equal—a partner in crime, if you will. The more you try to coddle and protect her, which is what it sounds like from your desperate note, the more she'll hate your guts. She's pretty simple to understand. She may be petite and gorgeous, but just don't treat her like a girl.

She'll warm up—it just takes time. (I know, it has been months, but that's not long in Rain's world.) Rain will always let you know that you matter and that what you do is worthwhile. That is one of her greatest gifts. She needs the same back. Do not take her for granted. Make sure you're honest with her, even if the words are hard or embarrassing. If you take a step, she'll take a leap. The trust and openness will come right after.

Now, about the girl thing... well, Rain is still a girl, after all. If you've joined forces then she sees you both as a team. But if you keep going around town trying to "smooth" things over with the ladies to make life easier, to Rain it still looks as if you're some sort of Romeo who doesn't know what he wants, which I suspect is not the case (I'm giving you the benefit of the doubt, here). Say something special or complimentary about Rain to the other girls that shows how you set her apart, and that shows she means something to you. Need I say, DO IT IN FRONT OF HER, otherwise your efforts will be for nothing. That'll go a long way . . .

Best of luck,

Nathalie

PS: I'm going to take a chance and read between the lines here, for the both of you. Rain's idea of a good time is a "French" picnic—fresh hot baguette, sharp cheese, fruit, and wine. Warm chocolate chip cookies are a bonus, but DO NOT get her to bake them for you. That'll just ruin the mood. I suggest you bribe one of the ladies in town—N

PPS: This information is going to cost you $40. Send it via Luke. I would never charge you normally, however, Sadie needs a new dress and she refuses to accept any help from Luke now that they've broken up, and her aunt is certifiable. He's very upset so I've decided to interfere. Thanks.

Barrington County
September 20

Dear Rain,

Thank you for "borrowing" the journal for me. It's absolutely priceless! All the information we've been trying to gather piecemeal is in this book!

Thank you for the information on the demon. It helps a lot.

Also, give poor Gabriel a break. I'm sure he's just trying to help you with the Superstition girls so you get the information you're looking for. You KNOW that you're not always that tactful, and, well… the Barringtons are very polished, and I'm sure he's using all his charm to get people to talk—for your benefit!

Otherwise… I might suspect a little possessiveness on your part. Are you jealous my sweet sister? After all, Gabriel is an extremely handsome young man… and you're a beauty in your own right! Perhaps you should be writing me about YOUR love life????

I'll write you soon,

Love,

Nathalie

Superstition County
September 27

Dear Nathalie,

Here is $100 to help Sadie. Buy something pretty for yourself at the same time. Your advice was… priceless.

Gabe

Wednesday, September 25
The Barrington Estate

Mid week the kids finally cornered John Barrington. He had aged in the last month. Heavy lines from stress marked his face, but he tried his best to be interested in the kids' project. They were sitting in the living room waiting for Luke to join them.

"So, what's this project Luke has been hinting to me about?" John asked, relaxing back in his chair and looking at Dean and Nathalie.

Luke walked into the room with a tray of drinks and snacks and deftly closed and locked the door before placing the tray on the coffee table.

John looked at his son oddly. "Is that really necessary Luke?" he asked, referring to the locked door.

"We think so," Luke said.

"Actually, our project is about the town's most famous historical moment, the burning of Willow Kellar and the hexing of the witnesses."

John Barrington didn't even try to sidestep them. He looked at Luke and frowned. "So you are the heir, the one they call The Seer. I was hoping the true sight would manifest in me," he sighed, "but it really does go only to one person in a generation. I'd hoped to spare you this."

"You're not the right age, dad. All of us are seventeen, except for the Browns, where there is no heir." Luke shook his head. "So, you knew what was happening to me? Why didn't you warn me? I had to figure this all out on my own," he said with heat.

"I'm sorry, son. I suspected when you mentioned something to me in July, but you never said anything again. Trust me son, this power doesn't come unless you need it. It's one of the first signs in Jacob's diary:

'... and The Seer will manifest his power in the presence of great evil, and what was hidden will now be revealed to his eyes ...'"

John quoted from memory. "Either that or the 'Lore Keeper' manifests first, as it did with Nettie. Of course, back then, no one knew what was happening, hence the written record. Anyway, you seemed normal, you had a new girlfriend, and I've just been so..."

"Distracted?" Dean offered.

"Well, yes, in a manner of speaking."

"Did you say 'Nettie,' Mr. Barrington?" Nathalie asked sharply.

"Yes, Dame Nettie Parquhar. She's your ancestor. The Parkers are one of the original families in Barrington. So, you're the Lore Keeper I take it?"

"Yes, it would appear to be. I didn't realize that Nettie was a... relation," Nathalie said slowly.

"Yes, she is. The spelling may be different, but not your blood. No one spelled names consistently back then. Your family's evolved into Parker."

"Spelling *is* important!" Dean exclaimed with wonder. "I'm sure my grade school teachers are smirking with satisfaction right now!"

"Things are clicking into place, little by little," Nathalie said ominously as she took out her leather notebook and flipped it open. "So, to confirm, the homes marked with blood are also the families that were hexed."

"Yes, but we kept the list from the press so as not to cause mass fear, in case anyone is keeping track. We've had a lot of proclaimed 'witches' and 'hex hunters' come through Barrington to monitor 'the signs' over the years. We try to keep information from those pests. They can cause a lot of trouble."

"Dad, our town is in trouble," Luke said wryly.

John sighed and rubbed his eyes. "And it's only going to get worse, buddy. Tomorrow the paper's going to print suggestions for citizens to keep themselves safe during the festival."

"Why? Have more things happened?" Nathalie asked curiously.

John Barrington hesitated before he answered. "The festival, the partying, the *energy* is attracting many types of people that do not always have... other people's best interests at heart."

"Why don't you just shut it down?" Dean asked curiously.

"We thought about it, but we don't have the authority anymore. I don't know if you've noticed, but the fairgrounds have swollen to twice their size. There are booths in the forest selling God knows what. It's a force unto itself now, and it has to run its course."

Nathalie shuddered at his ominous words. She'd heard them before from Taline.

"Until Halloween," Luke said.

"So we all have the same date," John nodded.

"Can't you get more police? From Limerick?" Dean asked.

"We tried. Sheriff Holt called the Limerick police, but the spell prevents outside intervention. The spell sent them home. They just drove right through—right by Sheriff Holt. We can call, and they'll keep trying to come, but they'll never arrive."

"The spell's a trap! How is it helping us?" Luke asked, worrying about Willow's growing power and influence and what that meant for Sadie.

"The spell doesn't trap us, it traps *her*, here. It had to be done to protect the other two counties. It was part of the deal Jacob made with Sean Kirkman, who was the Mayor of Limerick at the time when our cemetery was being moved, the windmill and barns were being built, and all the spells were being crafted. The information behind the "why" of the deal is sketchy at best, and Jacob does not have more information than what I've just told you. Apparently, Kirkman was secretive about why that spell was part of the deal, and he made it a condition to help us. We believe the purpose was to make sure she couldn't get help of any kind elsewhere."

Nathalie realized that Mr. Barrington didn't know about the demon and was unaware of Danner's part in all of this. *Old secrets,* Nathalie thought to herself, so she filled in the gaps.

"The deal was because of a demon Sean Kirkman was going to banish. Everyone involved believed that Willow Kellar would return during their lifetime. Elanah Von Vixen must have told Kirkman that if Willow returned *after* they banished Danner, her energy would seriously weaken the prison they were planning to put him in. He would then be strong enough to influence a weak mind to commit a mass murder in his name and walk free. So Elanah had Kirkman make a deal with Jacob Barrington to protect the future town of Superstition, and offered her services to work with Jacob and design the containment spell. Elanah was the witch in the group of five who banished Danner. Jacob didn't write any of this down because he didn't know. Eventually a Mr. Klaus Deitriche recorded everything in the demon's tome."

John Barrington was shocked into silence as he took it all in, but he looked at Nathalie with great respect. "That actually explains a lot. Thank you Nathalie."

He turned to Luke. "Not activating the spell wouldn't have helped Sadie, son. I'm sorry," he said with empathy. "Her path has been set and waiting for her for hundreds of years. What we have to do now is prepare for Samhain. That's when we're going to destroy Willow and end this hex once and for all. If we can do that, everything will right itself."

John got up and headed to the door. "May I?" he asked his son wryly. Luke blushed as his father unlocked the door and left the room. He returned with Jacob Barrington's diary. "This is for you, Luke. I've studied the spells and the steps needed to finish this. You need to study this and know it inside out."

He turned to Nathalie. "Nathalie, from what I understand from Jacob's writing, you're involved because Nettie blew the whistle on Willow. She ended up saving the life of the Croft child. You're meant to suffer and watch as everyone around you dies. It's her revenge for Nettie's interference. You get to witness everything, every horror, all the suffering, and *'write it down, lest we forget.'*"

"My sister found Nettie's journal in Superstition. How did it get there?"

"Donations by an heir, probably, or accidentally packed. Not everyone was conscientious about passing down family lore. The cursed families did for sure, but you must have had an unbeliever in your family tree at some point. It has been so long—hundreds of years. It's really no wonder."

"I have Nettie's *'Book of Record'*. I'm going to get some help reading it from someone who specializes in old language," Nathalie said dryly. "Maybe something will jump out at me that will help."

"So what do we do now?" Dean asked quietly. Of them all, he was the only one without an apparent part to play, even though his family was marked for some strange reason.

John looked at Dean with worry. "To be honest, I was surprised to see the Crofts on the marked list. I don't know what it means, but we're researching." He looked at the other kids. "For now we prepare for the worst. Nathalie, keep watch. Luke, study. Dean, keep an eye on the young kids. Don't expect much help, keep your eyes open and be aware at all times of your surroundings."

The news was bleak, but they weren't alone anymore. Mr. Barrington was watching.

"I know you've all spoken to Doc, so you know what we're up against on top of everything else. I'm proud of you all. I would never have thought to have that drink analyzed."

They all smiled, pleased.

"How is Sadie, son?"

Luke's friends looked at him with sympathy.

"So far, she's okay. But that may not be true for long," Luke said, worry lacing his voice.

His father tried to reassure him. "Willow Kellar was tough and ruthless. Sadie is cut from the same cloth, but this time, she's on our side, thanks to you. Don't worry too much about her. She comes from a line of steel."

Dean got up. "I need some air." He reached over and extended a hand to Nathalie. "My lady," he said with a toothy grin. "Would you care to accompany me to the fair to see the wonders therein?"

Nathalie laughed and grabbed his hand. "I think that's a great idea. I need a bit of fun, and to see Nettie. Luke, you coming?"

"Nah, I think I'll stay here and read about my heritage," Luke said, rubbing his hands over Jacob's diary.

"Just keep your eyes open, kids. The atmosphere is fun loving, but things can turn ugly, fast."

The Fairgrounds

The fairgrounds were packed.

"Where are all these people coming from?" Dean asked in wonder as he took in the mass of humanity before him.

Nathalie inclined her head in the direction of the gas station. "There must be twenty buses parked at the gas station, never mind the shuttles coming from Limerick and Superstition every half hour."

"Yeah, and apparently the attractions are doing really well. The Witch-Hunt Excursion is always packed, and I heard they tripled the price for Halloween night."

They held hands and walked through slowly. Night was falling and the twinkle lights around the fair were starting to show.

"It really is pretty," Nathalie said with a sigh. "The booths look mysterious; the things for sale are unusual. Look at that lantern shop. Have you ever seen anything like it?" The lanterns were all shapes, sizes, colours and made from all different types of papers and materials. "I'm going to get a set. I have to admit, the stuff for sale at the fair this year is really amazing. It's turning out to be a great festival."

"Yeah, where you can also get drugged beverages, buy wishing eyelashes that may give you a third eye you can't get rid of, and meet strange and unusual people who may kill you," Dean added in an undertone.

"True…" Nathalie said as she laughed. Right now, the fair just seemed fun, and without menace. After they paid for Nathalie's heart-shaped paper lanterns, they walked by Clara Innes and she flagged them down.

"Nathalie, me darlin'! Come over here a wee second!"

Nathalie and Dean weaved their way through the crowd to Clara's stall.

"Ye led me on a merry chase, lassie," she said disapprovingly.

"I did? I'm sorry..."

"You asked about your friend who was supposedly staying in my apartment."

"Oh, you said no so I didn't worry about it. I figured I got it all wrong."

"And ye did. I hadn't been at the place for a while, so I went to check. Can't be too careful about squatters, don't you know, especially during festival."

"Absolutely," Dean said with a charming smile.

Clara laughed. "Enough of that you shameless flirt."

"So, what did you find?" Nathalie asked curiously.

"Well, nothing."

"Nothing?"

"Nothing. The place was as bare as I left it."

"Well, that's a relief," Nathalie said, a bit mystified.

"Heathen!" Father MacGunne waved as he walked by.

"Father!" Clara yelled back. "Do your cards for ya?"

He barked a laugh and disappeared into the crowd.

"Begone with ya then," Clara said with a shooing motion.

"Bye Clara," they said and left. They waved at Taline as they walked by. Her stall was teaming with people attracted by her glowing gems. Nettie was busy feeding the hoards, but stopped to give them a quick wave.

"Nettie, do you have time for me tomorrow after school? I want you to help me read an old journal... by a Dame Nettie Parquhar," she asked nonchalantly.

Nettie's eyes twinkled. "To be sure, lassie! Come around four. Things are slow then as people don't want to ruin their dinner!"

"Hmmmph," Nathalie said, eyeing Nettie's smiling face.

They waved to Wayman as they cut through the barn towards the woods to see the expanded fairgrounds. "Stay on the lighted paths," Wayman warned as they left.

The new booths were wedged between the trees, and in some cases, built around them. The paths were lit from above by large, balloon-like lanterns, and on the forest floor, pathways were marked with mini-lanterns that looked like—

"Mushrooms! My God, Dean, they're little mushrooms lighting the way! That's adorable!" Nathalie was enchanted. The place was beautiful in its glowing busyness. The expression "hawking their wares" was never truer as it was here.

"Hot nuts, all types! Hot, meat filled pastries! Come and try! Free samples!"

"Try my nectar! It's sweet and refreshing. Reduces aging! Guaranteed!"

"Potions! All types! Wishes in a vial! Need love? Need to lose weight? Want revenge? I can help you!"

"Miss, try this perfume! It's guaranteed to attract and snare your lover! You will be irresistible!"

"She doesn't need that," Dean said smugly. "I'm already here." The seller just laughed.

They tried everything, the food, the nectar, and even the perfume. They skipped the potions table.

"Ella tried those wish vials. She's pretty brave," Nathalie commented.

"Or pretty stupid. Anything could have happened. One wish worked, her hair's still long. The other one still hasn't."

"Did she ever tell you what her second wish was?"

"Nah, she won't give, but she sure was disappointed."

Nathalie suspected what it was, but she didn't say anything.

The place was beautiful, and spread out as far as they could see. It was thronging with people laughing and shopping in the twilight. At a turn in the lighted forest path they snuggled in the darkness between two trees and kissed softly in the magical atmosphere. They stood there for a few minutes. Dean's warm mouth on hers was heaven. They hadn't had much time alone together with school starting and parents being stricter about bedtimes and visiting hours.

"I miss the freedom of summer," Nathalie said as she ran her hands through Dean's dark wavy locks. She was panting after a short kiss. She was keyed up and wanted more.

"I don't want to talk," Dean said, licking her neck, "Dean wants to kiss Nathalie—all over. And that perfume does smell *awesome*."

Nathalie laughed and speared an eyelash that was stuck to Dean's cheek. "You should have been a girl, with eyelashes this long."

"Make a wish," Dean said interestedly. "It's a superstition, so it may work. Wish to be alone!" he said rather desperately. "With a blanket and a flashlight!"

"Ever the woodsman..." Nathalie looked at the eyelash. "Oh, why not. I wish that Dean and I were alone by Crystal Falls with a soft blanket and a flashlight." She blew on the eyelash.

It was disorienting and immediate, and seemingly impossible, but they were no longer at the fair. They could hear the falls roaring behind them.

"It worked!" Nathalie screamed with surprise, looking around. "I don't believe it!"

Dean was already busy laying out the blanket he found on the ground beside them. "You have no idea how happy I am," he said, pulling Nathalie into his arms.

"But it's still light out..." she protested.

"And we are completely alone. And in a few minutes, I guarantee, you are not going to care, my sweet beauty," Dean said as they shared a hot, wet kiss and he pulled down her skirt and panties. She unzipped his pants and stroked him as he groaned and wiggled out of them. He was ready. She laughed as he tripped her and caught her on the way down, laying her on the blanket and falling on top of her. She moaned as he entered her and held him tight as his hips rocked back and forth and his tongue slid in and out of her mouth. Nathalie moaned with pleasure moments later, panting at the incredible sensations coursing through her. Seconds later Dean followed with another groan, pinning her hips and just pushing.

It had been a while.

They kissed slowly and deeply after that and Nathalie lost track of time when they switched positions. It was fully dark when they reluctantly made the decision to head home. Dean was resting on her, kissing her breasts and sucking on her nipples, one at a time. "They're so beautiful," he said worshipfully. He didn't want to leave. Every time Nathalie made motions to get up he grabbed her and kissed her until she was moaning again. This time it didn't work and she pushed him off her.

"Dean, we've been at it for *hours*," she said, giggling. "We have to go!"

"I know," he said getting up. He found her underwear and skirt, and she found his pants, but couldn't find his underwear.

"I went commando today," he informed her. "Didn't you notice?"

They laughed as they dressed each other. He fumbled with her bra, but Nathalie knew he was just taking liberties. She finally had to put her bra on herself. They packed up the blanket and were about to turn on the flashlight in the pitch dark when they heard shouts and horses. Dean stiffened.

"What is that?" she whispered.

"Hunters," Dean replied, pulling Nathalie to the falls. "I'll bet they're the hunters the newspaper has been writing about...the ones that killed Mr. Green. If that's true, then we're in danger. Quick, hide in the rocks on the waterfall side," he said in a rush. They scrambled across the shallow part of the pool and hid behind a large rock in the center. The water was knee-deep.

They were just in time, and they watched as the party rode through. In the lead were two large leather clad men with long tangled dark hair riding huge, snorting black horses, the likes of which they had never seen in a stable before. The men's eyes glowed in the night. The other five were just regular guys on regular horses, very drunk and trying to keep up with the rest of the party. They were holding burning torches. One of the large men looked in their direction with burning red-eyes, but kept moving. The rest of the party plunged forward, following. The horses' hooves pounded on the ground as they raced by. It only took seconds, but it was a terrifying few as they wondered if they would get caught, and what would happen then.

After about five minutes, Nathalie deemed it safe to come out when the sound of thundering hooves faded. The walk to the fair-grounds was a good twenty-minute hike on a fairly even trail. If they ran, they'd make it back in half that time. They heard horses again and splashed back to their hiding place.

"Nathalie!" a deep voice called. "Dean!"

"That's Wayman," Dean said, splashing to shore. "Wayman!" Dean yelled. "We're at the falls!"

Wayman appeared seconds later. He turned to them and his eyes were glowing a bright green. He had two horses with him.

"Get on and get going before they come back."

"What's wrong?" Dean asked with both nervousness and exhilaration as he helped Nathalie onto her horse before vaulting on his. Pain. The horse snorted at Dean and gave him a baleful stare, but didn't try to buck him off. "Is it the Wild Hunt?" Dean asked with excitement. He had been doing research on faerie folklore. It was fascinating.

"Not exactly. Something similar, but a smaller and more human version." He looked behind him. "But, it's still dangerous. Very dangerous. Let's get you both out of here," Wayman said, turning his horse and heading to the path.

"We hid in the water," Dean said, feeling his soaked runners and jeans slap against the horse, who didn't appreciate it one bit.

"You were lucky this time," Wayman yelled over the galloping horses. "They were just riding through. Once they start the hunt, they would have found you and hurt you."

When they arrived back at the stable, Wayman was quiet as Dean and Nathalie helped him with the horses. Nathalie approached Wayman and looked at him carefully. He grinned and Nathalie felt the same attraction and buzzing she always felt every time he turned on the charm. "So you're not human, but faerie. I've never seen anyone with green glowing eyes before."

"I'm a friend, Nathalie. One you can trust."

"Do red eyes denote the other side?"

Wayman hesitated before he nodded, "More often than not red is guaranteed bad, but you can't trust all blue eyes either."

"So how did you get here? Why are you here? Why are those two huge guys here?"

"The leather clad men with the glowing eyes are called dark riders. They're wild, murderous, lustful beings. If they're directed to hunt humans, they will. They were called here, like we were."

"You and Taline?"

"Yes."

"Do you know why?"

"Balance, maybe, for those two knuckleheads."

"What about Nettie?"

"She's a special case. You need to speak to Nettie about Nettie."

"Okay," Nathalie nodded and turned away. "Is one of those riders dating Beth?"

"I don't think 'dating' is the appropriate word. But yes, she has been linked to Venius, and yes, she's probably in thrall to him at the moment."

"He's the one with the blue eyes or the red ones?" Each rider had a different colour.

"Blue, his brother Clovis has the red eyes. But he's bad. Make no mistake."

Taline arrived with two necklaces and a sigh of relief. "I was so worried about you two. What happened?"

"Distractions," Dean mumbled, putting his arm around Nathalie and pulling her close.

"I see. You have to be more careful in the future. You could have been killed." Taline looked upset. "I've made you talismans. You need to wear them, along with your other amulet, from this point forward. Never take them off. Ever. Shower with them on. They will make you difficult to see, particularly by large, leather clad boneheads."

"Only for us? What about our families?" Dean inquired as they reached for his.

"Your families are fine. These beings don't care about them. They're after you. Nathalie, you've already been targeted by Danner. Dean, you're marked for some reason. Both of you are integral to the success or failure of their bosses' plans. It's you they'll be looking for."

"They're hearts!" Nathalie said, putting hers on. "Oh, my lanterns!" she said with a cry. She had set her bag in the trees before she made her wish.

"I have them," Wayman said. "Many of the shopkeepers saw you disappear and pointed me to the spot."

"Oh, what was the reaction? Shock? Screaming?" Dean asked with interest.

"That bunch? Hardly. Not much of a reaction at all," Wayman said dryly.

"A wishing eyelash. Wayman, it was incredible!"

"Mortals and magic...what are these people thinking?" Wayman muttered.

"It was my eyelash!" Dean said with awe.

"Even better..." he muttered. "Anyway, don't do that again. Just because you have access to something unusual right now, *like magic*," Wayman emphasized, "doesn't mean you should use it. You're untrained and bad things can happen when you take chances, like you did today."

"Let's get you home," Taline said.

She walked them through the fairgrounds, which were still teeming with people at this late hour.

"When do the grounds close? It's past nine o'clock," Nathalie asked.

"Generally around midnight these days. With the excursions and events, they stay open later. People like the magical quality the lights give off after dark."

"And Town Circle?"

"Wild. I don't recommend you go there in the late evening unless your plan was to get drunk, and...how do you say it? 'Hook up.'

There is nothing there but sin and despots. Those people are lost and easy prey for the night hunters."

"You mean there are more riders?" Dean asked worriedly. "Maybe we should be helping those people."

Nathalie nodded, thinking about her friend, Emma.

"Not more riders, Dean. *Humans*. Many humans hunt and prey on the weak of their own race. The people that go there…they make their choice every night. They don't want help. Any sort of police interference has been very negatively received. Like everything else, this part has to play itself out."

"Taline, can you explain the new amulets—the seeing part?" Nathalie asked.

"The hearts will push away the attention of any supernatural being with evil intent. Don't attract attention and they'll leave you alone."

"Kind of like Luke's amulet," Dean said.

"Yes," Taline confirmed.

They dropped Nathalie off first. Taline allowed them a few minutes to give each other soft kisses before ordering Dean to get going. "I have my own man to kiss, you know. I'm not a teenage babysitter," she said firmly, but they could hear the humour in her voice. Dean bolted when Mr. Parker opened the front door.

"Bye!" he yelled as he and Taline walked off.

"Where have you been, young lady? Your mother and I were worried! Not even a phone call!"

Dean laughed as he heard Mr. Parker's loud voice booming at Nathalie before he shut their front door.

"Are you going to get in trouble?" Taline asked archly.

"Nah, my parents don't worry if I'm home before midnight."

Taline left Dean at home and headed back to the fair. Like everyone else in town, she was touched by the amorous emotions, and she meant to take full advantage and enjoy it. She wasn't lying when she said she had her own romantic plans, and she couldn't wait.

The Kellar Residence

At the Kellar's, Willow had made a reappearance. "I'm only here briefly, Liora. Tell me how our plans are progressing."

"The demon's witch has defiled the church grounds. The town is in an uproar and blame Sadie for all that is happening."

"Good, good. How are the townsfolk?"

"Out of control."

"And Sadie? Not much struggle tonight."

"She's sad. The Barrington boy dumped her. She's better off without the idiot."

Willow was silent for a moment. "When was this?"

"Last week or so. She won't talk much about it. Just says they've had a falling out. Ashamed of the scandal and the slander in the paper was the excuse. He's worried about the Barrington name."

Willow was still and looked disappointed for a brief second before her face tightened and filled with hate. "Really! Worried about his name, is he. That I even thought for a second he was different. He should be so lucky to have her!" she hissed. "Well, no matter. We'll just see about young Mr. Barrington. A small visit... a little torture... let's see what damage I can do. Good work, Liora. Soon we'll both have our rewards."

The Parker Residence

After escaping her father and locking herself in her room, Nathalie picked up the journal Rain had sent her from Superstition and lay on her bed to have a look at it. It was very worn. The book's cover had a blue flowered wallpaper print, and the faded gold lettering on the front said simply "*Book of Record." What an interesting design for an official book,* she thought. She turned it over, but there was nothing on the back. The inside page had scrawled handwriting stating the town's name of Barrington County and "as Writ and Recorded by the County Scribe, Dame Nettie Parquhar."

My ancestor, Nathalie thought with wonder, *who is here helping at a bake table at the fair,* she thought in amazement. *Will wonders ever cease?*

The writing was faded and mostly legible, but some of the words were very hard to decipher. She started reading about the day-to-day activities as witnessed by the town scribe. While it was interesting, she didn't linger on the regular stuff. That would have to wait for later. Nathalie searched until she found the official record of the Kellar trial and execution. Nettie's description of Willow's death brought tears to Nathalie's eyes, but what shocked her more was what came afterwards.

Barrington County
Thursday, September 26

Dear Rain,

I need a favour. It's a big one.

I need you to go to the Barrington graveyard in Limerick's cemetery and tell me everything you see and everything that happens there. EVERYTHING.

Sorry, I'll explain later. Call me from Limerick. Don't go alone. Make sure Gabe goes with you.

Love you,
Nathalie

Friday, September 27

The Friday edition of the newspaper published "basic" safety rules at night for the expanded populace due to the festival. Broadsheets regarding appropriate public behaviour were printed and inserted into the daily paper and posted around town.

THE BARRINGTON BUGLE - FRIDAY, SEPTEMBER 27

Be Smart! Be Safe!
By Patrick O'Callaghan

The festival is an exciting time for Barrington. Business is booming and the festivities make the town THE place to be. However, not all visitors to our town have the same idea of fun.

A string of strange and violent acts have been plaguing the festival. For your own safety, and that of your family, the Sheriff suggests you follow these simple rules:

1. Do not walk alone at night. Stay in groups, particularly women.
2. Stay on the lighted streets and pathways. Do not go into Barrington Forest or Town Circle Park after dark.
3. Carry some protective spray in your purse. Smith's hardware has just

received a new shipment of MACE, at the Sheriff's request.

4. Kids and teens should be kept at home after nine o'clock.

Right now the Sheriff recommends all residents remain at home after eleven o'clock.

To all the men out there who left their balls in their wife's purse, like the Sheriff did, follow the rules!

BARRINGTON BROADSHEET

To be posted at all entrances to the Harvest Festival, on all poles around Town Circle and the residential quads, and placed as inserts in all newspapers.

By order of the Mayor of Barrington,
The Hon. John Barrington.

NOTICE TO ALL DENIZENS OF BARRINGTON

While visiting the town of Barrington County you are welcome to enjoy the sights, events and amenities of the town.

Certain behavior is not permitted, and you will be prosecuted to the fullest extent of the law if you are caught doing any of the following:

- LEWD OR LACIVIOUS ACTS
- DISPLAYS OF NUDITY
- VIOLENCE IN ANY FORM, VERBAL OR PHYSICAL
- VANDELISM, ARSON, OR THEFT
- LOUD AND DISTURBING BEHAVIOUR

You are welcome to Barrington County, but please respect the other visitors and the residents who live here.

THE BARRINGTON BUGLE – SATURDAY, SEPTEMBER 28
LETTERS TO THE EDITOR

Dear Editor:

What is a "denizen?" An animal? I got mighty insulted reading the Mayor's broadsheet before my wife gave me the definition and I got me some understanding. What the hell's wrong with plain English? That's the stupidest word I ever seen.

-Denying Dictionaries

Dear Denying:

Nice alliteration!

-Ed

Friday, September 27
Barrington School Grounds

Dean and Luke watched as one of the teachers put up the broadsheets around the school. Dean was worried about his younger siblings, particularly the terrible twin-duo. If they could read, they'd take it as a challenge.

"Are the little kids going to be taught about strangers?" Dean asked her as she walked by.

"This very day." She looked at Dean and smiled at him reassuringly. "Don't worry. With those twins, it's the bad guys who should run in the other direction."

"Are things that bad?" Dean asked Luke after the teacher continued on her way. He was looking at the broadsheet bleakly.

"I'm not sure. My dad is clamping down on the spread of information, even to me. There have been a few incidents. Some of them have made it into the paper, like Mr. Green's death and a few other hunts, but many of them have not been made public knowledge. The Sheriff is trying to control the outflow of information so there's no wide scale panic, so he's banned anyone in the station from talking to the press. Otherwise, Heimler would publish everything in his sensationalist way and happily freak out the town to sell papers. Just enough goes into the newspaper to keep people on their toes." Luke's anger at Heimler and the anonymous letter writer was still simmering.

"Yeah, I noticed that the 'Sheriff's Showdown' section hadn't grown. Maybe the Sheriff is getting back at Heimler for allowing O'Callaghan to write about his balls," Dean snickered.

"There's that too..." Luke trailed off and watched as Sadie walked by. The expression on his face was anguished. Sadie didn't even glance in his direction, but as she turned to go into her classroom, a folded paper fell out of her stack of books. Before Dean could blink, Luke dived for it.

"Getting a little desperate, aren't you?" Dean asked with sympathy. "Have some pride, dude."

"When you get used to kissing someone every day, it's hard to stop, Dean. Especially when you're in love with them. She's like a drug. Imagine if you couldn't touch Nathalie," Luke explained, putting the paper to his nose and smelling it.

Dean thought of their time in the woods. "Yeah, I can't fathom it. I am sorry man. Must be tough."

"Only another month," Luke said grimly, unfolding the paper. "Oh...it's a spell."

"A spell? Really? What about?" Dean said curiously, trying to glance at the paper.

"It's a mass spell..."

"A what? For church?"

"No, for a mass of people. It's to protect Barrington residents in their homes."

Dean froze. "Why would we need to do that?" he asked, fear flooding him. Where was Nathalie?

"This may have to do with a home invasion that happened a few days ago. It was kept out of the paper, but I overheard the Sheriff telling my dad. No one was hurt, but the jerks trashed the place and scared the family witless. Drunks. It wasn't reported in the newspaper because the family didn't want to draw any more unwanted attention. Fear of retaliation."

"That's an interesting tactic. Fear will keep half the population locked down in their homes, while immoral distractions take care of the other half. I think we're in deep trouble," Dean said gloomily.

"Sadie's warning us. She knows something, and things are going to get ugly. She wants us to cast this. The hex is escalating and so is the crazy and reckless behaviour."

"I'm in. So, what do we need to do?" Dean asked firmly.

"Sprinkle holy water on the houses, that's to keep out the unholy... like Willow or Danner. Then we need items imbued with a rejection spell so the 'unwanted' can't enter, like strangers. It's like an all-purpose protective shield." Luke frowned. "The only problem is that Sadie is the only witch I know."

Dean smiled smugly. "You need a witch? I think I know the perfect person."

The Croft Residence

After school, Dean brought the boys home and found his sister lying in her room with her best friend Max beside her.

"How did you two get home so fast?" Dean asked suspiciously, as a joke. "And what are you two doing in here?"

Max sat up and frowned, pushing his glasses up his nose. "We're reading. Why?"

That boy is so clueless, Dean thought to himself.

Ella sat up and smiled fondly at her best friend before scowling at her older brother. "What do you want, Dean?"

"I need to cast a spell."

"So? Is that my problem?" she said disinterestedly, twirling her long hair.

Dean stared at her silently.

Ella raised her eyebrows. "Are you asking *me*?" Her eyes shone with interest.

"Well DUH, and I know you can do it. Don't even bother to deny it," Dean said accusingly.

She didn't. "I wasn't going to. Fine. What do you need?"

"A protection spell for the homes in Barrington."

"All the homes? Why do we need that?" Ella asked in surprise.

Max answered. "Because things are going to Hell in town."

"Something like that," Dean hedged. He didn't want to scare his sister, but Max seemed to be somewhat aware... which meant Ella was too.

"A mass spell should be fairly easy for you, Ella," Max said confidently, patting her on the back, admiration lacing his tones.

Hoo boy, Dean thought, looking at Max's expression of adoration. "So how is it you two know so much about all this stuff, anyway?"

"We *read*, Dean," Max said impatiently.

"Yeah. We had a few false starts..." Ella said.

"Yes, we took out *Spells for the Modern Witch,* which turned out to be a total sham!" Max said with outrage. "We wasted a lot of material on her bogus spells."

"We even wrote Suzie Smaker and told her that her book was a load of crap," Ella said with scorn.

"But we didn't mail it," added Max.

"True, but writing the letter was fun!" she said. "Cathartic."

"I couldn't put it better," he added. "The worst, though, was *Herblore for Today's Naturalist,*" Max said laughing.

"Oh yeah!" Ella snorted, slapping his knee. "It was a cookbook!" They both giggled at their private joke.

"Hello…" Dean said in amazement, breaking up their two-man show. "Earth to Tweedle Dum and Tweedle Dummer! Got a serious problem here."

"Sorry," Ella said. "When we noticed all this strange stuff start happening, we decided to protect ourselves."

"Never know, with the history in this town," Max added.

Dean handed the spell to Ella who glanced at it and handed it to Max.

"Very good spell," he said thoughtfully. "The concept is sound. It uses common, available things and is simple but effective. May I ask the name of the witch who provided it?"

"Sadie Kellar."

Max nodded approvingly. He didn't blink an eye.

"So when do you want to do it?" Ella asked.

"Is tomorrow too soon?"

"Nope, just get the stuff." Max outlined what they'd need.

They both lay down again and picked up their books, signaling to Dean that he should leave.

Dean left with his list, feeling stunned at how easy that was. No shock, fear, denial, or comments that he was insane. *Ella should have been the boy and me the girl,* he thought. Then he heard Max ask Ella, "Did he think we were *fooling around*?" Max whispered curiously. "With the *door open*? If we were wouldn't we close the door? Geez, we're not stupid! Does he think we're stupid? He's stu…" he went on.

Clueless, Dean laughed to himself as he listened to his sister reassure him.

Saturday, September 28
The Barrington Estate

Luke dreamt of Sadie. She was standing in the woods, smiling at him and beckoning him near. Her hair was blowing in the wind and her dress rippled gracefully. Luke's longing for his girlfriend flared painfully. *Okay, only this brief moment, then we won't see each other anymore.* He went to her and took her in his arms but she suddenly went very still, and as Luke watched in horror, Sadie's eyes began to glow violet then white and within seconds she disintegrated.

Luke woke up sweating and shaking, sitting up in bed and taking deep breaths. He put his head in his hands and rubbed his temples. He could still feel the agony of Sadie's loss ripping through him and tightening his throat. After a few moments the feeling started to fade, like all dreams do, as reality asserted itself. Thankfully, he wouldn't remember the dream in the morning.

A tapping at his window made him turn his head and he yelled in surprise and fear. Sadie was at his window—on the second floor. He freaked and surged out of bed, heading to the window at a dead run. He wrenched it open. Sadie was floating in mid-air, purple energy flowing around her and lifting her up. He grabbed her hands and pulled her in. She was in her pajamas! A long, flowing white garment that looked like it came from the middle ages. It was very old fashioned and had a lot of material. He held her tightly and felt her arms go around him.

"I miss you, Sadie," he whispered urgently. "I love you so much."

She hesitated before she replied. "Me too, Luke," she said quietly, pulling back and bringing his head down for a kiss. The terrible ache in his heart began to ease as his mouth touched hers and they kissed deeply. Luke groaned at the feel of her body against his. He missed her desperately. He wanted her so badly. She gave a throaty laugh as she stepped back and he laughed with her as he swung her around the room, dancing to silent music.

After he twirled her around, she stopped and unbuttoned the front of her gown, which fell open to expose the swell of her breasts to her belly. She looked at Luke invitingly, moving her shoulders to expose some of her pink nipple. "Touch me," she whispered. Her voice held such power, such desire. "Take me, Luke..." she breathed, her chest lifting, begging for his caress.

Luke burned as he reached for her, but flashes of white in her eyes were disturbing him. Her hair was rippling, and so was her gown, but there was no air moving around the room. She took a step towards him, saying his name softly. His body responded. He was ready, but he was suddenly disoriented and the flush of mindless passion began to recede and was replaced with alarm. Something was very wrong. He stared into Sadie's eyes and his sight shifted and he knew. Sadie's body was here, but Sadie wasn't. It was Willow.

Luke pushed her and backed away a few steps. "I know what you're trying to do. It won't work."

"Don't you miss her?" Willow asked softly, suggestively, exposing one breast and rubbing the nipple invitingly with her fingers.

In that moment, staring at the face of the girl he loved more than himself, Luke understood why so many men had cheated and fallen under Willow's spell. Her sensuality was overwhelming, and the temptation to take her, a willing, wanton woman, and love her with no one around to witness...yes, he understood now.

"You'll get nothing from me," Luke said clearly, his breathing shallow. "I will NOT be used to hurt her! I do miss her, desperately. I *love* her, but most of all, I *respect* her, and her body. Shame on you, Willow Kellar, for using her, your own flesh and blood. She's your heir. You should have more respect for her, and for *yourself*."

"Like they respected me?" she hissed at him, suddenly insanely furious. Her eyes blazed demon white and Luke backed away in fear.

"So you'll perpetuate behavior you abhor?" he cried. "You are unworthy of her!"

"And you are worthy of her? You spineless cretin! Abandoning her when she needed you the most? Typical Barrington! I will see her rot in Hell before I allow her to be with you!" She hissed again then bared her teeth in a spiteful expression as she headed to the window. She sailed out of it forcing a cry of horror from Luke. He ran to the window and peered out in terror, but Willow was on the ground, stalking away.

"Your time has come and gone, Barrington," she said before disappearing into the woods.

Luke's heart was pounding. Love, fear, sorrow, anger all raged within his heart, but he was also filled with a bit of wonder. Beneath all that boiling hate that defined everything Willow was...tonight... well, tonight Luke had sensed disappointment...in him. He had let her down...which meant at some point in their brief interactions he had rated above a lowly worm in her estimation. *Something to think about.*

Sunday, September 29
A Phone Booth in Limerick/The Parker Residence

Pickup pick up pick up pick up pick up...

"Hello?" Nathalie answered the phone.

"Hello? Hello? Nathalie? Nat! I swear to God, I saw ghosts. Ghosts! My God! *People we know!* How is that *possible*?" It was Rain, babbling in a terrified panic.

Nathalie lunged for her journal and started scribbling furiously. "Tell me everything. Did it happen right away?"

"Did it happ...you knew!" Rain screeched at her sister, "My God, Nathalie. You knew this would happen and you didn't warn me!"

Nathalie flinched. "I, yes. No! I wondered if it was true. I read it in Nettie's journal. I was sure it was hooky! Crazy talk! To your point... how *is* it possible? I'm so sorry Rain..."

Silence on the line, and then a sigh. "The first half hour was fine, normal. The graveyard was beautiful, so Gabe and I looked around, reading the grave markers, paid our respects to Mr. Green. After that we started to feel strange, like we were being watched. Then I saw them, everywhere—filmy and flickering. We saw Mr. Green! Gabe shouted, and we ran! Not far though...because after a few rows we stopped seeing anything. Nothing at all, but we weren't in the Barrington graveyard section anymore!"

"Rain, Nettie writes that Barrington had a graveyard *in town* in 1595. It was right beside the church. After Willow was executed for witchcraft the families involved started to *see ghosts*. Not the whole town, *just the hexed families*. They were vocal about it at first, but the other townsfolk started to suspect *them* of witchcraft, or insanity, so the families had a meeting and agreed to keep it under wraps. This is one of the reasons only those families are on the council, so secret information like this doesn't get out to the general public and cause hysteria. Back then, bad things happened when people got hysterical. As a solution, the council agreed to move the graveyard, hoping distance would solve the problem."

"Are you kidding?" she asked incredulously.

"No, which is why I needed you to do a test. You wouldn't have gone if I had asked you to look for ghosts!" As Nathalie spoke her head cleared. "Willow's hex left a mark on all of us, a mark that's passed down from generation to generation. It's like a wedge in a door—something was left open, a tie to us and a way back for her when the time was right. If we get rid of Willow and cancel this hex that's been hanging over our heads for hundreds of years, then we'll be free of this too."

"But Nathalie, Parkers aren't on the hex list. Barringtons are, so I understand about Gabe, but not us. Why do I see ghosts? Maybe it's not limited only to hexed families."

"We're not directly on the list, but we are sideliners. Willow had a bone to pick with Nettie Parquhar, who is our ancestor. Parker is just an evolution of her name."

"Shitstinkle."

"You said it. Anyway, that explains why Barringtoners are not encouraged to go to Limerick with a body after the funeral. I understand having the funeral here, in our own church with our own priest, but I always thought the 'town goodbye' ritual for the body was stupid ... all to make it unnecessary, or even unusual, to go to the Barrington graveyard in Limerick."

Nathalie thought of the town design, the buildings, the rituals, the spells ... all the stuff The Circle secretly prepared to counter that terrible hex and protect their families.

"Do you think Father MacGunne knows about all this?"

"Who knows?" Nathalie said. "Maybe Father Brown left his diary, and instructions, for the next priest, and it's at the church. I'll ask Luke to ask his dad. After all, it's odd for a church not to have a graveyard. Any priest that followed must have wondered."

"This is weird shit, Nat. What does it mean?"

Nathalie was thinking furiously. "No strangers, no ghosts. It's funny. Every Barringtoner knows the saying, and repeats it, but no one ever asks why the saying exists or what it means. We just accept it as an oddity of our town, the fact that we have no hotels or graveyards."

"No one remembers because it has just always *been*. The explanation isn't part of our town history lesson, either," Rain argued.

"That's because this is trauma control circa 1590s. It happened so long ago now that no one remembers, and the people who did know the reasoning were trying to keep it a secret."

"Makes sense ... but you've got to wonder what the rest of the town thought of having their dead moved to Limerick."

"According to Nettie's journal, they told the townsfolk they were worried about plague, and they wanted to build a bigger church. They bought it. Everyone was afraid of disease back then."

Rain's voice was muffled briefly. "Relax!" Nathalie heard her yell with her hand over the phone. "What a spaz," she mumbled. "Nat, that's Gabe, nagging me like a girl. He wants me to get off the phone. I'm using his phone card, and apparently his mother gets uptight if she sees a conversation on his phone bill that is longer than one she's had with him herself. Gotta go, babe. I've got a date with a tome, anyway. You had better write me EVERYTHING," she threatened. "You owe me big for this one," she said before she hung up.

Silence. Nathalie was thinking and tapping her pen on her book. There must have been at least *one* person in a hexed family who'd experienced this, but then she tossed the idea aside. If council families have strict orders not to go to the graveyard, they don't go, so it's most likely a dead end.

Nathalie's Journal – Entry for Sunday, September 29

Dean and Luke just left. We've been crammed in my room for hours talking about the fact that we see ghosts. They have access to our mortal senses! It's a terrifying thought, and terribly wrong. We shouldn't be able to see them. It's not right. None of us want to see dead people.

According to Nettie, Willow was burned to ash, which was blown all over Barrington Forest. Does that mean she's everywhere? I know Luke was pretty horrified at the thought.

I think the ghosts are just by products of an open doorway, and Luke agreed with me. He thinks that the open doorway is something we need to be concerned about, and he made a very interesting point.

What if something else tries to come through?

Monday, September 30

The Residential Quads

Despite a couple of days delay while they waited for Father MacGunne to bless their water, the spell went well. Max and Ella were a great team. Max handled the technical set up while Ella handled the spell casting.

Nathalie was impressed. "Wow," was all she could say.

The first part of the spell required the residents' houses to be sprayed with holy water. Once Ella cast the spell, the holy water would keep out unholy beings such as ghosts and other non-corporeal troublemakers. To set that part up, Dean had kids in teams on bikes spraying holy water on the houses in each residential quad using squirt guns.

The second part of the spell involved—

"Trees?" Dean asked doubtfully.

Max grinned and explained. "The spell to keep non-resident jerk mortals from harassing citizens in their homes is a bit trickier. We can't do individual protection spells per house, which would take *forever* since we are doing all the neighborhoods, so we needed to use more general objects or things. The spell Sadie designed targets malicious intent of non-residents and makes them uninterested in coming near. By spelling the trees around the residential quads..."

"No jerk will even consider messing with the residents," Ella finished.

"Exactly," Max beamed at her.

"What about our *resident* hooligans?" Nathalie asked curiously.

Max shrugged. "That's why we still need Sheriff Holt," he said simply.

October

Tuesday, October 1
The Kellar Residence

It was very early morning. The room was as gray as the slashing rain outside. Sadie woke slowly, disoriented. Feelings of unease and fear were pulling her from sleep and she knew why. Something was manifesting in her room. A presence was forming, watching her. She sat up in bed, her heart pounding and her skin starting to prickle. She watched in horror as the entity solidified into the shape of Willow Kellar. Her hair and black dress were rippling as if she were standing in the wind. Sadie glanced wildly at her bedroom door and window and Willow laughed. Sadie could hear the locks turn.

"You're not going anywhere," Willow said lightly, staring at Sadie with her white eyes. "I need you now. There's no more playing around. No more visits. You're done."

Sadie frowned and responded coldly and evenly, even though she was freaking out inside. *Time's up,* she thought to herself. "Why don't you just leave me alone? None of these people ever did *anything* to you, you crazy witch. The people you want to punish are long dead."

"Crazy witch?" Willow's beautiful face contorted in rage before returning to its determined expression. "You know nothing of me, child. Nothing of what I endured at the hands of those people! Nothing!" Willow said vehemently.

Suddenly Sadie was furious. Three months of stress and fear launched her out of bed towards the apparition. Willow flowed back as Sadie screamed, "WHAT, WILLOW? WHAT THE HELL DID THEY DO TO YOU TO DESERVE MURDERING THEIR CHILDREN AND TAKING WHAT WASN'T YOURS TO TAKE? WHAT?"

"They took my husband and my child!" Willow raged back.

"You were just a harlot! You weren't married!" Sadie yelled.

Willow looked at Sadie with disdain. "Who says?"

"There's no mention—"

"No mention? So? You didn't find an official record...in Limerick? Where I *lived*. Just because you can't find a paper record that speaks of it does not mean it didn't happen, you foolish child!"

Sadie was stunned. *Limerick?* "What are you talking about?" she said tensely.

Willow considered her before answering. "I was married when I was fifteen and by sixteen had a babe of my own. He was a sweet boy. My husband's name was Jessie. He was a second generation 'half breed' as you refer to it these days—three quarters German settler and one quarter native Indian." Anger appeared in Willow's face.

"We had been sweethearts since we were small. We were frantically in love! We couldn't keep our hands off each other, like you and your Barrington boy. The town rejoiced at our marriage. The Kellars were a very popular family, and we were good youths. We were blessed with a child almost right away. We named our son Jessie Jr. Jessie didn't want that, but I wanted my son to bear the name of his father, the man I loved more than anything in the world. Jessie gave in, of course. He was the kindest and gentlest man. He always gave me everything I wanted." Willow hesitated and then continued. "But then the Von Vixen's arrived off the boat from Europe and settled in our town. Rich and entitled, they considered us all beneath them." Willow spat with disgust.

"The younger son, Karl, became obsessed with me even though I was a *happily* married young woman. Since he considered us all dirt anyway, he decided he could do whatever he wanted. The young men of the town followed him like dogs because he was 'pure' European stock and was very flashy with his fashionably cut clothes and sparkling jewels. He was the one who started to call Jessie a half-breed and made him seem less than human. He told people Jessie didn't deserve to have a white wife, especially one as beautiful as me..."

Willow's eyes glowed as she looked at Sadie. "I began to fear for my husband. Our families went to the town leaders and THEY WOULDN'T HELP US," she hissed, her white eyes shooting sparks. "Why? Because Elanah Von Vixen was the *honourable* Sean Kirkman's mistress, and he refused to interfere with her brother. I knew even then that those boys would take matters into their own hands and hurt my beloved husband. I warned the Kellars, but Jessie was incensed when he found out that Karl was harassing me, and in a rage, confronted him. Jessie was strong and Karl a stupid popinjay prancing around in his silly ruffles." Willow laughed, "Jessie, as you say, 'kicked his skinny ass' in front of all his friends that day."

Willow's look quickly changed to anguish. "That night a mob of young, brainwashed men came after Jessie. They broke into our home and dragged Jessie out of our bed. That's the night *my* power manifested itself, just like I knew yours would in defense of Luke when Liora attacked him and you thought she was going to kill him. I too attempted to defend my love, but I was too late to save my husband. They strung him up in our yard so fast and they made me watch as they hung him, all the while hollering and laughing! Karl meant to rape me and murder my son, who was now screaming in the house from all the noise and commotion. I was terrified, and slow, but when Karl said 'get the boy and string him up beside his half-breed father,' well, my fury overwhelmed my shock, and before anyone could move a muscle, I melted the flesh from the bones of every man in that clearing until you couldn't tell they had been human. Except for one. Karl Von Vixen got away because I let him. Death wasn't good enough for that man. He ran to Barrington."

Willow paused and Sadie was entranced, by the story and by the look of sadness on Willow's face. It didn't stay long. Her expression hardened. "I buried my Jessie while the Kellars packed and stole away with my son to hide him for his own safety. I left and tracked Karl Von Vixen down. But by then almost two years had passed and he had made a new life and changed his name to Knotts. He was married and had a child of his own by the time I found him."

Knotts... oh no. She didn't want to hear this, Sadie thought frantically.

Anger and hatred flowed out of Willow. "I moved into a little cottage nearby and set up shop. I found Karl and I seduced him. I made sure his wife discovered us in bed and saw her husband enjoying me. They were both *humiliated*. Then I took his child. He was so obsessed he just *handed* his little boy over to me. I killed his boy in front of him, and then I dumped him. I believe he killed himself a day or two later... I didn't care. I used that boy's life to increase my power. By then I had a new goal. I would have immortality and ultimate power as a demonness. I found the way in Elanah Von Vixen's spell book. That idiot, Karl, had stolen his sister's book when he fled, hoping to protect himself. What a fool. Once I transformed I would seek and destroy every Von Vixen alive. The world would be mine."

Sadie was trying to process all of this. "Elanah returned your grimoire and your diary to your family. I actually thought she was being nice, but she really went back to salvage her own book so she wouldn't be accused of being a witch herself!"

Willow shrugged, "I copied her spells, and made up a few of my own. T'was all the same. I had the one I wanted from her, the blood of three murdered children was all that was needed—the ultimate horrific act. I started with little Petie Knotts and then took Jenny Stone. Last was sweet Livey Croft...they always bred like rabbits, those Crofts. They still do, it would seem. I thought, who would miss one? But then someone squealed. Someone *noticed* despite all my spells, stealth and careful planning. I'm sure it was Nettie Parquhar."

"Did you say Nettie Parquhar?" Sadie said, involuntarily.

Willow looked at her. "Why are you so startled?" Her eyes widened and she smiled with pleasure. "Why, Nettie's here! How did I not sense her before? After all this time! Now I have no doubt my plan will succeed. She has to WATCH." Willow looked positively gleeful.

"I had slept with more men than I could count to manipulate events, hide my doings and get what I needed for transformation." Willow snorted in disdain, "Those rutting bastards. Ready at a wink to drop their pants and satisfy their lust. My beauty has been nothing but a curse, Sadie. Yours would have been too, if you were to live, which you won't. I was only twenty-one by the time they hung me and burned me at the stake. Every member of every family of the mob at my execution will be destroyed."

Sadie felt sad as she looked at the girl in front of her. A young girl whose life had held nothing but horrors. But to do what she did...

"You didn't deserve the pain and suffering you endured. Those people had no right. It was beyond horrific, but you deserved your ending," Sadie said quietly. "Many people suffer injustice and do not choose the vicious and evil path you did. Imagine how your son would feel if he could see you now."

Rage and loss boiled out of Willow, blasting Sadie with its intensity. "I lost my chance to be with my son!" Willow hissed angrily. "I could not find the Kellars even though I searched desperately. Then I decided it would be better for him if I didn't find him. I would get my revenge first, but then I was murdered by that Barrington bastard, Jacob. However, the Kellars have done right by me and have protected my line well. You are here."

Sadie started to back away. She looked furtively at her bedroom door. Her cell phone was on the bedside table. If only she could reach it and dial Luke's number.

"Forget it, child. You won't escape me. You are the catalyst that has made all this possible. You are the first female Kellar in my direct line since me. With your conception, the fulfillment of the hex became possible and was set in motion. If you hadn't noticed, each family implicated in the curse has a child the same age as you, Sadie."

"But I wasn't born here..."

"Your birthplace is irrelevant. Your conception was the key, the turning point. The fact that you're here *now* matters. Eventually, you would have been drawn here. Your father had his instructions."

Sadie was startled. "Do you know who my parents were?" Sadie asked, trying to keep the pleading tone out of her voice. Boris and Liora would never answer that question.

Willow stared at her, but then relented. "Irrelevant now, but anyway. Your father is still with you. Your mother died in childbirth," she said dismissively.

"You mean Uncle Boris—"

"Is my great, great, many times over great grandson, and your father."

Sadie was shocked at the news. Willow drifted closer.

"This still won't work," Sadie said desperately, backing away towards the wall. "There are no living Browns..."

"True, not in this time, there aren't. But Beth will take care of that. That's her little job. She's our mule. Our little time jumper. You remember Beth, don't you?"

Sadie looked at Willow in horror. Willow smiled evilly at Sadie. "Enough chit chat. Don't worry child, this won't hurt a bit."

DAY 1

Willow's Book of Record

I have control. I am gathering my faithful to wreak havoc on this town. In thirty days Barrington County will be a ghost town. I will destroy everything those murderers have built in the last few centuries. I exult as I see the Barrington boy staring at me and mooning over this form. "Die, Barrington scum," I said to him. "I will destroy all of you—your family, your friends—but I will start with you. This face, that you love so much, will be the last thing you see when you go screaming to your death." I tossed my hair and smiled as Sadie's power, now mine, rolled through me. Full access! I will not be denied! The look on his face was worth the struggle. I will devastate him. I will devastate this town. They will rue the day they meddled with Willow Kellar.

The Barrington Estate

Luke wasn't having a good day. Mind you, he hadn't had a good day since he and Sadie broke up. Today he hit rock bottom as he watched Willow in Sadie's body threaten him from the church grounds. He had been waiting for her. He had known something was wrong since very early this morning when he woke screaming from his dreams. The face of his beloved had already changed drastically. Her face was haughty and angry. Lines of cruelty appeared along the sides of her mouth as she sneered at him. She was going to kill everyone and dance in their blood. He shuddered. She started to drift over.

"Willow Kellar, you are not welcome on the Barrington Estate," Luke said simply. With his gift, he could see the natural magic take effect immediately, following the estate's property line and sealing Willow out.

She walked to the edge where the invisible boundary separated the Barrington Estate from the church lands—where she couldn't cross. Luke stood on the other side, an inch away. So close...but it might as well have been a brick wall. They stared at each other.

Luke frowned and looked at Willow intently. Sadie's dear face so near, but she nowhere in sight.

Willow snorted and stepped back. A few nights ago she had been kissing this boy, she thought to herself, and he had held her desperately. "Don't stare, boy. Sadie is gone. I have control now, and let's be very clear, we are mortal enemies," she said softly, cruelly, a smile playing around her mouth. "You can't stop me, you and your pitiful friends. You have no idea what's coming. The lore is lost, and you have no protection against me." Willow waved her hand dismissively at the barrier. "Child's magic. I will enjoy watching you all squirm."

"Effective magic," Luke said simply.

Willow turned her back on him in a final gesture and headed towards Town Circle. It was getting dark, but he guessed an entity like Willow didn't have to worry about being accosted. She could simply fry them with her power. He watched her turn on East Road with an ache in his heart.

He was about to leave when he looked closely at the church grounds. With his special sight he noticed that the land around the church was dark, only glowing ever so slightly near the church itself. Curious, Luke crossed the churchyard, keeping a lookout for Willow now that he had left the security of his estate. At the church he found the light coming from a crack in the side door. Luke opened the door and found the source. The sanctuary was glowing with a pure white light that sent beams of brightness into the darkening room. Nothing else glowed. Thoughts clicked through his head. "Uh oh," he said with a sinking feeling.

Later that evening Father MacGunne walked over to the Barrington Estate after receiving a call from Claire Barrington. He was humming a merry tune as he skipped along. *Ten people at vespers tonight,* he thought to himself, pleased. *A record turnout! The tide was changing in this town and he was responsible for it.*

With a cheery whistle he arrived at the manor and was welcomed in by Claire who lead him to the main sitting room. John Barrington was there with a few of his council members.

"Is there going to be a meeting? Would you be wanting a blessing, then?" he asked, magnanimously.

"No meeting, Father, although a blessing would be nice," John Barrington said easily.

Father MacGunne looked around and saw all the council members but one, but then noticed the Sheriff and a few teenagers. *Another type of meeting then.* He gave them a quick blessing.

"Spit it out already," he said briskly, helping himself to coffee on the sideboard.

It was the young Barrington, Luke, that spoke. "Father MacGunne, it would appear that the church grounds, well, everything except the sanctuary..."

"Yes, yes, go on," he said impatiently, waving his hand which now contained a large cookie.

"Well, it would appear that the ground is no longer...hallowed."

"Eh? What are you talking about boy?" he said with a mouth full of cookie. He took a moment to chew and swallow. "It's a church, with church grounds, consecrated years ago. What are you going on about?" His head whipped about as he looked between Luke and his father.

The Sheriff interrupted. "Father, are there any instances where consecrated ground could become defiled and require, say, another ritual cleansing or blessing to set it to rights?"

"To be sure," he replied, a bit bug eyed.

"We think this may have happened to our church grounds."

The priest stood still, his cheery mood gone as everyone stared at him. He looked at Luke, hard. "You have the sight, boy?"

Luke was taken aback. "The…the sight?" He stammered, not sure what to say and how much to reveal.

His father took care of it for him. "Yes, Edward. Luke has the sight."

"Great," Father MacGunne said despondently, putting the cookie back on the plate with a big bite out of it. "We all know what tha' means."

"How do you know about the sight?" Luke asked curiously.

"Laddie, I'm Irish. I grew up with stories of the wee folk." His face turned crafty. "Watch yourself, boy. They're sneaky little ba—"

"Ahem," Claire said disapprovingly as she swept into the room with fresh coffee.

"I was merely going to say bas—er… bug—er… brats." The priest sighed. Claire always caught his wayward tongue.

"So, you can see blessed ground, but only in the sanctuary now, eh? I have Brown's journals, you know. I read them all, as well as the journals from every priest who took care of this parish. The last ritual blessing that took place was right after Father Brown moved the graveyard to Limerick."

"Something has happened since then," John Barrington said worriedly.

"The animal killings?" Nathalie suggested. She and Dean were standing in the corner of the room, trying not to be noticed. "The Bugle reported that you found a string of dead animals on your doorstep."

"A dead animal wouldn't do it lassie, they'd have to be ritually killed on church land—"

"That's why they did it," Dean said. "Not to frame Sadie with 'witch-like' behavior, but to deflect suspicion while they defiled church property. But why?"

"Because they need headquarters!" Luke shouted and pointed outside towards the rows of fiery torches surrounding the church. Father MacGunne yelped, his coffee crashing to the floor as he dashed out of the room. Confusion reigned as people looked out the window, wondering what was going on, before dashing out to join the melee.

Father MacGunne was incensed. “What are you doing here?” he yelled at the mob, forcing his way through to the front of the crowd clustered near the main doors of the church.

Willow turned around and smiled. Her eyes were glowing white in the torchlight. “We need a place to stay,” she said simply, extending her hand and sending a surge of power towards the angry priest. It passed harmlessly around him. Willow pouted.

The priest was outraged. “You think you can harm me, witch? You have no power over me!” he roared. He was spitting mad.

“Pity,” she said in a bored voice, turning her back on him. Two very large leather clad men picked up the priest and tossed him back to the small band of spectators. He rolled and sprang up like a prize-fighter and was about to launch himself back into the fray when many hands grabbed him and held him back.

“You’ll have your chance, Ed me boy, you’ll have your chance. I guarantee it.” It was O’Callaghan speaking. He was pale as he scribbled furiously on his reporter pad, recording everything for The Barrington Bugle.

Father MacGunne only struggled briefly before he went limp and watched helplessly as Willow and her group opened the church doors and streamed in. The two brutes entered last. A large crackle and a scream of outrage came from inside the church, eliciting a laugh from the angry priest. “At least they won’t be getting in the sanctuary,” he said with extreme satisfaction. He turned to John Barrington. “I’m going to need a place to stay for now, it would appear.”

“I have a suite in the east wing available for you, Father MacGunne,” Claire said calmly before turning to her husband. “John, we’re going to need provisions. We have no idea what tomorrow will bring.” She turned to Bill Farmer. “I’m going to make you a list. Just put it on our account.”

“Will do, Ms. Claire.”

“We’ll collect them tomorrow morning. Now is not the best time to be roaming the streets.” She was right. Hooting and laughing could be heard from the church and partying from Town Circle. It was going to be another wild night.

That night Luke barricaded himself in his room and thought about Sadie. He lay in the dark, fully clothed, the horror of the day’s events washing over him. Tears leaked out of the corner of his eyes and he put his arm over them to stem the flow. His heart broke as he thought of the years Sadie had been alone and unloved, only to be used by an entity seething with hate. He could see it emanating from Willow's being, yellow and black stripes of hatred overlaid by Sadie's beautiful purple power. It was her essence Willow was using. His stomach knotted. Was she gone? Had Willow cast her out? If she was stuck with Willow, and her consciousness was alive, how would she fight? What could she do? Luke was tortured inside because there was nothing he could do to help. He could only pray that she was still there, somehow, and that she would hold on.

He missed her so much. Having her to talk to and hold everyday had been a blessing, a wonderful gift. He had reveled in it, loved her without bounds, only to have her taken away. He felt dead inside. He wanted to scream and rail and throw things and destroy. Instead he lay there, in the dark, and suffered by himself.

DAYS 2-7

During the first week of October, Dean organized the older teenagers into groups to walk smaller kids to and from school. Willow had murdered children before and Dean wasn't taking any chances with the little kids. They didn't publicize that, though. Barrington was teeming with strangers, and they used that excuse as a way to get the older teens to help out.

The other problem was that Danner's gold coins were appearing everywhere. Visitors picked them up regularly, and these were the strangers who stayed in town and caused trouble.

"Do not touch those coins," Dean had warned all the little kids. "They're poison. Poison you'll bring home to your families. Don't let anyone tell you differently." The kids obeyed and policed each other. They were good because they were scared.

By the end of the first week of October, both schools were closed indefinitely. An altercation between two teachers over a cheating husband left them both on medical disability due to stab wounds. Without a principal, or any sort of order at all, many of the teachers just stopped showing up for work.

"It's like the factory all over again. Just no beer in the fridge," Nathalie said.

"Why, did you check?" Dean asked with interest.

The so-called "wild hunts" had increased. There were a couple of deaths, but the men weren't Barrington townsfolk, so no one seemed to care. More strange incidents occurred during the Witch Hunt Excursion. Excursioners returned with burns and bloody cuts, and one woman was badly crushed in a mob of terrified jurors, but not one person lodged a complaint. They'd had "an incredible time." The complaints were from visitors because more excursions weren't planned.

Town Circle was overrun every night by out-of-control party packs of people who turned ugly when challenged. The Rotunda was a wild party, and many unusual folk arrived and took advantage of the willing party animals, their vices, and their frailties.

The Sheriff's office and the medical clinic were overrun with men and women of all ages who couldn't explain the bites and bruises on their bodies the next day, or what they had been doing the night before. They made complaints, but that didn't stop them from going out again that night once they were patched up. It was a crazy kind of hunger that drove them to experience more.

The Sheriff requested the excursions be cancelled because the woods were unsafe at night, and because of all the injuries.

Mrs. Throckmorton-Frosst definitely had something to say about that. "Don't be silly, Sheriff. The woods are perfectly safe. People are just enjoying themselves." She hesitated before she continued, "So get your…er…man parts back from your wife's purse," she said haughtily, her chin jiggling around her pearls.

The Sheriff growled and fingered his gun as he stared at the now flustered, and wild-eyed, Mrs. Throckmorton-Frosst, who backed away and left his presence.

He definitely had a score to settle with Patrick O'Callaghan, once he found him. It appeared that Patrick was now missing as well.

Word spread quietly that the Barrington Estate was officially the headquarters for the good gang.

"The GGHQ," Luke said quietly, "Good Gang Head Quarters," I came up with it myself.

"Guck?" Dean asked Luke.

Luke rolled his eyes. "Okay, Dean, THAT's what it sounds like."

"Just call it HQ, if you need an acronym," Nathalie said, ending the conversation. She looked at Luke. He was irritable and sad. She wished she could do something to help him.

The Bugle was full of strange stories every day now. When O'Callaghan wrote about how Sadie Kellar and a band of ruffians took over the church…well, that was crazy talk. Heimler thought for sure he'd caught O'Callaghan in a WUI, "writing under the influence," but he was unpleasantly surprised when he went to check himself.

"It's like 'The Bugle' has become 'The Inquisitor,'" Heimler was heard to have muttered in disgust. ("The Inquisitor" was a fanciful rag that reported on alien abductions and three-headed babies.) But his disgust didn't stop him from publishing enthusiastically.

DAY 4

The Barrington Estate

A few days after Willow took the church, Nathalie and Dean headed over to the Barrington Estate to see Luke, who had been pretty much non-responsive since that terrible day. They forced him out of his room.

"Get him to eat something," Claire Barrington said worriedly. "Nothing I've said has had any effect." She handed them a tray of sandwiches to bring to the living room. "I've left a jug of chocolate milk on the coffee table in the salon."

Dean had gone upstairs to get Luke. Nathalie could hear a slight scuffle and then stomping down the stairs.

"I got him," Dean said cheerfully, "but he looks like shit."

"No swearing," Mrs. Barrington said from the kitchen.

"She's got ears like a hawk," Dean said with awe.

"Yeah, and eyes at the back of her head, too," Luke said wearily. He took one of the larger couches and lay his long form on it.

Nathalie sat beside the couch and pushed his hair out of his eyes. "Eat something, Luke. You can't help Sadie if you get sick, or are too weak to fight."

"She's gone," he said with despair, flinging his arm over his eyes so they wouldn't see his tears. "Willow's so powerful, so ruthless, so mean. I saw! How is Sadie supposed to fight that? How *can* she? She's not like that."

Nathalie looked helplessly at Dean, but he just shrugged, at a loss himself. Then a new voice piped in.

"She can be defeated, Luke. She was defeated before. What you and Sadie share, she can't fight."

Luke sat up at the sound of Nettie's voice. Nettie walked over and squeezed herself beside Luke on the couch. She smelled like sunshine and baking. She smelled like hope. She sighed. "Luke, Sadie loves you so much it's painful to watch. She glows when you're around. She beams at your attention. Those types of feelings are anathema to Willow because they are polar opposites to her feelings of hatred and vengeance. When you feel love it's possible to put aside hate. Those feelings are torture for her because she's evil and has done very evil things. Love is the light that shines into the dark places we don't want to see into. I guess you could say her conscience kicks in."

Luke showed a spark of interest. "So, what are you saying?"

Nettie laughed. "Och, if I was you, boy, I'd torture her back. Use your love, and Sadie's, to give her a hard time. It's love that made Sadie strong to begin with. When she made the decision to protect you from her aunt, she was invincible. Made so over the summer. Love, romance, support, companionship, happiness, all contribute to a strong character and a strong WILL to endure and succeed. She needed you to build that in her."

Luke looked doubtful and unsure. Nettie sighed impatiently.

"Do I have to spell it out for you? I thought you were a genius!" Luke laughed as Nettie shook her head. "The summer solstice is the hardest time for a witch or a spirit to accomplish something evil. Their power is low when the days are long and bright. Yet, at her weakest point, Willow was able to manipulate Sadie. Once Sadie started hanging out with you, it became *more* difficult for Willow to manipulate and use her, and Willow was only getting stronger as we moved towards Halloween. What does that say? It says that Sadie was getting stronger, unconsciously maybe, but stronger. Love gives you confidence, and like I said, will and determination. You gave that to her."

"Nettie's right," Nathalie said firmly, grabbing and holding Luke's hands. "She's a different girl now."

"That's true," Luke said, relief and hope lighting his eyes.

Dean slapped him on the shoulder with approval.

Nettie put her arm around Luke. "Believe in her and believe in you, but don't go sobbing and crying to the lass. Nobody likes a sissy boy. If she feels bad she'll weaken. Shout your love at her. Be strong. Remind her what is waiting for her. Don't let her forget or despair. Don't worry about looking silly either. We're at war. All our lives are at stake."

Nathalie handed Luke a sandwich and a glass of chocolate milk. He started to wolf it down, looking at Nettie intently. *He could do that. No problem.*

In his room later on, Luke handled Jacob's diary gingerly as he found his place.

The Good Lord hath certainly shined his favor on his poor suffering Servant. For I, Jacob Gabriel Stratholm Barrington know now that I am, indeed, a sane and God fearing man. After living the last few months with the vision of the demon-witch continually beleaguering me—an aspect of such vileness it hath been a horror to look upon, I was certain madness hath come upon my very being. I prayed with Father Brown in our blessed church, which did not reject me, and asked for guidance and deliverance from these terrifying imaginings. To the priest, I asked him, curiously and cautiously, if he bore witness to an unusual aspect presented in Willow Kellar, but he hath denied anything unusual.

After conferring with my beloved wife, we paid a short visit to Dr. George Bingham at Blackbriar Sanitarium. Our desire was to investigate whether I should take the prerequisite steps to commit myself before the madness progressed further, thus ensuring the safety of my beloved family as well as the denizens of Barrington town from any hellish or daemon proclivities within myself. However, there are no words to describe the evil vileness of that stone prison. The insane live in cells made of the same moist and dripping black stone as the manor itself. The cries and screams of the committed echo along the halls and reverberate into the rooms. A glance into one cell showed a woman with wild black eyes and hair, unkempt, thin, and diseased. I asked the man in outrage how human beings can be kept in such vile conditions, but he was an indifferent soul. "This 'ain't no luxury accommodations, good Sir. You gets what you pays for." Promptly, I marched my wife out of the hellish place, but hath still deep concerns over mine own mental state and horrific visions. Perhaps after sometime there I, too, would lose all hope and would not deign to notice my pitiful and degraded state of living. Thankfully, Jane would hear none of it. She indicated to me that there was no way on the good Lord's green earth she would commit me there, even in my madness.

Still, my vision grows. Many of the council members rave over Willow's healing powers and gentle skills, but this is not what I see when I look at the witch. Her powers grow every day, and her demon eyes grow more white. Yet, she has the whole town under her spell.

It is with great thankfulness that Dame Parquhar hath finally come to my home and revealed her knowledge of the witch, and the evil the witch hath spread through the town. Together we have made a bold plan to capture Willow Kellar, putting an end to her vile beguilement of the good townsfolk of Barrington, and bring to them the true sight of what Willow Kellar is, witch and demoness, for the redemption of us all. Should I not survive this night, I pray that God have mercy on my soul.

Luke skipped forward a few pages.

I could see where the land had been diseased by the Kellar witch's foulness. One child was unearthed from the soil that lay under black shadows only I could see in that foul room. Little Jenny, her poor throat slit and her heart cut out of her chest. The Stone's were beside themselves with anguish. In Jenny's honour we have named Stone Creek for her, in memory of her sacrifice. Small Peter Knotts is still missing these past two years. We now suspect he hath died by Willow's hand and that it was the witch's evil magic that confused our minds then forced his poor father to take his own life.

Luke rubbed his eyes. The diary was hard to read because the scrawled writing was faded and the book so fragile. *Jacob thought he was crazy until Nettie barged in and made him act.* Luke smiled wryly. *I understand why he thought he was nuts. At least I have his journal, and we both have reason to thank the good Lord for Nettie.*

The sight was a terrifying gift, more of a curse than a blessing. It was like sight on two planes, one overshadowing the other. Luke could now see the desecration of the church grounds easily, without any concentration. How long it had been like that, he wasn't sure. What he was sure of was that he would probably become a target. With him around, it would be hard to do anything under the cover of magic, because he could see the alterations and aberrations around him.

Wow, he had come a long way from the hopeful boy he had been at the beginning of the summer, wishing for the chance to catch Sadie Kellar's eye and romance her a little, to falling desperately in love and losing her to possession by an evil and vengeful ancestor who plans to murder a good part of the Barrington townsfolk.

Life certainly wasn't boring.

Luke sighed, depression threatening to overwhelm him, but he remembered what Nettie had said. Sadie loved him. She loved him as desperately, completely and obsessively as he loved her. She wanted him and responded to him with great passion that shocked even her—a girl who was never taught how to love at all. He had brought that out of her. No matter what happened, he was going to make sure she survived, that she knew there was hope, and that love waited for her on the other side. He was going to fight like hell. Fight Willow and anyone else who got in his way. No more Mr. Nice Guy.

St. Thomas of All Angels Church

The church was dark. Night had fallen and Willow was alone. All her followers were out enjoying the revelry of a town full of visitors looking for a good time. Night was her time to reign as the pathetic denizens of Barrington cowered in their spell protected homes, meekly following the decrees of their idiot Mayor.

"Smart spell," she had acknowledged to the consciousness that was Sadie. "It has caused me no end of problems."

Her plans to terrify the Barrington residents with home invasions and other fun activities had to be killed. However, she had discovered an unanticipated boon. The happy, yet aggressive, party animals were doing much of her dirty work for her anyway, and providing great diversions. Fortunately, not all "denizens" followed the Sheriff's safety suggestions. The ones addicted to Bethiah's brew were out, ranging the fairgrounds and Town Circle for the magic elixir, and were fair game for her band of thugs and ne'er-do-wells. She thought of Venius and Clovis, her terrifying hunters. Both genders had to be wary of them because their favorite pastimes were killing and sex.

Venius stuck to killing men and fooling around with women, although lately Venius had been monogamous—sticking to Bethiah for carnal pleasure... *the devil knows why,* she thought, and realized that she and Sadie had both shared the same sentiment. Willow snorted.

Clovis wasn't so discerning. He liked men and women. Clovis was a bit more like an animal. But she didn't support rape, having herself been pursued for her looks and had her life ruined. However, she allowed him to use the full breadth of his coercive powers, which got him many seemingly willing partners. Too bad if they could be mind fucked.

In the end, she didn't care who they had sex with, or why, as long as they left her alone.

She had ordered Clovis to stay away from Ella Croft. Apparently he had caught her scent at the fair and had hunted her down. She was not sure why she forbade him from taking the girl. After all, who would miss one of the many Crofts? Still, it reminded her of when Karl had stalked her. She wasn't sure if it was her decision or Sadie's, but it didn't matter. She could ignore one little girl.

Thoughts whirled through Willow, and she burned with anger as she studied the sanctuary. Here was the only hallowed ground left in this rotten town. They had not been able to desecrate it and claim it—her way of turning up her nose at God. Her entry was barred. Was she surprised? This was the same God who had turned his back on her when she needed him most, all those years ago. She wouldn't allow the memories of her husband and child to haunt her. She felt Sadie's sadness for her and her fury grew. She wanted to tear the place apart and destroy it, but she couldn't get near. The force protecting the sanctuary absorbed whatever power was thrown at it and spat it back at her, and if she got too near, she began to burn painfully.

She understood the pain was physical and emotional. The physical she could take, but not the pain in her heart. She could hear a voice calling to her. A voice in the silence of the church. It called to her to come back, to turn back…but she wouldn't. It was too late for that. She was on her path and determined to win. So, she wasn't welcome in the sanctuary. A sound broke her thoughts. A sound from outside. Someone human was calling.

Willow turned and walked to the doors of the church and out into the night. It was warm for October and would remain so until she burned the town down to the ground and destroyed it's inhabitants.

"Sadie!" she heard called from the Barrington property line.

Luke Barrington, she thought with derision. *What the hell does he want? Doesn't the boy ever give up? It's over.*

She started to walk over to the property line. She was dressed in one of Sadie's new dresses, compliments of the Barrington clan. This one was white, but unlike Sadie, only buttoned up to mid breast and not the neck. She walked slowly, swaying her hips and straining the front of the dress. She could see that Luke devoured the sight of her. Such longing, always such longing. If she had a heart, she might actually feel sorry for the kid. She approached until she was just an inch away from his tall frame. She looked up and he looked down. They were close enough to share the same breath. She could sense he wanted to reach for her, touch her, put his hands on her face to keep it tilted so that he could kiss her, but he didn't do any of those things. He just looked into her eyes and spoke the truth.

"Sadie, I know you're in there my love. I want you to know that I'm here and I'm waiting. We're going to win, and we'll be together again. I love you, you beautiful, wonderful, gorgeous, incredible girl. I'm going to get you back. You belong to me and with me. There is nobody else for me but you. I live for you. You are my heart and my life." Luke's voice was low and sincere. The words were soft, fast, and pervasive. Willow swayed at the onslaught of the boy's feelings. His words, laced with the power of truth, were spellbinding, and she couldn't move or run while he was speaking. He poured out his heart. She could feel Sadie respond violently to the emotion and love pouring out of him. Willow forced her down and managed to take a step back from the magic of his eloquence.

"Very beautiful, Barrington. You've discovered the persuasive power of your true voice. Jacob did too when he convinced the town to hang me. Completely overturned my supporters. It was an unexpected twist. A voice like that can be a great asset..."

Luke smiled. "I cannot help you, Willow Kellar, but I love your many times over great granddaughter. I'll make sure she is cherished."

Willow was still for a moment, mouth agape in surprise, before her eyes filled with rage and madness. "It's too late for that!" she shrieked. She tried to reach for him but her hands hit a wall. Purple power arced from her, but it was just absorbed by the boundary spell. She stamped her foot. "It's not about *her*. It was never about her. It's about *me*. ME! You'll suffer for what you've done! I'll destroy all of you!" Sadie's face contorted in anger so deep it didn't look like her beloved face anymore.

"We aren't the people who hurt you," Luke said calmly. "What do you hope to gain? Jacob Barrington has been dead for over four hundred years! They're all dead and beyond your reach, Willow. You need to move on."

"You are wrong, Barrington," Willow hissed dismissively. "They WILL see and they WILL suffer. I have the power to touch them as well. I don't have to explain myself to you, *boy*, or the power I will bring to bear."

Willow turned and walked away, her hips swaying, taunting him, but there was a stiffness to her body that wasn't there when she first came out of the church. His words had made a difference.

Although Luke watched her go with pain in his heart, it was not as debilitating as it was before. His heart was lighter. Willow didn't know it, but for a split second, a second so brief that had he blinked he would have missed it, Sadie had won the struggle and looked upon him with eyes full of love. Thank God he didn't blink.

DAY 7

Willow's Book of Record

The plan is in motion and soon the town will shut down. I have given Bethiah the order to dispense with the drugged drink. Soon the town will begin to show the signs of withdrawal. People will be hollowed eyed. They will stop going to work and many of the stores and businesses will struggle to stay open without workers. I have ensured Dr. Peabrain can't treat one pathetic person going through withdrawal. Venius and Clovis intercepted the "antidote" medication they were going to use for the victims' symptoms. My snitch has revealed their master plan to me, which I have now crushed. Within a few days there will be madness and hallucinating, the crazed will roam, and there will be bloodshed in the streets while our sweet citizens withdraw from my special drug. I have Venius protecting Bethiah and have Clovis comforting as many deranged women druggies as he can.

These people are so pathetic.

They deserve to die.

DAY 8

The Barrington Estate

Mid-morning Dr. Peabody called the Barrington Estate and spoke to John. "No clinic is going to happen. Sheriff lost the shipment of meds."

"What! How?"

"Witness says the delivery truck got ambushed by two men, but he couldn't provide a very good description of them. Just said they were, and I quote, 'really large.' He claims he doesn't remember what they looked like. The bum smelled like beer."

"What about the truck driver?"

"Well, he couldn't talk on account of he's dead."

"So, if Holt wasn't there, why are you blaming him?" John asked curiously.

"Gotta blame somebody," the Doc said abruptly before he hung up.

Word had gotten out about the headquarters formed at the Barrington Estate. A safe route was set up through the woods from South Road for people to use without being accosted by Willow's ruthless gang members. They arrived in families—some of them because a child or a spouse was swept up in the madness of anarchy in the town, others because they wanted to help get control of their town back. The "supernatural" element of the town's problem was kept top secret.

Eric Sweet's wife Anna, and their son James, were just one of many examples of family members wanting things to go back to normal. "My husband can be a jackass on his good days, but he's the man who gives out free candy and ice cream to the poor kids in town, and I want him back!"

Cindy and Noah Baker were also active participants. "Hormones are ruling my son Reg…who comes home to eat and sleep the day away. We need that school reopened, and pronto!"

The gang of do-gooders was pitifully few. Many of the residents that weren't caught up in the frenzy stayed home. The citizens discreetly patrolled the streets in groups during the day, ensuring people could move about the teeming streets and fairgrounds freely and safely. They were armed with mace and rope and told to run if things got out of hand, but there was no need. Commerce was booming, and there wasn't much action on the part of the "Willow Gang" (as they were called) during the day. They owned the night, and the good citizen patrollers of Barrington left the evening shifts to the Sheriff and his deputy, who were properly armed. Many laughed at the Willow Gang's name, unaware of the mystical part of its makeup. That secret was tightly held within the town council families to contain any possible spread of panic over the witch they had executed all those hundreds of years ago.

"We also don't want people to think their leaders are insane," John Barrington said wryly. "They get enough of that at the country level."

The Barrington Bugle was no help at all. It published for both sides of the conflict. Some of the stories were so outlandish that now people read the paper for a good laugh as well as information.

"Poor Xander," Luke could be heard saying sympathetically early one morning as he read the paper. "People think he's a quack but he's right on the mark—and getting a bit personal!" Luke exclaimed.

THE BARRINGTON BUGLE - THURSDAY, OCTOBER 10

Town Teen Sadie Kellar–Leader Of Gang Terrorizing Barrington–A True Story Of Witchcraft And Possession

By X. Agerate

A high ranking source in Barrington's government has confirmed that Sadie Kellar is indeed possessed with the spirit of her executed ancestor, Willow Kellar, the witch burned in Barrington over four hundred years ago…

Barrington And Kellar Rematch–Will The Town Survive The Turmoil?

By X. Agerate

It's a well known fact that Luke Barrington and Sadie Kellar were sucking face for a while. Adolescent infatuation has turned bad as the two face off on different sides of rival gangs. Their love obviously wasn't strong enough to keep them together…

"Their love? Sucking face? What's Xander writing, a bad romance novel?!" Luke fumed, crumpling the paper in his hands.

His father coughed. "Well, he's being secretly contacted and given information."

Luke was shocked. "We're leaking our own information?"

"That's exactly what we're doing, and making it outlandish too. Who's going to believe Xander? The more he writes the truth, the less people believe it."

"So…we're using his reputation as a, well, *loser*, to get people off track."

His father had the grace to look ashamed. "Unfortunately, it's something we have to do."

"Is Heimler in on it?"

"No."

"Wow, so why is Heimler publishing his work?"

"When has Heimler ever worried about what he's publishing? He hasn't sold so many papers since—never. Right now there are people who won't go out and mingle, but they'll sneak out to get a newspaper."

Luke laughed. "You've got that right."

John looked at his son. "Did you notice any of the other contributors? Patrick O'Callaghan is missing now, so who else is writing?" he asked quietly before he walked out.

Barrington Mayor Slanders Gang Who Are 'Just Trying To Have Some Fun'

By H. Farmer

"What's wrong with making a little noise and doing some moonlight dancing?" partygoers ask. It's always the system trying to repress us...

"Slander?" Luke mused, and then saw the byline. "By Hannah Farmer!" he yelped and searched frantically through the paper for more of her work.

Barrington Mayor Imposes Martial Law And Suppresses People's Rights

By H. Farmer

Barrington's Mayor, John Barrington, posted his list of decrees effectively instituting martial law in the town. What right does he have to suppress our freedoms and treat us like children...

"What? Safety suggestions are martial laws and decrees now?" Luke was growing more furious by the minute.

Feeling Ill? That's Because Information On A Contagion Spreading Through Town Is Being Suppressed By The Town's Leaders!

By H. Farmer

This is a special alert! The town council has been suppressing information about something CONTAMINATED in the town causing many citizens of Barrington to become ill. Do you have the shakes? Are you hallucinating and vomiting? If so, then you've probably contracted the deadly virus...

Special Report: Doc Peabody In On Spread Of Contagion To Cash In On Sick
By H. Farmer
If you're sick, don't bother to see Dr. Peabody. He has no intention of treating you. When we went to interview him, he turned us out of his office and refused to answer any of our questions, especially the main one, why he won't help us...

Where Are The Drugs? Medications Suspiciously Low In Barrington Pharmacy!
By H. Farmer
David Croft, the town's pharmacist, is not able to explain the low volumes of stock at his pharmacy counter, and is making weak excuses: "Shipments just aren't coming in," he says. Well, this reporter says he's lying. He's working with Dr. Peabody in a racketeering scheme to raise prices and make a killing as the sick people in town get desperate. Are we going to take this...

Townsfolk Denied Exit From Barrington!
By H. Farmer
In a shocking display of police brutality, Sheriff Holt stopped partygoers from leaving town a few nights ago...

Luke was heartbroken and outraged at Hannah's betrayal of everyone who had raised her and supported her since she was a little girl. He knew she was being compelled and that Danner had her wrapped around his finger, but even before that she had chosen her side when she published her first anonymous letter. Of course the demon would choose her to do his bidding. The kernel of hate inside her was the prime element for Danner to manipulate and corrupt, allowing her to vent her anger against her "enemies." She'd attracted him with her vicious letters and meanness towards Sadie, and now she was stuck.

He still didn't understand how it all tied in. If the townsfolk had acted with a 1590s mentality, they would have lynched Sadie. How would that have fit into Danner and Willow's plan?

Such manipulation! Hannah's articles were carefully written and would effectively feed on the town's uncertainty and terror. With her writing, and Beth's mind-altering potion, they had created the illusion of a powerful conspiracy. People didn't realize why they were ill, and once they read her article, they would react.

The reaction came sooner than expected.

Doc Peabody and his wife arrived mid-afternoon with overnight bags. "Got some space for us, Claire? It's not safe at home and the office has been trashed," he said simply, dropping his bags on the floor.

"Absolutely," Claire Barrington said smoothly. Nothing ruffled his mother, Luke thought with admiration. "You can join Father MacGunne in the east wing. I'll prepare your rooms."

"Thank you Claire," Mrs. Peabody said quietly, fear lacing her words as she followed Claire up the stairs. "Your hospitality is legendary..."

Their voices faded as they left the central hall. Doc Peabody grinned, but it was more like baring his teeth. "To think I brought Hannah Farmer into this world. Where's her damn father?"

Luke thought fast. "She must be one of the druggies," he said quickly. "She's a hot chocolate addict... so, er, when Beth started her stall... she was a regular customer."

"Boy, you're a terrible liar. I know what addicts look like, and she doesn't look like an addict to me." The Doc shrugged. "Cover for your friend. That's what good friends do. John!" The Doc yelled as he spotted his friend. "I need some coffee!" The main salon had been transformed into a war room/headquarters. Coffee and snacks were always available.

"Follow me, Doc," John said and the two men left.

DAY 11

Farmer's Groceries & Goods—The Rx Counter

It started with a shoving match in front of the pharmacy counter at the back of the grocery store.

"You're hiding the drugs. I know it! The paper says so," a woman screeched at David Croft. "Look at me! I'm sick! I'm shaking all over. I can't keep any food down. I can't care for my family. I need something to help me!" Her eyes were dilated and she was shaking uncontrollably. Her hair was wild and unkempt.

David Croft looked at her helplessly. "I don't know what's wrong with you, and you don't have a prescription—"

"Forget the damn prescription! Doc Peabody has left, the damn coward! Left us to suffer this damn virus!"

"Virus?" he said aloud with a look of utter confusion on his face.

There was muttering behind her as a group of people waiting for their turn, and suffering the same symptoms, began to get riled.

"It's not a virus—" he began, but he never finished.

"Of course you'd say that!" the lady yelled, her patience snapping. She tried to push her way through the counter to access the wall of cabinets housing the prescription medications. The mob behind her pushed as well.

"Madam!" he exclaimed, to no avail.

Well, that's my cue to leave, David thought, looking at the crazed people who were trying to push themselves through and were now crushing the lady he had been dealing with. One of them was drooling.

"Try not to poison yourselves," he said with a shout as he exited via the back door. *Thank God the pharmacy's at the back,* he thought with relief as he checked the alley. It was clear, so he raced through and headed home. *Idiots,* he thought to himself.

The woman was badly hurt after she was crushed and then trampled by the people trying to get to the medications. After the melee was cleared by a roaring Bill Farmer, the citizen's patrol discreetly came in and brought her home to her family.

"We just didn't know what to do anymore," her husband said sadly, tucking the unconscious figure of his wife in their bed. "Without the Doc..."

"Do the best you can," Clara Innes said, being one of the party who had rescued the woman.

"And pray," Father MacGunne added in parting.

DAY 12

The Barrington Estate

Crazy twitching people wandered through the streets day and night mingling with the fairgoers and party animals, none of whom seemed to notice. There wasn't any point to their roaming, but mindless activity seemed necessary for their recovery.

"They're like zombies," Father MacGunne noted worriedly. They were all conferring in the Barrington's salon.

"Why are they doing that Doc?" the Sheriff asked curiously, watching a roving band head past the church.

"Weak minds on drugs—they probably think it's fun—maybe they're looking to score some more junk—more 'n likely they're just stupid."

Father MacGunne looked at the Doc with his mouth open. "That's it? That's your professional opinion?"

"I got nothing," he shrugged, taking a sip of his coffee and folding The Bugle he was reading. "I've never seen this before, and I have no way of examining one with my office closed. We never identified the unknown component to that drink, the hallucinogen, so like I said—I've got nothing." But watching the stupid zombies stumbling around had given him an idea. He called Xander.

THE BARRINGTON BUGLE - SUNDAY, OCTOBER 13

SPECIAL REPORT

A Message To All Barringtoners From Dr. Lance Peabody

A phone conversation with Dr. Peabody as transcribed by X. Agerate

My dear patients and fellow citizens, I HAVE ISOLATED THE CAUSE OF THE VIRUS. It is an airborne strain of areius idiotus aneoleus that has come from the north. I have contracted it, along with my wife, which is why we had to close our offices…along with the fact that you trashed them. There is no chemical cure for this virus, so using prescription drugs won't help you now. Only natural remedies will have any effect, combined with lots of rest. I'm writing the whole town a prescription and publishing a doctor's decree:

If you have contracted the Barrington Virus, you must stay in bed for the next two weeks. Call the number below and leave the names of the sick patients and your home address with the phone service. ***Within a day of leaving a message, the vitamins necessary for a speedy recovery will be delivered to your door.***

During your recovery you may experience headache, hallucinations, vomiting, stomach cramps, extreme sweating, diarrhea, a spastic colon, numbness in your hands and/or feet, tremors and/or twitching, temporary blindness, hair loss, dry mouth, ringing in your ears, bleeding gums, stupidity, rudeness, or loose teeth among other symptoms. If you have some or all of these symptoms, stay in bed. If you only have one or two, your case is mild, and you are very lucky, but you should still rest.

The Bugle will publish the clinic's opening hours once the missus and I have recovered ourselves and are back in business.

Good luck to you all, and may God have mercy on our souls.

LETTERS TO THE EDITOR

Dear Ed:

I'd like to address Hannah Farmer's article "Townsfolk Denied Exit" and her perspective on police brutality. Let's be clear—enthusiastic alcohol filled party people have been disturbing farmhouses in outlying areas by ringing doorbells and running like idiots, peeing on the sides of people's homes, and undressing "to be free" then passing out and becoming "naked-human-snoring-still life on lawn" sculptures. That is NOT art, and no family wants to see a naked man on their lawn in the morning.

The police "brutality" was my deputy and I shooting marshmallows from our 'mallow guns to get these artists to disperse before they headed out to try and "make someone's night." I hardly think their "giggling" constitutes police brutality.

-Marshmallow Shooter at the Police Station

DAY 13

The Barrington Estate

The Sheriff laughed when he read Xander's article. "Really, Doc. Bleeding gums? Hair loss? Stupidity?"

The Doc shrugged as he drank his coffee in the Barrington's salon. "At least they'll feel better if they only have the vomiting and the tremors and not all the symptoms."

Dean was impressed. "You're a genius! The streets are clear of hollow-eyed zombies. Just normal people enjoying the festival. I can't believe there are parts of this town that are still normal."

"Ain't nothing normal about that fair," the Doc grumbled.

Phone calls flooded into the hotline.

"Let's hope people don't call each other and compare vitamins," Dean said. "This house is getting cod liver oil. Yuck."

Nathalie laughed. "I'm giving these people orange-flavoured Vitamin C. They're delicious! We have them at home."

Teams of good guys biked the "remedies" all over town. It was nice to be out. The teens were tired of being trapped indoors and were restless.

"I didn't realize how much I enjoyed my freedom until I didn't have it anymore," Dean grumbled.

They spent their days at the Barrington Estate with their little brothers and sisters while their parents worked. With school out, babysitters were in constant demand.

The other problem causing Dean's irritability was since school disbanded, and the "gangs" took sides, Dean and Nathalie hadn't had much time alone together. Nights and days were spent at home or in the war room at Barrington Manor. Taline and Wayman came and went, reporting as the eyes at the fair. They were never alone.

So, after delivering the "remedies" in Nathalie's neighborhood, they found a quiet corner in the surrounding trees to steal some kisses. Dean's mouth was hot on Nathalie's. It was an unseasonably warm day and they were still in tee-shirts despite the changing of the leaves signaling colder weather. Dean's hands were gripping her butt tightly as he pressed her against a huge oak and rubbed himself against her. He was groaning loudly as he kissed her and Nathalie shushed him laughingly.

"I can't help it," Dean said, kissing her neck, his hand climbing up the front of her shirt and caressing one of her breasts. "I haven't held your ass or been inside you in ages."

His words made Nathalie breathless. Love and fiery passion for this man flooded her. His skin was hot under her hands and he smelled so very good. Somehow his jeans were open under his shirt and she found her hands in there stroking him. She missed his big naked body in her bed, tangled in her sheets. She missed seeing their clothes on the floor jumbled together, her underwear on his. It made her shiver. She wanted him now, even though Taline and Wayman had warned them against reckless and obsessive behavior, especially sexual behavior.

"You both need to be alert—more alert than most," Wayman had said sternly. "Look what happened in the woods. You threw caution to the wind to be together. You have to control it or—"

"Abstain," Taline said firmly.

"Abstain?" Dean had said, aghast.

Even Wayman had winced.

"Not touch Nathalie? Are you kidding? *Impossible,*" he had said flatly.

Nathalie had blushed in embarrassment.

"Willow's presence is heightening sexuality in people. Reckless behaviour is getting people into trouble, even killed," Taline added. "Have you walked down any of Town Circle Park's paths lately?"

It was true, and people had died. First their principal had been killed, then another teacher had been shot by her husband for having an affair, along with other crimes of passion...

"And dark riders are attracted to that type of behaviour," Wayman had said quietly. "The older teens in the town, like you two, have been hit hard with the amorous bug. You are already bags of hormones..."

"With no desire to control yourselves—" Taline interjected.

"The things we're seeing in the woods..." Wayman shuddered.

They had promised to be responsible.

The conversation ran through Nathalie's head in a blur as Dean kissed her. He had pulled up her shirt and bra and was sucking noisily on her breasts. She felt flushed and tingly. Her skin was so sensitive that every brush of Dean's hand had an answering tightness in her abdomen. She could feel Dean wiggling out of his pants while he pushed down her shorts and panties.

There's no danger at all. The woods are completely deserted. Just this last time, she thought.

Their kisses were deeply passionate, and Nathalie's arms were wrapped tightly around Dean's neck as his huge body pinned her to the tree. Any worries of danger were gone. They slid down, her bum hitting soft grass and Nathalie moaned as he pushed inside her with firm, powerful thrusts. Her head lolled back as pleasure flooded her, the incredible feeling spreading through her body. Dean groaned and bit her neck, holding her in a vice grip as he came. After a moment he mumbled, "sorry for biting," and kissed her.

"I love you, Dean," Nathalie said quietly.

He gripped her so tightly she thought her ribs would break. "I love you too, Nathalie. Only you, all of you, for ever and ever."

They stayed that way for a minute before practicality set in. Nathalie looked around as they reached for their clothes and got dressed. Dean had started to kiss her again when they heard the screams.

Dean whipped his head around the tree and saw two small figures struggling with a huge one at the edge of the forest. "Oh my God," Dean said as he bolted towards them. "It's my little brothers!"

Nathalie's heart dropped. She followed Dean at a dead run. What on earth were they doing here? They were supposed to be at the Barrington's!

Dean got there first. The figure stared at Dean as he held the little boys effortlessly. They had come on their bikes, which had been tossed carelessly in the undergrowth of the forest. The being was way over six and a half feet tall and dressed in black leather pants and vest. His long, tangled black hair fell to his waist. His teeth were sharp and rimmed with black. His eyes were red and blinking in the sun. It was a dark rider.

"Let them go," Dean said menacingly.

Nathalie stopped at the tree line and watched as the giant sniffed the air. "You smell the same as girl. Same as these two."

Girl? Nathalie thought and tensed. This was one of the guys the Sheriff had warned them about. *"The girls said they were compelled against their will,"* she had heard the Sheriff saying to Mr. Barrington.

He dropped the struggling boys. "Sleep," he said to them and they fell to the ground bonelessly.

"Sex," he growled, sniffing the air and looking at Nathalie. He lunged for her but withdrew with a howl at the same time she yelped in surprise and pain. She drew out the heart necklace Taline had given her. It was red hot. Dean was doing the same thing as the burning became unbearable. The being hissed and backed away, losing interest—his form flickering before he was gone.

"Oh my God, Dean!" Nathalie screamed as she knelt down beside one of the little boys. It was Eddie. His eyes flickered open and the terror in his face was replaced by relief at seeing Nathalie. Dean was crouched beside Zach, who was waking up as well.

"What are you doing out here?" Dean yelled furiously.

Zach started to cry with huge shuddering sobs and Nathalie could see Eddie's eyes fill with tears. Dean scooped the two little boys into his strong arms and was hugging them to him, his eyes suspiciously wet.

"We wanted to help deliver the medications to the sick people," Eddie said, clinging tightly to his big brother.

"We tried to find you but we couldn't! We biked down all the streets and then this guy showed up. He was smelling us like he was a dog!"

Dean shuddered and let them go. "That was a very dangerous thing you did. You know it's not safe to go outside by yourselves right now. There are a lot of strangers in town for the festival. Strangers like that big ugly guy."

Eddie and Zack got mutinous looks on their faces. "We're not babies. Everyone's not letting us help. We had ammunition." Nathalie and Dean looked. Sure enough, their pockets were full of rocks.

"Okay, but that guy was pretty big. The rocks would be like mosquitoes to him."

"Yeah," they said in unison, scuffing their feet.

Nathalie and Dean looked at each other. *Abstinence it is,* they agreed silently. Passion was too dangerous for them and the people around them. Wayman and Taline were right.

"We need some more information on those guys in leather," Dean said. "Why was he after my brothers?"

"I don't know," Nathalie said, looking at the spot where the giant had disappeared. "Let's get these two back and find Wayman."

The Barrington Estate

The boys were in big trouble when they got back. They had scared the hell out of all the adults, and a lot of yelling ensued by Ella (the babysitter). But it was facing Claire Barrington that put the fear of God into the boys for once and for all. She had lined them up against the wall in the kitchen and was staring at them. They were looking up at her with wild eyes, and they didn't move a muscle.

"Are you not guests in my house?" she asked them softly.

"Yes," they said in hushed voices.

"Do I not make you cookies and let you swim in my pool?" she asked quietly.

"Yes," they said with quivering voices.

"Are you ashamed of yourselves? You have scared me and many others who love you dearly," she asked in her calm and quiet way, looking down at them and folding her hands in front of her.

The boys hung their heads in shame, nodding. Big tears splashed to the floor in front of them. Sniffling could be heard.

Dean was amazed, especially when Luke hung his head and nodded with them.

"Dude," he said to Luke quietly.

"Habit," Luke hissed back, annoyed, but straightened his neck.

"I expect much better from you boys next time. I expect you to listen, and you are not to leave the estate again. Do you understand?" Claire Barrington asked in a firm voice.

They nodded miserably and were sent to the kitchen for a snack.

Luke looked at his mother with amazement and a big smile as realization dawned in his eyes. "That's a powerful voice you've got there, mother," Luke said. "Very, shall we say, influential." She was truly powerful in many ways.

"Even my family had special gifts, Luke, not just the Barrington line." She smiled and added, "how do you think I got seven boys through charm school and dance classes?" She hummed happily as she headed to the kitchen.

"What was that all about?" Dean asked quietly.

"Never mind, it's not important. Come on, time to call on my love, and then we'll head to the fair."

For the next hour, Nathalie and Dean listened in awe as Luke shouted his love and admiration for Sadie towards the inhabitant of the church. The first few times Willow had come out and openly taunted him, but his words and persistence were taking its toll. She never came out of the church anymore when he was there, but Luke knew she could hear him. His words reached her, even in the farthest and darkest part of the church where she cowered with her fingers in her ears. He did this every day; continually reminding Sadie to fight and that they would be together soon, in each other's arms.

"SHUT UP!" Hannah had cried the day before, storming out of the church and standing up to Luke nose to nose. "No one cares about your stupid feelings, Luke! Go away!" she screeched. They were friends no longer. When she found out Sadie and Luke's breakup had been a farce, she had had a meltdown. "I hate you," she screamed in his face.

Luke looked down at her coldly. "Unbelievable. Sadie's worth a hundred of you, no a thousand," he yelled loudly so Sadie could hear. Venius and Clovis had looked at Luke speculatively before dragging Hannah away, tossing her back into the church and closing the doors.

Luke had glared at the hunters. "If you touch one hair on that girl's head..."

They had just laughed.

In actuality, Luke was forbidden to leave the Barrington grounds. "Now that you're the *seer officialis*, you are in grave danger," his father had explained.

"She can't kill me. She needs me," Luke scoffed.

"That may be, son, but there are many other ways to destroy a man, not just by killing him. She can also capture you and lock you up—"

"Torture you and break your spirit," Father MacGunne added.

The Doc was nodding. "Cut off your fingers and your..."

"Whoa, Doc!" was the consensus around the room. "He gets the picture!"

Luke looked a little shocked, but became determined again. "But I can help. I can see things that no one else can see. The only ones who know about me for sure are Willow and her small gang, but she seems to be keeping the truth close like we are. She doesn't want any interference either. Besides, there are hundreds of people at the fair, plus, Taline's amulet makes me hard to see. I'll make sure I have escape routes and scream really loud if anyone tries to touch me, but I can't stay here. I'm going crazy and it's a waste of my abilities."

So with the help of Clara, Father MacGunne, Nettie, Wayman, and Taline, Luke's safety at the fair was fairly assured.

"I'll bash those buggers on the head with my staff," Clara had threatened, waving around a large wand-like stick with a huge crystal on it.

"It would help if the crystal were jagged," Father MacGunne had suggested. "More chance they'll die, or at least suffer a more painful wound."

Everyone looked at the priest in amazement.

"What?" he said, looking around. "I'm not advocating it. I'm just saying."

As he, Dean and Nathalie headed back towards the manor, Luke looked back and saw Willow staring at him balefully from one of the church windows. He smiled and blew her a kiss, but she turned away. This had better work, he prayed.

They took the safe path to South Road and headed to Town Circle and to the fair. Dean had one of the citizen's patrol walkie talkies in case of emergency. Bursts of static and talking punctured the air as they walked. Dean was fiddling with it, fascinated.

Luke warned him. "Don't do it, man."

Dean pressed the button and spoke, "ten-four Sheriff. All clear here." Dean snickered.

Sudden yelling came from the little machine. "WHO THE HELL IS THIS?" the voice shouted angrily. "BOY, THIS IS AN OFFICIAL LINE. YOU HAD BETTER NOT BE MESSING AROUND ON IT. IF YOU TOUCH THAT BUTTON AGAIN, YOU'D BETTER BE DYING," the Sheriff yelled.

Startled, Dean tossed the walkie talkie to Luke as if he'd been burned. Luke laughed and put the walkie to his mouth. "Won't happen again, Sheriff."

The fair was teeming with life.

"It's amazing how life just goes on for some people," Nathalie said wistfully.

"For most people," Dean said, pushing his way through the crowd.

They found Wayman saddling Pleasure and Pain for a ride. Dean looked longingly at the two horses.

"People are still doing the trail?" Nathalie asked curiously.

Wayman laughed, helping the youngsters up and patting the horses' rumps to get them going and walked over, dusting his hands off on his pants. "It's business as usual for everyone but you guys." He looked sharply at Luke. "What are you doing out?"

"We need more information on the two big guys in leather."

"Ah, Venius and Clovis. The dark riders. Wild hunters. Stay away from them. They're on the opposite side of the battle."

"Why would one of them recoil from my necklace?" Dean asked curiously, pulling it out.

Wayman scowled. His glower made him seem larger all of a sudden. Nathalie stepped back, afraid. Luke looked awed.

"You had a run in with one of them?" He looked at Nathalie as well. "I warned you both about losing your focus. Dean, you put yourself and Nathalie in grave danger."

Nathalie took Dean's hand. "It wasn't only his fault. It was my fault too."

"That type of *behavior* attracts them. Luckily, the amulets are linked by love, which will repel a being like that. BUT HE SHOULDN'T HAVE FOUND YOU IN THE FIRST PLACE."

They looked ashamed. Luke now looked confused.

"There was no harm done. He took off," Dean said humbly.

"What are you talking about?" Luke asked in frustration.

"Nothing, man, nothing," Dean mumbled.

"Dark hunters are strongly attracted to fear, blood or sex. They have an incredibly acute sense of smell that can differentiate between the different emotions humans give off."

"Emotions smell?" Dean snorted.

"Very strongly," Wayman said seriously. "Your body emits a scent when you're scared or aroused. How do you think Clovis found you?"

"I get it now," Luke said, waving a hand with an uncomfortable expression on his face. "I don't want to know!" He went to find a hay bale to sit on.

"He was smelling the air," Nathalie said. "He said Dean smelled like a girl *and* he had grabbed Dean's twin brothers who were out on their bikes looking for us," she said worriedly.

"He said you smelled like a girl?" Wayman asked.

"Whoa! Not like *a girl*, but like *the girl*!" Dean protested.

Nettie breezed in. "*The girl*, as in Ella Croft, his sister. A few weeks back Clovis bumped into her at the fair. He liked her smell." She looked at Dean sternly. "Keep those boys at home. I'm sure Clovis was on a mission for Willow. She needs a sacrifice, and twins double the power. You were lucky you were there."

Dean was aghast. "Oh my God..."

Nettie patted his arm. "I doubt she'll try again. She knows they'll be under lock and key now, but it never hurts to be vigilant."

She turned to Nathalie. "Did you want to continue with the diary this evening, lass?" Nathalie and Nettie had been meeting at Nathalie's in the evening to read her "*Book of Record*."

"Yes to the reading, but what do you mean he liked her smell?" *That can't be good*, Nathalie thought to herself.

Nettie smiled. "Crofts smell good. They're historical victims."

"I wish you'd stop saying that," Dean complained, looking a little pale.

"You know about the dark riders?" Nathalie asked curiously.

"Och, to be sure," Nettie said with a frown. "Dangerous buggers. Do not let those boys out of your sight."

"Don't you worry, Nettie. My mom has taken care of that," Luke said with pride.

Nettie smiled. "Yes, she's got a powerful voice, that girl."

"He didn't mark her?" Wayman asked Nettie, worried.

"I checked Ella right after it happened. He hadn't touched her," Nettie said confidently.

Wayman still looked worried. "He did catch her scent and obviously filed it away for another time," he mused. "That's not good."

Nettie agreed. "We need to keep an eye on the lass. If he gets obsessed with her, there'll be no getting rid of him until one of them is dead," she warned, "and this one has been a right player during this festival. He's had women willing and unwilling under him."

The kids gasped, but Nettie shrugged. "It's the truth. He's using his power a fair amount to compel the lasses, and a few lads. What we don't want is for him to abscond with Ella."

"Clovis isn't smart enough," Wayman said with disdain.

"Maybe, but he can be a determined and sneaky bastard when he wants to be," she said darkly.

"Willow must have forbidden it," Luke said thoughtfully, "otherwise he would have done it already. Clovis won't go against her for a mere mortal right now, but that won't stop him *later*."

"What about Venius?" Dean asked.

"He's busy with Beth. They're an item," Wayman said with distaste.

"Eww," Nathalie said, disgusted. "Still?"

"My sentiments... and yes," Wayman muttered.

"Advice?" Luke asked.

"Stay out of their way. They're bigger, stronger, faster and murderous. They have absolutely no conscience to speak of. If you find yourself face to face with one of them, run."

"Right," Luke nodded.

"No, I mean run now. Here they come," Wayman said, shoving Luke behind him towards the barn door at the back. The others followed.

Nathalie looked back. Wayman started to flicker with a blue light, cracking his knuckles and smiling.

DAY 15

Willow's Book of Record

Bethiah's suggestion for our sacrifice was a good one, but our attempt to take the Croft twins failed. Clovis, that idiot, got distracted. I doubt we'll have another chance to grab the two little brats. Such youth would have meant great power, and the power of twins on top of it! 'Tis a shame. After I punished Clovis I gave him leave to capture Ella Croft, but my spies tell me that she is also being kept on the estate for protection now. Too bad the other Croft children have no trace of magic in their blood. They're about as useful as rabbits—only suitable for stew. That leaves me only one other option, and that will be tricky.

Sadie grows weak inside me. She is still linked to her physical person, which I am starving. When I transform, the treacherous wretch will die along with her body. Regardless of all the rantings and ravings from the blathering Barrington bonehead, she will not survive to betray her family another day, and I will destroy her lover along with her.

DAY 25

The Barrington Estate

Not long now, Luke thought to himself. Six more days until D-day. He stood on the edge of the Barrington property. The evil emanating from Willow's presence had killed all the foliage around the church. The huge maple at the front was dying. The apple trees running along East Road were dying as well. Luke felt helpless fury at their situation.

They tried to change the tide. Waiting, guarding, protecting... all they did was bide their time. Frustration, boredom, sick anticipation and fear of the unknown were catching up with them.

A few days earlier the boys had wanted to storm the church the day Willow gathered all of her followers for a meeting. Nathalie was terrified they would.

Wayman had warned against it during a visit to the Barrington estate. "She's too powerful now. You go in, she'll take you."

"She can't kill us," Dean said. "She needs us for her spell."

"Actually, she could use you dead, Dean, being a Croft and all," Wayman pointed out. Dean paled. "And just because she won't kill you, doesn't prevent her from making you wish for death," Wayman said ominously. "You know, have a little fun first."

Echoes of his father's warnings ran through Luke's head.

"No one goes in there," Wayman repeated in his powerful voice, and Nathalie again got the impression he had grown a few feet.

Father MacGunne walked in as Wayman was giving the directive. "Quit yer yellin' and intimidation tactics. I'll go have a look."

Wayman scowled at the small man who had started calling him "Wee Wayman" because of his race. It made the priest snicker.

They watched as Father MacGunne snuck into the church through an outside secret passageway even John Barrington didn't know about.

"What?" Father MacGunne asked when he arrived back, in response to all the raised eyebrows in the room. "The church doesn't reveal all its secrets, you know."

"Tell us, Edward."

"It's all blather and hooky. She spoke of a new age and rewards for their loyalty. It's a load of crap, if you ask me," Father MacGunne said in disgust. "Those people will believe anything. They want to believe. They're lost souls," he said sadly.

Wayman looked at him. "That's your report? They're lost souls? It's a load of crap?"

"Yes, wee one."

Wayman growled. His eyes brightened.

"Did you see the hunters?" Dean asked hurriedly, attempting to stave off disaster brewing between the two men.

"The big leather fellows? I surely did. Those two just looked bored. Forced to be in church...get it? Ha, ha," he snickered, but nobody laughed, so he continued. "Bloodthirsty bastards they are, the lot of them. We're just sport for them, like animals. And then..." He looked uncomfortable. "I left."

"Then—what?" Everyone waited.

"They took off their bleedin' clothes, that's what! And started... you know...in my church!" Father MacGunne wailed. He was beside himself.

Luke froze. He hoped Willow wasn't putting Sadie through that, but somehow, he doubted it. Willow hated men with a deathly passion. Sex was a tool, not a pastime.

As if thinking about her willed her to appear, Luke could see Willow walk out of the church and head to the Barrington Estate. Luke shouted involuntarily and bolted out of the salon. It had been so long since he'd seen her. He stopped at the property line and watched as she came towards him, walking like a puppet on strings, jerking and twitching. Luke's heart tightened in his chest. He hadn't seen her in many days, and she had changed for the worst. Sadie was degenerating. She was thinner than ever and now looked gaunt. Her nails had grown unnaturally long and were gray with black streaks making her hands look like claws. It didn't look as of Willow bothered to wash. Her hair, clothes and body were dirty, and her skin was gray and sallow. Her white dress was filthy. She had trapped herself in that church without much fresh air or sun. Madness danced in her white eyes. He was pretty certain Willow was completely insane, and he tried not to panic when he couldn't see anything but a flicker of Sadie's life force.

She came close and smiled. "Soon she'll be dead, boy. Take a last look," she said with a sneer. "When I transform I'll shatter this body into pieces of meat." She looked at Luke, her cracked lips bleeding from smiling. "You'll all be pieces of meat for my brethren to feast on when I'm done with you."

Luke was horrified and fear wormed into his heart. They were beat. How do you fight something so evil? He took a step back and felt someone elbow him in the ribs. It was Nathalie.

"Fight, Seer," she whispered fiercely. Nathalie was trembling as well, but her voice was strong. "Willow is using her power to seduce you and suck your will. See. Win. Don't give up. Use your voice."

Willow's eyes narrowed. "Parker," she hissed. "You'll watch. You'll watch me destroy everyone you love until you beg me to kill you as well. Spy on me all you want. The end is near."

Luke said the only thing that was giving him any hope right now. "Six days, my love!" Luke boomed out. Willow hissed as she took a step back and then retreated. "Soon, Sadie! Six days! Hold on!" he yelled. He wasn't sure, but he thought he saw a flicker of life.

DAY 26

Waiting…tense patrolling of the Barrington grounds.

Willow attempts to send in armed townsfolk, under compulsion, to kill the senior Barringtons and snatch the Croft twins.

They are disarmed and detained in the Sheriff's office until Halloween, despite their confusion and protestations of innocence.

"Sorry folks," the Sheriff said without mercy.

No more strangers are allowed onto the Barrington Estate.

"How do we keep them out?" someone asked.

"We scare the hell out of them."

DAY 27

The following articles are published in The Barrington Bugle.

THE BARRINGTON BUGLE - SUNDAY, OCTOBER 27

Warning To All Citizens - Barrington Estate Cesspool Of Contagion!

By X. Agerate

This trusted reporter was contacted by the Mayor, John Barrington, himself to warn all citizens not to approach the Barrington Estate. "We're so sick we may die," the mayor himself informed me. "We have the virus. Do not risk yourselves! Do not go anywhere near the Barrington Estate!"

Even better, if you don't have to go out at all, STAY HOME!

Stop The Spread Of Disease! 10 Tips To Help You Stay Sanitary & Safe

By X. Agerate

Being sanitary isn't innate in people. This knowledge needs to be passed on. Here are some important tips to improve bacteria control in your environment. Post it somewhere visible!

1. Wash your hands with soap! Every time you sneeze, wipe your nose, or scratch your…

```
2. Cough or sneeze into your elbow and not
   your hands. Touching people with germy
   hands transmits more germs than kissing!
3. Close the toilet seat when you flush.
   It's true! Bacteria laden mist can jet
   up to ten feet and land on your unpro-
   tected toothbrush...
```

The Barrington Estate

They put contamination warning signs around the estate.

"Wow, the Doc was prepared in case something happened in Barrington," one of the council members said approvingly.

Sheriff Holt snorted. "He took them from his Halloween decorations. He never wanted to give the kids in town any candy, so he put those around his lawn and turned his light off."

Doc Peabody, who was sitting in the salon, just grunted.

"Well, I saw someone cut through the Barrington Estate a few minutes ago," Nathalie said. "The warnings didn't deter them."

"Because they look like Halloween decorations," the Sheriff said, sipping his coffee.

Dean chuckled as he read Xander's article on sanitation out loud, making Luke and Nathalie laugh.

With raised eyebrows, Sheriff Holt looked at John Barrington who had come in to help himself to coffee from the sideboard.

"Don't look at me," John said to the people in the room. "I only contributed to the virus article. The list of sanitation tips was Xander's brainchild."

"Xander's tips are accurate. You all *do* realize that, right?" Doc Peabody said to the room in general with raised eyebrows. "I mean, it's too bad the moron chose some of the more stupid ones to mention, but they're still accurate." He looked down at the psychic medical journal he was reading. "Now this stuff," he said as he waved the magazine in the air, "is crap."

DAY 28

The Barrington Estate

During a routine check of the estate perimeter, a vacant-eyed Austin Baker pushed Dean outside the protected boundary of the Barrington Estate. In the blink of an eye, Venius and Clovis appeared and grabbed a shocked Dean as Luke shouted for help. Luke was about to rush through to help his friend when Wayman appeared in a flicker of blue and streaked past Luke, pushing him back.

But it was too late.

It only took a second before Venius and Clovis were gone with their human cargo.

Wayman roared in frustration and turned towards Austin, who stood there with a puzzled look on his face. Taline appeared in a flicker of blue, an armed bow in her hands and took a second to assess the situation. Wayman was furious and had grown large and fierce in his rage.

"Leave the boy," Taline commanded sternly in a powerful voice. She relaxed her stance and put away her weapons.

"Traitor!" Wayman roared. Again, Luke could clearly see that Wayman was not human, and he no longer even tried to conceal it. Austin cowered in terror.

"STAND DOWN, Wayman!" Taline said aggressively. Her form flickered with blue light.

Luke was entranced by Taline's beauty and unwittingly diffused the situation. "Listen to her, Wayman!" Luke said with awe. "She's about to kick your ass!"

Luke's comment finally broke through Wayman's rage and got his attention. Startled, he laughed out loud and shrank back to normal size. His fury dissipated in the wake of a wide smile and sparkling white teeth. He took a final disgusted look at Austin and brushed by him at a run to the house. His form flickered and Luke could see that he was already an impossible distance away.

"Hurry up," he called back to them.

They bolted to the house, leaving Austin behind.

In the salon the good gang rallied and debated their next steps.

"Of course we have to get him!" Nathalie cried in horror when the adults considered and weighed the risks.

"It's no coincidence that Willow took a Croft," Nettie said firmly. "She needs him for her ritual."

"We don't even know what the ritual is," Nathalie said, despairingly.

Trapped on the estate, Luke, Nathalie, and Dean had been tasked with researching the Von Vixen spell book to see if Willow would be using one of her spells. They had given up once they had searched the book and discovered two pages towards the end of the book had been ripped out.

"It's no use! We know she wants to transform and murder us all... but none of Elanah's spells covers both, and we don't know what was on the missing pages. We just don't know what she's going to do or the ingredients she needs!" Nathalie said despondently. "It would only be our best guess."

"True, lass, and it's important we get him back. If she uses him she'll be unbeatable," Nettie said very seriously. "A life for a life is very powerful revenge witchcraft."

That comment halted the conversation in the room.

"Why a life for a life?" Luke asked her, his heart a tight ball in his chest.

Nettie looked around with surprise. "Why, Saul Croft was the executioner. He was the one who released the gallows."

There was a stunned silence in the room.

Nathalie was the first to speak. "Nettie, that's not written *anywhere* in your '*Book of Record*,'" she said slowly, her thoughts racing.

"Och, of course not lassie, to be sure. The executioner's name was *never* written down, out of respect for his privacy. It was a hard task, and an uncomfortable one, which is why they always wore a head covering, at a minimum, to hide their identity. It wasn't right to judge a God fearin' man doin' God's work."

"But you sent the Crofts home. Livey Croft was fine..."

"Saul was in a devil of a fury with Willow for having touched his child and terrifying his family. He offered his services to ensure the witch got her comeuppance."

Luke shook his head. "It makes sense now why the Crofts are on the list."

"If only we had shown the list to Nettie!" Nathalie said, angry with herself. "We *have* to get him back."

They all agreed, and the next hour was a flurry of activity.

The team armed themselves with whatever they could find, knives, baseball bats, two police officers with guns, and they stormed the church at sunset. A huge fight ensued between the people in Willow's gang and those in the Barrington gang, the results being black eyes, broken teeth, and many cuts and bruises.

Willow laughed as she watched them try to reach her.

"Did you think I would let you capture me *again*, Barrington?" she screamed incredulously. "You idiot! Where's your torch this time, foolish man? Last time you threatened to burn down my house! I dare you to burn the church! I dare you!" she sneered and laughed wildly over the din.

So that's why she chose the church, Nathalie noted. *She learned the hard way. You get burnt once, literally, you choose your hidey holes better next time.* Nathalie was jumping pews to get to Willow because the aisles were tangled with people fighting. "Where's Dean you crazy witch!" she screamed from one pew away.

Willow glanced at Nathalie and laughed again. "He's a dead man, PARKER! DEAD! You'll rue the day you told on me! You'll watch him die!" she said insanely and moved behind her wall of defenders.

Father MacGunne was hopping around like he was on fire. "Watch the pews! Don't smash the stained glass!! Don't kill each other!" He started to pray loudly.

"No, Father! Don't pray!" Nathalie screeched.

"She's leaving!" someone yelled.

Luke could see the sanctuary start to glow brighter. Willow hissed and bared her teeth. Venius grabbed her and she disappeared. Clovis followed immediately after.

"No!" Nathalie screamed with utter fury and burst into tears. After a few moments the fighting tapered off and stopped. The Barrington band watched warily as Willow's people milled around looking confused. Luke worked his way to Nathalie and put his arms around her.

"Now we'll never find him," she said, sobbing. Luke looked helplessly at his father. He understood exactly how she felt.

"What the hell?" one of the men finally exclaimed, looking around at his surroundings and at the bloody and banged up faces. "What is going on here? What the hell am I doing here?" he yelled in a panic.

One of the young women fainted while another one just looked at her bloody hands saying, "Oh my God, oh my God," over and over again.

"The last thing I remember is picking up a penny," another said with confusion.

Doc Peabody was ready. He had been waiting at the periphery of the fight in case he was needed to treat any serious injuries. "I'm a healer not a fighter!" he had exclaimed earlier when someone tried to give him a baseball bat as he ran with the mob to the church.

He put his arms up and shouted in a booming voice over the wails rising from Willow's victims. "Everyone, please! It's Doc Peabody here! Please, nobody panic."

Things quieted down somewhat and only some moaning and sniffling could be heard.

"You've all been suffering terrible hallucinations due to the contagion. Do not panic! The worst is over now and..." he was thinking frantically, "your fever has broken! We were using the church as a quarantine area."

Doc Peabody looked at Taline, who was standing next to him. "Missy," he whispered to her from the side of his mouth, "I need my doc bag *right now*." Within seconds Taline was back in the church with his bag. He took it from her as if her abilities were a normal occurrence. "Everyone, please line up in an orderly fashion and you'll get your antiviral shot."

What Doc Peabody really gave them was a mild sedative.

"What do we do with all the out-of-towners?" At least five of the people were not from Barrington.

Sheriff Holt joined them. "We'll take them to the precinct and check missing persons. We have four beds in the two cells and a couch. We'll put them up for the night and connect them with their families in the morning." All the victims were young adults. "Poor kids. Found the wrong party," the Sheriff said with sympathy and herded them out. The back entrance to the station was accessible through the trees on the church grounds, so they were inside the station, and safe, within minutes.

They organized into groups and got the rest of the young men and women home.

DAY 29

Willow's Book of Record

My sacrifice is in place. Bethiah's spell is ready. They're all dead.

DAY 30

The Barrington Estate

The Sheriff radioed Barrington HQ the next morning. "We have a problem, I think. Actually, I don't know what to make of it. I'm coming over. Make sure Luke and Nathalie are there."

Nathalie and Luke waited impatiently for the Sheriff. The huge manor house had become small and confined now that they were not allowed to leave. He finally arrived, taking off his hat and nodding to Claire.

He walked into the salon and handed Nathalie and Luke a piece of paper. It was a sheet with information on a missing teen. Both of them took startled breaths.

"That's Beth!" Nathalie said in a shocked voice.

It was and it wasn't. It looked like her but—

"It says her name is Tilly Black and that she's from Superstition," Luke said. He was shocked too because it also said she was severely autistic.

"This can't be right," Nathalie said, looking at a full colour photograph of Beth and looking for discrepancies.

"Just got this from Limerick. They got it from Superstition in July. Sent it over after I called for any missing person reports," the Sheriff said.

"The girl's eyes are turned up to the right corner," said Luke, pointing at the detail.

"So?"

"So... something's wrong," Luke said and ran upstairs to his computer. "Beth doesn't do that."

Nathalie and the Sheriff followed.

"How long has she been missing, Nat?" Luke asked as he ran to his desk and started clicking on the computer.

She checked the flyer. "Since... Shit!!! She's been missing since June 21!"

"The summer solstice," Luke said grimly. "When all of this started."

"Oh my God! Rain told me about this girl in her first letter! Her parents are frantic!"

Luke was typing rapidly. "What's Beth's last name?"

"Uh... Lace... Lacey, I think!"

"You said her first name is Bethiah, right? It's not short for Elizabeth?"

"No, yes, that's right. I remember thinking her name was archaic."

"I'm getting a hit on a Bethiah Lacey."

"Really? Where does she live?"

"Not where, *when* did she live," he said as he clicked on her name. There was a hushed silence in the room as the information came up. "This is from an article published in The Limerick Times. Bethiah

Lacey was a witch, and she was executed for witchcraft and grave robbing on June 21, 1860."

The Limerick Times—June 21, 1860
Public Execution Announcement

Hear ye, hear ye! It has been decreed by the most Hon. Grant Wraithstone that the following public executions be enacted on this day:

Bethiah Ingrid Lacey (19) is sentenced to hang for the practices of witchcraft, grave desecration, consorting with the devil, and moral turpitude.
Donovan Kirk (31) is sentenced to hang for murder in the first degree.
Old Ben (56) is sentenced to hang for using hoo doo and black magic to influence the prominent Drake Family and thus putting their souls in mortal peril.

The hangings shall commence at high noon at the town square gallows.
May God have mercy on their souls.

There was a grainy picture of the three condemned prisoners. Bethiah was short and plump with dark black hair parted in the middle and tied severely in a bun at the back of her neck. She was unsmiling and unattractive as she stood looking at the photographer. In comparison, Tilly was gorgeous with her long curly blond hair, tall physique, and slender curves.

"She was hung on the summer solstice in 1860. Why is that important? Why does Beth matter?" Luke was pulling his hair in frustration.

Nathalie was frozen. "It's important because it's the year Jedidiah Brown died of tuberculosis. Does it say in another article whose grave she desecrated?"

Luke searched. "No, but The Times has a list of grave desecrations... and Jedidiah is on the list."

"When did he die? What month?" the Sheriff asked curiously.

Luke checked. "Mr. Brown died in March."

"Any reports of grave desecration after the executions?"

Luke searched. "Nope. Interesting... according to the person who recorded the executions, only Donovan made a fuss, swearing and spitting. Beth went quietly, and so did Old Ben."

"So, did she die? Is she possessing Tilly's body? I don't get it. She didn't hex anyone... cast a spell... set a curse... something that would link her to this time."

The Sheriff shook his head. "Too much mumbo jumbo for me. Let me know if you need me to shoot anyone," he said as he left.

Nathalie was still. Her eyes were flicking back and forth as she processed the information on Beth.

"What Nat? Spit it out."

"It has to do with the door."

"What door?"

"The door to the dead—the one that's wedged open, and the reason we can see the dead."

"You're absolutely right, Nathalie," Wayman said. He had just arrived at the manor and had been directed upstairs by the Sheriff, followed by Taline and Nettie. "Danner the Demon used the open door to reach through time and pull his witch to your time."

"Luke was right, we needed to worry about what else would come through." Nathalie sighed.

"Beth's not a ghost," Luke said, puzzled. "I don't see an 'overlay' like I do when Willow's possessing Sadie."

"That's because she's not. We think Danner grabbed Beth from her time just as she was being executed, and forced her on Tilly—pushed Tilly's consciousness to the side. With a physical body to inhabit, Beth's a person. We figure they're 'living together,' so to speak," Taline said.

Wayman looked at Luke. "Have you ever really taken a good look at Bethiah, Luke? With your sight? It manifested with Sadie when the hex was activated, but you love Sadie. Even the littlest changes are noticeable. Perhaps to your mind that was just Beth's natural state, if you even noticed anything odd."

"It's possible," Luke said doubtfully. "I can't say I ever did 'sight' her. You asked me to once, but she was gone when I left, and I just forgot."

"But why choose Tilly, a disadvantaged girl? Why not a normal person?" Nathalie asked.

"Danner has probably been looking for a suitable and *amenable* human host for Beth for years. Tilly lives in Danner's town. He has probably been prepping her to help him since she was small—a voice whispering in her ear. Because she's autistic he probably considered her easy pickings—minimal struggle from the host intelligence. When he was ready, he called her and she went. I'll bet Tilly wouldn't even think to put up a fight." Wayman sighed. "The fact is, Danner's had hundreds of years to plan this. So has Willow."

"There's no doubt this situation is unique. Tilly's brain is wired differently and she may not be struggling. Maybe it's easy to hide someone else inside," Taline suggested.

"I wish I had thought to ask Rain to send me a poster," Nathalie said sadly, thinking of the type of girl Bethiah was and how she had abused poor Tilly's body with Venius. *Moral turpitude didn't even begin to cover it.*

"Nathalie, there's no way you could have ever made that connection. Who would have thought occupying someone else's body was possible? My God, it's unbelievable and improbable," Luke replied with disbelief. "I mean, the chances are..."

"Not calculable, resident genius, so don't bother," Wayman said dryly.

"So what do you think they have planned?"

"I don't know, but Beth is key for some reason."

"We'll know tomorrow," Nathalie said with a catch in her voice. She tried not to freak out when she thought about Dean, but it was hard. Her stomach was a constant storm of churning nerves. *Please don't hurt him,* she prayed silently in her head, over and over again.

Search parties were still out, knocking on doors and combing the woods.

"Nope, nothing," was all that ever came back over the walkie talkie from the volunteers. Nathalie was trying not to panic. The Crofts had been updated with what was happening and waited in anguish for news of their son.

"The fact is, Nathalie, it may not matter after tomorrow," Luke said, defeat creeping into his voice.

Nettie frowned at Luke's attitude, and tried to reassure Nathalie. "Timing is key for a spell of this magnitude, lass. We know a ritual will take place tomorrow and that she'll cast. Until then, she'll keep him alive. She'll no waste his blood." But it was obvious even Nettie was worried.

Nathalie touched her necklace, the match to Dean's. It was still warm and pulsed with life where it lay nestled close to her heart. She was sure it was a sign he was still alive.

The town was bursting with life. Even with all the crazy newspaper articles and threats of disease and violence, visitors to the town hadn't been fazed. Stores overflowed with people, and lineups were long due to missing staff going through withdrawal. Strange behavior was just perceived as poor manners. The fair was peaking. Even more strangers had arrived and set up shop, swelling the fair to three times its size.

Missing person posters with Dean's picture went up around Town Circle and the fair. A few false alarms were reported, but otherwise, nothing.

All those people and still no sight of him. Where was Willow hiding? Not even the woods were private anymore. Strangers were camping in there now. Thrill seekers ranged the woods at night, looking for the ghost of Willow Kellar, and daring each other to do stupid things. The Doc had reopened for business now that he and his wife were no longer "sick." They were treating a lot of alcohol poisoning cases, broken bones, and scrapes.

"Idiots," Dr. Peabody could be heard saying.

The suggestion to stay inside had become a decree to hit the streets at night for adventure. Others were feeling better after overcoming the "contagion" and were back out looking for fun. People had no fear.

"This town is going to be a shithole to manage come tomorrow," the deputy said with concern. "I hate Halloween."

"Yep," the Sheriff replied, not bothering to chastise his deputy for foul language. Today, he was right.

DAY 31

Willow's Book of Record

Today, they all die. The pigs.

The Barrington Estate

Halloween dawned sunny and windy. Happy visitors streamed into Barrington, and townsfolk of all ages dressed in costumes, determined to enjoy the last day of The Harvest Festival.

"What's going to happen? There are so many people," Nathalie said with awe. She and Luke were standing at the library looking at Town Circle. The restaurants had lineups. Even The Spells and Stars Restaurant was open for business. Joe's Java Coffee House was busting at the seams. The Rotunda was full. Waiters bustled through the tables placing food and hot coffee.

"Buses came early," the Sheriff said, watching with Nathalie and Luke as he sipped his coffee. He looked tired. His efforts, and those of his deputy, had been pretty heroic in the last month. Lines had been carved into his thin, leathery face.

"You look tired, Sheriff," Nathalie said kindly. She knew that he had pulled every string he could to try and find Dean. "I truly appreciate all you've done," she said sincerely.

He smiled at Nathalie. *Damn nice kid.* "I know I'll be sleeping tonight, one way or another, but thank you for noticing."

"The trams have been dumping full loads of people since seven this morning. They doubled the schedule to meet demand," his deputy added as he joined them.

"It seems so innocent. It's hard to believe all this bad stuff is happening at the same time. They're so…oblivious."

"Believe it," Luke said grimly. Of them all, he had changed the most. Gone was the goofy, carefree, infatuated boy of the summer. His face had hardened with what he'd had to endure. Luke was no longer the naive bookworm. He had a plan. He would win at any cost.

They watched and waited, nerves churning, but enjoying the breeze and the sun. There was no sign of Willow or any of her gang.

Where was she? What was she doing?

By noon the wind started to pick up.

By the time the sun had set, the town had been spelled.

Halloween Night

Visitors and partygoers reveled at the Halloween celebrations. The town was fully decorated. The Rotunda was bursting with diners and dancers. The festival was packed with visitors. Not one person noticed the hollow-eyed teenagers heading to The Rock. Not one parent noticed that their teenager was missing.

The call came softly and unremarkably, like a thought. The Circle's families were told not to let their children out of their sight, but slowly, one by one, they slipped away.

Tess Smith was certain Nathalie had called and asked her to meet her at The Rock, and that it was urgent.

Nathalie was suddenly sure she knew exactly where Dean was, but to rescue him she had to go alone. Too many people would raise the alarm and he would be killed. She left the Barrington's salon to use the washroom and didn't return.

Luke went to get some air, but his plan was to go get his girlfriend. He suddenly knew the spell to extricate Willow from Sadie's body and destroy her, but he had to do it himself.

Reginald was at The Rotunda with his friends when he realized that he could get Beth back by confronting her boyfriend, and his success was assured if he snuck up on him *right now*. Without saying anything to his friends, he walked away.

James Sweet finished his shift at Ye Ole Sweete Shoppe and left. His mother was busy with customers and his father was in Town Circle having beer with the boys. No one saw him go.

Not one visitor noticed that if they wanted to visit the historic landmark, they were subtly detoured to another activity or site. The Rock was reserved tonight for a private party. Willow had cast her spell and made the call to gather.

All the representatives from the original hexed families had arrived. Magic had slipped in and taken control, and Reginald, Tess, Nathalie, Luke, and James looked as if they were sleepwalking.

In the clearing, Danner was waiting beside Bethiah, his huge form flickering. Hannah stood on Beth's other side. Venius and Clovis stood back in the shadows. Everyone gathered in a semi circle with Willow in the middle. The Rock, with its menacing warning, cast a huge shadow that loomed over the assembled townsfolk, and with it a shadow that looked like gallows. More of Willow's followers appeared and ringed the chosen ones. They carried torches that burned and flickered wildly in the wind as it blew, bending the trees and causing the fallen leaves to skitter around.

Luke fought through the haze of the spell that was keeping him docile and inert. He had realized almost immediately that his idea to save Sadie was a lie, but he had allowed the spell to coerce him so he could find her.

He could see Sadie and Willow as they stood in the center. Sadie was still except for her black hair and white dress that whipped around her in the wind. She looked angelic in the torchlight, with her pale skin and blood red lips, and Luke felt a tug at his heart. Lightning flashed in the clearing, and between flashes, Luke could clearly see Willow's outline superimposed over Sadie. She was a few inches taller than Sadie, and the contrast between Sadie's billowing white dress and Willow's black one was startling. Luke stared at her, and he could see Sadie's essence! Relief flooded him. She appeared to be sleeping as Willow looked on triumphantly at the people gathered there. Then the amulet Taline had given him flared and emitted a burning pulse that radiated throughout his body, and suddenly Luke was clear headed.

Willow was holding a rusty, blood encrusted knife. Beth joined Willow in the center and presented her with a box, which Willow took and emptied into a large and elaborately cast cylindrical bowl on the ground at her feet. It was filled with a black liquid, and the object fell with a squishy plop. Willow took the knife and cut her hand, and then Beth's, and they clasped hands. Their mingled blood dripped into the metal bowl. Beth chanted as she held hands with Willow. Luke could see Sadie's purple power feeding Beth as she cast her spell. Above the cylinder a portal opened. Beth yelled a final word and the cylinder blazed and disappeared. In its place was a man.

Luke was shocked with disbelief. He suddenly knew what was happening and the identity of the man Beth had pulled through the portal.

Luke looked up and could see Nathalie motioning frantically to him. Like him, Nathalie was no longer entranced, unlike the others. He guessed her amulet and Lore Keeper heritage were kicking in as well. She also knew who the man was and there was a look of panic in her eyes.

Jedidiah Brown was crumpled at Sadie's feet, brow on the ground. Luke's heart leapt as he watched Sadie struggle with Willow for dominance, and win. Willow was gone and Sadie was there, looking around and then down. Sadie was horror struck as she crouched to touch the crumpled being and had to scream above the wind to be heard. "Jedidiah, are you okay?" she asked frantically, turning him over and putting her hand on his forehead.

"No, I'm dying. I've got TB. Tuberculosis," he replied weakly, pushing her hands away. "Who are you? Where am I? You shouldn't touch me, I'm contagious." Sadie's face was close to Jed's as he spoke in order to be able to hear him over the whine of the wind. So when Jed had a chest spasm, he coughed blood and mucus all over her.

Luke went white with horror. Sadie stood up and her face and dress were sprayed with blood. Luke frantically tried to reach for her but he couldn't move. Sadie's arm was out and her hand up. She had formed a wall of air around him so he couldn't advance.

"Don't come near me, Luke," she warned, her violet eyes flashing. "I'm contaminated. None of us are vaccinated."

"Of course not, because IT WAS ERADICATED," Luke screamed furiously, tying to beat his way through the barrier to get to Sadie.

"Not anymore," she said wryly, looking at the blood splattered all over her.

At that moment Beth grabbed Sadie's arm and whirled her around. "You fool!" she yelled, enraged. "How dare you interfere, you, you—"

"Who the HELL do you think you are, you insignificant witch?" Sadie said ominously as she wrenched her arm back and then lifted it, pointing a finger at her.

Beth hesitated and took a fearful step back, eyes round.

"Now, girls," Danner said warningly from the sidelines.

They ignored him. "Don't you *ever* touch me again," Sadie said angrily, taking a menacing step forward...but then she was gone. Willow was back, her black dress and hair billowing wildly around her. She hissed with rage.

Luke was furious and terrified. They brought Jedidiah to die and activate the hex. The boy was so close to death he was on the cusp. If he died, Willow's hex would kill every member of the original families and give Danner the required blood sacrifice to open his prison. If Jedidiah died here, they were toast. They had to send him back.

"I am going to kill you myself," Luke screamed at Willow.

She just glared at him. "Stay away from me, Barrington," she warned.

Danner was glowing with anticipation. Everything was going exactly as planned. He could taste his freedom. Bethiah watched with wide eyes. Hannah was staring sightlessly like the rest of the kids.

"It's time. Do it," Danner hissed to Willow. Willow bent down and grabbed Jedidiah by the hair and went to cut his throat. The boy was so weak he didn't even struggle. The knife was on his skin and a drop of blood appeared. Willow paused, her face had grown angry. Sadie was fighting.

"You dare fight me, you weak and pathetic little witch?" she was saying to herself, but her hand didn't budge.

Luke frantically looked for something to hit Willow with that wouldn't hurt Sadie. He couldn't see anything. He couldn't think. He saw Nathalie sitting in the clearing near Venius, watching as if frozen. Her face was wet with tears as she cradled Dean's head in her lap. Dean! He knew Dean was dying. He knew now that the black liquid they used to snatch Jed was his blood. Luke wasn't sure anything could save him now.

Time for his plan. Luke walked closer to Willow who was occupied with her internal battle. She was winning. She was so powerful and so determined, but he was going to tip the scales. He shouted over the wind. "So, do you mean to tell me that all the time we spent together in bed over the last month, it was with you and not Sadie?"

Willow and Sadie both stopped struggling instantly. Willow looked at Luke dismissively, "What are you talking about, boy?" she asked, taking a breath and then trying the knife again.

"You seduced me! I shouted all those loving things and you came to me every night and pretended that Sadie was free. In her white nightgown! You've run your hands all over me and kissed me in even more places. I've returned the favour frequently, passionately...and it wasn't real? I always thought it was Sadie with me, but it was you." Luke looked aghast.

Willow and Sadie stood up and looked at Luke full on. Sadie's expression was shocked. Willow's was derisive. "You lie," Willow said and turned her back on Luke, turning Sadie's body with her.

But Sadie, hearing this, turned her body back to face Luke while Willow struggled. She trained her burning violet eyes on Luke's face.

"We don't have time for this," Willow said angrily, attempting to force Sadie back to Jed, but there was nothing she could do. Sadie and Willow were coexisting and Sadie was in control.

Sadie was furious and JEALOUS. She was panting and her fists were clenched at her sides as fevered imaginings went through her head. She had WAITED. She had RESISTED while everyone else in town had been fornicating like rabbits in Babylon. *Waiting* to make sure there was no chance Willow could interfere. *Waiting* because she loved Luke so much she couldn't bear the thought of sharing him, not even with a ghost. Her fury rose as she looked at his sweet face, the face she loved more than anyone's, and realized what had happened. She would not be Luke's first. Not ever. Not even one memory, and with her body!

Danner was frowning now. *What the hell's going on here?* he wondered, but it didn't take him long to realize. "Ah, shit," Danner said with disgust as he watched Sadie explode with fury and then begin to glow violet as she brought the full force of her power to bear.

"No one messes around with my Luke! No one! You utter BITCH!" Sadie screamed with fury. "For that, you pay!"

"No," Willow whispered when she realized what Luke had done. "Nooooooo!" she screeched in denial.

Power filled Sadie and burst through her, and Willow was instantly annihilated. Sadie stood in the middle of the clearing, her body crackling with power. She could feel the power flow into her as she took the energy from everything around her. She was incensed. She glowed with purple light as it rolled around her and arced through her hands. It was not hot but comforting as it thrummed through her. She was insanely jealous, and powerful emotions rippled through her. She was starting to lose control of herself. She wanted to destroy something to ease the pain of Luke's betrayal.

She wanted to kill.

With an arc of purple light, The Rock was gone, shattered into a million pieces. People yelled and ducked as they were pelted with shards. Sadie was breathing rapidly and her nostrils were flared.

Luke looked at her with awe. His girlfriend was one scary bitch when she was mad.

"Sadie! My God, Sadie! Focus! Your necklace, you silly goose!" Luke yelled at her, waving his arms frantically and grabbing his neck. "Feel your necklace!"

Sadie watched him cavort wildly. Her throat was burning and she realized that her necklace was as hot as a lump of coal from the fire. Had he been lying? She narrowed her eyes. "You can't lie!" Sadie screamed at Luke, her anger causing tears to well up in her eyes. Her hands clenched and unclenched as she dealt with her rage and she tried to rip the necklace off her neck.

"Of course I can lie! I'm a teenage boy for God's sake!" Luke yelled back. "YOU can't lie to ME—that's why we got YOU the necklace in the first place—for when I WASN'T AROUND!!!"

Sadie stood very still as Luke's logic penetrated her brain and she thought through his argument. After a few moments she looked at Luke. "So..."

"Of *course not*!" Luke exclaimed.

Sadie smiled with relief. "Sorry, Luke. I should never have doubted you."

Phew, Luke thought. *That was close.*

Sadie turned to Bethiah. Bethiah was frozen in terror as she watched Sadie. Months of planning destroyed. Centuries, actually. Everything had gone horribly, horribly wrong. Sadie's eyes were as cold as ice. She looked at Bethiah, who had begun to back away.

"Compared to my power, you are but a worm beneath my shoe," Sadie said to her and pointed her finger. "I see you," she hissed. "Begone, parasite," she said with disdain as she flicked her wrist. Immediately, Beth grew still and her eyes rolled up to the top right side of her head as if she were listening to voices.

"My cue to leave," Danner said casually, looking around the clearing, but he didn't move. Sadie had wrapped a purple noose of light around Danner's huge neck. "Great," he said, and yawned. "Purple looks good on me."

Sadie smiled. "According to Klaus Deitriche, an entity 'demon in nature' betrayed his brothers and escaped to earth to avoid their wrath. This demon caused such havoc that the faerie actually helped a group of humans imprison him at Superstition and set a guard over him. His imprisoned presence caused odd but minimal danger. The deal was no power, or electricity, to weaken the cage, and in return they would always have plenty. Life does abound in Superstition."

He mocked her openly. "You can't kill ME, witch. Anyway, I'm not even corporeal." Danner looked bored.

"No, I can't kill you. But I can release you." Sadie said evenly.

"No, you can't *smarty pants*. You're not from Superstition, and you need a fairy." Danner said "fairy" with disdain and was blowing on his nails.

Sadie smiled. "Tilly, release Dannerlich, please."

Tilly smiled. "Release Dannerlich, please," she said automatically.

Danner was no longer checking out his nails. "That doesn't count. She's an idiot."

"She's not, actually, and she's a member of your community."

"What? *Whatever*." Danner waved his hand in a shooing motion. "You still need the power of the faerie."

"I release you Dannerlich," Wayman said loudly, arriving in the clearing with Taline and Nettie in tow. Wayman and Taline glowed, their bodies emitted soft blue light in the darkness. A big grin split his face, and he let out a wild laugh as he grabbed Tilly's hand and danced her around.

"I release you Dannerlich," Taline added for good measure.

"Sorry it took us so long. A spell kept us from entering the clearing," Wayman explained. "We could see what was happening, but we couldn't approach. It just broke a few minutes ago."

Danner's huge form solidified. He laughed out loud with glee. "Fools!!" he screamed insanely. He crouched, his huge body rippling with strength and power. His huge clawed hands flexed in anticipation. He was very aroused. "I'm going to rip all of you into bloody pieces and eat you one by one, starting with you, you stupid cow," he said to Sadie.

"I don't think so," Sadie said calmly, lifting her arms to the side and turning her palms up towards the sky. "Our play date is over," Sadie said and laughed. "It's time for you to go home." With that Sadie shouted a word and flung her head back. A steady stream of power flowed from the ground, through Sadie, and up into the night sky. The sky was black and boiling with energy. A tear ripped across the sky as Sadie opened a portal.

"NO!" Danner screamed in horror as his family collected him and pulled him back into the demon realm. As the portal closed, a gold amulet fell from the sky and thudded in Danner's place. Payment from them—a demon favour chit for Sadie to use in the future—the demon version of a thank you card.

"Sadie, it's almost midnight!" Luke reminded her. He realized that the wind had stopped. It was eerily quiet. People were still entranced. "We need to clean this up before All Saints Day!"

Sadie looked sadly at Jedidiah. *What a way to spend your last moments of life,* she thought. "I can't heal you Jed. You died in 1860 and if history changes... who knows what'll happen." Sadie bent over him and touched his chest. He struggled weakly to get away from her.

"You'll get sick..." he fretted, pushing at her feebly.

"No, my magic has killed the virus on me. Nothing can touch me right now," Sadie assured him. "I can take away your pain, but that's about it." She released power into his chest.

"The pain is gone!" He said with relief as he stared at her with awe. Sadie made a sweeping motion with her hand and a portal opened. It looked like a huge door filled with light.

"You'll end up exactly where you were when you were put in stasis," Sadie assured him.

Luke helped Jed up and steadied him. Jed thanked him and stepped through, and he was gone.

Sadie had turned to Nathalie and Dean. Dean was unconscious from blood loss. Willow had slit his wrists deeply to get the blood she needed for her spell. While not a healer by witch-trade, there was a broad knowledge in the power Sadie was wielding and she knew what to do to help. Sadie bent down and touched Dean's wrists and in seconds the gaping wounds closed. Sadie considered and then placed her hand, palm down, on Dean's chest. Nathalie could see a purple burst flow through him from the center of Sadie's hand.

"Can you wake him up?" Nathalie asked desperately between sobs. Dean's normally pale white skin was ashen.

"Give his body a chance to recover. I just sent it a..." Sadie struggled to explain herself, "a healing signal, and a little magical help. I think he'll be fine."

Sadie stood. Tilly was standing still, her eyes looking up to the right, lost in the voices. It was so strange to see Beth acting this way. Sadie looked at her and Venius stepped in front of Tilly.

"I can communicate with her. I am bringing her back with me. She is mine." His voice held power and possessiveness.

Sadie didn't move. "That's not Beth. Beth is gone."

"I do not want Beth. I saw the two entities after I had sex with Beth the first time. Before that I could not see the two, only after I gave my essence and Tilly was smart enough to grab it and use it to show herself to me. Tilly came to me and asked for me. After that I was never with Beth. I pushed Beth aside to be with Tilly."

Everyone was so focused on the giant they almost missed it. They saw, in astonishment, that Tilly was looking directly at Venius, *lovingly,* and had put her hand in his. "My power does this. She is better with me."

Sadie frowned. "Her parents may not agree," she said, looking with distaste at the dark hunter.

"I will make them," he said with bared teeth. "Humans worship us."

"Me go," Tilly said simply.

Sadie snorted but made no move to stop Venius from taking Tilly to the portal. Sadie could feel her own love just behind her and was getting impatient to move on and have some alone time with Luke. They had a lot to talk about and they had been apart for way too long.

The clearing had started to fill with all the strange folk that had graced Barrington's Harvest Festival this year. The potion seller smiled as she stepped through, stopping only long enough to make a rude gesture at Nathalie.

"Three months with the human race and that's what you have to show for it," Nathalie mumbled, insulted.

Dean laughed weakly. He was looking at Nathalie with his beautiful, if bloodshot, eyes full of love. "Maybe if you hadn't publicly insulted her, you'd be friends."

"You are never on my side," Nathalie said softly before she bent down and kissed him, holding him tightly. Dean laughed and struggled to get up. He was still weak, but Nathalie helped him and they watched as more of the magical folk arrived, drawn by the open portal.

Nettie stopped in front of Nathalie. "It's important that you record this, dear. Record everything you saw and heard. Do it immediately. People may have a need of this in the future."

"But Willow's gone," Nathalie said.

"Aye, her hex too. I can feel that Barrington has been freed. But lass, this land has had strong magic touch it. The earth remembers and this place is powerful now. You will need to know exactly what happened here." Nettie looked into Nathalie's eyes. "You are the Lore Keeper now. If you don't record it right away, you'll no remember. The faerie folk have a way of making human minds forget, and you are in close proximity with them."

"Okay, Nettie, I promise."

"You did me proud, lassie," she said, hugging Nathalie tightly, her eyes bright with tears.

Nathalie didn't know what to say, she just felt a rush of love for the woman. "I love you, Nettie. I'm glad I'm from such wonderful stock."

"I love you too, lassie. Oh, and while you're at it, be sure to write and tell the world that the Kellars are not to be shunned."

Shunned?

"Er, they don't shun people anymore Nettie," Wayman said casually.

"*Whatever*, as the young like to say. Now get me to my Henry," Nettie said as she walked through.

Strange folk were still streaming through. It was like watching the trams empty visitors at the fair. The basketball player who had played with the boys all summer appeared and grinned at Dean and Luke.

"I knew it!!" Dean yelled and Luke laughed. "No human is that good!" They high fived each other. Dean was feeling like his old self.

"Where are all these people coming from? How did they get here in the first place?" Nathalie asked. She looked at Sadie for an explanation but Sadie was lost in her power, her gaze turned inward as she held the portal open.

Taline walked over to the portal. "I'll try and explain. At the summer solstice the veil between realms is thin. Magic is very powerful. Danner took Tilly, brought Bethiah forward in time, and gave her Tilly's physical body to inhabit while she finished her spell work."

Wayman joined her. "Turns out Jedidiah didn't die from tuberculosis, like his family thought. Bethiah cast a powerful spell and put Jedidiah in stasis so he wouldn't die. He only *appeared* dead. His family thought he had finally succumbed to his disease and buried him quickly, as was the custom back then to prevent the spread of disease."

Taline was nodding. "The thing is, to meet the conditions of the hex, and this is unpleasant, Willow needed a "living" piece of Jed in this time to do a resurrection spell, which is what Beth and Willow performed to bring Jed to the clearing. The best part to use is a still-beating heart. But when Beth went to get it in 1860, she got caught desecrating his grave. That, along with her reputation as a witch, earned her a place on the gallows."

"Why didn't she just take what she needed at the hospital back in 1860? Why go to all the effort of digging up a grave and risk getting caught?" Dean asked. "Pretty dumb in my opinion."

Taline smiled with affection at Dean. "Well, Beth couldn't damage his body before his family buried him. It would have been hard to explain the gaping chest wound and missing heart."

"That is so gross," Nathalie said with disgust.

Taline's face mirrored her disgust. "It's the blackest magic. Beth and Jed were inextricably tied together by that spell, as caster and victim. In stasis, Jed isn't alive. He's nothing until the witch who cast the spell frees him. Beth's arrival in this time made Jed's existence possible, and with the Kellar heir ready, all the elements needed for Willow's hex, 'Gather and Die,' had been met."

"Beth finished her work. *The Limerick Times* carried a report of a grave desecration at the end of June this year. It was Jedidiah's grave. Stolen heart," Wayman said. "It's under investigation right now because Jed's body hadn't decomposed, of course, yet his grave marker says he died in 1860. So now they think it's a recent murder, so there's some confusion down there at the moment."

"Danner certainly was lucky he found Beth—living in the right time to help him *and* living in the same town as the last heir of the Browns," Dean said.

Taline agreed. "So to answer Nathalie's original question, when Beth came through, that's when the other strange folk did as well. When magical stress started to form around Barrington it attracted them. Many were drawn to the building tension and conflict that Dannerlich and Willow had planned for the town. Some were pulled involuntarily, for a purpose, like Nettie, and some of us came deliberately, like me, Wayman, and the various other folk you saw."

"So what about the rule of no interference?" Luke asked curiously. "Magical beings kept coming to Barrington, yet not one police officer from Limerick even stopped for a coffee!"

"Oh, that rule is for mortals and mortal things *only*, it turns out. Magical energy attracts magical things, and that didn't change. I think the information on the "no interference rule" was not clearly explained to future generations by your forebears."

"You think," Luke mumbled.

"Danner thought he was pretty smart," Nathalie commented.

"Not as smart as my Luke," Sadie interjected in a far away voice.

Taline laughed. Standing close to the portal, she had started to glow. Her long silver hair shimmered and her blue eyes twinkled like sapphires. Wayman was staring at her, spellbound.

"Danner underestimated the power of love," Taline said quietly. "It was brilliant to intoxicate the town with a drug mixed with a mild love potion."

"Is that what that mysterious ingredient was?"

"Yep. Many adults were so distracted that Bethiah and Danner got away with a lot." Taline laughed. "What no one took into consideration was the obsessive love of a teenage girl. The power of their hormones! The jealousy and rage... all for their sweethearts, as we saw with Sadie. In her rage, Sadie was so powerful she destroyed Willow, and his plan, in the blink of an eye."

Taline looked at Luke. "You are one smart kid," she said admiringly, "to have thought of capitalizing on that."

"Genius, actually," Luke said, and then smiled. "I know my girl," he said jokingly, "and I could tell that she'd had enough," but he did take a quick look at Sadie with a wild eye.

Wayman laughed and Dean looked at him suspiciously. "About your horse Pain, is he... smarter than most horses?"

"He is," Wayman confirmed with a wink.

"You tell him I'm going to kick him in the ass the next time I see him."

"Tell him yourself," Wayman said, inclining his head towards the trotting horse heading to the portal.

"Whoa, boy," Wayman shouted, and Pain halted, whinnying and pawing the ground. His white coat was glowing blue.

"You know, Pain doesn't bite just anyone regularly," Wayman laughed. "If he didn't like you, he'd just ignore you. Humans don't taste good."

Dean grunted as Pain nudged him with his nose and then tried to bite him, *again*.

"Geez!" he shouted, moving his hand in the nick of time. Pain nuzzled him and stepped on his foot before he galloped off.

"Ooof," Dean said in pain, but then he remembered his first ride with Nathalie. "I owe you one, buddy!" he yelled after the departing animal.

Just then a huge, black, snorting horse streaked through with a huge leather clad rider.

"That would be Clovis," Wayman said with satisfaction.

Taline smiled, but sadly this time. "We have to go too."

Nathalie hugged her tightly. She had learned so much from this confident, beautiful being. Nathalie started to cry.

Taline held her close. "Nathalie, you're a great girl. If you ever need us, we'll come." Taline took a necklace from around her neck and put it around Nathalie's. "This amulet is called a Summons. You invoke it by crushing it and calling our names. It acts like a mini portal. It's powerful magic, but only to be used in great emergency. Okay?"

Nathalie nodded.

She held her hand out to Wayman, and he pulled her into a great bear hug. His arms were heavenly. Dean started to make harrumphing noises, and Wayman laughed as they clasped hands.

Everyone said their goodbyes. Sadie inclined her head to the two in respect. Taline and Wayman did the same and stepped through.

The portal closed by itself when the last stranger passed. Sadie's power faded and she collapsed.

"Oh my God, Sadie!" Luke yelled as he rushed forward. He sounded panicked as he threw himself beside her.

"I'm fine, Luke." Sadie said gingerly, sitting up. She rubbed her head. Sadie was a mess. She was full of Jedidiah's blood and her hair was a tangled snarl from the wind. *Thank God there's no mirror around* Luke thought fleetingly. Sadie was beautiful, but she hated being dirty and disheveled. Sadie calmly looked around her and then into Luke's concerned blue eyes. She reached up and put her hands on each side of his face.

"I love you Luke Barrington," she said softly, her face tightening with dismay as her eyes searched his beloved face. "I was so scared when Willow had me. I didn't think I'd ever have the chance to tell you again. She was so strong and determined that I thought I was lost." Sadie pulled Luke to her and kissed him, stroking his face. She broke the kiss and put her cheek to his and wrapped her arms around his neck and he hoisted her up.

Sadie turned to look at the leftover crowd. Everyone was milling about, bemused. No one could figure out how they had gotten to the clearing. The torches were still burning and the wavering glow made the scene eerie and confusing.

Sadie curled her fingers with Luke's and turned to the crowd. She narrowed her eyes as she deliberated.

Tess looked at Sadie in astonishment. "What happened?" Tess exclaimed. She saw Nathalie. "You okay? I had a feeling you needed me."

Nathalie hugged her pal. "I'm fine, thank you for coming. It was just..."

"A big party at The Rock," Sadie suggested, glowing briefly as she sent the thought through the crowd.

Tess' eyes widened. "Of course, and it was..." she looked around, slightly bewildered.

"Awesome. It was just awesome," Sadie said confidently.

The word spread. The Halloween party at Kellar Rock was awesome.

"Where is Kellar Rock?" James asked curiously, looking around and then up, as if for help. "Are you sure we're in the right clearing?"

"It's dust," Dean said loudly. "I saw it get hit by lightening."

"Oh, that's awesome," James said, losing interest and drifting away.

The kids started to leave for home.

"Luke, make sure Xander writes a piece on The Rock for the next edition of The Bugle," Nathalie said, "particularly since it's on Barrington's list of historic things to see in this 'witch burning hexed' town."

Luke nodded distractedly. Blah, blah stupid rock. His eyes were fixed on Sadie hungrily. "Sadie, are we done? Can we go home?" Luke asked her quietly. The last few weeks had been murder. He missed her desperately and only wanted to hold her for the next hundred years.

Sadie laughed as Luke wrapped his arms around her waist and pulled her close. He couldn't stop touching her and they needed some time alone to reconnect.

"Can I sleep over at your place, Luke?" Sadie asked. "I really don't want to go home tonight."

Luke's face lit up with his old goofy grin. "Sure, my mom always has a spare room ready," he teased.

"I'll probably just stay in your room with you, Luke." Sadie said casually. "It has been a long month and a frightening night for both of us."

"Absolutely," he whispered. "You can wear my PJs and use my toothbrush."

Sadie put her mouth to Luke's ear and whispered back. "Neither of us is going to be wearing PJs tonight, Luke, but I'll definitely take you up on the toothbrush offer," she whispered.

Luke started to hyperventilate.

"Bend down and take deep breaths," Dean yelled behind him as he and Nathalie left the clearing.

Suddenly there was a lot of noise in the woods as adults streamed in with flashlights and dogs. Pandemonium ensued as teens were stopped by their parents and questioned, dogs barked, and the torches were taken and extinguished.

"Doesn't anyone realize how dangerous torches are in a forest?" Xander could be heard exclaiming. "I hope no kids were smoking! Oh, shit! Where's The Rock!?"

John and Claire Barrington found Luke and Sadie. "What happened? We couldn't find you..." John said, giving them both a rough hug.

"She's gone," Luke said wearily. "Sadie annihilated her," he said with pride as his mother looked Sadie over and gave her a hug.

Sadie smiled in embarrassment.

"We could feel it," Claire said quietly. "All that negative energy...gone."

John Barrington was nodding. "Other than a giant party still going on at The Rotunda, everything is well..."

"Normal," Claire said simply.

Luke nodded and yawned. He put his arm around Sadie and she sagged against him. "Sadie's wiped out, dad. I'm taking her home."

John was looking at the crater where the rock used to be. "Fine, son, we'll debrief tomorrow," he said, clapping his son on the shoulder and heading towards the Sheriff, who was shining his flashlight around the spot and whistling.

The Barrington Estate

They snuck up Barrington Manor's central staircase to Luke's room. His parents were out, but he didn't want any nosey siblings intercepting them. Thankfully, all was quiet. Once they closed the door to his suite, there was only one moment of awkwardness as they stared at each other. Sadie dispelled it immediately by pulling her dress over her head and tossing it to the ground, her underclothes following as she headed to the bathroom.

"Come shower with me Luke. I don't remember the last time I took a shower and I need to get this blood and dirt off of me *right now*," she said as she disappeared into the washroom. Luke was right behind her.

The shower was hot and steamy and filled with a lot of groaning from Luke and gasping from Sadie as they kissed and soaped each other up. They stayed in there a long time, enjoying the hot water rolling over them. Eventually Luke pulled her pink, heat flushed body out of the shower and tried to dry her a little as they kissed and stumbled to his room. Sadie fell back onto Luke's bed with him on top of her, holding her tight.

"Now," she said frantically as his mouth covered hers and he obliged with a thrust of his hips. As he slid inside her, Luke melted at her heat. "Sadie," he groaned against her mouth as he pumped his hips. She covered his mouth with hers and wrapped her legs around his body and moaned with pleasure. Within minutes she was writhing in ecstasy, and so was he.

Much later they were curled up together in Luke's big four poster bed. He was kissing the damp curls at the back of Sadie's neck. His arm was draped over her hip and he was rubbing circles with his hand on her flat stomach. She snuggled closer to Luke's large, warm body as the wind howled outside, causing the branches from the huge maple tree to knock and scrape at the window. Luke tightened his grip around the frail girl he loved so much.

Sadie felt safe for the first time in her life. Her eyes were closing and her last thought was a happy one. Luke was hers, wholly and completely, first time and everything.

The Parker Residence

When Nathalie and Dean arrived at Nathalie's house it was completely dark. They crept up to Nathalie's room and locked the door. Dean held Nathalie tightly. She was shivering from shock. In a matter of hours, their worlds had utterly changed.

"Nathalie, you have to record this," Dean told her softly. He gave her one tight squeeze and then pushed her towards her desk.

"It's already like a memory, and fading quickly," Nathalie said quietly, turning on her computer and seating herself in front of the screen.

"You can do it," Dean said sleepily. He had no recollection of where he'd been the last two days. His only memory was being in the clearing with the wind whipping around him while Willow slit his wrists and poured his blood into a cylinder. "A life for a life," she had whispered.

"It was really gross, and then I passed out," he had told her.

She watched Dean as he snuggled in her bed. She wanted to join him. She had almost lost him tonight.

"Nettie says that recording is part of your heritage. We'll do our best and talk through our memories tonight and get the bulk of it down. We'll let Luke have his time with Sadie, poor guy. He was in hell being away from her for so long. He can read it tomorrow and fill in the missing parts."

"Suppose he forgets too?" Nathalie said worriedly.

"I don't think he can. He's The Seer. With true sight, I don't think his mind can be tricked to forget. He *is* a genius," Dean mumbled... and started snoring.

And, I'm on my own... Nathalie thought as she stared at the bright screen. Unlike the rest of Barrington, Nathalie wasn't sleepy. A nervous energy animated her. A need to finish this pushed her to start typing. In the end Nathalie didn't have any problems recording the events of the summer or this past night as she looked back. The words flowed from her and her fingers flew over the keyboard. All the events and conversations came back to her. Even the times when her terror for Dean had distracted her, her mind seemed to have been recording events subconsciously.

When she was done it was almost dawn. Dean was out cold on her bed, snoring softly. He was still extremely pale. *He's going to Doc Peabody today if I have to knock him out myself,* Nathalie thought.

Nathalie's Journal – Entry for Friday, November 1

We did it. We all survived.

I wrote it all down, but no one will ever believe what's written in my little book. It's like fantasy. I wonder if Klaus Deitriche felt the same way when he wrote about his demon.

The good thing is that in the end, I didn't have to "watch" shit! Sucks to be you, Willow Kellar.

Bitch!

future

Friday, November 1 – All Saints Day
The Parker Residence

The next day Sadie and Luke dropped by Nathalie's in the afternoon. They were holding hands and laughing as they walked up Nathalie's street. Nathalie had called Luke and asked him and Sadie to come over and read her account. Dean and Nathalie were waiting for them on the front porch.

"She's a different girl," Nathalie said, looking at the radiant expression on Sadie's face.

"She sure is," Dean said, kissing Nathalie's hand.

Nathalie's mother popped her head out the front door. "I have snacks in the back and your dad's barbequing," Mrs. Parker announced. "So come and have something to eat!"

Nathalie's father drifted by humming, spatula in hand, wearing his new apron that said "I'VE BARBEQUED IN HELL. COME AND GET IT!" in big, bold letters. Nathalie sighed. Soon the snow will come and the barbequing will end. She hoped.

Dean led the way and Sadie followed him through the front door to the back yard. Luke was following when Nathalie stopped him.

"Luke, how much do you remember of last night?" she asked him curiously.

"I remember everything. You?"

"Me too, the memories aren't fading like I thought they would. Dean doesn't remember much from the last couple of days."

"Maybe that's not a bad thing. He was almost murdered. Wayman touched him when he left. Maybe he left a forget spell. That's why the faerie folk are considered myths—we can never remember encountering them."

"I'm not sure that's true."

"Why do you say that?"

"My dad was telling my mother how Patrick O'Callaghan and Shaemus O'Malley are back in town. I think Shaemus left when he saw the first faerie at the festival."

"Taline or Wayman?"

"Probably one of them. Anyway, he has some sort of sight...he went to Limerick and stayed hidden for over three months."

Luke whistled. "At the risk of his business and everything. What made him come back now?"

"Halloween passed and the festival ended. Apparently he asked Sheriff Holt if 'they' were gone now that the festival was over. Sheriff Holt threw him in the clink to sober him up, according to Patrick."

"Patrick left after Shaemus."

"Right after seeing Venius and Clovis at the church. Wrote his article and bolted. I'm not sure, and he's not saying. I think the Irish have a sixth sense about them."

Luke nodded. It made a weird type of sense.

"What about Sadie? How's she doing? She went through quite an ordeal. Being possessed, getting her power, blowing up The Rock, getting sprayed with TB..."

Luke blushed. "Oh, she's great. She's fine, physically and mentally, just extremely thin. Willow starved her, but that doesn't bother her. She wasn't abused in any way, thankfully. Even Clovis was terrified of Willow. Apparently she eventually gave him permission to grab Ella, but Sadie was so horrified she thinks she frowned at him briefly, so he didn't do it."

"Thank God," Nathalie said with relief.

"Well, they took Dean instead," Luke said wryly.

"It was hell, but I know he would prefer that than letting some beast put his hands on his sister," Nathalie said quietly. "It becomes a choice between two evils."

"The good thing is that Sadie can access her power at will, which is great, but she has no idea how she multiplied it *exponentially* by pulling all the energy from around her."

"Well, she performs well under pressure. She's always been able to use it the moment you're in mortal danger," Nathalie said wryly.

Luke blushed. "I have that effect on her," he said.

Nathalie could see that he was extremely pleased by that.

"I have that effect on *Sadie Kellar*, Nathalie. *The Sadie Kellar.* Who happens to be *my girlfriend*—" he emphasized.

"I get it!" Nathalie said, laughing. "Does she still have the demon token?"

"Yes. We've put it in a safe place. It looks as if all of Danner's pennies disappeared with him."

"Did she go home?"

"Yes, briefly. Her aunt was there, acting as if nothing happened."

"So..."

Luke shrugged. "It's her home. The Kellar legacy is over. Liora actually let me into the house for the first time ever. She just barked at me to take off my shoes."

"Just like that?"

"Just like that," he said. He didn't mention anything to Nathalie about Boris being Sadie's father. Sadie had no plans to confront him, yet. She needed time to think through how much Willow, and Willow's revenge, had manipulated her life, and all the Kellars, for centuries.

"Did you talk to Hannah?"

"No," he said curtly, "and I don't plan to. She showed her true self through all of this. I'm not sure I can be friends with her anymore. I still don't get the letters, particularly the hate mail. Why get the town riled up? I'm surprised Willow didn't want revenge on *her* for putting the spotlight on Sadie."

"The fact is, with everyone watching Sadie, no one was watching Beth. She did everything she needed to do without anyone getting in her way—right under everyone's nose."

"I hope Beth got what she deserved," Luke said. "She was one horrible witch."

"She was sent back to wherever she came from, and at the time she was being hung as a witch. I don't think she escaped that in the end." Nathalie handed the journal she had printed and bound to Luke. "Look through it and let me know if I missed anything."

"I will, Lore Keeper."

"Thank you, Seer."

They hugged each other and laughed.

THE BARRINGTON BUGLE - SATURDAY, NOVEMBER 2

Issac Heimler Fired From The Barrington Bugle!

By X. Agerate

Issac Heimler has been fired from The Barrington Bugle for "unprofessional conduct in the printing of the town newspaper."

Apparently the town council reviewed The Bugle's reporting over the summer and "[they] were shocked and appalled at the nonsense that was printed, especially the hate mail that was published in the 'Letters to The Editor' section."

Heimler didn't go quietly. He continued to yell his outrage and protest his innocence as he was escorted from The Bugle's offices.

According to friends, Heimler has been offered a very lucrative position at The Inquisitor, and will be joining their editorial staff as Editor in Chief.

We wish Issac much luck in his future endeavors.

Epilogue

November

By the end of All Saints Day, all the strangers were gone. Sheriff Holt, his deputy, and many determined citizens rounded up the party stragglers sleeping under tables and bushes in Town Circle and sent them packing. The town was theirs again. Over the month many of the adults in town had to live down their behavior during the Harvest Festival. It was especially painful for parents with teenaged kids. The reproving looks and repeated questions as to where *they* were going were difficult to swallow, but like all things, the novelty of torturing their parents passed and things went back to normal. By mid-November Barrington's schools reopened and kids went back to class. Both parents and offspring sighed in relief.

Liora disappeared in the middle of November. Sadie and Boris had no idea where she went, nor did they care.

Luke and Sadie were a bona fide couple again, and the teens accepted Sadie as one of their own. While they still had strange memories of Halloween night, they somehow knew Sadie had protected them all, even if they couldn't quite put a finger on what she had protected them from.

Hannah Farmer was the only one who refused to accept Sadie, and looked at her with hate-filled eyes. She hissed the word "witch" at her and tried to turn the kids against her, but they weren't interested in hurting Sadie anymore. Nathalie tried talking to Hannah, but she wouldn't listen. She was too far gone in her world of anger, so in the end they had no choice but to ignore her.

Despite the loss of his childhood friend, Luke was happy. He was ecstatic to have Sadie on his arm again as his beloved girlfriend. Their fingers were always twined together and he kissed her every chance he could get. While not accustomed to (or comfortable with) public displays of affection, Sadie allowed it. She knew he had suffered as much as she had during their time apart and his need to touch and kiss her was a physical thing.

She felt the same. Sadie glowed with happiness and confidence beside Luke. She stared at him with open adoration and love in her eyes. Dean teased Luke about it, but Nathalie often reminded him that he lived by a doubled edged sword, and that people who live in glass houses shouldn't throw stones. Dean just laughed.

Dean didn't suffer any ill effects from his near death experience. In fact, Sadie's healing pulse had made him practically invincible for months afterwards, as they discovered. His cuts healed instantly, he didn't get sick, and his muscles didn't hurt.

"Lucky," Luke would mumble painfully the next day after a strenuous bout of basketball the night before.

Dean and Nathalie were just happy to be a normal couple again, and able to enjoy time alone together that wasn't tinged with fear of attracting perverted magical beings. Her parents did eventually catch on that they were dating. Nathalie's mom was thrilled. Nathalie's dad was happy too. He liked Dean, but he did make frequent comments about the new shotgun he had ordered "for pests."

Dean made inroads with Nathalie's dad by allowing Mr. Parker to teach him how to use a barbeque.

"It's all in the distribution of heat," Mr. Parker would say zealously, staring at his Grill Master 4000 and rubbing his hands together.

"Sir, your meat is burning," Dean would very often point out.

December

By December, Barrington County was covered in snow and the town celebrated with Christmas lights and extravagant decorations. On weekends, hot chocolate and nut roasting stations were set up in and around Town Circle for Barringtoners to enjoy. At first *many* adults rushed to the drink stations. Memories of the summer's liquid treat danced like sugarplums in their heads...but after a few cups they realized it was really *just* hot chocolate.

Sadie and her father celebrated their first Christmas at Barrington manor. Boris thoroughly enjoyed himself. In the absence of his evil and controlling cousin (it turns out), for the first time in his life he finally felt free to enjoy the company of his daughter without the overwhelming obligation of fulfilling a hex passed down for generations. He enjoyed the festive atmosphere and the twinkling lights strung throughout the Barrington's home. Their scotch was also outstanding and he often just sipped his drink and watched the family interactions from a large stuffed armchair by the Christmas tree.

The family was boisterous and loving, and Sadie soaked it all in. She and Luke often marveled at the Barrington/Kellar family mix.

The Kellars stayed with the Barringtons for four wonderful days. The nights were just as sweet as Sadie slipped from her guest bed and curled up with Luke, sighing with pleasure in the deep dark of night as the snow and the cold swirled outside.

Nathalie and Dean spent the holidays with them as well. Sadie and Nathalie adored each other. "We're kindred spirits," Nathalie declared.

They often reminisced about the events of the summer.

"I'm looking forward to a *normal* Harvest Festival this year," Dean said.

The four were chatting as they got ready to watch a movie in Luke's sitting room. Luke was organizing snacks while Sadie put the movie in.

"Thankfully there's no reason why it wouldn't be normal," Sadie muttered as she fooled around with the DVD player.

Nathalie often caressed the amulet Taline had left her. She missed Taline and Wayman.

Luke was handing out hot chocolate. "What would be the attraction at this point?"

"Exactly," Nathalie agreed. "What could possibly happen? I'm not worried."

Acknowledgements

When you have great friends and family, no project you attempt is ever done alone. If my husband hadn't entertained our children and managed our household so I could write, HEX would still only be an idea. Hampton, Nikos, Shanna—thank you for leaving me alone.

To my bridal party reading group—Liz (my twin), Carolyn, Dominique, and Linda—thank you for the reading, editing, your suggestions and overwhelming enthusiasm and praise that made my book so much better. I do realize that I still need to learn how to spell, use commas properly, and conjugate verbs (in English!). I think I fixed everything.

Lastly, to my brother Rob, who never stopped saying to me, "Stacy, you should write a book. You're funny." This book actually started as an act of desperation to shut him up.

Thank you. Love you all.